MW00907797

Another Thriller in the Award-Winning Sam and James Series

Qisas

AA FREDA

iUniverse®

QISAS
ANOTHER THRILLER IN THE AWARD-WINNING SAM AND JAMES SERIES

iUniverse books may be ordered through booksellers or by contacting:

iUniverse
1663 Liberty Drive
Bloomington, IN 47403
www.iuniverse.com
844-349-9409

ISBN: 978-1-6632-1221-4 (sc)
ISBN: 978-1-6632-1220-7 (hc)
ISBN: 978-1-6632-1224-5 (e)

Library of Congress Control Number: 2020923639

Print information available on the last page.

iUniverse rev. date: 12/26/2020

For my brother John, my dear friend Richie, and all those who died too soon from the Covid-19 pandemic.

1

The Attack

A WHITE VAN WITH A "Pibbs Boiler and Repair" logo is parked at the back of the parking lot of the First Baptist Church in Lubbock Texas. A mujahedeen fighter is sitting in the front passenger seat looking over at the main entrance of the building as the people file in—the families are dressed in their Sunday finest. He has been staring at the church intently for the past twenty minutes. Over five hundred parishioners have made their way into the building. He rubs his hand over his chin and heaves a sigh. His assignment is finally coming to an end—he will be back home with his family in Mirabad, Afghanistan soon.

"Is it time yet Faakhir?" The driver of the vehicle asks.

Faakhir glances at the clock on the dash—ten minutes to nine. "Yes, Syed, it is time."

Faakhir turns to the four Palestinians huddled on the floor in the back of the van.

"It's time. Let's go over the plan one final time."

"Why? We know what to do!" One of the men answers. "Let's get going!"

Faakhir smiles warmly. "Yes Youssef, I'm sure you do know what to do. But we have a little time, let's go over the assignment once again. Tell me what you will be doing."

Youssef raises up on his knees. "We enter the church. On our right, there are two openings to the assembly, I'm to take one and my brother Nahid will take the other. As soon as we're in, we immediately start shooting."

"Shoot the people nearest to you first," Faakhir says. "That will discourage anyone from trying to take away your weapon."

"Yes, I know," Youssef answers. "After that we aim our fire at the exit doors on each side of the church. That will stop anyone from trying to escape."

"Good," Faakhir says. "Once that is done, you and your brother Nahid can simply go down the aisles and finish off the rest of the congregation. Most will be hiding under the benches."

He turns to another of the men. "What about you Omar. You have the most dangerous job, certainly the most complicated."

"I'm to go upstairs and eliminate any other people left in the building."

Faakhir nods. "Don't forget, the stairs to the second floor are at the end of the hall to your right." He looks over at the last of the men. "What about you Walid?"

Walid sits up. "I'm to guard the front entrance in case the police are called. It's also my job to make sure no one gets out of the church. While Youssef and Nahid are going up and down the aisles, they may miss someone. I'll make sure nobody gets away."

"Why do we need anyone to guard the front?" Youssef calls out. "What are *you* going to be doing?"

"I'll be heading for the rendezvous spot where we'll meet up after the mission is completed."

"What do you mean, 'meet up'?" Youssef says. "Aren't you going to wait for us? Are you just going to leave us there?"

Faakhir shakes his head. "No, Youssef. Listen carefully. After the shooting starts, the authorities will be called, I'm certain. The police will try to come bursting through the front entrance. That'll be their natural reaction. When Walid fires a couple of rounds at the incoming police, they'll head back to the parking lot for cover. At that time, Walid needs to round you guys up, and you'll make your escape through the back door at the other side of the building."

"Syed and I will be waiting for you with the van at the back entrance. There's no way you'll be able to get out through the front with the police lying in wait. You'll make your escape before the police have a chance to get to the back door."

Faakhir looks back at the church—a few congregants are making their way into the building. He turns back to the men. "We better get going—I'll get the weapons." Faakhir steps out of the vehicle and goes to the back of the van, opening the door and pulling out something wrapped in a blanket. He slides open the side door. "Here," he says and hands the bundle to Youssef.

Youssef opens the blanket and lifts up one of the four rifles. He cocks the bolt and looks inside the chamber. Each of the three men reach over, grab a Kalashnikov, and follow the same procedure.

"Reach back behind you . . . there're four bags of ammo," Faakhir calls out. "Each of you take a bag. There's ten magazines in each sack. That's over three hundred rounds for each of you—more than enough to wipe out the entire church."

The men reach back, and each takes a bag.

"Strap the bag around your shoulder," Faakhir orders. "Now reach back and grab the belts," Faakhir continues. "Strap them around your stomach. Remember; nobody gets captured alive, if there's any chance of being taken, you must press that button. To activate the bomb, just press on that button next to the buckle in the front."

"Hey, Faakhir, how do you know the bomb will actually work?" Youssef laughs. "Shouldn't you try the belt first?"

"Very funny, Youssef. Be careful not to press that button by accident. At least, don't press the button 'til you're very far away from the van and me."

Faakhir gets back into the front passenger seat and looks at the clock once more. Two minutes after nine.

Omar leans forward from the back seat. "What are we waiting for?" he asks. "Let's get this over with."

"Patience, Brother Omar, patience. There's plenty of time. I'm making sure that everyone gets in and is settled into their seats. We will go in at exactly ten after nine."

At ten after nine, Faakhir takes a final look around the parking lot and sees that the area is empty. All of the churchgoers are in the chapel. He smiles and turns to the men in the back. "OK, it's time. Everyone is inside," Faakhir says and looks over at the driver. "Start her up, Syed. Drive up to the front."

"Allah Akbar," he says to the men as they file out of the van at the main entrance of the church.

"Allah Akbar," the men respond in kind as they exit the vehicle and head for the church.

Faakhir watches as the men enter the church and turns to Syed. "Come on, start up the van. Let's get out of here."

"What…. about…. the men?" Syed stammers.

"Forget the men. I need to get out of Texas right away! You're driving me down to Nuevo Laredo. From there, I'll make my way back to Afghanistan. Come on, move! Let's get out of here before the authorities close the border to Mexico."

Syed speeds the van out of the parking lot. A smile comes across Faakhir's face as the sound of gunfire is heard coming from the church.

James is sitting in a pew in the front of the amphitheater. He is still out of sorts. Because Sam insisted that he talk at the church, he will miss out on an important business matter in New York. He's not paying attention to any of the services, simply going through in his head the speech he will give when called up. He vaguely notices his father in law the Reverend Powers walking up to the podium. Unexpectedly, he is startled back into the moment when the sound of gunfire resounds throughout the auditorium.

He turns and there are two men, one on each aisle, firing their rifles at the stage. Immediately he dives for cover under the bench. The automatic gunfire continues and his thoughts are trying to process his escape—cowering under the bench is no good. It will be only a matter of time before the gunmen get to the spot. There are people screaming in fear throughout the hall. The smell of gunpowder permeates through the air. He peers up and looks for the church exits on the side. Bodies are blocking the doors and the gunfire is aimed in that direction.

He notices a man trembling in the pew in back of him. The guy is holding a black semi-automatic revolver in his shaking hand. James crawls to the man and reaches for the pistol. The guy refuses to loosen his grip on the gun.

James gives the fellow an assuring smile. "It's okay," he whispers. "You can let go—I know how to use the gun, I was in the army."

When the man still refuses to let go, James says. "It's our only chance. We must fight back. The gunmen will soon be upon us. Let me have the gun, I will use it."

The fellow releases his grip and James takes the pistol.

"How many bullets does it hold?" James asks.

"Ten," he answers.

James, with gun in hand, crawls back under his bench. He's waiting for a pause in the shooting, which, will happen when the killers have to reload. He's targeting the assailant to his left. A moment later the gunfire stops and he hears an ammo clip hitting the floor. James quickly gets up from under the bench, rests his hands holding the pistol onto the back of the pew and aims to where he last saw the shooter. The man comes into view, James fires off two shots. The attacker drops. James ducks back down under the bench.

'Youssef, Youssef!' James hear shout, and he hears someone running. He peeks back up and sees a guy running on top of a bench toward the man he had just shot. Once again, he rests his hands on the back of the bench and takes aim. As soon as the man reaches his partner, James fires off two more shots. The second shooter drops.

He hears gunfire coming from somewhere upstairs, and he realizes that there are more gunmen in the building. James makes his way quickly to the two men he had just shot—he wants to get to the automatic rifles.

When he gets to the bodies, he reaches down to pick up the AK-47s. That's when he notices that one man is wearing an explosive belt. He puts the pistol to the man's head and fires, making sure that the guy is dead. He repeats the same process with the other corpse.

He reaches down for the bag with the other magazines and straps it around his shoulder. Loaded with an automatic weapon and ammo, he's ready to confront whoever is doing the shooting upstairs.

James let's out a breath and notices a young boy huddled under the bench. He gives the child a comforting smile and says. "Keep your head down."

As he is headed up the aisle, another shooter, with rifle in hand, pops into the entryway. James reaches for his rifle but the man fires first emptying an entire magazine at James.

2
The Hallelujahs

JESSICA, THE VICE PRESIDENT OF public relations at the Coppi Company, walks down the aisle toward the back of the company Boeing 727 jet that's on its way to New York. She walks up to the lounge area of the plane where Sam, one of the company's owners is reading a magazine. She takes a seat across from Sam, pushes back a lock of her black hair away from her face and crosses her long legs. "Why are we doing the closing on a Sunday?" Jessica asks and fixes her skirt.

Sam puts down the magazine on the coffee table in front of her. "We weren't supposed to. We were scheduled to close a few days ago, but the lawyers couldn't get the documents ready in time. Anyway, the closing itself shouldn't take long. The money for the deal has been wired and is sitting in escrow. James has already signed his share of the documents."

"I can't believe that James isn't coming," Jessica remarks. "We're selling the fashion business, and he's not here. A multimillion-dollar deal. I thought for sure that James would be here. Is he sick or something?"

Kathy, James's assistant and Sam's lifelong friend, who is also sitting across from Sam asks, "What happened, Sam? Is James all right?"

"Yeah, he's fine. Something else came up."

"Like what?" Kathy asks. "At the office, on Friday, James told me he was coming. What could be so important that he'd miss this closing?"

Sam pauses for a moment and then smiles. "James is giving a talk at my father's church in Lubbock."

"Really?" Kathy asks and bursts out laughing. "That's why James is missing this deal? How'd you rope him into doing that? James hates talking at your father's church. Calls all the congregants a bunch of *hallelujahs*."

"Yeah, I know." Sam says, laughing. "But this time I had enough. We had a full-blown, knockdown fight last night. I'm just tired of all his excuses, that's all—I finally had enough. I'm sick and tired of how he keeps avoiding my father. My family came over during Easter, and James gave a pretext of an important business matter and just disappeared.

"James hasn't seen my father in over a year. James promised my dad a month ago that he would speak at the church, but then he tried to wiggle out of this one, too. It's only one day. Not even one day— just a morning. It's the least that James can do. Even this morning he carried on. His last words to me before he left were, 'don't blame me if the church blows up when I show my face.'"

"Well, I'm not going to be in the office on Monday," Kathy says. "James will be in *such* a foul mood."

"Just Monday?" Jessica says. "I'm taking a week's vacation. It'll take James at least that long to get over going to Lubbock and giving a talk at the church."

"Yeah, well—stop complaining, ladies," Sam says. "I've got to live with the guy."

"Amen to you," Kathy laughs.

"What about this deal?" Jessica asks. "Are you happy to be selling the fashion line? I thought you guys were going to wait for a while and let the business grow."

"We *were* going to wait," Sam answers. "But Henry Greenwald approached James about selling his railroad to us. The purchase of the railroad is something that we just can't turn down. It's a really great opportunity. James felt that running all these businesses would just be too much for us.

"That's why we hired Vernon Dixon," she continues. "Vernon is going to be running the day-to-day operations of all the remaining companies. James and I are going to concentrate on the strategic planning. Running the fashion company would be too much of a headache for us."

"What's going to happen to Penelope?" Kathy asks. "What do you think she's going to do?"

"James and I came up with a plan for her. Penelope is coming over to our hotel this afternoon. Hopefully, she'll like what we're offering her."

"Who is Penelope?" Jessica asks Kathy.

"Penelope is Henry Greenwald's granddaughter," Kathy answers. "She was James's first case, back when he worked as a private detective."

"Was that the teenager who was kidnapped and then rescued by you guys?" Jessica asks Sam.

"Yes. She was only fourteen at the time," Sam answers. "Ever since that rescue, James and I have grown very fond of Penelope and have looked after her welfare. We gave her a job as a fashion designer, and she really took to the job. She's designed some of the most successful lines."

Vernon Dixon and Maxwell, the firm's legal counsel, come walking back from the front of the plane. "Samantha, may we speak to you?" Maxwell asks.

"Girls, can you excuse me?" Sam says to the women, who get up and leave. Vernon and Maxwell take the ladies' seats.

"OK, guys—what's up?" Sam asks.

"Maxwell is a little concerned about this performance clause that the other side has inserted into the agreement," Vernon tells her.

Sam looks at Maxwell. "What's bothering you, Maxwell? What don't you like about the provision? I'm told that it's a standard clause in this type of deal."

"It's too vague, Samantha. The other party is holding five million dollars in escrow for five years. The money will be released to you at the end of that period—provided you have kept up your end of the bargain. They've inserted language like 'they expect you to make personal appearances,' you 'need to be available for interviews,' and so forth.

"I'd like to tighten the language a bit. You know—precisely how many personal appearances do they expect? How many interviews? And so on. Have the other party specify exactly what they expect. What do you say? Do you want me to make that demand?"

"Maxwell, did you speak to James about this problem?" Sam asks. "What did James say?"

"James said he likes the section being vague. James doesn't want you tied to any formula. What if you can't keep up with the requirements of the agreement? 'If it's vague,'" James said, "'we can always argue that the other side is being unreasonable.'"

"What's wrong with what James is saying?" Sam asks. "Isn't that better?"

"It leaves too much in doubt—I just feel that it's going to create a problem down the road when we try to collect our money," Maxwell says and then pauses for a moment. "What do you say? Do you want me to tighten up the contract?"

"No, leave it as it is. Maxwell, let's go over some of the other requirements in this deal. Like the noncompete clause."

"The noncompete clause?" Vernon jumps into the conversation. "What's wrong with the noncompete? Are you planning on going back into the business?"

"No, Vernon, I'm not," Sam says with a smile. "I've had enough of running a fashion business for now."

"Well, if you're not going back in the business, then what's your concern, Samantha?" Maxwell asks.

"If I lend someone money and that someone starts a fashion business, am I violating the agreement?"

"Is that person a competitor of our fashion business right now?" Maxwell asks.

"No, she's not."

"Do you have knowledge that she's going to use the money to

start a competing business?" Maxwell asks, continuing to probe. "In other words, why are you lending this person the money?"

"Maxwell, can you excuse us for a few minutes?" Vernon says. "I'd like to speak to Samantha alone for a moment."

After Maxwell leaves, Vernon turns to Sam. "What's up, Sam? What's this all about? What do you and James have in mind? Don't forget, Sam; this is an eighty-million-dollar deal. You and James own eighty percent of the company. Your cut is sixty-four million.

"In addition to your cut, you have a licensing agreement that gives you two percent of all sales. That's at least another two million a year, based on last year's sales. The 'no compete' clause is a very important part of this deal. I hope you guys fully understand the consequences if you break that part of the agreement."

Sam smiles. "We know that, Vernon—that's why I'm asking questions about it."

"All right; let me see if I can help you." Vernon looks around and lowers his voice. "Tell me what the loan is all about."

"We want to lend Penelope Campos half a million to start her own business."

"Are you guys going to get a cut of the action?"

"Not immediately. Penelope may cut us in down the road."

Vernon rubs his chin. "What's your relationship with Penelope? Are you guys friends—I mean, do you trust her?"

"Yes, of course! Penelope is completely trustworthy."

"Here's my suggestion," Vernon says. He leans forward a little more, looks around once again, and lowers his voice. "Lend her the money. No strings attached. And certainly, don't make it a condition that she use the money to start a fashion business. At least—don't let anybody know that the purpose of the money is to start a fashion line. Then, when the noncompete agreement expires, go back and have a talk with her about a partnership. Don't do it before then."

Sam smiles.

"Thank you, Vernon. Thanks for the advice."

Vernon gets up and walks away. He goes a few steps and turns back around. "No more discussions about this with anyone except Miss Campos, please."

Sam smiles. "Yes, Vernon, I understand."

"Penelope, I do believe you've gotten even more beautiful than when I last saw you," Sam says to the young woman sitting across from her in the hotel room. "And you dyed your hair! You're a platinum blonde now."

Penelope sips her mineral water and smiles. "Yes, I did. This is the second time in three months that I changed my color. I tried dyeing it strawberry blonde, like you, but that didn't work, my hair turned all red. I'm not thrilled with this color either. Maybe I'll just go back to my natural color, ash blonde. But what's up, Sam? You're not really interested in my hair. Why are you buttering me up?"

"You must have heard that we're selling the business."

"Yes, I heard—I was wondering when you and James would get around to speaking to me."

"All right—let's have that talk. What are you going to do after we sell? Are you staying with the new company? You're quite good; I'm sure they'd keep you."

"No, I'm not staying, Sam." Penelope looks away and is quiet. She turns back to Sam. "I don't like working with the Cinelli brothers. Don't get me wrong—the brothers are quite talented. But I'm just not comfortable working with those guys, especially now that I won't have you to act as a buffer between me and them."

"What are you going to do?" Sam asks. "Don't you like designing women's clothes anymore?"

"Sam, I love what I do—in fact, I can't imagine doing anything else. I'll take some time off and see what I can come up with. I've got some money saved. There's no pressure on me to make a quick decision."

"Why don't you start your own line? You know—start your own company."

"Start my own company?" Penelope asks and laughs. "Are you losing it, Sam? I know nothing about running a business. Besides, where would I get the money? I've got a little money saved up, but nothing like I would need to start a company."

"How about your grandfather, Henry? I'm sure he'd give you the money."

"No! I'm sorry, Sam—I wouldn't feel right asking Pop Pop for the money."

Sam leans over. "Why not, Penelope? Your grandfather has more than enough. You'd need only five hundred thousand—a drop in the bucket for Henry. It's your legacy. The money would eventually come to you, anyway."

"No. I'm sorry, Sam," Penelope says, shaking her head. "I wouldn't feel right asking for that. If the business failed, I would feel awful that I lost his money."

Sam sits back in her chair and smiles.

"How about if James and I lend you the money?"

"You?" Penelope's eyes widen. "You'd give me money to start a company that would compete against yours? Why?"

Sam waves her hand dismissively. "Don't be ridiculous. You're not our competition. The fashion world is big enough for both of us. However, if we do lend you the money, you can't tell anyone. You need to let everyone believe that it's your grandfather that helped you out.

"The contract I'm signing this afternoon has a 'no compete' clause," Sam continues. "I don't mind your getting into the business and competing against me, but I'm sure the new buyers wouldn't take too kindly to my helping you out."

"What about the fact that I know nothing about running a business?" Penelope argues. "You'd probably lose your investment in two days."

"You have access to one of the best minds when it comes to starting up companies. I'm sure James would be very helpful to you. He absolutely loves you—looks out for you like you're his little sister."

"That's true—I know he's very fond of me," she smiles wistfully.

"I've known that ever since he rescued me from that monster who kidnapped me when I was a little girl."

"Well—is it a go?"

"What do you guys get out of this? Would you be my partners?"

"Silently," Sam whispers. "And I do mean *silently*. No one must ever know."

"All right," Penelope smiles broadly. "If you're my partners, it's a deal. But first, I'm taking some time off. Maybe a month—maybe even two. Get myself recharged. I'm excited, Sam. Thank you, and thank James. As always, you guys have come through for me."

"All right, honey," Sam says, standing up. "We'll talk some more when you're ready to get started. There's no rush—take your time. As soon as you're set, give me a call." Sam looks at the clock. "I better start getting ready—I've got to get downtown for the closing."

Sam looks at the clock after she returns to her hotel suite that night. "Ten thirty! I can't believe the closing took so long," she says out loud.

"I was beginning to wonder if we'd ever get finished," Kathy says. "That damn lawyer of theirs was so picky. Kept changing every little thing."

"Well, it's done now," Jessica says. "And you and James are a whole lot richer. What do you say? Should we order a bottle of champagne to celebrate? Are you going to spring for a bottle, Sam? Spend a little bit of that money."

"Yeah," Sam says with a smile. "It's worth celebrating. Call room service." She pauses and frowns. "I wonder why James hasn't called? That's not like him. He's usually very curious. I'm going to take a quick shower, and I'll join the celebration when I get out. If James calls, come and get me—I need to speak to him."

After Sam heads to the bathroom, Jessica walks to the phone. "Kathy, turn on the television," Jessica says as she dials room service.

"It's time for the nightly news. Let's see what's going on with the rest of the world."

Kathy is standing in front of the television when Jessica finishes ordering the champagne. Kathy's eyes are glued to the set.

"What's up?" Jessica asks. "What's so interesting?"

Kathy points to the set. "*Look!*"

"The death toll has reached thirty-eight," the newscaster says. "At least eighty-three others have been wounded, many in critical condition. The death toll could go even higher. There are many people still unaccounted for.

"Some of the casualties are children who were there for Sunday school. The situation is very confusing and chaotic. The Lubbock hospitals have been flooded with victims since the shooting this morning at the First Baptist Church."

Jessica turns to Kathy. "Isn't that the church where James was supposed to speak?"

"Yes, it was." Kathy runs toward the bathroom. "I've got to tell Sam." She knocks on the bathroom door. "Sam, open up. It's important."

There's no answer. The shower is running. Kathy opens the door and walks in. The bathroom is foggy from the steam. Sam is showering behind the sliding glass doors. Kathy bangs on the glass. "Sam, I need to speak to you."

Sam slides open the door a crack and peeks out. "Christ, Kathy, you banged so hard, you nearly gave me a heart attack."

"Towel yourself off and come on out, Sam. I need to speak to you. It's important!" Kathy scurries out of the bathroom before Sam can ask any questions.

Sam walks out after a moment wearing a white robe, still dripping wet. "What's wrong?"

Jessica pushes her down into a chair and squats in front of her. "There was a shooting at the church this morning in Lubbock—the church where James was due to speak."

Sam turns pale.

"What happened? Where's James? Is he all right?"

"We don't know," Jessica answers. "A lot of people were hurt."

Sam stands up and walks quickly to the phone. "I've got to call my father."

The phone rings as she's about to make the call. Sam lifts the receiver. "Hello?"

The shaky voice on the line says, "Sam, it's your dad."

"Dad, are you all right? What happened? Where's James?"

"I'm fine, dear. There was a shooting at the church today. Gunmen came in and began shooting up the church. I was able to crawl out through a back door behind the altar."

Sam feels her body getting weak. She feels faint and holds the edge of the table for support. She takes a deep breath, "Where's James, Dad? Is he all right?"

"It was James who killed the gunmen," her father responds.

"Dad, please—tell me what happened to James." Sam's hands are shaking so badly that she can barely hold the phone.

Her dad lets out a sigh. "I don't know, dear—I don't know what happened to James. The situation here is so unclear. There was an explosion. James was taken away in an ambulance and I've been calling all the area hospitals, but I haven't been able to locate him."

"Dad, I'm leaving right away. I should be in Lubbock by morning. Keep looking for James, please! Find him!"

There's a knock at the door. Jessica opens it.

"Here's the champagne you ordered," the waiter says as he enters the room. He looks over at Sam. "Where would you like me to put the ice bucket?"

"Put it down anywhere," Sam tells him.

"I'm sorry, I didn't hear you. Where did you say you wanted the champagne?"

"Anywhere!" Sam shouts. "I don't give a fuck!"

Jessica walks over to him. "Put it on the coffee table," she says, and signs the tab, handing the man a tenner.

"Thank you, ma'am," he says and heads for the door.

Sam reaches for his arm. "I'm sorry."

He nods and leaves.

"Kathy, call Captain Jeffrey," Sam says. "Tell him to get the plane ready. We're going to Lubbock. I need to get to James right away."

The three women are walking on the tarmac toward the company jet. Mary the stewardess and Captain Jeffrey are on top of the steps of the gangway. When the women climb the stairs, Mary grabs the bags from Kathy.

"Are we ready to go?" Sam asks Jeffrey.

"Yes, ma'am," the pilot replies. "I radioed ahead. There's no news on James yet. If I hear something, I'll bring it right over. We should be in the air in ten minutes."

"Thank you, Jeffrey."

Sam walks inside and takes a seat. Kathy sits next to her and holds on to her hand. Mary comes over to them.

"May I get you something, Mrs. Coppi?" Mary asks.

"I brought a tote bag with me. Inside the bag, there is a Bible. Can you please bring the book to me?"

Mary walks to the front and fetches the book. Sam opens the Bible to a passage and begins reading.

Two hours into the flight, Sam lifts her head up from the book and notices the pilot, Jeffrey, walking toward her.

"Oh God!" she utters, and grabs Kathy's hand. She shuts her eyes tightly and whispers under her breath, "Please, God, please let him be all right!"

"I've got good news for you, Mrs. Coppi," Jeffrey tells her. "I just got word that James is alive."

Sam snaps open her eyes. "Oh—thank you, Lord!"

"James is at University Medical Center in critical but stable condition," the pilot adds.

"James is critical? How bad is he?"

"They didn't know. There will be a police motorcade waiting for us when we land to rush you to the hospital."

"A police motorcade? Why?"

"Sam, your husband is a hero. James was the one who killed the shooters. If it weren't for him, hundreds more would've been killed."

"I don't understand. How could James kill anybody? He doesn't have a gun."

"They didn't tell me what happened." Jeffrey says and then squats in the aisle next to her seat. "Sam, at last count, forty-three people were killed. There are another seventy-eight victims in hospitals, many in very critical condition. Some fifty others are still unaccounted for. There were some five hundred parishioners at the church. The killers were armed with automatic weapons. I don't know how James pulled it off—but if he hadn't, it would've been a whole lot worse, I can assure you."

Sam closes her eyes after the pilot leaves. "Please, God, help James pull through. Look out for my baby; he is a good man."

Sergeant Vince Ormond is leaning against the police cruiser on the taxiway at the Lubbock airport, smoking a cigarette and waiting for the private jet to arrive. There are two other cruisers and two police motorcycles lined up.

"What's taking them so long?" One of the two cops standing with him asks.

"Yeah, I'd like to get back to the station and look over the casualty list." The other copper says. "I might know some of the victims."

"Take it easy guys," Vince answers. "They'll be here." Vince looks down the runway. "In fact, here comes the plane now." Vince tosses out his cigarette. "Get the boarding ladder ready."

The jet taxis to the men and they push the ladder to the doorway. The door opens and three women appear at the top.

"Holy cow," one of the coppers lets out. "Those dames are gorgeous," he smiles broadly and looks over at the two men. "I'll take the brunette; you guys take the blondes."

"Cut it out!" Vince says.

"Mrs. Coppi?" Vince calls out when the women get to the bottom.

"Yes," Sam replies faintly.

"I'm Sergeant Vince Ormond. I'm here to escort you to the hospital." The sergeant opens the rear door of one of the cars. "Please—right this way."

The cop turns to Jessica and Kathy. "You ladies can hop into one of the other cars." Ormond moves quickly to the other side of the vehicle and gets into the back seat with Sam. "Whenever you're ready, Mike," he says to the driver. The caravan puts on the sirens and speeds out of the airport.

"Sergeant, do you have any news on my husband's condition?" Sam asks the policeman.

"No, ma'am—I'm sorry. I don't know much. I was just instructed to take you to the hospital immediately."

The caravan pulls up to the main entrance of the hospital. Sam jumps out and runs for the entrance. The Sergeant dashes after her.

"We're looking for James Coppi," the policeman tells the woman behind the front desk.

"Straight ahead in ICU," the woman says. Sam and the sergeant bolt down the hall.

At the ICU nurse's station, the policeman yells, "James Coppi!" to one of the nurses. "Number six," the nurse says and points to one of the cubicles. By now, Jessica and Kathy have caught up with Sam.

The three women walk to station six, and Sam pulls open the curtain.

3

"I Told You the Place Would Blow Up if I Showed"

SAM HAS TO GRAB KATHY'S hand to keep herself from fainting when she first lays eyes on James. The bed sheet is partially off his body, which is completely wrapped in bandages from head to toe. Only his face and his right arm are visible and unwrapped. There is an overwhelming stench of medicine—and another odor that she doesn't recognize. Tubes are sticking out of him everywhere. James' eyes are closed.

Tears trickle down Sam's face as she gazes at her husband.

"Is he asleep?" Kathy whispers.

"Am I dreaming, or are there really three beautiful women in my room?" James asks.

"Just exactly how good *was* that dream?" Sam answers, and a smile forms through her tears.

She walks up to the bed, leans over the railing, and gives him a kiss. "How do you feel?"

James winces, and his face contorts. "You mean, apart from the shooting pain going throughout my entire body?"

"Is it that bad?"

James lifts up a cord with a red button at the end and begins pressing the button. "I don't think this damn thing is working. It's

20

supposed to be a pain medicine release contraption—but I keep pressing, and nothing is coming out."

He looks over at Kathy. "Do me a favor, Kathy. My nurse's name is Anne. Go to the nurse's station and ask her to come in here, please. I want her to check this damn device—it's probably out of medicine."

"What do the doctors say?" Sam asks. "Are you going to be all right?"

"The doctors say the surgery went well. Other than that, they haven't said much. They've been very busy. A lot of people need attention—I haven't seen the doctors since right after my surgery."

"What kind of surgery was it?" she asks but doesn't get an answer as the nurse walks in.

"What can I do for you, Mr. Coppi?" Nurse Anne asks when she walks in. She walks to the side of the bed and adjusts the pillow behind his head. Then she looks to the floor and checks the urine container.

"This pain pump isn't working," James says, showing her the cord. "I keep pressing the button, but nothing is coming out."

"That's because you've used up the maximum dosage of the medicine. It's set on a timer for a refill."

"When is the next refill?"

"At six o'clock."

"What time is it now?"

"Twenty after four."

James groans. "Just fucking great," he says and tosses the pump away.

"James, your language!" Sam calls out.

The nurse turns to Sam. "That's OK, ma'am, I've heard a lot worse. Are you his wife?"

"Yes—my name is Sam."

"Pleased to meet you, Sam. I'm his nurse, Anne."

"How's he doing?" Sam asks.

"Your husband was in surgery for about eight hours, and he appears to be recovering nicely. His vitals look good, and his complaining is a good sign. The doctors will be in a little later. They'll give you a full report." The nurse looks over at James. "Do you need anything else, Mr. Coppi?"

James shakes his head.

Anne turns to Sam. "I'll be at the nurse's station if you need me."

"Thank you for all of your help. I'm sure James is very grateful."

"No, Sam, *I* should be thanking your husband. My mother was in that church yesterday morning. If it hadn't been for your husband, I'm sure she'd be dead. He saved her life." Anne fixes his bedsheets and walks out.

James looks over at Jessica and Kathy. "If you guys are tired, you don't have to stay here. There may be a place to get some rest in the waiting room. Besides, I want to talk to Sam alone for a few minutes."

He is silent after the ladies leave.

"What's the matter?" Sam asks. "Are you all right? What did you want to speak to me about?"

His eyes moisten, and he turns his head away from her. She leans over him and caresses his face. "What's the matter, dear?"

James turns back to her. "Sam, I killed four men. Shot them dead at close range. All the time I was in Vietnam, I never killed a man. At least, not directly. I called in artillery on the enemy, and I'm sure that the bombing must have killed someone, but I was always detached from the deed. Not this time—I actually saw the men die."

"Oh, James," Sam says as she continues to stroke his face gently. "You *had* to. You had no choice. Those men would have killed you and murdered hundreds more if you hadn't stopped them."

"Yeah, I know. The doctors and nurses at the hospital say that I'm a hero. If that's true, why do I feel so fucking miserable?" James pauses and smiles. "Let's talk about something else. Get my mind off it. How did everything go yesterday?"

"Everything went fine. Stop worrying about the business, James. Just concentrate on getting better."

"What about—" he begins. Then he recoils in pain and lets out a breath.

"What's the matter? Are you all right?"

"The constant pain is bearable, but every once in a while, I get a shooting pain throughout my back." James tries to adjust himself on the bed.

"Do you need help?" she asks. "What are you trying to do?"

"I want to raise myself up in the bed a little."

"Here, let me help." Sam reaches under his arms and lifts him up.

"Ow, ow!" he cries out. "Bad idea! Let go—it hurts."

"I'm sorry."

"Not your fault." James turns slightly to her and lets out a breath. "I'm the one who asked for help. What about Penelope? Has that been worked out?" James forces out a cough.

"Yes, she's all set."

"Good."

Jessica and Kathy come back in the room. "Here, Sam, we got you a cup of coffee," Kathy says and hands Sam the cup. "We found a vending machine."

"Have you called home?" James asks Sam as she takes a sip of the coffee.

"No. I came straight here."

"You should call. Let everybody know that I'm alive. Michael and Christopher are too young to understand, but Molly isn't. If Molly saw the television news, she may be very frightened. Molly knows that I was supposed to speak at that church."

"It's only a quarter to five," Sam answers. "No one is up yet."

"Call anyway. Let Billingsley know."

"OK, I'll go call."

"We'll come with you," Jessica tells her.

When the women get back, they see that James is now sleeping. They leave him and find the waiting room.

Sam falls asleep in her chair. When she wakes up, she looks at her watch. It's quarter to seven, and she gets up and stretches. Jessica and Kathy are both sleeping in their chairs. Sam goes down the hall into James's cubicle. James is awake and smiles at her.

"I thought you'd gone home."

"You're in a good mood," she tells him.

James lifts up the handle of the pain medicine pump. "It's

working. Come on, go grab a chair and sit next to me. Let's talk before the effects of the medicine wear off."

Sam comes back with a chair and sits next to him.

"Did you call home?" he asks.

"Yes, and you were right. Molly was very frightened. She was up when I called. I assured her that you were fine. Told her to go to bed and that you wouldn't be happy if you found out she was still up."

"Maybe you should go home later today."

Sam gives him a long look. "No, James, that's not happening. I'm not leaving until I know you're out of danger."

Jessica and Kathy come walking in. "Listen, guys, you don't have to stay," James tells them. "Go home. Kathy, do me a favor and look in on my children later today. Jessica, when you get to the office, tell Vernon to give me a call. There're a few things I need to go over with him."

"Are you sure that you don't need us here?" Jessica asks. "I'm sure reporters are going to want to speak to you."

"All right, Jessica. Stick around—you're right, I might need you."

"What do you want from Vernon?" Sam asks after the ladies leave. "I can't believe you're conducting business from a hospital bed."

"There's something important that I need to discuss with him."

Two men and a woman in lab coats come walking in.

"How's our favorite patient doing?" one of the men asks.

"You tell me . . . you're the one who cut me up," James says. Then he gestures to one of the men. "Sam, this is Dr. Folroy—he did the surgery. This is my wife, Samantha."

"It's a pleasure to meet you, Samantha."

"Thank you. It's a pleasure to meet you, too. How's my husband?"

"Well, he lost a lot of blood. We also pulled out a lot of shrapnel caused by the explosion. We stopped counting at forty-four—it filled up a couple of small buckets. Most of his wounds were superficial. Three were very serious, but fortunately did not damage any vital organs. James has three busted ribs. His back was partially burned. That's the odor you smell in here."

Sam gasps. "Burned? How bad?"

"Not too bad, near his right shoulder blade. The main risk to him now is from infection," the doctor continues. "We need to keep the wounds clean. Overall, your husband is doing quite well, all things considered. I'm changing his status from critical to serious but stable."

"When can I go home?" James asks him.

"As soon as we can be sure that the wounds have healed nicely, and there's no more risk of infection. I'd say in seven to ten days."

"Doc, can you remove some of these tubes? Especially the one that's up my boy, down there—the tubes aren't needed any longer. I can go to the bathroom on my own."

"Not quite yet, James," the doctor answers. "You might still be too weak—you lost a lot of blood. Give it another day, and then we'll take another look. There's a bunch of law enforcement people waiting outside to speak to you. Are you up to speaking with them?"

"Yeah—send them in."

A few moments later, six men come into his room—three in civilian clothes, three in police uniforms.

"Good morning, James," one of the men in civvies says. "I'm special agent Floyd Mayweather, and with me is Sheriff Thomas Johnson." He points to one of the uniformed men. "I know you're in pain and very uncomfortable, so we won't keep you long."

"How bad was it at the church?" James asks the agent.

"Forty-three dead, seventy-eight injured. Eight are still critical, so the death count could go up," Mayweather replies and looks directly at James. "Would've been a lot worse if it hadn't been for you. The four men were packing more than a thousand rounds of ammo. Can we go over your story? Tell us what happened."

James lets out a deep breath, collects himself and begins telling the story. When he gets to the part of when he is confronted by the shooter that empties an entire magazine at him, he pauses as he contorts his back. "Sorry," he says, and lets out a gasp.

As she listens, Sam is silent, but her hands are trembling.

James takes a breath and looks at the men in the room before continuing. "As I was headed up the aisle, another man popped into the entryway. The man kept firing till he ran out of bullets. He had emptied his whole magazine at me."

At this, Sam gasps and starts to cry quietly.

"I fired off a burst back at him, and he dropped. I checked myself to see if I'd been hit—miraculously, he'd missed." James laughs a hollow laugh. "The shooter had emptied an entire magazine clip and hadn't hit me once. What are the odds?

"I got to the man's body quickly and put a bullet in his head for good measure. Again, I heard shots coming from upstairs, and I began making my way there. Just before I got to the steps, I turned to go back to the auditorium. I wanted to tell the people to start evacuating. There were more gunmen in the building, and I didn't know if I would make it. Better to play it safe and get the assembly out while I could.

"Before I could make it back to the hall, I heard someone running down the steps. The guy and his rifle came into view and I let loose another volley. He fell backward against the wall and slid to the ground. I turned back to the auditorium to get the people out of the church. I started yelling for people to hurry up and get out—that it was safe now. That's when the explosion happened. My last thoughts were, 'Oh shit, I fucked up!'"

"Wow!" Special Agent Mayweather says. "You are truly a hero! A lot of people owe you their lives."

"There's a press conference at one this afternoon," the sheriff tells him. "Are you up for it? We'd like you to be there—let the country know who you are."

"Not today, Sheriff. I'm just not up to it. I've got all this medical stuff sticking out of me every which way. Maybe tomorrow. They're supposed to begin removing these tubes this afternoon."

"OK, we'll see you tomorrow."

After the men leave, James looks over at Sam. "Are you OK?"

"Yes, I'm fine now," she says, smiling through her tears. "I'm never asking you to go to church again."

James manages a grin. "I told you the place would blow up if I showed." He reaches over and takes her hand. "How many times did you *pray* on the way here?"

"The entire plane ride—I prayed and clutched the Bible the whole way."

James smiles at her. "I'll go to church with you the first chance I get after I get out of here."

"Really? That's a change, I thought you didn't believe in divine intervention."

"After the shooting, I'm rethinking my view. There's a reason that I'm still here. And, I'm pretty sure *He* had something to do with it."

4

Qisas

THE NEXT DAY, JAMES IS sitting in a wheelchair in his hospital room, waiting to be wheeled out to the press conference. He was moved out of ICU earlier that morning. The tubes have all been removed. A hospital robe hides from view the bandages covering his body, except for the bindings still covering the top of his head. The doctors have upgraded his medical condition to serious but stable.

"Are you sure you don't want to go over some of the talking points?" Jessica asks him.

"No, I'm fine, Jessica—I know what I want to say," James says. Then he turns to the nurse. "I'm ready."

The nurse wheels him next to the stage where the press conference is being held. The nurse stops before the curtains. Jessica is standing alongside James. A woman comes off the stage.

"Hi, James," she says as she squats down in front of him. "I'm Marjorie Baxter, the hospital's spokesperson. The press conference is getting ready to begin. The other officials will be talking for a few minutes. When the speakers are done, they'll introduce you, and we will wheel you in.

"There will be a row of microphones at a lower level just for you on the stage next to the dais. We will place you right behind the microphones. Take your time and try to speak as loudly as you can. You'll have a chance to say a few words before taking any questions from the reporters. If you get tired or fatigued, give me a wave, and we'll end the talk. Do you have any questions?"

"No, I'm fine. Let's get this over with."

"I'm going back on stage to start the news conference," Marjorie says. "I'll come back to get you when it's your turn."

Fifteen minutes later, Marjorie is back. "Are you ready?"

"Yes, I'm ready."

Marjorie holds back the curtain as James is rolled in by Jessica. As soon as he is on the stage, the audience stands up and gives him an ovation. James notices a row of dignitaries, including his medical team, also on the stage. The wheelchair is rolled behind a bank of microphones.

"Thank you," he says to the audience—they keep applauding. "Thank you," James says once again. The audience is still clapping. "Thank you," he repeats and smiles. "You people need to sit and stop clapping, I don't know how much longer I can hold out."

The audience sits, the room quiets, and James begins, his tone is serious. "Before I take your questions, I'd like to say a few words. My thoughts and prayers go to all the victims of this senseless tragedy. I wish there were more that I could have done to save those who perished.

"I'd like to thank the medical team here at University Hospital Medical Center. Everyone at the hospital did miraculous work—not just with me, but with all of the victims that they treated." James pauses to cough. "I'll take some questions now."

"Mr. Coppi, can you give us the details of your encounter with the terrorists?" the first reporter asks.

James goes over the details, as he did the day before with the police authorities in his room, leaving out only what he'd said afterward to Sam.

"Were you frightened?" the second reporter asks.

James laughs. "I'm pretty certain that I soiled my underwear," he replies and turns to the medical team on the stage. "Dr. Folroy, am I right? My undies were pretty stained?"

Dr. Folroy laughs and shakes his head no.

"To answer your question," James continues, "when the shooting first began, I hit the ground, as I said earlier. At that point, I was pretty scared. But, more than that, I was quite confused. I didn't know what was going on or what to do. Once I had the revolver in my hand, I felt a lot better–I had trained with a 45 pistol when I was in the army so I knew how to use the weapon. With the gun in my hand, I felt that I had regained some measure of control.

"After I began fighting back, my fear completely disappeared. All of my thoughts were concentrated on killing the enemy. I knew how important my mission was. If I failed, a lot of lives would be lost—I was the only person in the way of the killers carrying out their homicidal plan. There was no room for fear in my emotions."

James pauses and twists his back, clearly in pain. "I'm very sorry, but I need to cut this conference short. The pain medicine appears to be wearing off. I'll try to make myself available again at another time when I feel a little better."

Marjorie walks over and wheels James off the stage. On the way out, Jessica leans over and says, "Good job. You did great."

Sam is on the phone when he's wheeled back into his room. "He's here, Vernon," she says into the phone. "James just got back to his room." She hands the phone to James. "It's Vernon—you wanted him to call you."

"Thank you," he says, taking the phone from her.

"Hello, James," Vernon says. "How do you feel?"

"They tell me I'll survive," he answers. "I should be good to go in a week or so."

"That's good to hear, James. Everyone here was really worried about you."

"Listen, Vernon, I need you to get Charlie and Rodney involved in this church investigation. I need to know who was behind this operation."

"What, the guys who work for you? Why waste the company's time? Shouldn't you let the FBI and CIA take care of the investigation? They have plenty of manpower. Besides, they're far better equipped to take care of these types of situations."

"That may be true, Vernon, but I want to stay involved in the case. Tell Charlie and Rodney to get started. I'll give the guys a call in a few days to discuss the investigation with them."

"OK, James—will do. Get well. We're all looking forward to having you back real soon."

⊣——⊢

Faakhir walks to the window and opens a slat of the wooden shutters, looking out from the second floor of the compound. Across the courtyard, a guard with a rifle strapped to his shoulder is pacing along the wall. His steps leave footprints in the dry dust. Out of sight, on the other side of the wall, another guard would be pacing around the perimeter. Barbed wire is fixed to the top of the wall.

It took Faakhir nearly two weeks to make it from Lubbock to Peshawar, a Pakistani town on the border of Afghanistan. He had taken a flight to Egypt where he spent a week when he finally was able to board a ship to Karachi. From Karachi, he hitched a couple of rides to the compound. He would like to get home to his family. He hasn't seen his wife and three children in nearly six months. It will take at least another week after he leaves Peshawar to make it home.

The mission in Lubbock had gone well, he thought. Over a hundred casualties, of which forty-three were deaths. There would have been a lot more if that American had not intervened. Still, the message was delivered to the Americans: we will strike you right in the heart, at your holiest of places. Mafrouz, his superior, should be quite pleased. It was the exact message Mafrouz had wanted to send. Best of all, because all of the shooters were Palestinians, the Americans would not be able to trace the job back to the Afghans. The money from the Americans for the fight against the Russians would continue pouring in.

What kind of fools must these Americans be? Do they really believe that we like them more than we do the Russians? The only solution acceptable is for all westerners to get out of the Middle East. Not just Afghanistan—the entire Middle East. We are ready to fight for a thousand years, if necessary. Eventually, we will win. No sacrifice is too great for our cause.

Faakhir watches the wooden front gates swing open and the black van pull in. It parks at the front door and three men get out. To his surprise, along with Mafrouz, the prince is also there. He smiles and thinks; *the prince is here to personally congratulate me on a job well done.* Faakhir heads downstairs to greet the men.

"Mafrouz, it is a pleasure to see you." Faakhir says, still smiling, when he gets down the stairs.

"Yes, Faakhir. I'm glad you arrived back safely," Mafrouz answers, a slight coldness in his voice.

"Your Highness," Faakhir says and bows.

"Nice to see you, Faakhir," the prince says. "Come, let's sit and talk. We have a lot to discuss."

They squat down on a rug.

"I'm sure you've heard by now, Mafrouz, that the mission was successful," Faakhir says. "We struck at the church, just as you instructed. Over a hundred casualties."

"I'm sorry, Faakhir. The prince and I don't share your belief on the success of the operation," Mafrouz answers indifferently. "There were over five hundred people in that church. Your men should have taken out a lot more."

"We would have killed more if that one American hadn't intervened," Faakhir explains and extends his arms in a pleading manner. "How could we have anticipated an armed man being there? Despite the interference, we were still able to inflict a lot of casualties. More than any of the recent operations we have had. This was a tremendous defeat for the Americans."

"Faakhir, you're missing the point," the prince tells him. "It's not about the casualties. It's about perception. It's concerning public opinion. The Americans are claiming victory. They say that this man who defended the churchgoers is a hero. He defeated a superior force to save hundreds of lives. The entire world is celebrating this infidel's heroic deed. This operation is being painted as a defeat to our forces."

Faakhir bows his head. "I'm sorry to disappoint you, Your Highness."

"Faakhir, you'll have to go back and finish the job," Mafrouz tells him.

"Finish the job?" Faakhir's eyes widen. "You want me to go back and strike that church once again?"

"No, we want you to go back and take care of that American," Mafrouz explains. "We need to demonstrate to the world that there are no such things as American heroes. The infidels cannot win.

"This next assignment is very important, Faakhir—more important than that strike on the church itself," Mafrouz continues. "This American, this so-called hero, must be dealt with immediately. We cannot allow him to be glorified. The world must see what we do to anyone who tries to stand in our way."

"Not just the one American," the prince speaks up. "Faakhir, it's *Qisas*."

"*Qisas*? You want me to kill his entire family? Even the children?"

"Yes Faakhir," the prince answers. "We need to send a strong message that if you try to stop us, this is what will happen to you. You will be killed, and your entire family will perish with you. It must be made very clear. This man must not be looked upon as a champion. We must put fear into the hearts of all Americans."

Mafrouz places his hand on Faakhir's shoulder and smiles. "Go home, Faakhir. Visit your family. You have been away from them a long time. Get a little rest. We are assigning another man to help you in the next operation—he will contact you in a few weeks. His name is Moshar Malik. You two can plan this next mission. Can we count on you?"

Faakhir looks up. "Yes, of course."

———— ╬————— ╬————

"What do the doctors say?" Sam asks James on the phone. "I thought they were letting you out today. Something must be wrong. I'm coming back down."

James had talked Sam into going home the week before. He's now been in the hospital over two weeks.

"The medical team just left my room. The doctors are concerned about the low-grade fever that I have. Dr. Folroy believes that the fever may be a sign that there's an infection. The blood tests didn't show anything, but Folroy is still worried.

"I'm back on antibiotics since yesterday. The doctors want to give it another day or two and see if the fever comes down. No need for you to come down. There's nothing that you can do. Stay home and take care of the children. They need you more than I do."

"I miss you!" she says.

"I miss you too, baby. Anyway, I'm giving the doctors another two days and then I'm coming home. The doctors can treat me just as well in Colorado as they can here in Texas."

"Are you still in pain? Yesterday, you complained that your back was still hurting you."

"Yeah, I am, but I stopped taking the pain medicine. Just Tylenol, which doesn't seem to help at all."

"I've got a few things to do this morning, I'll call you later," she says and hangs up.

The phone rings as soon as he puts down the receiver.

"Hello, James, it's Vernon."

"Hello, Vernon. What have you got for me?"

"James, I want to update you on a couple of things here at the office. First of all, Greenwald is OK with the delay on the closing date for the purchase of his railroad."

"That's good. What else have you got?"

"On the investigation into the shooting, Charlie says that the gunmen were Palestinians. They belong to a sect that's broken off from the PLO."

James shakes his head in frustration. "Vernon, I already got that information on the television news. Tell me something I don't know. You got anything else?"

"No, that's about it."

"This is very disappointing, Vernon. The shooting took place over two weeks ago and you guys have nothing. Tell Charlie and Rodney to stop pulling on their peckers and get to work. I'll be back home in a few days—I want them to come out to the ranch and map out a proper plan for this investigation. I hope the guys have something more substantial to tell me when I get back home than what you just reported."

5

Back Home on the Ranch

PULLING BACK THE CURTAINS OF her bedroom window, Sam peeks out. She's looking up the roadway to the gate of the ranch. James is on his way home today—he was released from the hospital early this morning. The chauffeur had called from the airport to tell her that his plane had arrived—he should be home any moment now. Sam is about to walk away from the window when she spies the limo coming into view. She hurries out of the room and hollers, "He's here!"

Sam hurries into the next bedroom and picks up baby Christopher. Molly and Michael are in the hall.

"Is Daddy really here?" Molly yells.

"Yes, his car is coming," Sam replies and moves quickly toward the door. Billingsley is holding it open for her.

The household staff, dressed in their best uniforms, are already lined up on the porch. The limo pulls up and Max, James's bodyguard, gets out of the front seat and opens the rear door. James holds on to the sides of the car as he slowly lifts himself up.

"Daddy!" Molly yells out and runs down the steps to leap into his arms.

"Oh God," James cries out, visibly in pain as he reels back against the vehicle with Molly in his arms.

"Daddy, I missed you," Molly says and gives him a kiss.

"I'm sorry about that," Sam says and reaches for Molly. "Come on, Molly, get down—you're hurting Daddy." Sam gives James a kiss. "Are you OK? Did she hurt you?"

"You have no idea." James turns to the baby in Sam's arms and gives him a kiss. "How's my little boy?"

The baby smiles, looks at Sam, and points to James. "*Dada.*"

"Yes, Christopher, *Dada,*" she says.

James bends down. "And how's my other little guy?" he asks Michael and gives him a kiss. "Have you been a good boy?"

"Yes, Daddy. I've been good. Are you home for good?"

"Yes, Michael, I'm home for good."

"Welcome home, sir," says Billingsley, who is standing nearby. The butler turns to the staff on the porch. "Guadalupe, Gilda—get Mr. Coppi's bags, please."

"It's good to be home," James says and carefully walks up the steps.

"What do you want to do?" Sam asks him when they are inside the house. "Are you tired? Do you want to lie down?"

"No, Sam, I'm fine. If you don't mind, I'd like to sit outside on the patio. Take in some of that clean Colorado air."

"You go ahead. I'll be right out with you—I'm just taking Christopher to his room."

A few minutes later, Sam comes out and gives him another kiss. "Welcome home, darling."

"Thank you, dear," he says, and looks up at the majestic mountains. "Oh, how I missed this place!"

Sam sits next to him. "I told the children to leave you alone. Are you OK?"

"I am now!" James says. He takes a deep breath and turns to her. "Sam, can I tell you something? When they brought me to the hospital after the shooting, I regained my consciousness. There was blood all over my gurney." He pauses for a moment. "I became very frightened—I honestly didn't think I was going to make it. Then, you popped into my head, and I knew I had to keep fighting. I'm so blessed to have you in my life."

Sam leans over and kisses him again. "We're blessed to have each other."

That night, James is lying in bed, propped up by three pillows behind his head. Sam comes out of the bathroom, gets into bed, turns off the lamp, and leans her head on his shoulder. "It feels so good to have you in bed next to me," she says.

James begins stroking her hair. "Yes, it feels wonderful to be here next to you."

Sam's hand slips into his pajama bottoms and she begins fondling his member. James kisses her on the top of the head. "This is going to come as a complete shock to you, dear, but I'm not going to be able to do anything tonight. As much as I want to, I'm still in a lot of pain. Especially my ribs and back."

Sam lifts up her head. "You don't have to do anything at all. And your guy down there is disagreeing with you—he's already at attention!"

"I'm sure he is."

Sam unbuttons his pants and lets his boy free—continuing her gentle caress. Moisture is accumulating on her hand. She leans down and licks the head.

"Oh, that feels good," he moans.

She looks up. "No pain?"

"Absolutely no pain!"

Sam places his member into her mouth and gently starts her slow, deliberate up-and-down motion, sliding her tongue over the head of the member with each stroke. His hand is caressing the back of her head and she knows that he's enjoying it. She continues her methodical movement. He's purring with delight.

"Oh God, you're driving me wild," he says.

That is her cue to increase her pace. Sam takes the penis a little deeper into her mouth. His excitement is building until he cannot take it any longer and finds his release. She looks up, and he has a huge smile on his face.

"Thank you," he says. "That was wonderful."

Sam slides up to give him a kiss. "Welcome home, dear."

<hr />

James rises early the next morning and gets dressed quietly without waking Sam. They had stayed up talking until nearly two in the morning. He's walking down the hall when Billingsley notices him.

"Good morning, sir. Would you like a cup of coffee?"

"No, thank you, Billingsley. Not right now. I'd like to go for a walk first. I need to stretch out these aching legs of mine."

"Yes—certainly, sir. Enjoy your constitutional."

James steps out onto the front porch and immediately feels the cool, crisp Colorado air. The sun is barely rising on the horizon. He looks out at the vast paddocks that abound at the ranch. The horses are already in the fields, grazing on the moist grass. One particular mare in one of the paddocks comes into view. She is in an enclosure with half a dozen other mares.

This steed is James's horse Clementine, the first horse that he had ever owned. She has been with him since he first bought the ranch. The old matron is under her favorite tree, that she'll use to shade herself from the Colorado sun that will soon be overhead.

Clementine guards that particular spot and allows only horses that she likes to have access to the area. The mare chases off intruders and lets any young filly quickly know who is in charge. Jeff, his ranch boss, and Billy one of the ranch hands, are coming out of the corral.

"Welcome back, Boss. How do you feel?" Jeff asks as he closes the wooden gate.

"I'm getting there, Jeff—slowly but surely," James says and turns to the other ranch hand. "Good morning, Billy."

"Good morning, sir. Welcome home."

"Thank you." James turns back to Jeff. "Have you got a few

minutes, Jeff? Take a walk with me. Get me caught up on what's going on around here."

As they begin their stroll, Jeff tells him, "Boss, I just want to say how proud we all are of you."

"Thank you, Jeff." James clears his throat. "How are you getting along with the breeder reproduction specialist that I hired? Are you still feuding with the man?"

Jeff lets out a laugh. "No, we're doing better." The ranch boss stops and looks at James. "Boss, I'm just an old-fashioned cowboy. These modern gizmos scare the crap out of me. It's a business—I get that—but it's just not something that I can understand. All these tubes and stuff—I really don't know what they all mean." The two men take up their walk again. "I'll come around—I promise. I'll get along with your new guy."

"Good," James says.

"Speaking of business, are we making any money, Boss?" Jeff asks. "I know that for the longest time, we were in the red."

"Yeah, Jeff, we are. The horse business turned the corner last year, and now we're in the black. This breeding part of the business is what's doing it for us. That's why I brought in this specialist. He's going to be very useful." James stops and looks around the yard. "Jeff, can we move these turnouts a little farther away from the houses? I'm considering putting in a practice track, and the turnouts are in the way."

Jeff takes off his cowboy hat, rubbing his hand through his blondish-gray hair. "What if we also moved the barns?"

"Is that really necessary?" James asks. "That's going to cost a lot of money."

Jeff has a look around. "No, we don't have to move the barns. It would just be more convenient if the barns were closer to the turnouts. Do you really need the track this close?"

"No, the track can go anywhere, but I'd prefer it in this spot."

"Can I have a few days to think about the plan? Let me mull it over a bit."

James nods. "Anything else important going on that I need to catch up on?"

"No, Boss. Everything is running smoothly."

"Come on, Jeff. Let's head back. I've got some people coming in this morning."

On the way back, James notices Cardiz, another of his ranch hands and an old army buddy of his, with his two young sons, Santiago and Afonso. The famous Cardiz smile broadens the man's face.

"Well, look who's back," Cardiz yells. "I hear you had a little trouble, Coppi. You needed your old army buddy. If I'd been there, you would've just sat back on your ass and let me take care of the problem—just like you used to do when we were in Vietnam."

"Yeah, you're right, Cardiz. So? Where were you?" James asks, laughing, and looks over at the boys. "I see you got your sons here for the summer to help you. Maybe some work will get done around here, finally."

Cardiz turns to his sons. "Boys, go and clean out the barns. I want to talk with Mr. Coppi."

"I'll see you later, Jeff," James says.

"Yeah, Boss. Take care."

"It must be nice having your sons around," James says to Cardiz. "I'm sure you must miss them. At least you'll have your boys for the summer."

"Not just the summer, Coppi. I'll have them for good!"

James stops and stares at Cardiz. "For good? What happened?"

"My ex-wife is here. We're going to try to work things out. I won't be living in the bunkhouse any longer."

James grins. "That's great, Cardiz. Just great. Anything that I can do to help, just let me know. If you need some time off . . ."

"Thanks, Coppi. I appreciate that."

"What happened?" James asks. "How did this all come about? What made you two try to reconcile?"

"It was you, Coppi! You were the influence on me."

"Me? What did I do?"

"You lived your life—that's what you did. When you and I were in Vietnam, you were the same screwed-up guy that I was. But you changed yourself. Now, whenever something knocks you down, you get right back up and try even harder. I've been asking myself—if Coppi can do it, why can't I?

"I see how you are with Sam," Cardiz continues. "You guys have your problems, but you never quit."

"That's because I love Sam," James responds. "I can't imagine living my life without her."

"Yeah, I know. And, I love my wife, Mattie. But I screwed it all up," Cardiz says and lets out a sigh. "Two weeks ago, I called her and asked if she would give this marriage another try. Told her that I had changed. I can't believe she said yes. This time, I'm not going to screw it up—you'll see. You'll like Mattie, Coppi. She's a lot like Sam."

"I'm sure I will. Why don't you bring Mattie for dinner tomorrow night? I'd love to meet her, and I'm sure Sam would, too."

"Yeah, I'd like that. You sure that it wouldn't be too much trouble?"

"No, no trouble at all. OK, I'll see you tomorrow. Bring the boys, too."

Sam rolls over on the bed and notices that James's side of the bed is empty. She gets up, slides her feet into her slippers, and heads for the bathroom. When she's back out, she picks up the robe from the chair and heads out of the bedroom. Sam sees Billingsley in the hallway.

"Mr. Billingsley, have you seen James?" she asks, tying her robe.

"Mr. Coppi went for a walk," he responds. "There's a Mr. Vernon Dixon waiting for Mr. Coppi in the sitting room. I just brought him a cup of coffee."

"Vernon," she greets the silver haired gentleman in the sitting room, "I didn't know you'd be here today. What brings you out here?"

Vernon sets down his cup and smiles. "James set this up yesterday. He wants to meet with his management team this morning. Me, first."

Sam immediately feels furious. *Not even a day home and he's already back at work.* She hears someone coming through the front door. James walks in and gives her a kiss.

"Good morning, darling," he says, and turns to Vernon. "I'll be right with you. Can I have someone get you anything?"

"No—I'm good, James. Your butler brought me a cup of coffee."

"OK, good! Just give me a few minutes to get cleaned up."

Sam marches into the bedroom with him. "You're working today?" she hollers at his back.

James turns to her and smiles. "Not all day—just a few hours this morning. Why are you so upset?"

"I can't believe you! Not even one day home from the hospital, and you're right back to working! Don't you even want to spend some time with your family?"

James smiles and reaches for her. "It's just a couple of hours," he says as he gives her a hug and a kiss. "After that, I'm all yours. I'll tell you what—pack a picnic basket. We'll get the wagon out and take a family outing this afternoon. How's that? No more interference. Just a picnic and the family."

Sam gives him a side glance. "Very slick, Mr. Coppi. You got yourself out of that one really fast. You better keep your promise—I don't want to hear this afternoon that you're in a lot of pain."

James gives her another kiss. "I'll keep my word. Although, I am in pain. Can you get me a couple of Tylenols please? The pills are on the top drawer of the medicine cabinet."

As Sam is getting the pills he shouts. "Oh, by the way, I invited Cardiz and his wife for dinner tomorrow night. His sons are coming, too."

Sam comes out of the bathroom. "His wife? I thought Cardiz was divorced."

"They've reconciled. At least, he's trying to put the marriage back together. I thought it would be nice if we had them for dinner. You don't mind, do you?"

Sam hands him the pills. "No, of course not. "As he pops the pills into his mouth Sam asks. "James you're only taking Tylenols for the pain, nothing stronger, right?"

"If I was taking something stronger why would I be asking you for Tylenols?" He walks up to her and holds her in his arms. "I'm not back on drugs, I swear. That's why I stopped taking the pain killers at the hospital, I didn't want to take the risk of getting hooked again."

"All right, Vernon, let's get started," James says when he walks backs into the study. "The rest of the staff will be here shortly. What's been going on at the company? Bring me up to speed."

"Well, James, you'll be happy to hear that the company is doing just fine. We are five percent ahead of our goals. We're having our semiannual management meetings this week, and we're planning on updating our forecasts. I'm going to ask everyone to push even harder in the second half. Keep the momentum going that we built up in the first."

"That's good, Vernon. Really good. Nice going. How about the railroad? When are we going to get that back up and going, now that I'm home?"

"James, I think we should wait a little longer—until you're completely one hundred percent. Once this railroad venture gets going, we're going to have to put on dog and pony shows for the financing that we'll need to buy out Greenwald. That means at least a month of nonstop traveling for you around the country to meet with the bankers."

"OK, Vernon, I guess you're right. Call Greenwald and make sure he's aware of the postponement."

Mr. Billingsley knocks and opens the door. "Pardon me, sir, but the rest of your party has arrived."

"Thank you, Mr. Billingsley," James answers. "See if they want anything, please. We should be done soon." James turns back to Vernon after the butler shuts the door. "Have you got anything else?"

"Yes, James, I have," Vernon replies and clears his throat. "Your real estate development and golf course design companies—is there a reason that I'm not involved with these? You have put me in charge of all of your business interests except for those. I should think that you'd want me running those companies, too."

"Yes, I do want you involved," James responds. "The only reason that I haven't turned over that responsibility to you as yet is timing. I wanted you to come up to speed on the other side of my business—I was planning on turning over the remainder to you by the end of this year. That is, if you feel comfortable by that time."

Vernon sits back in his seat. "All right—that sounds mighty fine. I'm sure that I'll be ready to go by the end of the year."

"Good! Now if there's nothing else, why don't we bring in the rest of the crew and get started? I promised Sam I'd take her on a picnic this afternoon."

The next few hours are spent with the remainder of his senior staff. The meeting is about to conclude when James brings up one last point.

"What about the investigation on the church shooting? How's that coming along?"

Charlie McGill, the head of the domestic investigative side of the business answers. "We've identified the four shooters as being Palestinian nationalists."

"Yes, I know that, Charlie. You told me that once before—and I can read the newspapers as well as you. What else have you got?"

"They arrested an Imam from a Brooklyn mosque. The FBI believes that the Imam was part of the conspiracy," Charlie answers as he is loosening his tie.

James throws up his hands. "That's it? So basically, you've got nothing? Have you done any investigating at all? All this information that you just gave me, I already got from just watching the television."

"James." Vernon speaks up, bringing up an old argument. "Why are we getting involved? Why not leave this up to the FBI? They're far better equipped to handle this than we are."

"Gee, I don't know. I've had a small bucket of shrapnel pulled out of my body. I'd kind of like to know who put them there. And, just as importantly, you guys aren't seeing the big picture. Our security business is advising our clients on how they can protect their assets and personnel. This attack on the church is very troubling. Can you imagine if such an attack occurred at a stockholder meeting held by one of our clients?

"These terrorist attacks represent a new kind of danger," he continues, looking at each of them carefully. "We need to know exactly what that danger is so that we can advise our clients on how to protect themselves from these types of attacks. This investigation that I've asked you to undertake will give us insight as to what these extremists are all about. What are their motives and how they operate? This may be the most important investigation we conduct this year.

"As far as the FBI being better at handling this investigation, I totally disagree. It's been nearly three weeks since the shooting, and all they've got is that the gunmen were Palestinians.

"The FBI has this poor religious sap from Brooklyn locked up," James adds. "I doubt very highly that the cleric had anything to do with the shooting." He turns to Charlie. "What about the inside man, Charlie? Why hasn't the FBI identified him?"

"What inside man?" Charlie says.

James shakes his head in disbelief. "Damn, Charlie, you really haven't given this any thought." James lets out a sigh. "How did a bunch of Palestinians come up with an idea to shoot up a church in Lubbock, Texas? Explain that to me, Charlie? How do the Palestinians even know where Lubbock, Texas is?

"Trust me, Charlie, there must be someone on the inside. A delivery man—or maybe someone on a construction crew. Or possibly a temporary worker who knows something about the place. Check around, Charlie. Look for that person. The inside source is probably

Muslim—or at least a sympathizer. That person shouldn't be very hard to find in Lubbock."

James stands up and tries to stretch. He winces in pain. "OK, guys, we're done. Thanks for coming. Vernon, Prince Khartami is coming over in a little while, and I want you to be here for the meeting."

A few minutes later, Billingsley looks in. "Prince Firuz Khartami is here."

"Thank you, Billingsley. Do me a favor—get my wife and have her come in here. After that, you can bring in the prince."

"What does the prince want?" Sam asks when she's come into the study.

"Honestly, Sam, I don't know. This is a spur of the moment meeting called by him. His father, is under political pressure in his country. I'm having my sources in the Middle East look into the shah's problems to let me know if it's anything serious."

"Prince Khartami!" James calls out, and leaps from his seat when the prince enters the room with Billingsley. James walks over and gives him a hug. "I'm so happy to see you. How is your father?"

"My father is fine," the prince unbuttons his suit jacket. "And, I'm happy to see you too, James." The prince notices Sam. "Mrs. Coppi, I'm so glad to see you!" He walks over and gives her a hug. "I did not know that you'd be here at this meeting. How have you been?"

"I'm just fine, Your Highness. Thank you for asking," Sam replies. "You don't mind if I stay for the meeting, do you?"

"No, not at all," the prince answers, smiling. "I know how much James relies on your advice and counsel."

"Would you like a cup of coffee, Your Highness?" Billingsley asks him.

"Yes, thank you," he says, and Billingsley closes the door.

James gestures to Vernon. "You remember Vernon."

"Yes, of course." The prince walks over and shakes his hand.

"Come on, Prince Firuz, have a seat." James motions to a chair. "Let's talk for a while and get caught up. I haven't seen you in over a year. How've you been? How is your family?"

"My family is fine," Firuz replies, taking a seat "I, on the other hand, am another story. I'm not feeling so good."

"Really?" James asks. "What's the matter? Anything serious?"

"No, I don't believe it's anything serious. I've just been having headaches. They're probably from flying. My father has me traveling all over the world. I should feel better after things calm down and my traveling is done."

"Speaking of your father, how is the shah doing? The last time I spoke to him, he wasn't feeling too well, either." What James really wants to know is what is happening in their country. Recent reports from his sources indicate some problems with a religious group.

"My father is doing a little better," Prince Firuz replies.

Billingsley walks in and sets the coffee on the table. "Will there be anything else, Your Highness?"

"No, thank you," the prince answers.

"I hear there is some political turmoil back home," James says after Billingsley leaves. "Some sort of religious unrest in your country."

The Prince waves his hand and shrugs the question off. "Just some small-time agitators—nothing serious. We've handled thousands of these troublemakers before."

"OK," James says and smiles. "Now I'm completely baffled—why did you call for this meeting? If everything is going great, why travel halfway around the world for a face-to-face with me?"

The Prince takes a sip of his coffee and looks at James. "James, as you know, my father just recovered from a very serious illness. He is fine now, but it got him thinking about his legacy. What will happen to the family if he's not around?

"So my father began to create a contingency plan. He's in the process of moving roughly two billion dollars out of the country. We purchased property in France where the family can have an escape haven if the unrest turns violent in our country.

"My father wants you to review the plan and make sure we have taken the proper precautions. Will you do that for us?"

"Yes, of course," James says, leaning forward. "I'd be more than happy to help."

"Wonderful!" The prince puts down his cup, wipes his mustache with the napkin and gives James a sly look. "What is your fee?"

James stares at the man intently for a moment, quietly doing calculations. "I want a five-year agreement to manage the money. The fee is one percent per year of the outstanding balance. My firm will also need another agreement for five years to supply security for your family—which is vast—if they are forced to leave your country."

James peeks over at Sam who is shaking her head. He turns back to the prince.

"My estimate for the security service is around a million a year, if that happens. All of the money is to be paid up front. Your Highness, if you choose to go ahead with my proposal, I want twenty-five million as a retainer at the start of the assignment."

"What you're asking is ridiculous!" Prince Khartami says, his voice becoming progressively louder. "My family doesn't need a long-term commitment from you. We just want you to review our plan—nothing else."

"I've already reviewed your plan," James says, letting out a breath and sitting back. "It stinks! It won't work."

"What do you mean, it won't work?" the royal almost shouts. "Why won't the plan work? You haven't even looked over anything that we've done. In a matter of minutes, you say you know that the plan won't work. How could you possibly be so sure?"

James waits a moment before responding, letting the conversation lull a bit while the prince calms down. Once James senses that the prince has collected himself, he continues. "Look—I don't need to review what you've done. I already know that what you have in mind won't work. If all you need from me is to review your plan, save your money. The conclusion I reach at the end will be the same as I've reached today."

James leans forward in his chair. "Listen to me, Your Highness. If something should happen back home—I'm not saying that it will—but if something should happen, the new government in power is going to want this money that your family took with them returned.

"It's probably already widely known in your country that your family is in the process of moving this money into a foreign account. Even if it isn't known, the new regime will find out as soon as they're in power. Two billion is not pocket change.

"And since you didn't use my people to make the transfers, I'm sure the funds will be easy to trace. The first place the new government will look for the money is Switzerland—it's the obvious choice." James looks shrewdly at the prince. "Isn't that where you're going with the money?"

The prince's eyes widen.

"So what will happen when the new players find out that your money is hiding in Switzerland?" James continues, shifting in his chair to get more comfortable. "You know what's going to take place—the new regime will put pressure on Switzerland to hand over the money. Believe me—the Swiss government and their banks will fold under the political pressure. The Swiss authorities will hand over the money in a heartbeat. Even if the Swiss banks don't give the money back, they'll put a freeze on your account. How will you get the money out of Switzerland? Switzerland provides no protection or security for your family's money.

"And your plan to relocate your family to France is no good, either. Your entire clan living in one location is perfect for the opposition. The new regime can send in a commando unit to wipe out the entire family in a single operation. The French government will not provide you with any protection. You'll have to provide your own security detail."

"What do you suggest?" the prince asks.

"You need to spread your money around the world, not just in Switzerland. The money has to have layers between your family and the banks. We must completely obscure the paper trail. You need to place the money in financial institutions in places like the Cayman Islands, Panama, South Africa, Israel, Singapore, and so on. Countries that usually don't pop up on the radar of normal financial channels. Not all of these organizations will be banks. My company knows how to move money around the world quickly and also secretly."

James peeks over at Sam to see her reaction. She shakes her head and frowns.

James smiles at her and turns back to the prince. "On a personal note, your family will have to spread out, too. Your residences can't be located in just one country. What if France kicks your people out? What will your family do then?

"Doesn't it make sense to cover all of your bases? You have a large family. The security detail that will be required will be large and complicated. We will need to monitor threats from all around the world."

James pauses for a moment and tries to gauge the prince's reaction. The prince appears to be looking thoughtful and James knows that his talk is having an effect. In a much calmer, more reassuring voice, he continues.

"Come on, Your Highness—you know I'm right. The only way to protect your family is to have someone like me involved. If something were to happen in your country, and you lost power, all of the other nations would abandon your family.

"You need me. My fee is reasonable, when you consider the amount of work that needs to be done. I'm not trying to take advantage of you because you're in a tight situation. What do you say? Is it a deal?"

Prince Khartami swallows audibly. "I will need to speak to my father. Is there a place in this house where I can call and speak to him privately?"

"Yes, of course. You can use Sam's study. It's right next door to mine."

"You know that his father will never agree to the deal," Vernon says after the prince has left. "You asked for way too much."

"Frankly, Vernon, I really don't care if the Khartamis take the deal or not. This religious group that's trying to overthrow his government are true devout zealots. I don't agree with what the prince is saying—this opposition group is not just a bunch of troublemakers. Rodney called his sources at the CIA and was told that the agency is contemplating abandoning the support of the shah. Without the CIA backing the royal family is finished. And these fanatics won't be happy with just coming into power. They'll want to kill the shah's entire family and wipe them out completely. To do the job that's required if the country does fall apart will require a Herculean effort on our part. Nearly all of our company's personnel will have to be involved.

"Believe me—we will have earned every nickel of the money that I asked for. All the transactions on the account will go through our Singapore subsidiary. We need to keep the details as far as possible from our company.

"If we become involved, then just you and Ian, from our London office, will be involved in moving the money. No one else at the firm will be made a part of the process until the Khartami family is ready to be expatriated. This is going to be handled very hush-hush."

At that moment, Prince Khartami comes back into the office and smiles. "My father says we will take the deal," he tells James.

James looks over at Vernon and smiles. "That's great, Your Highness. Vernon will drive you to his office and will draw up the initial binder. You will deal with Vernon directly."

Sam walks up to James after the two men leave. "That was some deal you worked out. I hope you know what you're doing?"

"Yeah, maybe," he says, looking worried. "I hope I didn't outsmart myself."

"Why? Do you really believe there will be a problem?"

"Oh yeah—for sure, there'll be problems. The prince didn't speak of his true fears. There are big problems in his country—much bigger than what he admitted to today. There were riots at the capital last month. The police opened up and fired on the demonstrators, killing over two hundred. It's never good when you have to kill your own citizens to keep the peace," James says. Then he shakes his head. "Yeah, there'll be problems. I just hope the problems are manageable."

The next night, after dinner, James, Sam, Cardiz, and Mattie are sitting on the patio having a cup of coffee. The children are all playing in the yard—except for Cristopher, who is near the adults, in his highchair.

"This place is beautiful," Mattie says. "Thanks for having us over."

"You are most welcome," Sam answers and smiles at the seven generation New Englander.

Mattie points to the children. "I love Molly's red hair. Who does she take after?"

"My hair was red when I was younger—it turned blonde as I got older. I hope Molly's stays red."

"Yes, I do too, that color is beautiful." Mattie smiles and turns to Sam. "You know what I just realized? You have one of each! Molly has red hair; Michael's hair is jet black like James, and the baby, Christopher, is a blonde."

Sam laughs. "I guess that's true. Now all we need is a child with golden brown, like your beautiful hair and we'll have the entire match."

"Where are you staying?" James asks.

"I've got a room at a cheap motel downtown," Mattie replies. "Antonio and I have started looking for a place of our own, but there aren't many rentals available. The soldiers at Fort Carson have snapped up everything that's affordable and any good."

"Why don't you stay in our guest house?" Sam says. "It's empty."

"We wouldn't want to put you out," Mattie responds.

"It's no problem at all! I insist. The place is only sitting vacant. You can have it until you find a place. Move in right away and save yourself some money."

Mattie looks over at Cardiz who nods. "Thank you! That's very generous. With that out of the way, I can begin looking for a job."

"What kind of work are you looking for?" James asks.

Mattie shrugs her shoulders. "Most anything. Probably an office job. That's what I did back in Massachusetts."

"What about being a receptionist?" James asks her. "There's an opening at my place. Diana, our current girl, is leaving. I think you'd be perfect. That wonderful Bostonian accent would be a big hit with our visitors."

She grins. "Sure, that would be great!"

"Good! I'll let Kathy, my assistant, know. I'll call her in the morning, and she'll set you up. Give her a call tomorrow afternoon after you're settled in at our guest house."

Cardiz smiles and looks at Mattie. "See? I told you these are good people."

Mattie smiles, too. "Yes, they certainly are."

Out in the yard, the children start yelling and shouting. Molly comes storming over.

"Mommy, can you get Daddy's medals, please?"

"Why do you want the medals?" James asks her.

"Because Afonso said that his daddy is braver than you."

"All daddies who went to Vietnam were brave, sweetie. I'll tell you what. Why don't you take the boys into the game room and show them your new pinball machine instead? I think the boys will like that much better than some rusty old medals."

When the kids had run inside, James turns to Sam and frowns. "I didn't know you went around showing off my army medals."

"Why not?" Sam asks with a smile. "Like Molly, I'm very proud of you." She stands up. "I've got to change the baby's diaper." Sam leans over toward James to whisper, "And they're not *your* medals. You gave them to me, remember?" She lifts Christopher out of his highchair and heads inside.

The next morning, Sam walks into her husband's study. "James, did you complain to Billingsley that the silverware was all stained and dirty?"

"Yeah, I did." he responds without looking up.

"Why?"

"Because the silverware was all stained and dirty." James raises his head. "You know, Sam, I think things are falling apart around here—I let Billingsley know that, too." James gestures at his desk. "Just look at all that dust. This table hasn't been cleaned in months." James leans forward, looks toward the door, and whispers, "You know what, Sam? I think the women who clean are taking advantage of our good natures."

"The help is not taking advantage of us!" Sam's voice goes up. "The reason the women don't clean your office is because there are papers scattered all over your desk. The women are afraid to touch anything. The last time you misplaced a file, you crucified these poor girls, remember? You were convinced that one of the ladies threw out your file. And if I remember correctly, the folder was actually in your office at work."

Sam stands up. "Now you've got Billingsley all worked up—and you know Billingsley, he'll do anything to make sure you're happy. Heaven forbid that Lord Coppi isn't pleased! Billingsley is meeting with the entire household staff right now, threatening to fire them all if they don't shape up. The whole place is an uproar—thanks to you!"

"Good! Maybe the staff will get into shape now. Do some work around here. This place is falling apart."

"You have no idea how hard everybody works around here!" Sam says. "We give nearly a dozen parties a year. Do you know the amount of work that goes into putting on one of those affairs?"

When James looks away from her, she continues. "No, of course not, you don't. You just stand around at the social event and accept all the compliments on what a great party you've put on."

Sam warns him. "The next time you have a complaint, you tell me! Don't get Billingsley involved."

"No, I don't like that idea," James shakes his head. "It's emasculating. Besides, who made you the boss? I have just as much a say around here as you do!"

Sam crosses her arms and warns him with a deathly stare.

James laughs. "All right, I'll behave," he says as the phone rings. It's Charlie.

"Syed Bakhil," Charlie says immediately. "He's your inside man. He's the guy who set up the attack on the church—an immigrant from Afghanistan. Bakhil works for a boiler company. This guy does some maintenance work at the church from time to time."

"Afghanistan? The guy is an Afghan? He's not Palestinian? Are you sure?"

"Yes, I'm positive. Bakhil is from Afghanistan. I checked with immigration. What the fuck is the difference that this guy is from Afghanistan? They're all the same, aren't they?"

"I don't know—maybe it makes no difference. It just seems odd, that's all. How do you know it's him that set this thing up?"

"I'm not absolutely sure he's the guy, but he's the only one that fits the profile. He's the only guy who's a Muslim and who also had access to the church." Charlie pauses, waiting for James to speak. "So what do you want me to do? Turn this guy over to the FBI?"

"Where is this fellow Syed now?" James asks. "Can we get to him?"

"Yes. Syed lives in Lubbock. He has a wife and two kids who also live there. Bakhil works for Pibbs Boiler and Repair. This is the company that does the work at the church. The Bakhil family got their visas by claiming political asylum—they're not going anywhere, as far as I can tell."

"OK, good. Don't do anything yet—don't give the FBI Bakhil's name. Give me a little time to come up with a plan."

Before he hangs up, James says, "Good job, Charlie!"

6

On the Hunt

MOSHAR WAITS AS A HERD of goats crosses the road. There's a small town not too far away that has come into view. That town, Mirabad, is his destination. He's been traveling on foot for the past week. It was a torturous trek through the desert in the searing heat that wouldn't have been necessary if Faakhir had made the trip to Saindak, Pakistan, as he'd promised he would. Instead, Moshar has had to make the long trip to Mirabad to find out what is going on.

Has Faakhir changed his mind? Mafrouz had told Moshar that Faakhir could be trusted. "He is extremely reliable," Mafrouz had said. *Well, if that's true, then why had Faakhir not shown up for his appointment?* Now, Moshar wants to find out for himself just how reliable this fellow Faakhir really is.

Moshar, wipes his brow, unlatches his waterskin and takes a swallow. The pouch is nearly empty. He will be arriving at his destination just in time for a refill. When the herd has passed, Moshar continues walking toward the village. He's not worried about being seen by the Russians. This part of Afghanistan is pretty safe from Russian air reconnaissance. Besides, who would waste their time on a lone traveler? There's no one in the streets when he gets to the Mirabad. It is midafternoon and most of the townsfolk are indoors sheltering themselves from the sweltering sun. Eventually he comes upon two young boys kicking a soccer ball.

"Do you know the house of the man called Faakhir?" he asks the boys.

One of the boys points to a house on the left. "It's that large house over there."

Moshar knocks on the door, and a youngster comes out. "Is this the house of Faakhir?" Moshar asks him.

"Yes. He is my father," the boy answers.

"Can you tell your father that Moshar is here?"

Faakhir comes to the door.

"It is nice to meet you, Faakhir. I'm Moshar. May I come in?"

Faakhir invites Moshar inside with a gesture and then signals to his son. "Please get our guest some water. He has come a long way and must be very thirsty. Then tell your mother to bring our guest some food."

When the boy has gone, Faakhir motions to a rug. "Please, make yourself comfortable. Or would you like to wash up first? I'm sure it's been a long journey."

"Let's talk first," Moshar says and squats down on the rug.

Faakhir squats across from him. The boy comes out with a pitcher, pours water into a cup, and hands it to Moshar.

"Thank you," Moshar says, and drinks down the cup.

"Leave the water," Faakhir says and dismisses his son with a wave.

"What happened, Faakhir? You didn't show." Moshar reaches for the pitcher and pours himself another drink. "Have you changed your mind?"

"No I haven't changed my mind—there are things that I need to tend to here at home. The American can wait."

"Well, Mafrouz doesn't agree with you," Moshar says, raising his voice a bit. "He feels that we need to handle this American right away. I've already sent men out to Colorado where this man lives. The men should be reporting back to me before too long."

A woman comes out, places two dishes in front of the men, and leaves. "We have only *badenjan* and *nan*," Faakhir tells Moshar. "If you stay a little longer, I can have my wife make Palaw."

"The *badenjan* will be enough," Moshar answers as he tears off a piece of the bread and scoops up the dip. "It is good," he says as he wolfs down the food and looks over at Faakhir. "I can't wait any longer, Faakhir—I must have your answer. Are you coming back with me?"

"As I said, I cannot leave now. There are things that I need to do at home. I will come in two weeks."

"Two weeks—are you sure?"

"Yes, two weeks—no more. That's all the time I will need."

"OK," Moshar says and smiles. "Two weeks. But no more." Moshar looks around. "How many children do you have?"

"I have three children. My son, the one you just met, is eleven. I have a daughter who is thirteen and another daughter age nine."

"Thirteen. Your daughter will be marrying soon. Do you have someone in mind?"

"Yes, we are working out the details. It is the reason that I need to be home."

Moshar tears off another piece of bread and scoops up some more *badenjan*. "Faakhir, if you don't mind, can you pour me a bowl of water? I'd like to get cleaned up a little before I start back."

"No, I don't mind. But can we go over the plan first? You must have thought this through. What is the plan?"

"No, I haven't, Faakhir. I don't have any plan. When we meet again in Saindak in two weeks, I should know more. As I said, I have men on the way to America right now. I'll know more about how we should proceed when they give me a report."

The ranch hand Billy is riding his horse along the edge of the Coppi ranch. He's inspecting the fence. A massive storm had passed through the previous night, and he's making sure that none of the fence is down. In the distance, he spots a blue pickup truck inside the ranch.

"Trespassers!" he utters.

Billy pulls his rifle from its holster and gallops toward the truck. The truck speeds away from Billy, toward a hole in the fence.

Billy gallops alongside the truck at full speed. "Pull over!" he yells at the two men in the front seats. The driver ignores him and instead guns the engine, kicking up mud as he drives off. Billy watches the truck escape through the gap in the fence. Billy hops off his horse and watches the truck disappear into the distance.

Ten minutes later, there's a knock at the door of James's study, and Billingsley sticks his head in. "I'm sorry to disturb you, sir, but Jeff and Billy would like a word with you."

James looks up from his paperwork. "Send them right in."

The two men come walking in, hats in hand. "I'm sorry to bother you, Boss, but there's something that you might like to know," Jeff begins. "Billy was out inspecting the fence after the storm we had last night. There was a blue pickup truck on the property with two men inside. Billy tried to catch up with the men, but they sped off."

James looks at Billy. "Any idea what those men were doing out there?"

"None at all, sir," Billy replies. "There's no reason for anybody to be out in that part of the ranch. It's pretty far from the main road. The barbed wire was cut clean, not damaged by the storm. Those men cut a hole in the fence—that's how they got onto the ranch."

"What did the men look like?"

"They were a little older than me. Tanned faces—but not Mexican or Indian. Something different."

"Tanned? Middle Eastern, maybe?"

Billy shrugs. "I don't know Middle Easterns, sir!"

"Mediterranean? Palestinian? Arab?"

Billy nods. "Yup, Arab. That's it, sir. They looked a little like the men you shot at that church. Just like the pictures I saw of those men on television."

"OK—thanks, Billy."

"Is there anything you need us to do, Boss?" Jeff asks. "Maybe these guys will come back."

"Just have someone ride the entire perimeter of the ranch every day for a while and look things over, Jeff. Let me know if they see anything else."

After they leave, James mutters, "Arabs? What the fuck are Arabs doing out here? And what do they want on my ranch? Does this have anything to do with the church shooting?"

Sam walks in with car keys in her hand. "I'll be gone the rest of this morning. I'm going to the beauty parlor."

"By yourself?"

"Yes, of course by myself," she laughs. "I'm a big girl."

"Where's Ronan your bodyguard?"

"You gave him the week off, remember? You gave both bodyguards the week off."

"I gave the guys the time off because we were staying put all week. I didn't know you'd be gallivanting all around town." He makes circular motions with his hands.

"I'm not 'gallivanting all around town'!" she protests, laughing and aping the circular motions. "I'm just going to the beauty parlor."

"Ask Jeff to have one of the men go with you."

"But I don't want anyone to come with me!"

James stands up and walks toward her. He pulls her into his arms. "Please, make me happy. Have someone go with you."

Sam looks up at his face. "What's wrong, James? Why are you being so careful?"

"There's nothing wrong. Ever since this church shooting, I'm just a little anxious—that's all. Have someone go with you, please. Ask Cardiz. I think he's free."

Sam shakes her head. "All right—I'll do it this time. Are you happy?"

James gives her a kiss. "Yes, very happy. Have a nice trip."

After she leaves, he makes a call. "Charlie, are Gurney and Hiawalah on assignment?"

"Yes, of course," Charlie replies.

"How fast can you get them back?"

"Two days, I guess," he responds. "That should do it. Why? What do you need?"

"Get ahold of the men and meet me at my plane in two days. We're going to Lubbock. It's time to have a talk with this guy Syed."

James makes another call to his head of government security.

"Rodney, you worked at the CIA—get in touch with the people you used to know. Find out everything you can about the four shooters at the church. Also, get me some information on a Syed Bakhil. He's an Afghan nationalist who is living in Lubbock now."

"OK, James. Is that all?"

"Yeah, that's it for now. Get back to me as soon as you can. I'll need the information on Syed by tomorrow."

James gets back on the phone with Ian Wadsworth, the head of his London agency and European operations.

"Ian, this is James. I need you to contact your Israeli sources. Find out what they know about the Palestinians that I shot at the church. Also, see if they know anything about a connection between Palestinians and Afghans."

"Afghans and Palestinians?" Ian comments. "That's an odd combination. What makes you think that these two groups are connected in any way?"

"I don't know if there *is* a connection. That's why I'm asking you to find out. If there is a connection, the Israelis will know about it."

James taps his pencil on his desk after hanging up. *Arabs, eh?* he thinks. *What are you guys up to?*

"So what's our plan for this guy Syed?" Charlie asks on the plane as James and his men are flying to Lubbock.

"Here's what I got," James leans forward toward the three men. "When we touch down, we'll pick up two car rentals. Charlie, you and Frank will go and pick up this fellow Syed. Frank, you used to work at the FBI, show Syed your old FBI identification, he won't know the difference. Have Syed believe that you guys are FBI agents. Tell Syed that he's wanted for questioning in the church shooting."

"What if he doesn't want to come with us?" Frank asks.

"Make him come," James answers. "Do whatever it takes. But I don't believe that anything else will be necessary. This guy knows that he was part of the crime. He'll come. Hiawalah and I will get a motel room. There's a HoJo's not too far from the airport. Bring him there as soon as you have him."

An hour later, Charlie drives the car into the parking lot of Pibbs Boiler and Repair and looks around. There's a lone blue Pontiac parked in the front.

"Is this where this guy works?" Frank asks.

"Yeah, this is the place."

"It doesn't look like anyone is around. I hope we didn't make the trip down here for nothing."

"There's only one way to find out," Charlie says and opens his car door.

When they walk into the shop, there's a young woman sitting behind a glass partition and chewing gum. She slides open the glass, takes off her glasses, and puts them on the desk. "Can I help you?"

Frank waves the wallet with his identification in front of her. "I'm Frank Gurney with the FBI, and with me is my partner, Charlie McGill. We're looking for a fellow that works here named Syed Bakhil. Is he around? We'd like to speak to him."

"Syed is out on the road, on assignment," she replies. "What's this all about? What do you need from Syed?"

"We need to speak to Mr. Bakhil. It's extremely important. Where can we reach him?"

"Hold on a sec. Let me get the assignment log." She reaches back and pulls a clipboard off the wall behind her. "He's at the college— Texas Tech," she reads off the sheet. "Not too far from here. He's working at the gymnasium. Do you want to tell me what this is all about?"

"No, I'm sorry, I can't," Frank says, and they walk out.

"There's the van," Charlie points out when they drive into the university's parking lot. "Hurry, pull up—I think that's him getting into it."

Frank pulls the car alongside the van and they jump out. "Excuse me, Mr. Bakhil," Frank yells out. He takes out his wallet with his ID and sticks it in front of Syed's face. "I'm Frank Gurney with the

FBI, and this is my partner, Charlie McGill. May we have a word with you?"

"What about?" Syed asks, holding the door of the van open.

"It's about the shooting at the church. I'm sure you've seen it on TV."

"Yes, I saw it. What do you want from me? I don't know anything about what happened."

"Actually, Mr. Bakhil, we'd like you to come with us. We have a few questions that we'd like for you to clear up."

"I'm working right now. I can't just leave."

"Mr. Bakhil, it's not a request." Frank shuts the door of the van. He opens the door of the car and motions for Syed to get into the front seat. "Please. Come quietly. It'll only take a few minutes."

"What about the van?"

"Leave it here. We'll bring you back when we get done."

"This is a motel?" Syed asks as they drive into the HoJo's parking lot.

"Yeah, we're from Washington," Frank responds. "We're here to help out with the investigation. There's no room at the police station."

"Make yourself comfortable." Frank motions to the lone chair in the motel room. "This shouldn't take long."

James and Hiawalah come out of the bathroom.

"Hey! You're not policeman!" Syed yells, jumping up. "I know this guy." Syed points at James. "He's the one that shot the four men."

Charlie pushes him back down onto the chair. "That's right. We're not policemen. So just sit there and shut your fucking mouth."

"I'm not staying." Syed jumps back up and tries to make it to the door. Hiawalah slugs him with a straight right to his midsection. Syed drops down to his knees, clutching his stomach. Hiawalah pulls him up by his hair and flings him back onto the chair.

"The man said sit down and shut your fucking mouth," Hiawalah says, putting his mug right in front of Syed's face. "Do you understand?"

Syed nods, gasping for air.

James sits on the bed, facing Syed.

"Your name is Syed Bakhil?" James asks.

Syed nods.

"You're from Afghanistan, is that right?"

Syed nods again.

"Where in Afghanistan? What city?"

"Mirabad."

James smiles. "Tell me, Syed. What's a nice man from Afghanistan doing getting himself mixed up with a bunch of Palestinians?"

"I don't know any Palestinians."

James's smile gets wider. "Really, Syed? Is that how you want to play it? Do you really want to do this the hard way?"

Syed doesn't reply.

James turns to Hiawalah. "Sarge, do you remember how you got Jimmy Johnson to cooperate? I do believe that Mr. Bakhil needs a little bit of that medicine."

Hiawalah grabs Syed by the collar and drags him into the bathroom. They hear a commotion and Syed gagging as his head gets shoved into the toilet.

James goes over to Charlie. "Charlie, do me a favor. There's a vending machine downstairs—get me a Seven Up."

James walks over to the bathroom where Hiawalah is still pushing Syed's head into the toilet bowl. "That's enough, Sarge."

Hiawalah pulls Syed's head out of the toilet. Syed lies on the floor, coughing and spitting out the water.

"Bring him back into the room," James tells Hiawalah.

Hiawalah throws Syed onto the bed. James hands the man a towel. He turns to Frank and Hiawalah. "Do me a favor, guys. Take a walk outside for a few minutes—I want to talk to Syed alone."

James sits on the coffee table. "Come, Syed, sit up." Syed raises himself up and sits on the side of the bed facing James. "You do know that they're not going to stop. This is only the beginning. But I don't want to talk about that right now. Let's talk about you. You have a family, right?"

Syed nods, mopping his face with the towel.

"A wife and two children," he says. "A son and a daughter."

"How old are the children?"

"My son is eleven and my daughter is nine," he responds feebly.

"What's going to happen to them?"

Syed looks up at James but doesn't answer.

"Have you thought of that, Syed? What's going to happen to your family after we're finished with you today?"

Syed still doesn't respond.

"All right, Syed. Since you don't know, let me explain it to you. After we're done with you, we're going to hand you over to the police. Eventually, they'll convict you of the killings at the church and you'll get the chair. You're in Texas; there's no way that they'll let you live. Your wife will probably get arrested, too, and she'll get executed just like you."

Syed shakes his head and raises his voice. "My wife had nothing to do with anything."

"You might know that, Syed. And that might even be true. But the police won't know that. And, quite frankly, they're not going to give a shit. Forty-three people are dead, and they're looking to make someone pay." James straightens himself on the table.

"And your son and daughter? What'll happen to them? The children will have no parents. They'll get deported back to Afghanistan, probably. Perhaps our government will hand your children to that puppet government that the Russians are backing.

"And what do you think that Russian government will do with your kids? The children of a known terrorist who wants to overthrow the Afghan government? You know what they'll do, Syed. I don't have to tell you."

James pauses to let everything sink in. "That's one possible outcome of what's going to happen after today. Let me give you another possible result. You cooperate with me today, and I'll make sure nothing happens to your family."

"You can do that?" Syed asks faintly.

"I can, if I can show the authorities that you're helping."

"What about me?"

"Forty-three, Syed. That's how many you killed. Would have been more, if not for me. You need to pay. No one can save you."

James looks intently at Syed, who is looking away from him. "Are you going to help, or do I get the guys back in here?"

"You will help my family?"

"I give you my word!"

Syed exhales. "All right. I'll cooperate."

"Good." James leans forward. "Whose idea was the shooting? Who was behind it?"

"Prince Aba al bin Faikil and Muhammad Mafrouz."

"Who are these guys? They're not Palestinians?"

Syed shakes his head. "They're the leaders of the resistance in Afghanistan against the Russians."

"Why did they attack America? I was under the impression that the US was helping the rebels in Afghanistan."

"They attacked the US because they don't like what the Americans are doing in Lebanon. They wanted to send you a message: stay out of the Middle East. But they didn't want the Americans to know who was behind the attack. You know, because of the American support in Afghanistan. That's why they sent Palestinians. So that no one would suspect who was really behind the attack."

"Tell me a little about those two men. Start with Mafrouz. Who is he, an Afghan?"

"No he's Egyptian"

James's brow goes up. "Egyptian? What the heck is an Egyptian doing in Afghanistan?"

"I don't know."

"What about this other guy, the prince? Where's he from?"

"I don't know for sure, I think maybe Saudi Arabia."

"Saudi Arabia? How come I never heard of him?"

"I don't know why you never heard of him, maybe he's not that high up. You know, there are a lot of royals in that country."

"What about the Palestinians? Who do you know that's Palestinian? Who was your contact?"

"I don't know *any* Palestinians. My contact was an Afghan named Faakhir. He comes from my same village in Afghanistan—Mirabad."

"What about the two men at my ranch? The guys that my man Billy saw a few days ago."

Syed furrows his brow. "I don't know anything about any men at your ranch."

"What else can you tell me? How can I find this fellow Faakhir?"

"You can't find him. Faakhir went back to Afghanistan. The day of the shooting, I drove him down to Nuevo Laredo. He made his way back home through Mexico."

"Anything else? Can you tell me anything else?"

Syed shrugs. "No, that's it," he says, then hangs his head again. "Now what?" he asks James.

"Now I turn you over to the police. Keep cooperating and they just might spare your family."

On the plane back to Colorado Springs, the men are sitting in the lounge area, "Thanks for all of your help, guys," James says. "I couldn't have done it without you."

The men nod.

"By the way, Charlie, is Mark Malone in town?" he asks.

"Yeah, I think so. Why? Do you need our security specialist?"

"Yes, I do. Tell Malone to drop by the ranch tomorrow, around nine. I've got a job for him."

7

Problems at Home

SAM, JEFF, AND CARDIZ ARE standing at James's front door when he gets home. His limo driver, Marvin, is carrying his suitcase.

"I'll just put your suitcase inside, sir," Marvin tells him when James stops to talk with the trio.

"Thank you, Marvin," James says and turns to Sam. "What's going on?"

"Your dad just clocked Antonio," Sam says and gestures to Cardiz, who is sporting a shiner on his right eye. "Look."

James looks at Cardiz. "What happened? Are you all right?" He lifts up Cardiz's chin and takes a closer look at his face.

"I was trying to help your father with some farm work," Cardiz explains. "Your dad yelled that I was doing it all wrong. Before I knew it, the old man belted me." Cardiz looks meaningfully at James. "You know, Coppi, your old man is lucky that I respect my elders."

"I know, Cardiz." James continues to inspect the black and blue. "Thanks for showing such restraint. Are you OK?"

"Yeah, I'm fine. You need to have a talk with your old man," Cardiz says, twirling a finger around his temple as he and Jeff walk away. "That guy is *loco.*"

Sam walks up and gives him a hug and kiss. "I'm sorry you had to come home to this, dear."

"I'll be right back," he says. "I'm going to go have a talk with my dad."

James walks down the dusty road to his parents' house. His mom greets him at the door. "Giacomo!" She grabs his cheeks and gives him a kiss. "Come esta?" *Vuoi qualcosa da mangiare?* Can I get you something to eat?"

"No, I just need to talk to Pa," he says, walking toward the back.

His mom grabs his arm. "Giacomo, be kind. He is feeling ashamed."

James turns to her. "I will, Ma. I just want to understand what's going on."

When James gets to the porch, his dad is sitting in a rocking chair gazing out at the field. James sits on the chair next to him.

James looks at the old man's sun-drenched face. Age spots from years of working outside pepper his face. James sits quietly, saying nothing. He knows his dad—he'll speak when he's ready.

Without looking at James, his father finally speaks.

"It wasn't supposed to be like *this*, Giacomo," his father says in Italian, since he can't speak any English.

James says nothing.

The old man turns to him and repeats, "It wasn't supposed to be like this. What happened?"

"I don't know, Dad," James answers back in Italian. "What happened, Pop? How was it all supposed to be?"

The old man doesn't respond but begins gazing at the open field once again. "You are a good businessman, Giacomo," he states.

"That's because I learned from you, Pa. You taught me. I remember when I was a little boy sitting in your grocery store and watching you work—I was so proud of you."

Papa Coppi turns to him and smiles. "Yes, I remember." Then the old man waves his hand dismissively. "But you didn't learn anything about running a business from me—I was a terrible businessman. The store closed because I couldn't pay my bills."

The old man sighs.

"Dad, you taught me two things when I was a young boy that I will never forget. If you run your own business, you will control your own destiny. And if you own your own land, your family will never starve. That's advice that I will remember forever. As you can see, I have followed that advice faithfully.

"The reason your store failed was because of your kindness," James continues, leaning toward him. "You were too generous, and people took advantage of your compassion. You kept extending more and more credit to all of your customers. When the patrons couldn't pay, you kept selling more merchandise to them, anyway. The customers' tabs kept going up and up. You never turned down anybody—even when they couldn't pay."

"How could I refuse those poor *paisans*?" Papa Coppi asks with a shrug. "It was right after the war. Nobody had any money. Those people were our neighbors—neighbors who needed food to feed their families." The old man looks over at James. "What could I do? Let those poor people starve?"

"Oh, Pop, you can't help anybody if you can't help yourself. When you couldn't pay your suppliers because you had no money, the suppliers cut you off. Then you had to close the store. Somehow, your *paisans* found a way to feed themselves and their families without you. When our store closed down, these so-called starving people still found a way to get food on their tables, didn't they?"

His father does not respond.

"All that your kindness caused was misery for you and your family. If I remember correctly, none of those *paisans* came to help you. To this day, a lot of those neighbors still owe you money."

"I know, Giacomo." His father's eyes, yellow with age, start to moisten. "That's why I say—you are a good businessman. You didn't take after me. I made one mistake after another.

"You remember after the store closed," the old man continues. "My *cugino* Fiore said there was work in Germany. My cousin said he'd lend me the money for the train tickets, and we went together. After six months in Germany without any work, Fiore and I had to give up. We came home empty-handed and broke. Now I owed even *more* money. I was afraid that we would lose our house and the small piece of farmland that we owned.

"Then my other *cugino*, Fortunato, suggested I go to America. 'The streets in America are paved with gold,' my cousin said to me. He said there would be plenty of work here. One year in America and I would come back home to *Italia* with so much money that I'd not only be able to pay off what I owed, but I'd have plenty left over to get back and restart my store. Fortunato said that he'd lend me the money for the boat fare."

James has never heard this story, but he keeps quiet and gazes out at the field, too, letting his father speak.

"But America was not much better than Germany. It took me a year to find a job as a bricklayer and to get my union card. I missed my family. So I borrowed some more money for my family's sea voyage and sent for you children and your *madre*.

"The plan was for me to work a few years, get out of debt, and for us to go back to Italy. I was so determined to get back to Italy that I refused to learn English. Time passed, and when I finally had enough money stashed away to return to Italy, none of you wanted to go back. How could I leave you in America without me to support you?

James's father wipes at his eyes.

"By now, I'm much older—in my midfifties. So I decide I'm going to continue working until I am 62. At that age, I will retire. My plan was to collect social security and my small union pension. With that money, I could retire and return to Italy.

"By that time, all of you would be settled and wouldn't need me any more for support. I could live a comfortable retirement at our house back in Italy and work that small piece of land that I still owned. But when I finally turned 62, your mother did not want to go back to Italy. Your mamma did not want to leave her children and grandchildren."

His dad turns to him with a sad face and shrugs. "Now what do I do, Giacomo? How can I ever go back? What happened to my plan? That small piece of land that I have back in Italy is still sitting there, fallow and untilled."

"But you have land here, Dad," James protests. "You can work the land here that I set aside for you."

Papa Coppi gives him a sweet smile. "Giacomo, you're a good boy, and I know you mean well. You provide this house for me and your mother. You gave your brother a good job. You pay all of the bills for your two sisters' educations and—most of all—you take good care of your own family. But, Giacomo, for me, I'm still not happy.

"This place and country is not the same. Here, nobody understands me. Look at what happened today—I got very frustrated with that young man. He was only trying to help."

The old man leans toward his son. "Giacomo, don't worry about me. This will pass. I'll get over it. Stop worrying about me. Go back to your family. They missed you."

James gets up and squats down in front of his dad. "How about if we reach a compromise"

"A *compromesso*?" Papa looks at him.

"Yeah, a middle ground." James says. "When you do the farming in Italy, you're only busy for six months—am I right?"

His father thinks for a moment. "Yes, the planting is in April and the harvesting is in September. In between, I do some pruning, some irrigating, and some other chores."

"But after September when you've sold the harvest, there is little to do," James points out. "The crops are sold. There's no need for you to be there."

"What are you trying to say?"

"I'm saying that you can spend six months in Italy and six months in America. This way, both you and mom can get something that you want."

Papa Coppi is quiet for a moment. "You think your *mamma* will go along with this idea?"

"Yes, I believe that Mom will," James says, smiling. "Especially when I tell her I'll bring my family to visit every year. Mom can teach my daughter Molly the Italian way of life."

His dad smiles. "She does love that little *mascalzona*. She can't get enough of her."

"Is it a deal?"

"Yeah, sure. If you can talk your mother into it, it's a deal."

James stands up. "Now, Dad, you need to go over to Cardiz and apologize. He's in the guesthouse."

"Can you say you're sorry for me? I'm so ashamed."

"No, Dad, you need to go say you're sorry. I already apologized. Now you need to go over there yourself. You owe that to Cardiz—Cardiz needs to hear it from you."

"All right." *Papa* Coppi gets up out of his chair.

"How did it go?" Sam asks James when he's back at the house.

"It's all cleared up. We reached a resolution. I'll tell you all about it later. Where are the children?"

The butler Billingsley comes over. "Are you hungry, sir? What would you like for dinner?"

"Something light, Billingsley. Something Mediterranean, if Mrs. Billingsley is up to it. Give me a little time with the children, first. I'll have my dinner on the patio in about an hour."

"The children are in the den," Sam informs him when the butler has left. "Are you going to tell me what happened with your father?"

"I will, dear." He gives her a kiss. "Let me look in on Christopher and spend some time with Michael and Molly. I haven't seen the kids in a week. It's all been worked out with my parents."

"What happened with your dad?" Sam asks him again later on the patio, once James has finished with the children.

"My father is very unhappy here," James tells her as he dips a piece of bread into a tzatziki dip, and he begins telling Sam the outcome of his talk with his dad.

"So we'll be visiting for a few weeks every year when my parents are in Italy," James concludes when he's finished telling Sam the arrangement he reached with his father.

"That's great," Sam says and smiles. "It'll give me a chance to practice my Italian."

"How *is* your Italian coming along?" James asks her teasingly. "You've been taking lessons for more than a year now."

"Not very good," Sam admits. "Even little Michael can speak Italian better than I can, and he's not taking *any* lessons. Molly is great. She speaks perfect Italian. I'm hoping that when we spend time in Italy, my Italian will get better. I *really* want to learn. When we get to Italy, James, I want you to speak to me only in Italian. No English."

"OK, I'll do that," he says, taking a final bite of a *dolmade*.

"James, what was it like growing up in Italy with your dad? You don't talk about that part of your childhood much."

James stares out at Cheyenne Mountain. "Growing up in Italy was great," James says. "I learned everything I know about business from my dad."

"Really? How so? I thought your dad was a working man. You know, pulling a salary."

"No. When I was a little boy in Italy, we owned a grocery store." James looks out at his vast ranch. The sun is beginning to set behind the Rockies, and the sunset is spectacular—there is an orange and yellow glow.

"You know, Sam, we talk a lot about when I went off to Vietnam and how tough it was for me," James tells her. "But you may not know that my dad was in a German prison camp for over two years.

"The Germans called the Italian soldiers 'civilian workers' instead of 'war prisoners.' Because of that label, the Italian soldiers had no rights under the Geneva convention. The Red Cross was not allowed to inspect their camps. The prisoners were put into forced hard labor.

"The conditions in those camps were brutal. Thousands died. After the war, it took my father nearly nine months to get home. He had to hide from the French, who wanted to put him in their labor camps. My mother didn't even recognize my dad when he got home—that's how emaciated he was. Somehow, Dad managed to scrape up some money and open a grocery store.

"I'd go in every day after school to help out. People didn't have much money, what with the war and all. Most of the townsfolk were farmers or seasonal workers. The villagers would buy their food on account and pay when they got some money. My dad used to keep accounting books on what all the villagers owed him.

"It was my job to do the entries in the book for him. I was so proud of him. I felt so important. Everybody in the village owed us money. They all knew my dad."

James pauses for a moment and fiddles with his beer bottle. "One day, after school, I went to the store, and the front door was locked. Immediately, I thought something had happened to my dad. I ran upstairs and Dad was sitting in a darkened room, crying.

"I'd never seen my father cry before. Here's a man who suffered all those horrible atrocities during the war and never shed a tear—but on this day, he was crying."

James looks at Sam. "The creditors had shut down the store because my dad couldn't pay the bills. I was so humiliated that I ran away from home. The whole town went out looking for me. They found me at around four o'clock in the morning sitting on a branch of my favorite tree that overlooks the town." James says and takes a swig of his beer. "Sam, that's never happening to us—I swear."

"On another topic," he adds suddenly, "I almost forgot to tell you—we're going to have some visitors staying at our guest house for the next month—Prince Firuz's family will be staying with us. I'm going to arrange for extra security detail while they're here. The ranch is going to look like a fortress over the next month."

"But what about Mattie and Cardiz?" she asks. "They're living in the guest house right now."

"They'll have to move into the main house with us until the Firuz family leaves. I'm sure they won't mind."

"Why is the Prince's family staying with us?"

"Prince Firuz called me while I was out of town," James replies. "His dad, has to come to the US for medical treatment. The Prince is worried about his family's safety if both he and the shah are in the US. The family shouldn't be here much longer than a month."

8

Building a Fortress

THE NEXT MORNING, SAM WALKS into James's study as James as hanging up the phone. "There's a Mark Malone here to see you," she tells him.

"OK, good."

"He works for us, doesn't he? What does he do?"

"Malone is a facilities security specialist. Bring him in and then stick around for the meeting—I'd like you to know what's going on."

After introducing Mark to Sam, and they are seated, James says, "Mark, I'd like you to check the security here at the ranch. Not only the ranch, but the security surrounding my entire family."

"What's this all about, James?" Mark asks. "Is there something in particular that's worrying you? Both you and Sam travel with bodyguards."

"One of my boys, Billy, noticed a truck that trespassed on our property a few days ago. There were two men in the truck—Middle Eastern-looking men he said. The men ran off when Billy chased after them.

Sam jumps a little in her chair.

"After the church shooting, I'm a little worried," James continues, his eyes still on Mark. "So I want you to do a thorough analysis of this ranch and of my family. I want to know how to best protect everyone—find all the weak spots and make suggestions on how to fill the gaps."

"James, there were strange men on the ranch?" Sam asks. "Why didn't you tell me?"

"I *am* telling you, dear. That's why you're at this meeting." He turns back to Mark. "Anyway, Mark, get busy right away. Do a thorough check. Report back to me when you're done."

"Will do, James." Mark stands up.

"How long is this going to take?" James asks.

"It shouldn't take long—a couple of days."

"All right, James," Sam says after Malone leaves. "Tell me what's going on. Are we in some sort of danger?"

"Sam, I really don't know, I'm trying to put the pieces together. I just got off the phone with Ian from our London office. At my request, he contacted his Israeli contacts. They said there was a meeting in Lebanon between an Afghan and a Palestinian, Aalam Salvar. This happened before the church shooting. The four shooters at the church were Palestinians."

James looks over at Sam. "Do you see where this is going?"

Sam furrows her brow. "You think there's a connection?"

"Yeah, definitely a connection. A few days ago, I met with this Afghan in Texas. This Afghan was involved in the church attack also—he was the one that provided the layout of the church. I turned him over to the police. He gave me three names. The first was an Afghan, Faakhir, who ran the attack. He also gave me two other names, an Egyptian and an Arab prince. These two guys are fighting to kick out the Russians in Afghanistan."

"What's all this have to do with us?" she asks.

James shrugs. "I don't know. But two men suddenly show up on our ranch. Arab looking fellows. Something is up—I need to find out what these guys are up to. Please do me a favor: try to have everyone stick around the ranch for the time being. If you and the kids go off the property, make sure that you have Ronan with you. Don't take any chances. I'm sure that I'm overreacting, but I'd rather play it safe."

The phone rings, and James picks it up.

"James, this is Jessica," the caller says. "You got a minute?"

"Yeah, Jessica. What's up?"

"You're going to receive the Presidential Medal of Freedom with Distinction. The president's press secretary just called me.

Congratulations! That's quite an honor. They'd like you to come to the White House this week for the ceremony."

"Jessica, I can't do it this week. I'm leaving for New York for some meetings. It'll have to be next week."

"OK, James, I'll work out the schedule with the White House. I don't think it will be much of a problem."

"You're leaving for New York?" Sam asks. "Should you be traveling? Last night you said that you were in a lot of pain."

"Yeah—I need to go. I've got to meet with Prince Khartami. He's in the country and said that he needs to meet with me about an important personal matter.

"By the way—Jessica just told me that I'm going to receive the Presidential Medal of Freedom. There'll be a ceremony for me next week at the White House. You'll come, won't you?"

"Yes, of course I will. That's quite an honor." She walks up to him and gives him a kiss. "I'm so proud of you," Sam says and smiles deviously. "That's another one of your medals that I can add to my collection." She gives him a light tap on the shoulder. "I'm still angry at you for running off to New York. Please don't stay too long."

"It shouldn't be long. Two days—max."

The trip to New York to meet with Firuz and his father turns out to be timely, as James got a chance to head out to Belmont and watch his two-year-old filly race.

"Sir, we're here," the limo driver says when they get to the Plaza hotel.

"OK, thanks." He opens the door to let himself out. "I should be out in thirty minutes, so don't go too far."

There are two men standing in the hallway on the floor of Prince Firuz's suite.

"May we help you?" one of the men asks as he steps in front of James.

"I have an appointment with the prince. I'm James Coppi."

"Oh yes, of course." The big man smiles and gets out of the way "They're expecting you, Mr. Coppi."

"It's good to see you again, James," Prince Firuz says when he opens the door to the hotel suite.

"Nice to see you, Your Highness." James looks around. "Is your dad here? I thought he wanted to speak to me."

"My father is next door on a call back to my country. He'll be here as soon as he gets done." The prince motions to the sofa. "Have a seat. How did your horse do at the track yesterday? Your horse did run, didn't he?"

"Actually, the horse is a she," James says after he's taken a seat. "It's a filly. She came in third. She'll get better. I'm happy with her performance. The horse is only a two-year-old." James moves forward on the couch and lowers his voice. "What does your dad want to speak to me about? What's going on?"

"I really don't know," the prince responds, also lowering his voice. "My father didn't say anything to me about what he wants to discuss with you. Listen, James, on another matter—my family will be in London next week. Can you have your plane pick them up and bring them to your ranch?"

"Yeah, sure, I can do that. I'll send Rodney there to personally escort your family to my ranch."

The prince leans forward. "Have all the arrangements been made for my family's arrival at your ranch?"

"Yes, all the security is being put into place right now. I've got my security specialist working on additional protection at the ranch. We hired extra household staff for your family. The staff has all been checked and screened. Does your dad know that your family will be out there?"

"My father has been told that the family is going on holiday." The prince turns to look at the door. "So please don't dwell on the matter too long if the subject comes up."

Both men jump up when the shah enters the room. "Hello, James," says the shah, smiling, and reaches for his hands. "It's so nice to see you again."

"The pleasure is all mine, Your Majesty." James replies, extending his hands. "How are you feeling? I hear you are a little under the weather."

The old man waves his hand dismissively. "You know doctors. Once they get a hold on you, they never let go." The shah motions to the sofa. "Please, have a seat."

James sits back down, and the royal takes a seat across from him. "James, how are the plans coming along for the money transfers and the housing for my family?"

James clears his throat. "Your Majesty, I just got started. I only recently got the assignment."

"How much time do you foresee that you will need to complete the mission?"

James takes a long look at the shah. "Is there something wrong? Something that I should know about? Prince Firuz never mentioned any urgency about the matter."

"You know, James," the shah says, smiling. "This is the fourth time I have met you in person, and I'm more impressed each time we meet. You are very fast in picking up even the subtlest clues. Yes, there has been a new development. But before we get into that, let me ask you: can you complete the assignment in three months?"

Prince Firuz across the way creases his brow and stares at his father.

"Yes, I can do that. I'll get to work on the project immediately when I get back."

"Good." The shah smiles and gets up. "Then you better get working on it."

James jumps to his feet. "Excuse me, sir. Are you going to tell me what's going on? What *are* the new developments?"

"No, James." The sovereign becomes stern. "You don't need to know. Just do the assignment that was given to you."

"Your Majesty, with all due respect, I cannot do my assignment adequately if I don't have all the facts. This is a very delicate matter that I will be working on. I need to know all of the players—both friends and foes. It's time you brought me into your circle of confidantes."

The monarch is quiet for a moment. "Yes, you're absolutely right," he says and sits back down. "Please, sit."

James takes a seat.

"There is a good possibility that within three months, I and my family will be abdicating the throne."

"What?" Prince Firuz nearly comes out of his seat. "When was this decided? Why haven't I been told?"

"Please, Firuz," his father says. "Lower your voice. You weren't told because the negotiations are ongoing. I'm meeting with many heads of governments to negotiate the transfer of power."

"So that's it, then." Prince Firuz stands up. "You decide that you don't want the throne anymore, and then it's all over. What about me? What about my birthright? Did you even give that any thought?" Firuz storms out of the room, slamming the door on the way out.

After a moment, the sovereign turns back to James. "James, my son Firuz does not understand that my abdication is the best for my family. Your CIA has made it very clear that we are losing American support. Without that support, we are finished.

"My family won't be able to hold on to power," the shah continues. "There will be a civil war if I stay, and thousands will die. I don't want to be a ruler that causes such pain to my subjects. This is the only reasonable course available to us. Please, get busy and take care of my family. The situation can turn grave at any time, so don't waste a moment."

"What about you, Your Majesty? What can I do for you?"

The monarch gives him a sad smile. "Thank you for your concern, but don't worry about me. There is a king that owes me a favor. I lent him a hundred million a little while back, and he doesn't have the money to repay my loan. This king has agreed to provide me with sanctuary when I leave—I will be just fine. Take care of the rest of my extended family."

James runs into Prince Firuz when he gets to the lobby. "Come on, Your Highness, let's go to a bar. Let me buy you a drink."

They go to the Oak Room lounge at the hotel and get a table in the back, out of sight of anyone entering the bar. James stares out at

AA Freda

the room, which features walls of Flemish oak, frescoes of Bavarian castles and wine casks carved into the woodwork. A smile comes to his face when he looks up at the ceiling at the chandelier that is topped by a statue of a barmaid hoisting a stein.

"I can't believe that my father is such a coward," the prince says as he sips on his martini.

"Prince Firuz—your dad is no coward. He has been in power nearly fifty years—you don't stay in power that long by being a coward."

"Oh yeah? Well, if you're so smart, tell me what's going on. Why is he abdicating"

"Your family has lost its support," James says, taking a sip of his beer, and looks at the prince. "Your father came into power with the help of the American government. Now he's lost that backing, and your family has fallen out of favor. Your dad doesn't have any more cards to play. He's doing the best possible for his family.

"If you want to rule, Your Highness, then you need to negotiate with the CIA and get that support back. You've got to secure that backing, just like your father did fifty years ago. Don't blame him for your loss of a legacy. Either go get that CIA support, or stop sulking and help your family with this transition. I'm going to need your cooperation. Frankly, Prince, I'm with your father on this one—I also believe that you can't stay in power any longer. Times have changed, and royalty has fallen out of favor."

———

Three days later, James is in the study with Sam and Malone, reviewing the report on the security at the ranch.

"James, with a piece of property of this size, you'd need a battalion of men to do a proper security job," Mark tells him. "Fortunately, I don't believe that's what will be needed. If an attack does come, it won't be done by more than one or two men. The men will either come at night in a covert operation or in broad daylight, disguised as delivery or maintenance men. Or something of that nature."

"What do you recommend?" James asks.

"To safeguard the ranch from a night attack, I suggest we set up security cameras and sensors."

"Mark, do you realize how many cameras we would need to cover over ten thousand acres? Hundreds! And what about the sensors? Won't they go off every time an animal passes by?"

Mark sits forward on his chair. "No, James. I'm not suggesting that we build a fortress around the entire ranch. There's no need for that. We need to fortify the compound where the houses are located. I'd like to set up a security zone around your residences. We'd need no more than a dozen cameras to do the job.

"We won't need more than two security men per shift to monitor the area. Maybe ten—possibly twelve—men, total. As for the sensors—yes, some animals might set them off. But so what? The cameras would quickly reveal the presence of an animal. This security measure should be enough to safeguard you from anyone trying to get into the ranch at night.

"As for the daytime entry, that's a different problem. You've got people coming onto and going off this property all the time. Vets, farriers, and delivery men. There's construction workers coming everyday working on the practice track that you're building. It's nonstop activity. We need to establish new procedures that define who gets onto this ranch and under what circumstances.

"I'd also like to have a conversation with your entire household staff about what to watch out for. If someone is trying to get on this ranch, potential trespassers will need to know more about what's going on inside the place."

Mark stops as James stands up, rubs his back and sits back down.

Mark continues. "Your staff needs to be aware of the type of people they might encounter—especially when they're off the ranch. People who may act friendly but are actually trying to ply them for information.

"It may seem like an innocent conversation at a supermarket, for example, but it probably isn't. I'll need to bring everybody that works for you up to speed as to what they need to know. Conduct a couple of drills with the ranch hands and the domestics. I might even put a few of my people undercover to see how your staff reacts to certain situations. The more your people know about how to respond, the safer you'll be.

"Truthfully, James, I don't think there's going to be an assault on the ranch. That's not how I think an attack will go down. If they want to get to you and your family, it will be while you're in the outside world. Far easier than here at the ranch—there's just too much that can go wrong.

"For that reason, I think that you and Sam should double up your bodyguards. One for each of you is not enough. Also, we should begin providing security for your daughter Molly, especially when she goes back to school at the end of the summer.

"The other children are too young as yet—they don't leave the ranch, so no security is necessary for them. But Molly is going to need a detail of her own. Also, the school will have to be advised of the threat."

"What?" Sam sits up in her chair. "The school?" She turns to James. "James, this whole thing is making me very scared. Is all this necessary? What is it that's got you so worried? What, exactly, are we being protected from? Who are these people? And why do they want to harm us?"

"I don't know, baby—I just don't know. Something just doesn't feel right. And, when I don't know something, I worry." James turns back to Malone. "When can you get started?"

"I'll get going right away. First thing tomorrow morning."

"OK, good." James turns back to Sam. "You heard everything?" She nods.

"Do you have any questions?"

She shakes her head no.

"You and the children stick around the ranch for the next few months," James tells Sam after Malone leaves. "It's summer, so Molly won't be going to school. Have her friends come here instead of her going to their homes."

"So we are to be prisoners?" she asks, scowling. "Can't we ever leave the ranch?"

"No, we won't be prisoners. Just limit your outside activities as much as you can. At least until I know more about what's going on. If you need to go off the property, follow Mark's suggestion and take two bodyguards with you."

He gives her a serious look and says, "Sam, please don't take this lightly. Give this your full attention. This is very serious stuff. I wish I could spare you knowing any of this, but I can't—I need your help. Just be very careful."

"OK, I get it. You'll have my full cooperation. I just hope this is over soon."

9

Eliminate the Hero

SAM AND JAMES ARE AT the White House. James is to receive the Presidential Medal of Freedom with Distinction. They are being briefed by an aide as to how the ceremony will unfold.

After the aide has left, Sam turns to James. "You have no idea how proud I am of you today."

"You do know that you're completely embarrassing me," he says.

Sam gives him a kiss. "I don't care—I'm proud of you. Hold on a sec, you have lipstick on you." She reaches into her small purse to pull out a tissue.

"Leave it," he says, smiling. "It'll give the reporters something to write about."

She rolls her eyes.

"Hold still," she tells him, and wipes the smudge off his face.

"Isn't this exciting?" Jessica asks when she walks into the room. "My boss is the biggest hero in the whole country. I've got every major news organization covering this story."

"That's it. I'm leaving." James tries to walk out. "I knew that I should have stayed home."

"Cut it out," Sam says, grabbing him by the arm. "Behave yourself."

"What's the matter?" Jessica asks her.

"James is embarrassed," Sam responds. "He hates all the fuss that everyone is making over him."

"Forty-three people are dead," James points out. "I'm sure their families are not celebrating. This just feels wrong. It's like a big party."

"A lot more families would've been sad today if not for you, James," Jessica points out. "Come on, let's go. They're calling us in."

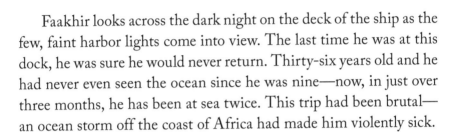

Faakhir looks across the dark night on the deck of the ship as the few, faint harbor lights come into view. The last time he was at this dock, he was sure he would never return. Thirty-six years old and he had never even seen the ocean since he was nine—now, in just over three months, he has been at sea twice. This trip had been brutal—an ocean storm off the coast of Africa had made him violently sick.

Faakhir is feeling tired—and not just from the two weeks that it took him to get here from Afghanistan. It's this war—it's wearing on him. He hasn't lost his fervor, though. He still believes entirely in the cause.

It's being away from his family that is weighing on him. The children need him. His daughter is of marriageable age. His son is becoming a man. The boy needs a father to teach him the ways.

"It shouldn't be long now," Moshar says as he comes alongside Faakhir and looks out from the deck.

"No, not long—maybe twenty minutes," Faakhir agrees. "What time is it?"

"It's a quarter to one," Moshar replies. "What about this fellow, Aalam, who's meeting us? Is he reliable? Will he be there?"

Faakhir turns to him. "I guess so—I only know him from that one last mission. That's the mission you and I discussed in Pakistan. Aalam was here when I came the last time."

"Well, I hope this man comes up with better fighters than the ones he provided you on your last mission. I can't believe that a single guy with one little pistol was able to take all four fighters out."

"If you feel that way, why are we using this fellow Aalam again?"

"Because we *need* the Palestinians. They have a network all over Europe, and we need access to the network." Moshar taps him on the shoulder. "Come on, let's get down below and get our gear. We should be docking soon."

In the parking lot at the end of the dock, Aalam is waiting for the men in a green Peugeot. Faakhir hops into the front seat as Moshar slides into the back.

"What happened to your Mercedes that you had the last time I was here?" Faakhir asks him.

"I needed to switch cars. The Zionist spies are everywhere. Who is your bearded friend?"

"This is Moshar," Faakhir replies. "Moshar, this is Aalam."

Moshar nods to Aalam, and the Peugeot pulls out onto a road.

"Where are you taking us?" Faakhir asks.

"Same place I took you the last time you were here. You know, because you left so fast, you didn't finish your meal. You ran out of the restaurant just as fast as you ran out on my men at that church. Four of my best men were killed. Where were you?"

"If those were your best men, I'd hate to see your worst," Moshar cries out from the back seat. "One man with a cap pistol was able to take them all out. Who trains your men? A schoolteacher?"

Aalam slams on the brakes and turns back to Moshar. "You can both get out now," he says, pointing to the door. "Go back to your own country and get some of your goat herders to help you. Maybe the goat herders can do a better job!"

"Calm down, Aalam," Faakhir says softly. "Let's not fight among ourselves. We're all very upset. Nobody likes losing good men. This American at the church is a lot better fighter than we had any reason to expect. I'm told that he was in the Vietnam War. No one could have foreseen that he'd be at that church. We won't make that mistake again. The next time we meet up with this American, we'll be ready."

Aalam puts the car back into gear and drives off. Faakhir turns to Moshar and shakes his head, signaling not to bring up the subject again. When they get to the restaurant, Aalam parks the car in the same side street as last time.

When they turn the corner, Moshar calls out, "Who's that?" as he points to the lone man sitting on a wooden box, talking to himself.

"Don't worry about him," says Aalam, waving his hand dismissively. "That man is the village fool." He points to his temple and makes a sad face. "Soft in the head."

Aalam opens the door and lets himself into the darkened restaurant. "Hassad, are you here?" he calls out.

A man comes out, carrying a lit candle.

"Hassad, have you got a little time to cook us some food?" Aalam asks. "We're all very hungry."

Hassad gestures to a table. "Please, sit." He walks over and lights the candle on the table. "I will be right back."

"So what's going on with this American?" Aalam asks. "Why did you have me send out men to check on the guy? Are we planning on killing him? If so it's not going to be easy, the report was that he lives on a large property in Colorado. The place is very well guarded."

Hassad comes out with a pitcher of water. He fills the men's cups. Moshar takes a drink.

"Initially the idea was to kill the American and his family," Moshar says. "Avenge the killing of our men at the church. But now the plans have changed—we no longer want that man or his family killed."

Hassad brings out a dish of flatbread. Faakhir breaks off a piece and scarfs it down.

"I don't understand," Aalam says, looking over at Moshar. "If we're not to kill this man, what do you want to do?"

"We want to take the American alive," Moshar explains. "We need him for trade. The Americans have our Imam in jail. We need to get him out. And not just the Imam—all the political prisoners. Not just in America, but also in Israel and in Europe! We're going to use this American as ransom for a swap."

Aalam lets out a laugh. "Have you guys been using the poppy that you're growing in Afghanistan? No one will ever agree to such an exchange. Especially the Israelis—they'll never agree. That American is not that important to the Israelis."

"That's where you're wrong, Aalam," Faakhir says, joining the conversation. "This man is a national hero. The President of the

United States just gave him a medal. How would it look if the Americans didn't come to his rescue?"

"Even if that's true, the Israelis will never participate," Aalam shakes his head. "These people that you want to barter with are American. Why would the Israelis care if the American that we kidnap is killed or not?"

"Yes, you're right. The Israelis will not care about the American," Moshar says, getting back into the discussion. "But the Israelis get all their support from the Americans. They wouldn't dare turn down such an offer to trade."

Aalam pauses and takes a drink of water. Then he shrugs. "I still don't think it will work."

"Let's say you're right," Moshar says. "Let's say the plan doesn't work. The Israelis don't agree to the swap. What's the worst that could happen? We kill the hostage, just as we wanted to do in the first place. And the Americans come out looking weak and pathetic. They couldn't even protect a national hero."

Aalam gets quiet for a moment. "All right! That makes sense. Even if they don't agree to the exchange, we still end up the victors. How do we do this? We can't get on the ranch—it's too well guarded. Where do we grab him?"

"We don't need to go to the ranch," Moshar explains. "We wait for him to come out. The American has a lot of business in Europe. We wait for him there. It'll be much easier to snatch him in Europe. When he's in Europe, he'll have maybe one or two bodyguards— at the very most. It should be really easy to grab him. We've got a man working at the airport in America where this man keeps his plane.

"Our inside contact will call us as soon as the man's plane takes off. Give us the location of where the flight is heading, and we'll be ready. That's what we need from you, Aalam—we need you to find us a place in Europe so that we can move quickly when we get the call. Have you got such a place?"

"Yes, I've got a place in Belgium," he answers. "A small farmhouse. It's convenient to most places in Europe."

"How about some men?" Faakhir asks. "Can you supply us?"

"I thought you said my men weren't any good."

Moshar laughs. "They'll be a lot better with us in charge."

Aalam's face turns red. "Faakhir was in charge of the last operation and four of my men are dead!"

Faakhir tugs at Moshar under the table. "Let's not get into an argument again. As I said before, we made a mistake the last time and didn't anticipate this American—we won't make that same mistake again."

Aalam continues to glare at Moshar.

"Aalam, what do you say?" Faakhir smiles. "Will you help?"

"Where are you going to keep the American, once you have him? They'll be looking for him all over Europe."

"That's why we're not going to keep him in Europe," Moshar answers. "We're going to bring him here to you, Aalam—he will be your prisoner. Once we hand him over to you, Faakhir and I are finished with the job. You'll be in charge of all the negotiations.

"The Afghans can't be seen as being complicit in this plot. We still get a lot of military aid from the Americans in our fight against the Russians. We can't afford to have that aid cut off.

"Besides, it's Palestinian prisoners that are going to be released, not Afghans. Aalam, this is a great moment for you and your people. The whole world will know of this kidnapping. Everyone will be riveted to the negotiations. Your name will be known throughout the world. The entire world will all know you as the man who took on both the Americans and the Israelis. What a moment in history—for you!"

Moshar looks over at Aalam. "So do we have a deal?"

"The plan sounds too complicated to succeed. But if we can get to this American—somehow, it's worth a shot." Aalam looks at the other two men. "OK, it's a deal. I'll provide the place and supply the men."

Hassad comes out carrying a platter and three empty dishes. "I made *shish taouk* again." The cook looks pointedly at Faakhir. "I hope you have time to stay and eat this time."

Faakhir smiles. "Yes, Hassad, I have time. Thank you for the food."

When the men have finished their meal Hassad walks them to the door and waves good-bye. The old man that was sitting on the box walks over.

"Who were those men, Hassad?" he asks. "I thought I recognized one of them. They were Pakistani's, weren't they?"

Hassad frowns. "Well you are wrong old man. They were Afghans not Pakistani's. And where would you have met any of them anyway, you have never been more than twenty miles from this village. Go to bed you foolish old man."

———⌐————⌐————

In Metula, Israel the general is in his bunker reading reports. "I'm sorry to bother you, sir, but I just received a dispatch from one of our lookouts in Lebanon. He noticed two Afghans having a meeting with the Palestinian named Aalam."

The general looks up from his papers. "Afghans? Again? Is this report from the same source as last time?"

"Yes, it is."

The general scratches his head. "Are they still in Lebanon? Last time they left immediately."

"Our source didn't say."

"Well, tell him to find out. Get a team together in case we need to go in. Let's get to these guys before they have time to hatch a plan."

"What about alerting the Americans, sir? Last time we noticed an Afghan, there was a shooting in America."

He raises his brow. "You think the two events were connected?"

"I don't know, sir. The two incidents *could* have been connected. The Afghan disappeared soon afterward. Won't it make sense to put out an alert and not take any chances?"

"All right—go ahead. Let the Americans know. And get back to your source in Lebanon. Tell your informant to get us more information. If the Afghans are still here, I want to dispatch an intercept team right away. I don't want to give them any time to carry out something over here."

———†———†———

James is propped up in his bed with three pillows, reading the report that Malone did on the security at the ranch. Sam comes out of the bathroom wearing sheer lingerie. James glances up from the files.

"Wow! I guess someone has plans for this evening," he says.

Sam smiles coyly. "You said you were feeling much better. It's been a while. I've missed you. What do you say? Are you up for it?"

James closes the files and places them on the night table, dims the lights, and then pats the bed. "I say, come on over—I've missed you, too."

An hour later, after the act is done, James is on top of Sam's sweating body, trying to catch his breath.

"Wow, that was wonderful." Sam reaches up and pulls him to her. "Thank you!" She gives him a kiss.

"I hope no one woke up," James says as he pulls himself out of her and falls back onto the bed beside her. "You were really loud at the end."

Sam laughs. "I'm sorry—I guess I got a little carried away. It's been a while." She turns to her side and whispers in his ear, "What do you say? Can you go another round? I'll give you a little break. I'll even get on top this time."

James gives her a kiss. "You're a horny little girl. You've got a deal—but only if you promise to be a little quieter. I wouldn't want the entire house breaking into our bedroom in the middle of the act to make sure I wasn't murdering you."

Sam laughs. "I'm not making any promises about the noise. But I'll tell you what! I'll lock our bedroom door," she says, leaping up and turning the lock. "There," she says after jumping back into bed. "Now I can make all the noise that I want!" She pulls herself on top of him.

———†———†———

The next morning, James is in his study when he gets a phone call.

"James, this is Rodney. I just got a call from one of my sources at the CIA. They have received a dispatch of a recent meeting between two Afghan fighters and a Palestinian operative, Aalam Salvar."

"Where was the meeting?"

"In Lebanon," Rodney answers.

"Are they still there?"

"I'm not sure. The meeting happened last week." When James falls silent, Rodney calls out, "James, are you still there? What do you want me to do?"

"Call Ian from our London office. Tell him to contact the Israelis and find out what they know. We need to get to these guys before they can carry out their plan, whatever it is. You can bet that something is in the works—we need to find these guys right away!"

"What're you going to do when we find them?"

"I've got a call out to Ernie, our South African mercenary. I'm going to have him put together a reaction team. When we find these guys, we're going in to take them out."

"You do know that's only a temporary fix, right?" Rodney asks. "They'll just send out another team. James, you got to get to the top guys. The men giving the orders."

"I know, Rodney. But right now, I don't know where those top men are. All I can do is to try to stop the attack that's about to happen. Call Ian and tell him to get in touch with the Israelis right away. Keep me informed if anything new develops. Call me immediately if you hear anything—timing is crucial."

"All right, James. Will do."

"Thank you, Rodney. And by the way—good job."

After he hangs up, James stares at the silent phone. He's called the mercenary at the usual number but hasn't been able to reach him. He left a request for a callback.

Come on Ernie, call. Where the hell are you? Why haven't you called? I really need you!

He's hoping that nothing has happened to Ernie Bauer, a South

African former army colonel who is now a soldier of fortune. James has used Bauer in nearly a dozen missions. The Afrikaner is extremely reliable and fearless—perfect for this type of operation.

James is about to get up from the desk when the phone rings. He dives for it.

"Hello!" he says.

"James Coppi, how the fuck have you been?" the caller with the clipped South African accent says. "Long time no speak, you *domkop!* I hear you had a little skirmish in Texas?"

"Yeah—just a little, Ernie."

"How are you doing? I guess you're recovered?" There is static on the line.

"Yeah, I'm doing fine. It sounds like we have a bad connection. Where are you?"

"I'm in Afghanistan. Doing a little job for the Russians."

"Russians? How the hell did you get mixed up with them?"

Ernie bellows out laughter. "Because James Coppi hasn't given me much business lately. Russian Kruger's are as good as any other money when you need some dough."

"Listen," James says, "enough of the small talk. Let me get to the point before we get cut off. Have you got time for me? I've got a job for you."

More laughter into the phone. "Always got time for you, *boet.* You're my best customer."

"OK, good. I need to put together a rapid deployment team. The squad needs to be able to move out at a moment's notice."

"How big a team?"

"Ten to fifteen men should do. Light infantry. How fast can you get it done?"

"It's available now. They're fighters I'm using right now, in Afghanistan."

"What about Gary Pator? Is he with you?"

"No, Gary is back home in South Africa. Why do you need him? I should be able to handle anything you throw at me."

James laughs. "Just in case you chicken out, I need a backup."

"Thanks a lot, buddy!"

"All kidding aside, can you get Gary? I might need him."

"All right—I'll get in touch with Gary. I'll be ready in three days. Just give me the word. Where and when?"

"All right—stand by. I'll let you know when I'm ready. Listen, Ernie, I need you to check in with me every day. You know—in case I can't reach you for any reason. If you can't reach me, call Ian in London. You got that?"

"Loud and clear."

"All right Ernie—and keep your head down. I wouldn't want anything to happen to you. I wouldn't want to have to rely on just Gary."

Ernie bellows out another laugh. "For a moment, you had me worried, James—I was beginning to think that you were actually concerned about me."

After the call, James walks to the master bedroom, opens the door, and looks in. Sam is still sleeping. He's given everyone strict instructions that she shouldn't be disturbed. He walks over and sits on the bed. Bending down, he gives her a gentle kiss on the cheek and sees her stir.

"Are you ever getting up?" he asks. "I guess you're getting too old to keep up with me. I must have really tired you out last night."

Sam rubs her eyes and smiles. She stretches and yawns. "What time is it?"

"It's quarter to eleven."

She wraps her hands behind his head and pulls him to her. "Thank you for last night," she says, kissing him tenderly. "It was glorious." She sits up. "What're you doing today? You're not going to the office, are you?"

"No—I'm staying here at the ranch. In fact, I'm not going to the office the entire summer. If anything needs to be done, the office can come to me. This summer is going to be devoted entirely to my family and the ranch. I'll spend my time working with Jeff and the boys."

She nods and stretches.

"How about you?" he asks. "What will you be doing?"

"I'm free, too. I've got nothing until next month."

"Next month? What do you have next month?"

"I need to go to Milan. You know—as part of our agreement to sell the fashion business."

"Milan?" James gets very annoyed with her. "Didn't you listen to anything that I said? I want the family to stick around home. At least until I figure out if there is anything to worry about. This whole thing with these Arabs has me really worried. Now you're going to go galloping off five thousand miles away."

"Well, I'm sorry, James. That was the agreement we made when we sold the business."

"Can't you postpone it?"

"It's only for two days. I'll be in and out of Milan. Just a few quick meetings with the company's best customers."

"I'll come with you."

"No, that's OK. You'll just be in the way. Jessica is coming with me. I'll be back before you have a chance to miss me."

"All right, but you're taking two bodyguards with you—both Ronan and the new guy, Regis. Don't even *consider* going to Italy without the two of them."

"OK, I'll do that."

"And no going off shopping or taking some other side trip. Strictly business. In and out. Come right back."

Sam puts her arms around him and pulls him to her. "OK, I'll be a good girl. Come on, let's have a little more fun."

"I'm not in the mood. I've got a lot on my mind."

Sam gives him a kiss and presses her breasts against him teasingly. "Come on, please?" She pulls him toward her. "We'll do it doggie style. You can come at me from the back. How's that?"

James gives her a huge smile and jumps up. "All right—just let me lock the door so no one comes in."

10

The Middle Eastern World, It is Exploding

SAM AND JAMES HAVE JUST finished their romp when there's a knock at the bedroom door.

"Mr. Coppi!" Billingsley hollers from the other side. "Mr. Davis is on the phone. He says it is extremely important."

"OK, Billingsley—I'll take it in the study," James yells back. He gives Sam a kiss on the back of her neck. "You better get dressed."

When James comes back after the call, Sam is walking out of the bathroom. "What happened?" she asks. "What did Rodney have to say?"

"There was a sudden uprising, Shah Khartami is abdicating his throne and going into exile," he tells her. "The whole country is in revolt. This happened faster than I expected. We need to get there and get the shah and his family out. I'm leaving as soon as Rodney and Charlie get here. Billingsley is packing my bags as we speak."

"You're going personally?" Sam asks, pulling at his arm. "Are you crazy? It's too dangerous. You'll be right in the middle of a revolution. Send someone else."

James smiles at her. "Who do you suggest I send? I already have Rodney and Charlie coming with me."

"How about Anthony?" she offers.

"It's too dangerous for me," James asks her, shaking his head, "so I should send my brother in my place?"

"I'm sorry, James." Sam embraces him. "I'm just very frightened.

99

Our family has gone through so much the last few months—we don't need anything else to go wrong."

James pulls away from her. "Don't be alarmed—it's just in and out of the country. We're meeting everybody at the airport. If all goes as planned, I shouldn't be on the ground for more than an hour or two. We just need to get the royal family out and situated in their new location. I should be back in a few days."

James is having a meeting with his men aboard his plane while it is headed for Washington, DC. "We will use three planes in all," he tells the men. "Rodney, you and I will be on the jet carrying the shah and queen to Egypt. Charlie, you'll be on the 747 with the largest part of their entourage heading back to the States. Ian will be on the third plane with the families of the royal's close relatives going to Paris and London."

"What about security?" Charlie asks. "Because of the suddenness of the shah's abdication, we haven't finished setting up all of the security details for the refugees when they get to their new homes. Many will arrive without any security in place."

"We'll have to improvise," James responds. "I've got security set up for the shah, but we'll have to manage the rest of the refugees as we go. It's chaotic, I know, but I don't believe that—in the short term—any of the lower-level refugees are in any danger. There's too much confusion going on in their home country for anyone to create any problems for the people that are fleeing. Let's concentrate our security efforts on the immediate royal family and their higher-level advisers. They're the ones most at risk.

"We're meeting Sester and the CIA in Washington when we refuel," James continues. "I'm not really sure what role, if any, the US government will take in this affair. We shouldn't count on any help."

He shifts the pillow behind his back, which is still healing.

"Prince Firuz is going to meet us in Washington, DC, as well, but I don't believe he'll be much help, either. Until we know better, it's safe to assume that the entire project will be our responsibility."

"What's our job?" Max, his bodyguard, asks him. "Why do you have Ronan and me on this assignment?"

James looks at him and smiles. "Your job, as always, is to make sure that nothing happens to me."

———†———†———

Sester, Prince Firuz and two CIA operatives board James's plane when it stops to refuel in Washington. After the introductions, Sester says, "James, Carl and Henry are here from the CIA and will fly over with you as advisers. The men will have no direct role in the operation. You'll be in charge of the entire affair. There'll be no direct US government involvement.

"With that understanding, what is your plan?" Sester asks. "I know it's a sudden event, but you must have anticipated that something like this could happen."

"Yeah, Sester—I fully understand the government's position, and I'm prepared," James replies. "I have a temporary security detail ready to escort the shah and his immediate family to Egypt. Egypt is only a temporary home for the former monarch until we can work out the details with the people in Morocco. We made arrangements for His Majesty to stay at a secret retreat with a security detail that has been picked out by me. Once the shah makes it to his final destination in Morocco, we'll put a permanent security team in place for his long-term safety."

"James, my father doesn't need your security men. He has his own loyal bodyguards," Prince Firuz says.

"No, I'm sorry, Your Highness—we're leaving your father's personal guard behind. We can't trust anyone from your country. One of the revolutionaries in your country may be contemplating becoming a hero or a martyr. The men I hired have no political ambitions. Your father will be a lot safer with my men.

"Once the shah is settled in his new home, if he then wants to bring over some trusted men, we can arrange for them to be brought to him. In the meantime, your father will be a lot safer with my security."

James looks at all the men intently. "Here's the immediate plan, guys. Three planes will land at the capital. Rodney and I, along with a security detail of some thirty men, will escort the shah and his entourage out of the country. We'll be stopping in London to refuel and pick up the security team that I've hired. Charlie will board one of the other planes waiting in London and accompany the members of the royal's family who are heading for their new homes in the States on that leg of the journey.

"Unfortunately, we didn't have time to set up security for all the evacuees, but Charlie will make sure that everyone at least arrives safely to their destinations. That's all we can do for the time being. Once we have everyone settled in, we'll try to set up a tighter security apparatus.

"Ian, from my London office, will come on a third plane. He'll be responsible for situating the remainder of the monarch's entourage, who are destined for their new homes in England and France. It's my understanding that as many as three hundred are fleeing the country. We haven't made permanent arrangements for everyone, as yet, so these new housing assignments are, in most cases, temporary. We'll work on getting everyone permanently settled once they're safely out of the country."

James looks over at the CIA operatives. "Since you have no direct role, just try to stay out of the way." They nod.

"When are we going to get started?" Prince Firuz asks.

"As soon as we finish refueling," James answers. He gets up and stretches. "Your Highness, can we go to the back? I'd like to speak to you privately."

When they are alone in the back, James says, "I spoke to my finance man in London, sir. He says that only 1.3 billion dollars has been transferred from your Swiss accounts. You told me there would be two billion. What happened to the rest? Is there more coming?"

"No, that's all we could get out," the Prince replies. "There's no more money coming."

"I hope you're not expecting a refund of part of the twenty-million-dollar advance," James says, smiling.

"The deal was for one percent." Prince Firuz's voice gets a little louder. "One percent of 1.3 billion is thirteen million dollars."

"Thanks for pointing that out to me, sir. I couldn't have done the math. You forget that you said that your father would make his own arrangements. But here I am, flying all over the world to take care of his needs.

"Besides, it's not my fault that you didn't come up with the money," he continues. "That's your problem. There'll be no refund!"

Firuz looks around the plane as men are preparing for the trip. Some are checking their rifles. Others are stowing their gear in the overheads. He turns back to James. "I'm very disappointed in you, James. You're taking advantage of me and my family. You are using this desperate situation to squeeze money out of us."

"I'm sorry you feel that way, Prince, but I don't agree with you. We made a deal, and I'm living up to my end of the bargain. That's why I asked for the money to be paid up front. You can cancel this agreement at any time." He pauses to let this sink in. "However, whether you cancel or not, the up-front money is not refundable. You knew that from the beginning. Now, I have a lot of work to do. Are we in agreement?"

Prince Firuz gives him a long look and nods. "OK, let's get going," he says.

"Where do you think you're going?" James asks.

"I'm coming with you, of course."

"No, sir, you shouldn't come." James's voice is stern. "You're not needed. We can do this just as easily without you."

"My father will be expecting me."

"That may be true, Your Highness, but you're not thinking this through completely. Hundreds of your family members are going to be scattered all over the world. They'll need you to coordinate and make this exodus happen.

"Your father is in good hands," James points to the men on the plane. "These men are professionals. Your father will be well guarded and treated. You stay here and get this part of the project completed. I'll explain to your father that because of the suddenness of the mission, you couldn't make the trip."

James is staring out the window of the jet as it makes its final approach to Mehrebad Airport.

All air traffic around the capital will be stopped until the shah is on board and the planes have departed. There will be two more planes to follow, which will airlift the rest of the entourage. Those two jets won't land until this plane is back in the air, with the shah on board. There's a rumbling noise beneath James's feet, indicating that the landing gear is coming down under the aircraft.

James stares out the window. A pill box some twenty yards off the runway comes into view. The barrel of a machine gun sticks out of one of the holes of the bunker. Sandbags and barbed wire surround the bunker, and three soldiers are sitting outside the fortification. A little farther down, the opening of a fox hole that is surrounded by sandbags can be seen. A fifty-caliber machine gun is mounted at the center of the pit. Four men in military uniform lounge around the crater. The military scene reminds him of other airports he's witnessed in his travels.

The big jet, touching down, bounces as its tires make contact with the runway. The noise of the engine going into reverse reverberates throughout the plane as the pilot applies the brakes. The suddenness of the maneuver pushes James first forward and then back in his seat. The plane slows, and the pilot banks to the right to taxi to the terminal. The men of his security force begin gathering their equipment on board.

"Are you ready, sir?" the commander of the detail asks James when the security officer sits alongside him.

"Yes, Ernie, I'm ready," he responds and unbuckles his seat belt. "Where's Rodney?"

"I'm right here, James," Rodney answers him from behind.

James glances at him and then turns back to Ernie. "Remember, the local police detail will drive the shah from the terminal to the plane. Your men need to make a perimeter around the jet. I will escort the monarch from his vehicle onto the plane."

Commander Ernie smilles. "Yes, sir! We all know the plan; we've gone over it a dozen times already. We'll load back up immediately, as soon as everyone is on board. We shouldn't be on the ground for more than ten minutes. Please stop worrying, James—everything will be just fine. My men and I are ready."

James looks at the commander and smiles. "Yes, of course. Thanks for getting to me so fast," he adds. "I know it wasn't easy getting out of Afghanistan."

James knows that there's no need to worry about Ernie. He's used the South African Ernie Bauer in a dozen missions. The mercenary has never failed to come through. Cool and calm, this particular leader is always well prepared. James thinks back to the last mission he did with Ernie.

They were in Kinshasa, Zaire. Everything had gone smoothly up to that point and they were just waiting for the planes to pick them up at the airport. Suddenly, there was a surprise attack from one of the warlords. Some sixty fighters—mounted in jeeps and trucks—attacked them at the airport. Ernie was not fazed at all by the unexpected assault. The Afrikaner, with only six men, fought off the insurgents like it was routine. Within minutes, half of the raiders were dead. The rest retreated as quickly as they had come. This commander was a good man to have on a mission.

"Was there a problem with the last-minute change of plans?" James asks Ernie. "You know—the shah going to Egypt instead of Morocco?"

"No problem at all," Ernie says and smiles. "I spoke to our squad leader, Gary Pator. He was already on the ground in Egypt before we flew out of London. Pator had already finished his reconnaissance of the new locale. Gary is a good man; he'll have everything worked out before we get there." The jet slows its taxiing on the tarmac. "We're good to go," Ernie tells James and walks toward the door.

James goes over to the CIA men, who are now standing. "You guys sit back down," he tells them. "No direct involvement. Remember Sester's orders—we'll get the shah on board. You can have your turn speaking to him at that time."

James gets in the back of the line of the thirty mercenaries, with rifles strapped on their shoulders. Ernie is standing in front of the line. James looks to the back of the plane. His bodyguards, Max and Ronan, are there. James gives them a nod. The bodyguards nod back.

The jet comes to a halt. The door opens, and Ernie looks out. The airstair on the taxiway is fastened to the plane. Ernie steps out first. The remaining soldiers move out quickly but don't run. The soldiers' movements are deliberate. Each man knows his assignment and the position he'll take out in the field.

James emerges, scurries down the steps, and stands next to Ernie, gazing at the terminal as the remaining soldiers form a perimeter around the plane. The men have their weapons at port arms.

Six dark limos are making their way to the airstairs of the jet. When the first limousine arrives, Ernie hurries to open the door. Ernie helps a well-dressed, gray-haired gentleman out of the car. James walks over immediately.

"Good morning, Your Majesty," James greets him, and he shakes the king's hand.

"Good morning, James," the shah replies. Then he turns to help his wife out of the limo. Two other men follow her out of the vehicle. More people are getting out of the other limos as well.

"I didn't expect this many people," Ernie whispers in James's ear. "Who are they?"

James shakes his head and whispers back, "I don't know. This wasn't in the plans. We'll just have to make the best of it."

To the royals, he says, "Right this way, please." He motions to the steps and escorts the shah and queen up the stairs. The soldiers get back on board after the entourage is safely on the plane. Ernie takes a final look outside and locks the door.

Within minutes, the jet is speeding down the runway for takeoff. The whole operation has taken less than half an hour. As soon as they reach altitude, James takes a seat across from the royal couple. The two CIA agents come over and sit across the aisle.

"Why couldn't I bring my own security detail?" the shah asks James. "I don't know these people—I'm not sure that they can be trusted."

"I'm sorry, Your Majesty, but this is the best course of action," James responds. "With all that's happening in your country, we don't know who is your friend and who is your enemy. These soldiers are all professionals, and they're all trustworthy. I have used them before— they are extremely reliable.

"None of these men have any interest in your political affairs. To these guys, this is just another mission, and their assignment is temporary. Once you get set up in your new home, we can begin turning over your security to your own staff."

The shah and queen briefly confer, and the king gives James a tight nod.

"Who are all of these other people who boarded with you?" James asks. "It was my understanding that only a few close advisers were coming with you."

"These *are* my close advisers," the former monarch replies.

"How many are there?"

"I don't know," the shah says, shrugging. "Forty—fifty, maybe. What difference does it make?"

"It's a matter of accommodations, Sir. We may not have enough room for your entire entourage. Remember, you were originally scheduled to go to Morocco. Egypt was a last-minute change of plans. We not only have to find rooms for your entire entourage, we must also be able to provide all these people with security."

James runs his hand through his dark hair. "All right—I'll just have to manage. I'll take care of it. These two men are from the CIA," James adds, gesturing to the men sitting alongside him. "I believe they want to speak to you. I'll leave you alone now." James stands up. "I'll be back when you're finished."

James walks over to Rodney. "Get a list together of every person that came with the king and do a thorough background check on each as soon as we land," he says. James then walks over to Ernie. "Are the additional people going to be a problem?"

"No problem at all, as far as security is concerned. The living accommodations are another matter. I hope these people are used to sleeping on the floor," he says, laughing. "We don't have enough beds."

"We'll figure something out when we land," James responds.

The problem was solved rather quickly. There turned out to be an empty military compound a few blocks from their location. They were able to get access to the place and to house everyone safely with a minimal amount of security.

———————

Two days later, James is back at the ranch and is entering the front door of his home. Molly spots him and comes running. She leaps into his arms. "Daddy! You're home!"

Sam walks out and gives him a kiss. "Welcome home, darling."

"See? I told you it would be an easy affair!" he says.

Sam gives him a wry look. "I hope these easy affairs come to an end soon. I don't know how many more of these easy affairs I can take. I haven't had a full night's sleep since you left."

11

A Princely Act

A FEW WEEKS LATER, JAMES is in California for a brief meeting with Prince Firuz.

"Do you need me to wait, sir?" the limo driver asks as he pulls up to the Bel Air Hotel.

"Yes, Spencer, please wait. I shouldn't be more than an hour."

The doorman of the hotel opens his car door. Max, his bodyguard, gets out of the front seat and stands beside him.

"Are you ready, Max?" James asks the bodyguard.

"Yes, sir," Max replies.

Upstairs, they are greeted by a scantily dressed blonde who opens the door of a penthouse suite. James looks closely at the lady and checks the door again for the room number. "I'm sorry, I must have the wrong suite," he says.

"Who are you looking for, honey?" the blonde asks.

Before James can answer, Prince Firuz comes up from behind her and opens the door wider.

"You've got the right place, James," the prince says. A familiar, wide smile is on the royal's face. "Come in." The prince moves aside.

There's another blonde in a cocktail dress sitting on the sofa in the parlor. Her legs are crossed, and she's showing plenty of legs.

James turns to the prince. "If we came at a bad time, Max and I can come back later."

"No, James, you're fine." Prince Firuz says, and then he gestures to the women. "This is Ginger, and on the sofa, is Marge." The prince turns to the ladies. "Could you please excuse us for a few minutes? I would like to speak to James in private." He opens the door to the terrace.

As the women are leaving, Ginger turns to James. "You look familiar. Do I know you? Have we ever met?"

"No, Ginger, we've never met. I'm sure I would've remembered you." James turns to his bodyguard. "Max, why don't you accompany these fine ladies to the patio?"

Prince Firuz motions to the sofa after they are alone. "Have a seat, James," he says.

Before James can sit, the door of the terrace flies open and Ginger comes barging back in. "Now I remember where I saw you!" she tells James with a grin. "You're the guy that shot those terrorists at the church!"

"Yes, that's me," he admits pleasantly, with a small nod.

"I was just *sure* that I knew you!" Ginger adds, standing and grinning at James.

Prince Firuz finally breaks the silence. "Ginger, can you please excuse us?"

"Oh, sure." Ginger turns to James with another smile. "I hope you stick around for the party afterward, I'll do something special, just for you."

James has just taken a seat when another man walks into the room. James jumps back up. "Prince Farsad," he says, walking over to the man and giving him a hug. "I didn't know you were in town. I thought that you'd be in Paris, handling your people who are relocating to Europe."

Prince Farsad smiles. "It's nice to see you again," he says to James. "I came to the States to help my brother. Please, have a seat." Prince Farsad motions to the sofa again. "We will explain."

"James, my brother is going to take over for me," Prince Firuz says when they are all seated. "Farsad will be your contact person from now on."

"Really? What will you be doing? Is everything all right?"

"We can discuss my situation after I bring you up to date with Farsad. Let me just say that I've bought an estate in Virginia. My family and I will be moving out of your guest house in the upcoming week."

Prince Firuz clears his throat. "James, I want to thank you and your lovely wife Samantha for all of the warm hospitality that you shared with my family," he continues. "Especially Samantha—she is truly a most gracious host. My wife tells me that she comes over every day and caters to her every need. Samantha went as far as to teach my wife how to ride a horse."

"Don't mention it. It was no trouble at all—I'm sure you would've done the same for us."

The prince bows his head in acknowledgment of the compliment, then says, "I will be over next week to help the family move. Will you be there?

"Yes, I'll be there."

"Good—because, I have a present for you and Samantha."

James waves his hand dismissively. "The gesture isn't necessary, Prince. Truthfully, it was no problem at all."

"I know it's not *necessary*, but it is something that I want to do. Please don't offend me."

"No, of course not—I wouldn't want to offend you. I look forward to your gift."

"Good. Now let's get started on our discussion," Prince Firuz says, motioning to his brother. "Go ahead, Farsad."

"James," Prince Farsad begins, "there are a few things that I'd like to discuss. First of all—have you seen how much your company has billed us for your services? It's astronomical."

James ignores Prince Farsad. Instead, he looks over at Prince Firuz and smiles. "That was quick, Your Highness. I went from being a gracious host to a low life in a matter of seconds." James turns back to Prince Farsad.

"Prince, when we first began this project, we were told that no more than a hundred people would need to be evacuated, and also that your father would be responsible for his own expatriation," James says.

"Not only have we had to move your father—the shah—and his

immediate family, but we also had to move his entire entourage. We have had to transport—at last count—nearly seven hundred of his close associates, each of whom required housing and security. There were four planeloads of your close relatives and friends.

"My entire company has been bogged down by this project," James informs them "Many of my other customers have suffered because of this assignment."

"But James, many of the people you moved are lower level," Prince Farsad's voice goes up. "They don't *need* the security details that you have assigned to them."

"That may be true, Your Highness, and we may know that now," James responds. "But we didn't know that when we started the assignment. These people just showed up and boarded our planes unannounced. We were given no lists of who they were and how important they truly were. All of these good folks just appeared, and we flew them to safety. We had no choice. With the situation in your country becoming deadly serious, we needed to move quickly.

"I'm sure that the costs to you will drop once we have everything sorted out. You must appreciate the confusion that we were thrown into. Let me remind you that each person was transported safely. No casualties whatsoever—quite a feat!"

"Yes, I believe James is right," Prince Firuz cuts in, looking at his brother. "The matter was all very confusing. Under the circumstances, James and his company did an amazing job." Prince Firuz looks back at James. "The expenses should begin getting much lower now that we know the situation—am I right? Everyone appears to be settled in, and the situation is stabilizing."

"Yes, Prince, the costs should be coming down considerably—all but the expenses associated with your father. If the shah comes to New York for medical treatment, we will have to provide the security detail."

"Good," says Prince Firuz. "Now that this is settled, there's another matter that we need to speak to you about." The royal turns again to his brother. "Go ahead, Farsad."

"James, it is my understanding that you are in the process of

AA Freda

building several real estate developments. My family is also interested in investing in these types of ventures. You know— homes on golf courses, just like you're doing. We're considering buying some land in Palm Springs. We would like your opinion—is this a good move on our part?"

"Yes, real estate development is a good move for you guys," James tells them. "Palm Springs is perfect. Great weather, beautiful scenery. You should do well. Just make sure you're ready for all the headaches that come along with real estate development—construction unions, permits, environmental impact statements, real estate boards, and politicians who will have their hands in your pockets."

Prince Firuz smiles and looks at his brother. "I told you we have the right man."

His brother Farsad leans forward in his chair. "James, we know of the problems that you mentioned. If what you say is a headache for you, it will be a major pain for us. We are foreigners—no one will trust us. That's why we would like you to join our venture. We'd like you to become one of the partners."

James frowns. "I'm sorry, Your Highness. I'm already fully invested in my own real estate projects. I don't want to put any more of my money in any other development until my ventures are completed."

"There's no money for you to put up," Prince Farsad explains. "We will be responsible for the entire investment. We already have sixty-two investors who are ready to fund the project. The investors will be limited partners. All of the capital needed for the project will come from the partners.

"What we need is a general partner to oversee the entire enterprise and to become the public face for the venture—that would be your role. Someone who can talk to all the politicians and other officials. Again—there's no need for you to put up any money. James, I must tell you, we are also looking at a possible second project on the Monterey Peninsula. This could be a very lucrative arrangement for you."

"What's my cut?" he asks.

"Five percent," Farsad answers.

"Pass," James replies immediately. "Not interested."

"What percentage did you have in mind?" Prince Farsad asks, getting louder. "You'd earn five percent without putting up any money. That's a pretty good deal."

"No, not really, Prince. You don't know a lot about this business— so let me enlighten you. The general partner is the one who assumes all the risks and liability. If something goes wrong, I will be the one on the hook." James gets up to stretch. "If you want me, it's twenty percent and a salary of $200,000 a year."

"Wow!" Prince Firuz says with a whistle. "That's some deal. Is there any room for negotiation in that proposal?

James sits back down. "All right, I'll lower my share to fifteen percent, but that's my final offer. You'll provide me with an indemnity agreement from each of you and from all of your other investors, protecting me from lawsuits. That's it, fellows—that's my best offer. Take it or leave it—I'm not going any lower."

Prince Firuz looks over at his brother, who nods. "All right—it's a deal. We'll get the agreement to you right away."

"Now that that's done," James says, looking over at Prince Firuz, "let's talk about you, sir. What are you going to be doing? While your brother is handling these affairs, what will you be working on?"

"James, I just bought an estate in Virginia. That's going to be my new home. There's a reason I chose that location. It's close to Washington. I want to get to know all the key players in your country. Throw plenty of money around. Build plenty of allies and support." Prince Firuz leans forward. "James, I'm going to get my country back. I'm going to fight back against the groups that forced my family out of power. I'm getting back my legacy that my father foolishly squandered."

"Are you sure you want to attempt this, Your Highness?" James asks. "Have you read the reports on what's happening in your country? There's a revolution. Thousands of people are being killed. The communists are at war with the religious fundamentalists. The ruling council that's in control has no power at all. Someone just murdered the leader of the central government."

"Yes, James—I'm well aware of this turmoil. That's my point exactly—the country is in utter chaos. With all the forces on the extremes fighting each other, the middle class is becoming afraid. This is the middle class that foolishly thought things would get better when they forced my father out of power.

The prince lets out a breath. "The panacea that the citizens hoped the abdication would bring never materialized. It is only a matter of time before the middle class becomes disenchanted and wants the old system back.

"I need to be ready to make my move when that change in mood happens. There are still allies of my family in the country. These supporters are keeping me informed of all the different factions and the moves that these groups are making.

"James, you could be of help to me. You have contacts within the CIA. Introduce me to your connections. Let me have access to your sources. Will you do that for me?"

James looks pensive for a moment. The princes wait.

"Yes, of course I will. Anything for you, Prince. I'll have Rodney personally introduce you to all the players. I'll call Bill Sester myself. Sester will be a key person for you. He's very close to the president."

"Thank you, James." Prince Firuz says, visibly relieved, and sits back in his chair. "I knew I could count on you."

"Your Highness, I'll help in any way that I can—but I must warn you. Your plan is risky. The political landscape in your country has changed. You and your family are not wanted there any longer. Based on what I see of the political climate in that part of the world, I can't envision any way that the populace will allow you back into power. Except for a small minority that's left behind, all of your political allies have fled the country. There's no one there any longer to provide you with any meaningful support.

"Even your old head of secret police was recently assassinated. The situation is totally out of control. Please consider my advice carefully before you embark on this plan."

The prince smiles politely.

"James, thank you for your concern, but I have to follow what I consider to be my destiny. If I lose my life in that attempt, so be it—nothing is going to stop me from making the attempt."

"All right, Prince. As you say, so be it. You can count on me to provide whatever help I can." James stands up and walks over to the terrace door. He knocks on the glass and gestures to his bodyguard Max to come inside. The ladies follow Max back into the suite.

"You're not staying for the fun?" Ginger asks James.

"I'm sorry, my dear. I have a date with another filly this afternoon," he replies.

"She's a lucky girl," Ginger responds.

"I hope so—she's running at Hollywood Park in about two hours." James smiles and turns to his bodyguard. "Come on, Max. If we hurry, we'll still have time to see my horse race."

Prince Firuz escorts them to the door. Before leaving, James turns to him. "I guess I'll see you at the ranch. When did you say you'd be there?"

"I'll be there on Wednesday." The men shake hands.

James walks into his home that evening.

"I'll take that, sir," Billingsley says, walking over and grabbing the handle of his suitcase.

Sam is walking down the hall. "You're home!" she calls out, and she hurries over and gives him a kiss.

"Where are the children?" he asks.

"Molly is in her room, playing with her friend Marcy. Michael is in his room, being punished for refusing to stop teasing the girls. And here comes Christopher, waddling down the hall right now, naked except for his diaper."

James squats down and holds out his arms. "Come here, baby."

Christopher calls out, "Dada!" and comes running.

James scoops Christopher up and begins walking toward the bedroom with the baby in his arms. "What else is new?" he asks Sam.

"Princess Khartami was here earlier. Did you know they're moving to Virginia?"

"Yes, the prince told me when I saw him this weekend in California."

"I wonder how they decided on Virginia? Isn't that a strange choice?"

"It's a long story," he says. "I'll tell you about it later. By the way—make sure you're around on Wednesday. The prince wants to say goodbye. He says he has a gift for us." James sees one of the maids, Gilda, walking toward him. "Gilda, take Christopher from me, please."

<hr />

On Wednesday, there is a knock on the door of James's study. Billingsley pokes his head into the room. "I'm sorry to disturb you, sir, but the royals are here and would like a moment with you. They are in the parlor."

"Thank you, Billingsley," James says and gets up. "Please let my wife know that the Khartamis are here."

"Princess!" James calls out when he enters the room, and walks to the princess who looks striking wearing a silk Persian blue gown. A string of black pearls circle her neck. The jet-black hair flows down to her shoulders. "I hear you're leaving us."

"Yes, James," the princess smiles warmly. "As much as I have loved my stay at your beautiful ranch, it is time to move on. I want to thank you for the warm hospitality extended to me and my family— especially from your lovely wife." The princess looks around. "Where is Samantha? I would not want to leave without saying goodbye."

"I'm right here, Princess Khartami," Sam replies as she enters the room. Sam walks over and gives the royal a kiss on the cheek. "I hope you're not leaving for good. You will come for back for a visit, won't you?"

"Yes, of course I will. And you must come to visit us at our new place, once we have our home all arranged. And, please, no more 'Princess.' It's just Yasmin, now."

"I would be delighted to visit," Sam smiles. "But, I'm sorry, it's not plain Yasmin—you will always be my beautiful princess."

"I'm glad that you are here, Samantha," Prince Firuz says. "My wife and I would like to present you with a gift as a gesture to show our gratitude for the warm welcome you have extended to us during our stay."

"The gift isn't necessary," Sam responds. "It was our pleasure."

"Yes, I know it is not necessary—but still, we want to offer this gift to you and James." Prince Firuz turns to James and speaks sternly. "James, I do have one condition on the gift. This present is for both for you and Samantha. You are not permitted to take control."

"All right, sir. As you wish," James responds and looks around. "Now you have piqued my curiosity. Where is the gift?"

"It is outside." The Prince heads for the door.

James gives Sam a look and whispers, "Outside . . . I wonder what it could be?" They follow Prince Firuz out the front door.

When they get out onto the grass, they see one of the ranch hands holding a beautiful chestnut thoroughbred by the reins.

"That's our gift?" Sam exclaims in disbelief.

"Yes. I hope you like him," the prince says with a smile. "I purchased him at a private sale three weeks ago. The colt's breeding is impeccable. Both his sire and dam were successful stake winners at a mile and a quarter. His sire was also third in the Kentucky Derby and won the Preakness. I'm told that this two-year-old is ready to race—he's been in training."

"Prince, this is too much," James says. "We cannot accept him. I know the breeding. This horse must have cost you a small fortune."

"James, please—do not insult us. Both my wife and I want to offer you this gift. You and your wife Samantha are the warmest, most genuine people that we have ever met."

"All right—we'll accept your gracious present." James says and turns to the ranch hand. "Billy, bring the colt down to the stable.

Tell Jeff to put him into a stall away from the other horses for the time being." He turns back to the Khartamis. "Thank you! We are honored to accept your most generous gift. You will come and see him race?"

"Yes, of course," Princess Yasmin answers. "But don't forget, James—he is not just for racing. Sam owns one half. I would love to see her ride the horse, most of all—I have witnessed Sam riding. She is so elegant and graceful."

"Whatever you say," James replies and turns to Sam. "I'll tell you what, dear—you can be in charge of his training."

"It will be my honor and pleasure," Sam tells the royal couple. "Thank you both very much. It is a beautiful and most thoughtful present. I would like to second James's statement; we are honored to accept your gift."

"They are such nice people," Sam says when they are back in the house and the royals have left. "I hope it all works out for them here in their new country. And I hope the prince stops this foolishness about trying to get his throne back."

"No, Sam—Firuz won't stop," James tells her. "The prince feels that it's his destiny—that his legacy was torn from him. He is the crown prince. Prince Firuz has a meeting with Sester next week; I set the meeting up for him. Firuz is determined to see this through, at whatever the cost."

"The cost could well be his life," Sam says. "Has he seen the accounts on television of what is going on in his country? There is a bloody civil war going on. Thousands are being killed."

"Yes, Firuz is following the action in his country closely. For some reason, he believes he can turn the commotion to his favor. With all the different factions fighting against each other, he sees an opening to work his way back into power.

"Sam, I don't agree with him. I'm with you. I feel that Firuz is tilting at windmills. His father had much more backing than he does, and even he couldn't stay on the throne. But who am I to give Prince Firuz advice? My lineage doesn't go back a thousand years in the history books, as the prince's does. I don't know what I would do if I were in his shoes.

"Anyway, next time you're at church, say a prayer for him," James adds. "The Prince will need all the help he can get—especially that of the Almighty."

12

Kidnapped

FAAKHIR PACES UP AND DOWN a room inside the small chalet in Belgium. Moshar has gone out for supplies and to make his daily call to Lebanon to get the status on the Americans that are holed up in Colorado. Faakhir is stuck in the farmhouse with the four Palestinians. Stuck with them in Belgium for over three weeks so far. And there seems to be no end in sight.

It's nearly August. It will soon be harvest time back home—he needs to return. His family can't manage the harvest without him. There has been no news from America. The Americans have not moved from the ranch.

Faakhir is beginning to wonder if he will ever see his family again. There's no way to get in contact with them, and there is no way for him to get any news about how they are doing. He looks across a field and notices a car speeding along the dirt road, kicking up dust. That would be Moshar. When the vehicle gets to the house, it screeches to a halt and Moshar comes rushing in.

"Come on, everybody up!" Moshar shouts excitedly. "Get ready to move out!"

Faakhir grabs him by the arm. "Our man has left America?"

"Not him, her!" he smiles. "His wife! She's leaving for Milan tomorrow. We've got to hurry! We've got to get to Milan immediately and get everything set up." Moshar looks at the men, who are looking at him but not moving. "Why are you just standing around? Let's go!"

"His wife? A woman? She's worthless," one of the Palestinians cries out. "They won't exchange the prisoners for a woman. It's a waste of time."

"That's where you're wrong, Mohammed. *We* wouldn't swap for a woman, but the Americans will. They have a soft spot for women. They think that women need special treatment and protection. In any event, it's either her or nothing. Let's go. We've wasted too much time already! We've got to get into town and pick up another car."

On the ride to Italy, Faakhir asks, "What's the plan? I'm sure this woman will have bodyguards."

"Yes, I'm sure she will," Moshar answers. "We'll know more tomorrow when she leaves the US. Our source in Colorado will tell us how many men are with her when she boards the plane." Moshar looks back at the other car, which is following. "We'll take the woman on the street. Drive her down to Genoa, where a freighter is waiting for us. It's all set—the ship will take her and us to Lebanon.

"Come on, Faakhir—let me see a smile. You should be very happy. It's almost over for you. As soon as we drop the woman off in Lebanon, you can go home to your family."

"What about the man on the ranch in Colorado? He's still out there. Won't you need me for him?"

"No, Faakhir, we won't. I spoke to Prince Faikil, and he said you can go home. This completes your assignment. You deserve a rest. Besides, if I know the American—now that we have his wife, he'll come out of his little hole that he's been hiding in. There's no way he'll stay in that fortress that he's set up for himself. Once he comes out, we'll be able to take care of him, too. It's all falling into place— just like we planned."

———————✦———————✦———————

James is in his study at the ranch, staying home and watching over the family. Kathy is there to give him the weekly reports on his companies. Yesterday, Sam left for Milan with Jessica for the fashion trip.

"How's your precious daughter, Marlene?" he asks Kathy.

"Getting big," Kathy says, smiling.

"I haven't seen her in a while. Next time you come to the ranch, bring her with you."

Kathy laughs. "I'm afraid that we wouldn't get any work done. Marlene is getting to be quite a handful—always getting into things that she shouldn't."

The phone rings, and James picks up.

"Hello, James, it's Jessica."

James can tell by her tone that something is wrong. "What's up? Is everything all right?"

"No, it isn't, James! Sam has been kidnapped!"

"Kidnapped!" James yells into the phone. *Did I just hear that right? Sam was kidnapped?* "What the hell happened?"

"Who was kidnapped?" Kathy shrieks.

"Oh, James, it was horrible!" Jessica says, bawling into the phone.

James's head is spinning. He can't focus. Doesn't know how to proceed or process what he has just heard. *Collect yourself,* he says to himself. *This is important.*

"Who was kidnapped?" Kathy cries out once more.

James puts up his hand out to Kathy to quiet her. "Jessica, collect yourself. Tell me what happened—from the beginning."

"We were breaking for lunch. Sam and I decided to take a walk and do some window shopping."

James shakes his head. *Damn, Sam, you just won't listen—I told you not to wander off.*

"Men attacked us, and they took off with Sam!"

"Where were Ronan and Regis, the bodyguards?"

"Ronan is dead! He was shot. Regis was also shot, but I think he's still alive. He was taken to the hospital."

"Which hospital?"

"The same hospital that I'm in—San Raffaele."

"You're in the hospital? Are you all right?"

"I was knocked unconscious when I tried to help Sam. I should be fine. Aside from a swollen cheek, I'm OK. They're keeping me overnight as a precaution. James, there's a police lieutenant here who wants to speak to you. He's right outside my room. Hold on—I'll call him in."

"*Pronto*, this is Tenente Giovanni Alfano. Is this Signor Coppi?"

"Yes, it is, Tenente Alfano," James answers, switching into Italian.

"Signor Coppi, may I say how sorry I am that this has happened."

"Thank you, Lieutenant."

"May I ask you, is there anyone that you can point me to in this matter? Someone that you might believe could have done this?"

"Yes. Palestinians or Afghans—we've received threats from both those groups."

"Palestinians or Afghans? That is a strange combination. Why would they threaten your family?"

"Because of the church shooting that happened in Lubbock, Texas. I was the one that foiled their plan."

"Oh, now I recognize the name!" the lieutenant yells into the phone. "I knew the name sounded familiar."

James shakes his head impatiently. "Lieutenant, what are you doing to find my wife? Do you have any leads?"

"No—no leads yet. But you can rest assured that we're doing everything possible. We have posted an all-points bulletin. All escape routes out of the country are being monitored—both at the airports and by land. We will catch the kidnappers—you can be assured!"

"What about by water?"

"By water?"

"Yes, by water. Genoa is nearby, and it's a main port. Have you done anything to make sure they don't escape on a ship?"

"Yes, I see—I will get on that right away, Signor Coppi."

James now realizes that the Italian police are not going to be of any help. "Lieutenant Alfano, I will have some men coming to Milan tomorrow. I would appreciate you giving them an update and your cooperation."

"Yes, of course. Have your men contact me as soon as they get here."

"Can you please put the *signora* back on the phone?" When Jessica is back, he says, "Jessica, Charlie McGill should arrive tomorrow. Don't leave until he gets there."

"All right, James. I'll wait for Charlie."

"Good. Feel better. I'll give you a call in the morning."

"What happened to Sam?" Kathy asks after he hangs up.

"You heard—she's been kidnapped."

Kathy gasps. "Kidnapped? By who?

James is gazing up at the ceiling, deep in thought. He picks up the phone again and dials.

"This is James Coppi. Let me speak to Charlie McGill. It's urgent."

"Yes, Mr. Coppi," the receptionist responds.

"Mr. Coppi, Mr. McGill is currently in the conference room, conducting a meeting," Charlie's secretary informs him.

"Yank him out of the meeting, Susan. It's extremely urgent."

"Right away, sir."

"Hello, James," Charlie says after a brief moment. "What's up?"

"Sam was kidnapped!"

"What? Where? When?" Charlie can barely speak.

"In Milan, earlier today."

"Oh shit!" Charlie takes a deep breath and lets it out.

"Charlie, I need you to round up Gurney and Hiawalah and get to Milan right away. The company plane isn't available, so you'll have to fly commercial. When you get there, find Jessica. She's at a hospital called San Raffaele. Jessica will fill you in on everything. Please get going immediately. You might be able to catch a flight out today if you hurry."

"All right, James. I'm on my way."

James looks at the clock on his desk. "Ten to eleven," he mutters. "He should still be in the office." He dials the phone. "Ian Wadsworth, please," James says to the woman who answers. "This is James Coppi,"

"Hello, James!" Ian says brightly. "How's everything in sunny Colorado? It's raining here in London, as—"

"Sam was kidnapped!" James says, cutting Ian off.

"Oh fuck!"

"Ian, what's the name of our man in Italy?"

"Paolo Rizzi! What happened?"

"Get in touch with Rizzi." James tells him, ignoring the question. "Have him get to Milan right away. Tell him to get to Jessica Force—she's at San Raffaele hospital. Jessica will fill him in on the kidnapping. McGill should be there tomorrow with a couple of men. They'll need a translator—someone who speaks the language and who knows his way around. Then you'll need to pack your bags and head for Israel."

"Israel? Why Israel?"

"Sam was kidnapped in Milan, but my hunch is that she's not in Italy any longer. I'm guessing that they've moved her to Lebanon. The Israelis might know something. At least, they can be of help.

"Listen, I don't want to waste any more time talking!" he adds impatiently. "Get going. Try to make tonight's flight. Call me when you get to Tel Aviv."

James hangs up with Ian and takes a deep breath. The phone rings immediately.

"James, this is Rodney. Charlie just told me that Sam was kidnapped. This is terrible—I feel awful. What can I do?"

"Rodney, I'm glad you called. I was about to call you. Get in touch with your CIA sources. I want to know everything about Palestinian organizations in Lebanon."

"Lebanon? I thought we were dealing with Italians?"

"No. She was taken in Italy, but Italians have nothing to do with the kidnapping. This is a Palestinian operation. It might have an Afghan connection. Find out if your sources know anything about that.

"An Afghan named Faakhir has popped up," James continues. "He might have something to do with Sam's kidnapping. See if the CIA knows anything about this man and his connection to the Palestinians, especially a Palestinian named Aalam Salvar."

"OK, James. I'll get right on it."

After they hang up, James looks at the clock once more. He dials the phone. "Ernie, I was hoping that I'd get you. I know it's late in South Africa."

"What do you need, James?"

"I need you to go to Mirabad. It's in Southwest Afghanistan. Look up a fellow named Faakhir. Find out what this guy has been up to—I need this information right away."

"James, I'm sorry—I really can't help you. I'm in the middle of a mess right now here in South Africa. The government is trying to charge me with war crimes for my part in the fighting in Angola, and they've taken away my passport."

"Where's Gary? Can you get in touch with him?"

"Gary can't get there right away, either. He's part of this Angola mess, too. How fast do you need this information?"

"I need it right away. I'll have to make different arrangements. How long will you guys be tied up?"

"It shouldn't be too long for Gary. I don't know how long my situation will take."

"OK—have Gary call Ian Wadsworth as soon as he can get away. I want him to get to Israel."

"OK, I'll do that. What about me? I can sneak out of the country if you really need me."

"Yeah, you better start thinking about making your way out of the country. Head for Israel and join up with Gary and Ian as soon as you can get away."

"Who is our man in India?" James asks Kathy after he hangs up. "Omprakash, right? What's his number?"

"It's in your Rolodex," Kathy says. She gets up, opens the file, and pulls out the card. "Here."

The phone rings as he reaches for it to dial the number.

"James, Rodney just told me the terrible news," Vernon says. "What can I do to help?"

"Vernon, I need you to keep a handle on things at the company. Everyone else is going to be very busy. You'll have to step in and cover for them."

"Sure, James—of course. You can count on me. Anything else?"

"Do you know where my brother Anthony is?"

"Isn't he in New York City?"

"Do me a favor, find and call him. Tell Anthony I need to speak to him."

After he hangs up, James immediately begins dialing. "Omprakash, this is James Coppi. I'm sorry to bother you at this hour of the night—I wouldn't be calling if it weren't extremely urgent."

"It is no bother at all, Mr. Coppi. What can I do for you?"

"I need you to send a man up to Mirabad, Afghanistan. It's on the border of western Pakistan. He needs to get me information on a man named Faakhir. Who he is? Where is he? What's he been doing? And anything else they can find out about this Afghan."

"All right, Mr. Coppi. I'll get to work on it."

"Omprakash, it's extremely urgent. I need this right away."

"I'll dispatch someone first thing in the morning."

James hangs up and takes a deep breath. He feels like the weight of the world is on his shoulders. He's so lost in thought that he's almost forgotten Kathy is still in the room.

"What are *you* going to be doing?" Kathy asks, jolting him back. "You've got everyone hopping all over the world. What will you be doing?"

"Waiting for the call."

"Waiting for the call? What call?"

"The call with the demands. The demands of what they want in exchange for freeing my wife," James says and stands up. "Kathy, I need a big favor from you."

"Anything, James. Anything! What do you need?"

"I need you to go home, get your daughter, and then come and live here at the ranch until this thing is over. I've got a feeling that I'm going to be quite busy, and I'll be leaving quickly once this thing really gets moving. My children will need a steady presence to help them get through this crisis. Will you do that for me?"

"Yes, of course. I'll move in tonight."

"Good!" James says and frowns. "Now for the hardest part. Breaking the news to the children."

James walks out of the study and heads for his daughter Molly's room. He knows that it's his daughter who's going to be hit the hardest. His sons Michael and Christopher are too young to really understand. He lets out a sigh and walks into the room.

"Hi, Daddy," Molly looks up from her desk and puts down the book.

"Are you busy, darling?" he asks. "I'd like to speak to you about something important." James sits on her bed. "Come on, jump up. Sit on the bed next to me."

"What, Daddy?" she says after she hops up on the bed.

James faces her. "Mommy is not going to be home for a while."

"Why, Daddy? Where is she?"

"You remember that book I read to you? The one where the bad men kidnapped the princess?"

The child furrows her brow, trying to understand.

"Yes, Daddy, I remember. Did a bad man take Mommy?"

"Yes, baby, he did, and Mommy is going to be gone for a little while."

The worried child sits for a moment, trying to absorb this. Then she looks at her father with an expression of total trust.

"Are you going to rescue her?"

"Yes, I am, darling. I'm going to go get Mommy. It's just going to take a little while. So you won't see her for a little bit, until I get her home. You need to act like a big girl and be brave. Do you understand?"

Molly reaches up and gives him a hug. "Yes Daddy. You go get Mommy. Make her safe and bring her home."

13
The Demands

SAM GETS UP FROM THE mattress that's on the floor and raises up on her toes to peek out of the porthole. The sun is beginning to rise over the blue horizon. This is the second morning that she's seen the sunrise. She's beginning to wonder if they'll ever reach shore. No one has told her anything. The fear that had first come over her is now completely gone.

She didn't see much of what happened during the fight. But the sight of Ronan being shot and falling to the ground horrified her. She hopes that he's all right. She hears the sound of a key going into the lock on the door.

Two men walk in. "I brought you some food. You haven't eaten much," one of the men says to her. "Here's some hot tea." The man puts the tray on one of the cargo wooden boxes that are in the room. The other man pours a jar of water into a basin. "You might want to clean up," he says.

"What do you want from me?" she asks the men.

The man turns from the basin and smiles, showing his yellow teeth. "You, nothing. We'll be discussing what we want from your husband once we reach shore."

Sam walks over to the box and pours tea into a metal cup. "When will that be?" she asks, taking a sip.

"Tonight. We arrive tonight."

"Where are we landing?"

"That's not important right now. You'll know soon enough."

Sam puts down the tea and looks at the men defiantly.

"You know, my husband is a very powerful man. He will hunt you down."

The man smiles once more. "Yes, I know he's very formidable. And very rich, too. But most of all, he's very clever. That's why we picked you. Your husband is very smart; he will not try to do something stupid. He will listen to reason and follow our instructions carefully."

"Why are you doing this? I have three children. How can you be so cruel as to deprive those children of their mother?"

"Palestinian mothers have children, too," the man tells her, his voice rising. "Every night, the mothers try to sleep with their children. When the Israeli bombs drop on their houses and the children are afraid, it's those mothers who try to give them comfort. When the Zionist soldiers come in the middle of the night and break into their homes, stealing away the children's fathers, it's the mothers who are left to pick up the pieces. Do not expect any pity because you're a mother."

The two men turn to leave. "Don't worry," the man adds. "If your husband is as clever as we think he is, you'll be home with your children very soon. He'll accede to all of our demands. Please eat something. You need to keep up your strength. We wouldn't want something to happen to you and upset your children."

He gives her a sardonic smile.

───┤────────┤───

"James, I've been here four days—and nothing," Ian tells him from a phone on the border between Lebanon and Israel. "How long am I supposed to wait?"

"As long as it takes, Ian."

"The Palestinians are attacking this camp with rockets every day. We're no more than five hundred meters from the border. Do you have any idea of what it's like during a rocket attack?"

"I might have some idea. After all, I was in Vietnam. Anyway,

I'm sure the bunkers are well fortified. If I know you, you haven't even seen the sun."

"How sure are you that Sam will be taken to Lebanon?"

"I'm not totally sure. It will either be Lebanon or Afghanistan. I have a man headed for Afghanistan. He should be reporting back to me any day now. Has Gary arrived yet?"

"Gary just called from Tel Aviv. He's on his way up here. What do you need him to do when he arrives?"

"Nothing until I hear something from the other side. Have Gary give me a call when he reaches you," James says and hangs up. He's about to go get a cup of coffee when the phone rings.

"James, this is Rodney. The American embassy in Beirut just got an envelope. Inside was a picture of Sam holding a Lebanese newspaper headline. It was yesterday's date. Sam is alive and looks unharmed."

James is so relieved that he can't speak.

"James, are you still there?"

"Yes, I'm here," he manages. "What else was in the envelope?"

"There was a demand. They have conditions for Sam's freedom. They want the Imam that was arrested in the US to be released. Also, they're saying that all Palestinian political prisoners being held by Israel need to be freed. And they're demanding that all the Palestinian political prisoners being held in Europe and Africa be freed, too."

"I see."

"James, it's going to be impossible to meet these demands."

"I know. What else does it say?"

"There was an ultimatum—they want an answer within seventy-two hours."

"Did they give a way to reach them?"

"They want the answer posted in the classified section of a certain Lebanese paper."

"OK."

"What are you going to do?"

"I'm going to reach out to the heads of these countries and see if they'll agree to the swap."

"You know that they'll never agree," Rodney says gently, as if breaking bad news.

"I know. But I can ask!" James says and forces out a laugh.

"What are you going to do when they turn you down?"

James pauses. "I've been working on a plan."

"What is it?" Rodney asks eagerly.

"Let's not talk about that right now. Rodney, run an ad in that newspaper just as the kidnappers instructed. Just say something like, 'Message received, working on your proposal.' That's it—no more. You got that?"

"Yes, James. I'll do it right away."

"I'm going to call the president and see what he says," James tells him. "After he gave me the Presidential Medal, the president told me that if I ever needed anything, to just let him know. Sam also made friends with the president's wife Jennifer, I'll reach out to her too."

It takes fifteen minutes and four people before James gets through to the president. Well, not really the president—he is able to get to the chief of staff, who says he remembers the promise the president made. Aside from a general comment that the country was doing everything possible to free up Sam, the aide wouldn't disclose anything definitive as to how the administration will help. Which to James means that they are not doing much. He also contacted the president's wife and while she took the call, and expressed her sympathy, she wasn't much help either. She agreed to pass on the information to the president.

It's amazing how these politicians can look directly into your eyes and lie so easily, James muses.

He does not expect the president to accede to the kidnappers' demands. James fully understands the political problems that the president would face if he were to give in to terrorists. But can't the man at least take his call—instead of hiding behind all these people? What does that say about the man leading this country? That he doesn't have the guts to even take a call?

James gets up and walks out of the study. It doesn't matter if the president calls back or not. James has a plan. The demands made by the kidnappers can never be met. Even if the president agrees, the other countries never would. James walks out of the house and heads toward the bunkhouse. A smile comes across his face as he notices Cardiz sitting on the fence of the corral—doing nothing, as usual.

"You're consistent, I've got to admit, Cardiz—you *never* work."

"A man is allowed to take a break, isn't he, Coppi?"

"Yup—but for you, a break usually lasts the entire day. Come on, get your ass off the fence. Walk with me for a while—I want to talk to you about something."

"Any news on Sam?" Cardiz asks.

"Yeah, I just heard this morning. Sam is alive and well. She's being held somewhere in Southern Lebanon."

Cardiz looks startled.

"Why don't you look happier? That's good news, isn't it?"

"Yeah, Cardiz, that's good news—Sam's alive. But the good news ends there. The kidnappers have made demands for her release that can't possibly be met.

"Anyway—I've got a plan, and I could use your help," James continues. "You may have to come with me to Israel. I know you just got back together with your wife, so if you can't come with me, I'll understand."

"Of course I'll do it," Cardiz says, putting his arm across James's shoulder. "Anything for you, buddy. What's the plan?"

"Do you remember how Hall and Goyette got killed in Vietnam?"

"Yeah, I do. By friendly fire. They had to call in the artillery on themselves when they were surrounded and being overrun."

"Right. And I'm going to do the same thing."

Cardiz eyes widen and his voice rises. "You're going to call artillery on yourself? How the fuck does you getting yourself killed help Sam get rescued?"

"I'm not going to get myself killed. Listen to my idea." James tells Cardiz the strategy that he's come up with.

"Christ, Coppi that's one hell of a plan. Are you sure? You're really putting yourself at risk." Cardiz pauses. "Listen, Coppi, I always considered you one of the smartest guys I've ever met, but this idea is just plain stupid. You're going to get yourself killed."

"Well, it's the best plan I can come up with," James says, his voice rising. "Listen, Cardiz, I've got to get Sam home. I'll do whatever it takes. If I die and she gets out safely, the mission will have been a success. I'm ready for death—just as long as I know that Sam got out safely. That's all I ask of my life—that Sam gets back home alive and well. I'll exit this world a happy man knowing that Sam is back with our children. I've felt like such a failure the last few days—I couldn't protect my beautiful wife from this horror."

Cardiz looks at him. "OK, compadre—just let me know when you're ready. You can count on me."

The telephone is ringing when James gets back to his study. He runs over to get the call. It's Omprakash.

"James, my man called. He just got out of Afghanistan. This fellow Faakhir isn't in Mirabad—he hasn't been home in weeks."

"Yeah, I figured as much. What else did your man find out about this guy?"

"This man is apparently very well off; my man says he has the biggest house in Mirabad. He lived in England as a child. His father at one time was a very important official in the Afghan government."

"Okay thanks, that's all very good information."

"Is there anything else that I can do for you?"

"Yeah. I need your man to go back to Mirabad and get one of the villagers to work for us. I need to know when this fellow Faakhir makes it back to his home. If I'm right, this fellow Faakhir should be back soon."

"OK—I can do that."

James walks out and knocks on Kathy's door. She opens and lets him into her room.

"I'm going to be leaving in the morning," he tells her. "I'll be gone for a few days."

"Where are you going?"

"I'm going to go rescue Sam and bring her home."

"You heard something?" Kathy's face lights up. "That's great!"

"Yes. She's being held in Southern Lebanon, as I suspected. I'm going to Israel to negotiate her release."

"Oh, James." Tears flow down Kathy's face. "That's so wonderful. I'm so happy."

"Yeah—I am, too. This ordeal will soon come to an end. The children will have their mother home again." James clears his throat. "Kathy, sit down for a sec. I want to speak to you about something really important."

After she takes a seat on the bed, he sits on a chair across from her. James reaches into his pocket, takes out a key, and holds it out to her. "Here. This is a key to the upper drawer of my desk in my study. If, for some reason, I don't make it back, you'll need to get into that drawer.

"Inside the drawer are all the legal documents that Sam will need to keep going. I worked out all the legal papers with my attorneys, and everything is in good order."

Kathy reaches out and takes the key. Her eyes are starting to well up again. "James, what are you saying?" she asks. "Are you saying that you'll not make it back?"

"There's always that possibility—these are very dangerous men. You must be prepared for any news—good or bad." James squeezes her hand, gets off the chair, and then squats in front of her. "There's a letter in there from me, addressed to Sam. It's to be opened only if I don't make it back.

"There are also letters addressed from me to each of my children. Those letters should be read to my children when they're old enough to understand. Molly should remember me, but I don't believe Michael or Christopher will. Those letters—and the stories that Sam tells the boys about me—are the only way they'll know who their father was."

Tears are now streaming down Kathy's face. She reaches over to the nightstand, grabs a tissue, and blows her nose. James clears his throat.

"Now is the most difficult part. If, in the highly unlikely event that neither Sam nor I make it back, I'd like you to be the guardian to our children. The papers appointing you as guardian are also in my desk."

He pauses and takes a deep breath.

"Kathy, I know, I'm asking for a lot. You have your own child to raise. So if you don't want to be the guardian—tell me now, and I'll change the papers."

Kathy is weeping. She's trying to speak, but no words come out. She reaches over and pulls James to her, squeezing him tight. "Oh, James, please don't talk like that. You *will* make it back. Both of you."

James pushes her off him gently and looks into her face. "I know. I'm almost absolutely certain Sam will make it back—otherwise I wouldn't be attempting my plan. But in case we don't—will you take care of our children? There's no one else that I trust more than you."

She hugs him tightly once more. "Of course I will. Do you think I can handle all of your financial affairs? Your affairs are very complicated."

"I've got a couple of people lined up to help you. But I don't believe you'll need anyone else. You've been working by my side for over ten years. You know as much about my affairs as I do. Kathy, you know exactly how I think—you'll do just fine."

James stands up. "Now—one last item," he says. He pauses for a second and clears his throat. "Kathy, you must know by now that I have a special place in my heart for you. Aside from Sam, you're my best friend—have been for quite some time now. There's also a letter that I wrote to you. It's pretty personal. That letter reveals a lot of my inner feelings about you. Under no circumstances are you to read that letter unless I don't make it back. You got that?"

Kathy forces out laughter through the tears. "Now you've got me all curious. All right, I'll agree. But when you make it back, I want to read the letter."

"You know what? I'm going to take that letter out of my desk and put it someplace else. Have someone else give it to you. You are far too curious." He pulls another tissue out of the box and hands it to her.

"Your makeup is all smeared," he points out with a laugh, then says, "Thank you, Kathy. You have no idea how much better I feel knowing that you'll be here to take care of things." James heads for the door. "I'm going to speak to the children now."

Five minutes later, James is in Molly's room. James in on the bed, holding Christopher in his arms. Michael and Molly are sitting in chairs, looking at him expectantly. James swallows hard and begins.

"Daddy is going away for a few days. Auntie Kathy will be here with you."

"Where are you going, Daddy?" Molly asks.

"Just like I told you, I'm going to get Mommy and bring her home."

"You're going to rescue Mommy from those bad men?" Molly says. "Just like the prince rescued the princess from the evil queen?"

"Yes, Molly, just like the book that we read. Now, listen, Molly— you're a big girl now. You need to help Aunt Kathy with your brothers—do you hear?"

Molly clutches her stuffed rabbit and nods. "Yes, Daddy, I'll help."

"I want you to read the Bible every night to your brothers. I won't be here to do that."

"I will, Daddy," she says solemnly.

"Good." He gets off the bed and squats down in front of the older children with Christopher in his arms. "Come on—both of you, give your dad a hug." As they're hugging him, he adds, "Remember: no matter what, your daddy loves you very much, and will love you always. I will always be with you, even when I'm not around. I'll be just like the wind. If you ever need me, just let the wind touch your face, and you will feel your dad touching you, too."

The next morning, before his flight, James gets on the phone with Rodney.

"Any news?" Rodney asks. "Have you heard from the president?"

"Yeah, I heard this morning. Not directly from the president;

the call was from his chief of staff. The coward didn't even have the courage to turn me down directly. Anyway—it doesn't matter. I knew he wouldn't help.

"Listen, Rodney, I want you to get a message to the kidnappers. Tell them that the negotiations are very complicated and are taking longer than expected. Let them know that I'm worried about Sam's health. I'd like to propose a swap, in the meantime. While the negotiations for the release of the prisoners are going on, I'll take Sam's place. I'd like to swap me for Sam."

"James, are you crazy? If the prisoner exchange doesn't work out, they'll surely kill you. They might take pity on a woman. But they'll show *you* no mercy."

"Yes—I know all this, Rodney. Make the offer!"

"What makes you think the captors will even go along with the proposal?"

"Oh, they'll go along with the plan. Don't you see it, Rodney? It's *me* that they are really after. They took Sam when they couldn't get to me. With me as their prisoner, the kidnappers can't possibly lose.

"If they don't get the exchange that they're demanding, they'll execute me. I'm a national hero. It'll make the US look weak and pathetic—the whole western world. These western governments can't even defend their own heroes.

"That'll be quite a feather in their cap," James continues. "Almost as good as getting the prisoners released. No, Rodney—the kidnappers won't turn down the offer. They're dying to get their hands on me. Make the proposal."

Cardiz walks down the aisle of the jet and sits in a seat directly across from James. James places down the paper he was reading on the table in front of him. Cardiz looks around the cabin of the plane. "This is quite a setup you got here, Coppi. Do you always ride like this?"

"It's my plane—how else would I fly?"

"This is un-fucking believable! You've got couches and even a bed in the back." Cardiz smiles broadly and rubs his hands over the seats. "Feel these seats. This leather is softer than a baby's ass."

"I know what the leather feels like, Cardiz—I'm the one who picked it out."

Mary comes over to them. "Can I get you something to drink?" she asks Cardiz.

"What have you got?" Cardiz asks.

"Just about anything," she answers. "What would you like?"

"How about a boilermaker? Do you know what that is?"

"Yes, I do," Mary says, smiling. "Would you like a bourbon or an Irish whiskey?"

Cardiz looks at Coppi. "Holy crap, Coppi, this lady is amazing."

James looks at Mary. "Any whiskey or beer will do, Mary," he tells her. "He won't know the difference."

"Yes, I'll see to it," she replies. "How about you, Mr. Coppi?"

"Just mineral water, please."

"Water!" Cardiz cries out, looking around the plane again. "All this money is being wasted on you, Coppi. You should give some of that money to me—I'll show you how to live and have some fun." Cardiz looks out the window. "How long before we get to Israel?"

"It'll be a while. We need to make a couple of stops: New York to pick up my brother Anthony, Ireland to refuel, and Paris to pick up some people I'll need for the mission."

"You don't need your brother or anybody else," Cardiz tells him, smiling. "You got me—that's all you'll need. Just you and me. Like the old days back in 'Nam. The two C-boys—Cardiz and Coppi."

James smiles. He's happy that he brought Cardiz along—Cardiz has a way of dispelling his worries. James furrows his brow. "I don't remember anybody in 'Nam ever calling us that. The two C-boys? When did that happen?"

Cardiz sits back in his chair and smiles. "Just now! I made it up. Pretty good, huh?"

Mary comes over with the drinks. Cardiz immediately downs the shot of whiskey. He shuts his eyes and shakes his head. "Ay, caramba!" he shouts. "That's good stuff!" Cardiz hands his empty shot glass to Mary. "Keep it coming, sweetheart."

Cardiz lifts his glass of beer and salutes James. "To the two C-boys!"

James lifts his mineral water and gestures back. "To the two C-boys."

After the fifth drink, Cardiz finally falls asleep. James was going to say something to Cardiz about hitting on Mary. Luckily, Cardiz fell asleep, and he didn't have to butt in. Mary comes over and picks up the empty shot glasses.

"I'm sorry for my friend," James tells her.

Mary smiles. "It was no trouble at all," she says. "He's harmless. I've handled hundreds like him."

14

It's All About the Timing

MARY IS PUTTING A BLANKET on Cardiz, who had been fast asleep in his seat. He stirs and opens his eyes. "Oh, my aching head!" Cardiz says, putting his hand to his forehead.

Mary smiles. "Five boilermakers will do that to you every time. I'll get you a couple of aspirins."

"Who's doing all that shouting?" Cardiz asks when she comes back with the pills.

"That would be Mr. Coppi's brother, Anthony," she replies, handing him the pills and a glass of water.

Cardiz pops the aspirins in his mouth and washes them down with the water. "Anthony? When did he get on the plane? Did we land in New York already?"

"Landed and took off, over an hour ago. Would you like anything else?"

"Not right now."

They hear Anthony yell, "I can't believe anyone could be so fucking stupid and stubborn!"

"I'll see you later," Mary tells Cardiz and leaves.

Anthony comes storming over and sits across from Cardiz. "Cardiz, you need to speak to my brother. He might listen to you. If he goes through with the plan, he's going to get himself killed. I can't believe my brother could be that fucking stupid!"

"Yeah, your brother is really fucking stupid," Cardiz says and smiles. "James is so stupid that he can't run all these companies that he's built. So dumb that he has to pay smart guys like you to run the businesses for him. Coppi is such a dope that he buys a huge ranch and has to pay geniuses like me to work it for him. He can't work the ranch by himself, I guess.

"Your brother is such an idiot that he doesn't know how to take a commercial flight," Cardiz continues. "He has to travel on this fancy plane, where everything is brought to him. That's how fucking stupid your brother is."

Cardiz sits up in his seat, suddenly very serious. "Now, you listen to me—and listen good, little brother. You can use a lot of words to describe your brother, but 'stupid' isn't one of them. There's no one that I have higher respect for than James. That man would do anything for you or me.

"He needs our help right now. Stop bitching and give him that help. I don't know if this is the best plan, but I do know one thing—it's not stupid. If anyone can make it work, it'll be your brother. Just do your part of the scheme as he lays it out. If we all do our parts, the plan will work."

James comes to the front and sits across from the guys. Cardiz turns to him. "Where's our next stop?"

"Ireland. We're going to refuel there, and then go on to Paris. In Paris, we'll pick up the men that we'll need for the mission. When we stop in Ireland, I'll call Rodney and find out if the Palestinians have agreed to the swap."

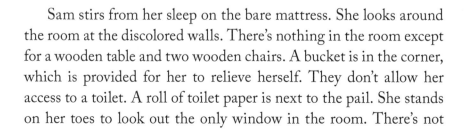

Sam stirs from her sleep on the bare mattress. She looks around the room at the discolored walls. There's nothing in the room except for a wooden table and two wooden chairs. A bucket is in the corner, which is provided for her to relieve herself. They don't allow her access to a toilet. A roll of toilet paper is next to the pail. She stands on her toes to look out the only window in the room. There's not much to see. Except for a dog that's sniffing through the garbage, the back alley is almost empty.

This is the third house that she's been in since her abduction. They are moving her constantly. Always at night, and she is always blindfolded. She doesn't quite understand the reason for the blindfold. Why bother? She wouldn't know where she was, anyway.

Sam hears a key in the lock of the door, and Najla, her keeper, comes in.

"I brought your breakfast," the teenager says and sets a dish on the table. She turns to Sam. "You must eat—you will get weak."

"I'm not hungry."

"That was very stupid, what you did," Najla says. "Escaping! You could have gotten yourself killed. How could you ever have hoped that you'd get away? Where would you run to?"

Sam doesn't answer—she's staring out the window again.

"What happened?" Najla asks. "How did they capture you? How far did you get?"

Sam turns, walks back, and sits at the table. "Not very far at all. I was totally lost, and I hid in a tree during the night. As soon as it was daylight, I climbed down and ran into a policeman.

"The fellow didn't speak English, but I somehow made him understand about my difficulty. I asked him for help. The policeman took me to a store and told me to wait there until he got back. He told the store owner to keep an eye on me." Sam looks at Najla. "Needless to say, the cop didn't help me. Instead, he turned me right back in to the kidnappers."

"Please, eat something. This will be over soon. They are negotiating with your husband. You do not want to get sick." Najla motions to the dish. "Please."

Sam looks at the food. "I'm not hungry."

Najla walks to the corner of the room and looks into the pail. "Good, it's normal—I was beginning to worry. I'll just empty the pail and I'll be right back."

Sam hears the door being locked. She begins nibbling on the food. A few minutes later, Najla comes back with the empty pail.

"Good—you're eating," she says. Najla sets the bucket down and sits across from Sam. "What is your husband like? The men say he is very rich and powerful—is that why your family arranged for you to marry him?"

Sam smiles at Najla. "No one arranged our marriage. We fell in love as soon as we first met. Neither James nor I come from wealthy families. The truth is that we were very poor when we first met. Everything that we have comes from our hard work."

She pauses for a moment as she thinks of James. "People might think that James is powerful because of his money—but he's the kindest, sweetest man that I have ever known. Always has been."

Sam looks at Najla. "How about you? Why is a pretty young lady like you not married?"

"My *makhtuba* is in an Israeli prison," she replies sadly.

"Your what?" Sam asks.

Najla laughs. "Oh, I'm sorry. My *makhtuba*—it means my betrothed. He's been in prison for nearly two years. My brother Aalam says he will be set free if these negotiations are successful. You will go home, and I will be married."

"So that is what they're asking in exchange for my release? Your boyfriend's freedom?"

"No, not just for him—for all Palestinian prisoners!"

Sam laughs. "I'm afraid that you're in for a big letdown, Najla. I'm not that important."

The jet is on its final approach to Ben Gurion. James has picked up Ernie and eight other mercenaries from South Africa in Paris. The team is now complete—he just needs to finalize the plan. He spoke to Rodney during one of the stops. As James assumed they would, the Palestinians have agreed to the switch. They just want to know where and when it is going to take place. James has chosen a location in Lebanon that will be perfect.

Ian and Gary are already waiting for him in Metula, right across the border from the place that he has picked out for the exchange. All that's left is to discuss the upcoming operation with the Israelis. He could use their help. But whether the Israelis give him that help or not doesn't really matter. He's ready, either way. It'll just be that much easier if the Israelis cooperate.

Ernie comes over to where James is sitting.

"Are we chartering a small plane to get up to the border from Tel Aviv?" Ernie asks him.

"No, we're driving. I've got three jeeps waiting for us," he answers.

"Wouldn't it be faster if we flew?"

"Yeah, it would be. But we'll need the vehicles for the mission when we get there."

Ernie laughs. "What're you saying? The Israelis have no jeeps?"

"No, but the Israelis might not let us use their vehicles when we get there. At the very least, we would have to requisition the jeeps and explain to the Israelis why we need them. That'll take days, and we'll have to answer hundreds of questions. Finally, we'll have to put up collateral reimbursing the Israelis if one of the vehicles is damaged.

"More delays. To tell you the truth, Ernie," James frowns, "I don't know how much help the Israeli military will be. The less I ask for, the better off we are. Anyway, it's only a two-and-a-half-hour car ride from Tel Aviv to Metula. It shouldn't be too bad. Give everybody a chance to see the Holy Land."

Five hours later, James is sitting in an Israeli bunker with maps strewn across a table. Major Rubin and Captain Moishe, from the Israeli military, are present. James got good news when he arrived—the Israelis have agreed to help out in his mission. That is a big relief.

"Right here," James says, pointing to a spot on the map. "See—a little west of this village, Zaqiyeh. There's a bridge that spans the Litani River. That's where I want to make the exchange." James looks at the Israelis. "What do you guys think?"

The men lean over and look at the spot. "Why there?" Major Rubin asks. "Couldn't you choose a place a little closer to the border?"

"I didn't want the Palestinians to get suspicious that we might be setting a trap. The bridge is far enough inside Lebanon to make them feel comfortable, but not so far as to be out of range of the artillery." James looks at the captain. "It should be well within the range of your guns, Captain Moishe. Don't you agree?"

"Yeah, we've hit that spot before. We have the coordinates."

"What kind of battery do you have?" Ernie asks.

"Six one oh fives," the captain answers. Moishe looks over at James. "Will that be enough?"

"More than enough. I'd like to go out this afternoon and target some practice rounds—if it's all right with you guys?"

"Sure, we can do that," the major answers. "We'll make a helicopter available to you for a flyover."

"Why do you need spotting?" the captain asks. "I already told you that we have the coordinates. You're just increasing the chance of getting yourself noticed and letting the other side know that something may be coming down soon."

"No, I won't give anything away. We'll fire just two nonexplosive practice rounds into the river. No one will know what happened. The artillery coordinates need fine tuning; I want to make sure we hit the bridge and nothing else. I don't want any civilians hurt."

"All right—it's your call," Captain Moishe responds.

"Let's go over the dispersion," James says. "The bridge is approximately 90x30 feet."

"With that small an area, you should probably go with a converged sheaf," the artillery captain suggests. "With a six-gun battery, you should be able to cover at least 75x100 feet. That should be more than enough."

"What are you guys talking about?" Anthony yells out in exasperation. "I'm totally lost!"

"They're talking about the kill zone," Ernie tells him. "That's the area where the explosions will occur." Ernie turns to James. "You know, James, it's five miles away. Maybe you might want to go with an open sheaf. Broaden the area of dispersion a bit."

"Yeah, you're right," James replies. He looks at the captain. "Let's go with Ernie's suggestion—let's go with an open sheaf."

"OK," the captain says. "As I said before, it's your operation. How many volleys?"

"I'm figuring three?" James asks and then looks at Ernie.

"Yeah, three should be plenty," Ernie agrees. "That's eighteen rounds. More than enough."

"All right," Captain Moishe says. "Then the whole operation should be completed in less than three minutes."

"James, let's go over your movements for that day," Gary says, cutting in. "Especially after we make the exchange. I'm a little worried about the timeline. As you know, the timing is critical if you're going to come out of this alive. So can we take some time now to go over the plan carefully?"

"All right—go ahead, Gary," James answers.

"We're driving up in three vehicles. Ernie and I will be in the first jeep with you. Your brother will be in the jeep that's going to carry your wife Samantha back.

"Your wife will probably be very confused and frightened. It's good to have a face that she's familiar with. We'll have one of our men inside the car with her and Anthony. The last and final jeep will have Cardiz and the rest of the men."

Gary puts a map on the table.

"Let me show you." He points to a spot on the map where the bridge is located. "When we get to the bridge, we will turn the cars around so that we can make our escape quickly after the exchange. Ernie and I will accompany you to the center of the span. As agreed to in the arrangement that you're trying to negotiate, we'll be unarmed. The rest of our men will form a wall on our side of the bridge. They will be *fully* armed in case the other side tries anything funny.

"The other side will also walk out with two unarmed men and Samantha. We'll walk out slowly, trying to get a fix on the two men. See if any weapons are hidden under their clothing. We'll all meet at the center, where the exchange is supposed to take place. I'm sure they'll let you say something to Samantha—but, James, try not to take too long. You don't want anyone getting nervous."

Gary points to the map. "Ernie and I will walk back and have

Samantha get into the car with your brother. We'll get into our vehicles, too, and drive off. Immediately after driving off, we'll call the fire direction center and have the batteries commence firing.

"This is the tricky part, James." Gary stares fixedly into James's face.

"Every second is vital. One second lost can cost you your life. From the time we drive off, it'll take no more than three seconds to call in the artillery. Another maybe three seconds for the message to get to the gun batteries, and then they'll start firing. And it'll take maybe fifteen seconds after they commence firing for the first barrage to hit the bridge." Gary looks at the captain for confirmation. "Am I right?"

"Yes." Moishe replies, nodding. "Fifteen seconds, give or take one second."

"That's twenty-one to twenty-two seconds, James. That's how much time you'll have from the time we drive off. That's how much time you've got to get off that bridge and find shelter from the artillery barrage.

"You got that? Twenty-one to twenty-two seconds," Gary repeats. "So tell me how you're going to get it done. Let's go over your timetable, second by second. The timeline is critical. If you make your escape too soon, the artillery won't have hit yet, and the other side will have time to hunt you down. Remember, you'll be unarmed. Leave too late, and you'll die in the bombardment."

James clears his throat. "Yes, Gary, thank you. I fully understand. It's all about the timing. Before we get to that, let's discuss Sam's escape. What's to stop these guys from ambushing her vehicle on the way out of there?"

Major Rubin speaks up. "James, I have two squads ready to go from our camp. Once we get the message that your wife is safely on her way here, I'll dispatch the squads to her. The artillery barrage won't be over for at least three minutes. We should be able to meet up with her car before anyone can recover."

"Thank you, major." James turns to Gary. "Here's what I came up with, Gary. It'll take me two seconds to ditch the men escorting me and jump into the river. Another second to make the twenty-foot drop to the water."

"James, make sure you enter the water feet first," Ernie tells him. "The river may be shallow."

James laughs. "Thanks, Ernie. I'll try to remember that. All right—back to my time. Another second in the river to stand up, if the water is shallow—or start swimming, if it's deep."

"Make sure you get under the bridge right away, James," Gary says. "There'll be men on the bridge trying to shoot down at you. You're much harder to hit if you're under the bridge."

"Yes—I know that, Gary. In fact, with this particular bridge, it's almost impossible to shoot from above at anything directly underneath. That's why they'll soon give up shooting and try to get to the riverbank for a better shot. Let's put ourselves in their shoes for a moment. That'll give us a better picture of their timeline.

"During the first second, the men on the riverbank will see me shove aside their men on the bridge. In second two, I'm running to the edge of the bridge. Three seconds in, they watch me jump into the river. Seconds four to seven, they unhitch their rifles and run up the bridge to the center where I leapt into the water. They fire a couple of bursts aimlessly into the river at where they think I am. That takes us through seconds seven to ten."

James looks around at the men before continuing.

"When they realize that the gunfire is useless because they can't see me, they'll run off the bridge and back to the riverbank to get a better fix on me. That'll take about four seconds. Maybe five. Where were we? Oh yes, we were at ten. Add the five and now we're at fifteen seconds. They'll notice me on the other riverbank and begin firing at me. About three seconds after that, I'm hit—probably fatally.

"Where are we now, timewise? Oh yes—around eighteen seconds. In three to four more seconds, the first artillery barrage will begin dropping on their heads and wiping them all out."

James turns to Gary and smiles. "Too late for me, though—I'm already dead. Have I got the timing perfectly correct? Even if I'm a few seconds off, and the shooters are a few seconds late, they'll still have time to take me out."

Gary sits back. "That's about right. You made your escape at least five seconds too soon. What are you going to do about that?"

"Maybe I can have a conversation with the Palestinians on the bridge? You know—ask what the weather is like in Lebanon at this time of the year?"

"Quit fucking around, James," Gary says, scowling. "This is serious stuff."

"I'm sorry—I know it's serious," James leans toward Gary. "My plan is to tell my escorts that I want to see Sam leave. Basically, I'll say something like, 'I'd like to see her drive off, please.' After Sam and the cars have left, I'll count to five and make my move."

"What if they refuse?" Ernie asks.

"They're unarmed. I'll find a way to convince them. Anyway, that's my problem—not yours. I know the timing, Gary. I'll get it done. You guys do your job. Make sure you have a backup radio in case one doesn't work. Test all the equipment before we start out. Make sure that all the men know what their roles are.

"The most important part of this mission is getting Sam to safety. I'm just the side show. Six o'clock tomorrow morning— that's when we have to be at the bridge. I want to get there early so that there are no civilians on the road." James turns to the artillery captain. "Why don't we get that helicopter ready? I'd like to get to the targeting rounds after I call Rodney and let him get in touch with the kidnappers."

James leaves the bunker and walks over to Cardiz, who is standing outside. "I'm going to call in a couple of targeting rounds. You go and observe the batteries. Let me know your opinion of the gun crews. Let me know if the men reliable. The last thing I need on this mission is a team that doesn't know what it's doing."

James is looking out of the open side door of the chopper as it hovers over the target area. He's holding a map in front of him, and has just finished plotting the coordinates for the firing of the first round. The round, if accurate, should splash down upriver about three hundred meters from the bridge.

The pilot's voice comes over the radio in his helmet. "If I were you, I'd get my head a little farther inside the helicopter, sir. This area has a lot of sniper activity."

"Thanks," he says, and moves himself a little farther away from the door and into the chopper.

"Shot! Over!" a voice says over his radio. It's the signal from fire direction center that they fired off the first round, and it's on the way.

James places binoculars to his eyes and aims them at the spot where the round is supposed to land. He notices a splash shortly thereafter.

"Down four hundred, left one fifty, over," he says, calling into Fire Direction Center the instructions of where he wants the next round to land.

"Down four hundred, left one fifty, over," the voice on the other side confirms.

If on target, the next round is expected to hit a hundred meters downriver from the bridge.

"Shot! Over!" the voice comes over the radio a few moments later.

Once again, James lifts up his binoculars and has a look. He notices the splash exactly where he was expecting.

"Up fifty, right seventy-five, over, out," he says, calling in the final coordinates. The crew won't be shooting another round. That's the exact spot on the bridge that the artillery will fire at tomorrow.

"Up fifty, right seventy-five, over, out," the voice repeats.

"We're done—we can head back," he tells the pilot over the mike.

"Roger. Heading back."

⸻

"How did it go?" Ernie asks him when James returns.

"Looks good. We're all set."

"Now what? Anything else?"

"There's nothing else to do, Ernie. That's it. Just waiting for the call from Rodney confirming that the meeting is all set for tomorrow."

"What if they don't agree to the location that you've chosen?"

"Well, then—we're pretty well screwed, aren't we? But I think the Palestinians will agree—they're pretty eager to get their hands on me. The area we chose for the exchange is unassuming and safe for them. Well inside their area of operations and also wide open so that we couldn't set a trap. They shouldn't have any problems with the location."

15
The Operation

JAMES IS SITTING ON A cot inside one of the military bunkers just outside the border of Lebanon. It's early evening, just after dinner. The bunker is getting dark. Rodney still hasn't called, so James is not sure if the mission is a go for the morning or not. It doesn't matter. If not tomorrow, then the next day. He's certain the Palestinians will take the deal. The mission itself is weighing on him. Doubts have crept in.

Not the doubt that Sam will get out safely—he's confident that she will. It's *his* outcome that he's worried about. He's not sure that he will make it out. And it won't be because his men will fail to do their part. Ernie, Gary and the rest of the men are pros. They will know exactly what to do—and they won't get rattled. Cardiz has reported back that the artillery is competent. No problem there.

It's those damn bombs. He knows firsthand the devastation those 105s can do. He used to call in those same shells all the time, in Vietnam. And that old bridge—he's pretty certain that it won't hold up to the shelling. If he makes it under the bridge without being shot, he's sure that the structure is going to collapse on him. There's no way that shaky old bridge will stay up after a pounding by 105s.

What will my family do without me? That's the question going through his mind endlessly. The faces of his three children keep appearing in his thoughts. That last hug in Molly's room slips into his mind. He's been in tight spots before—and he knows full well that he needs to get those feelings out of his system to be on point tomorrow.

In the past, he would pop a few pills and get through the night.

Not anymore. He had made a promise to Sam long ago—no more drugs. If he does leave this world, he doesn't want to leave breaking a promise that he made to her.

A soldier enters the bunker. "Sir, there's a telephone call for you."

Thank you, Lord. His mind was beginning to spiral out of control. James lets out a deep breath and gets up from the cot.

"The phone is in the command bunker, sir," the soldier says. "Two down on the right."

Inside that bunker, another soldier points to a phone on a desk. "Right over there, sir."

James nods.

"Hello?" he says when he gets to the phone.

"James, it's Rodney. I just heard back. It's on for tomorrow morning at six. The spot you picked out. The other side agreed to everything."

"Good," he says.

"Good luck!"

"Thanks."

An eerie calmness comes over him. All his trepidations have disappeared. Now that he knows the mission is on, he's absolutely ready to carry out the operation. No more doubts.

When James is back in his bunker, Cardiz comes walking in carrying two beers. "I thought you could use a beer."

"Thanks." James reaches out and takes a bottle.

"Are you OK?" Cardiz asks as James takes a slug.

James looks at Cardiz and raises one brow.

Cadiz lets out a laugh. "Yeah, I know. Stupid question."

The men sit silently, drinking their beers. "Anything else you need from me?" Cardiz asks, breaking the silence.

"No, I'm good." James says, and then he sees the concern on Cardiz's face. "The plan isn't bad, Cardiz. It has a shot. A lot better than the mission that Goyette and Hall went on. Those poor guys never had a chance—their plan was faulty from the beginning. They lost control of the fighting when they were overrun by NVA soldiers. Hall and Goyette had nowhere to run to find shelter when the bombs landed on them. I'm not making the same mistake. If everything goes as planned, I'll be under the bridge when the first artillery round hits the bridge."

Cardiz takes a final swig of his beer. "Yeah, I know. I'll see you tomorrow." He heads out of the tent.

James stares at the bottle in his hand, takes a final swig, puts the bottle down onto the ground, then goes to his bunk. He sets the alarm for four thirty and lies down, fully clothed. Within minutes, he's fast asleep.

The alarm wakes him the next morning from a deep sleep—no restlessness whatsoever during the night. James stretches and looks for the washbasin next to his cot. He lifts up the basin and goes outside to the water tank to fill it.

Outside, it's still dark. No one else is up yet. The ground is wet from the dew that's formed during the night. He takes a deep breath, inhaling the crisp morning air. After filling the basin, he walks back into the bunker and takes out his shaving kit—he wants to look good for his reunion with Sam.

When he's done, he heads back out to dump out the washbowl. It's twilight now, and there are men walking around the camp. He tosses out the water.

"Are you ready, Boss?" Ernie asks as he walks up from behind.

"Ready as I'll ever be."

"You know, James, I was thinking—maybe you should wear a flak jacket?"

James gives him a side glance. "Yeah, maybe I should wave the flak jacket up in the air. Let the other side know that an artillery barrage is coming."

Ernie lets out a laugh. "No, that's not what I meant. The jacket won't be visible. It can be worn under your clothing."

"I'm not doing that, Ernie. I don't want to do anything to give our plot away. Remember what I told you—the most important part of this operation is for Sam to get out safely.

"Round everyone up," he adds. "I'd like to get started by

five-thirty—arrive at the rendezvous area before the other side has a chance to get set up."

———————†——————†———————

Sam is awakened by the sound of a key in the lock of her door. It's still dark out. Najla walks in with a lit candle and has a smile on her face.

"I've got good news: you're leaving today," she says.

Sam jumps up. "Really? They agreed to let me go?" Sam looks up at the ceiling. "Thank you, God!" She looks over at Najla and smiles. "It's good news for you, too, I guess, your *makhtuba* should be released." Sam notices that Najla isn't smiling anymore. "What's the matter? Aren't you happy to see your fiancé?"

Najla sits at the table. Sam looks at the teenager—she's grown very fond of Najla.

"What's wrong?" Sam asks.

"It's this conflict—I should be very happy that my man is getting out of prison. But what will happen after he is free? He will be right back to fighting. This fight will never end. The Israelis say they want peace, but that's not true. They don't want peace! What the Jews want is us out of this land." Najla takes a deep breath and looks up at Sam. "I've lived in three different houses in Palestine. Each time I get settled in a place, the Israelis come and confiscate the land. The first time was when I was thirteen."

Najla looks at the window and back at Sam. "My brother Aalam and some of his friends through some rocks at an Israeli convoy passing through our village. They arrested Aalam and my father went to the police station to get him out. That night Israeli soldiers broke into our house and tossed us out. They said are home was condemned and unsafe to live in. That house had been in our family for over a hundred years."

Najla lets out a breath. "My father had tears in his eyes as we walked away in the darkened street looking for a place to live."

"There is no room for us—the Jews just keep coming from all

over the world. Some have two homes—one in Palestine and another in Europe or America. Isn't one home enough?"

Najla wipes a tear from her face with the back of her hand. Her voice turns angry.

"The Jews say they want peace—if that's so, why do they keep taking our homes? And what will happen to my boyfriend? He'll either get killed fighting in the war, or he'll go back to prison. What kind of future is that for us? Look where we have ended up—we're in a foreign land, far from my home. What is to become of us? No one wants Palestinians in their country."

A man comes bursting into the room. "Hurry up get dressed," the man barks at Sam. "We're leaving." The man looks over at Najla. "Help her to get ready quickly and get outside. You can ride in the car with her. Hurry—we don't have much time. The cars should be here very soon."

James looks at his wristwatch. Twenty to six. His team is all lined up on the southern end of the bridge. The Palestinians haven't shown up yet.

"Where are they?" Anthony, who is standing next to James, calls out. "What if they don't show?"

"Calm down, little brother," James answers. "They'll get here. You just remember your part. Get Sam into the car and then get her the hell out of here."

A few minutes later, two cars and a pickup truck pull up on the other side of the bridge. James watches as men pile out of the cars and hop off the truck.

Ernie walks up to him. "I count fifteen men," he says, "but I don't see your wife." He pauses. "James, when you leap from the bridge, jump off to your right—toward the east. The rising sun will get in their eyes, and it'll be a lot harder for them to see you."

"Got it." James walks up to the bridge. "I don't see Sam." He turns back to Ernie. "Maybe they're trying to pull a fast one?"

Ernie walks up to him. "She must be in the car. Wait here, James. Gary and I will walk out onto the bridge and meet with them."

James grabs Ernie's arm. "That wasn't part of the plan."

"I know—but we've got to make absolutely sure that the men who come out with Sam are unarmed. Give you a chance to jump off that bridge safely."

James releases his hold. "All right—go ahead."

Gary and Ernie walk out to the center of the span and stand there, waiting. Two Palestinians approach them with rifles strapped to their shoulders.

"Do you speak English?" Ernie asks.

One of the men nods. "Yes."

"The deal was that you'd be unarmed. As you can see, we're not armed." Ernie raises his arms. "You can frisk us, if you like."

One of the Palestinians frisks the two men.

"Now you need to go back and put down your weapons," Ernie tells them. "We'll be frisking you when you get back, so don't try anything funny. Come back with Mrs. Coppi. We'll get Mr. Coppi. Agreed?"

The Palestinians nod. "Agreed," they say and head for their end of the bridge. Ernie and Gary turn back.

—

Sam looks out the window of the back seat of the car when they get to the bridge. Men are milling about. She turns to Najla. "What's going on? Why have we stopped?"

Najla reaches over, cranks down the window, and leans out to have a look. "We've reached our destination—I think they're making the final arrangements."

A man opens the door of the vehicle. "Come! Get out! It's time."

Sam turns to Najla. "Goodbye," she says.

Najla leans over and gives Sam a hug. "Goodbye. I hope we meet again someday. In much better circumstances."

"Yes. I hope so, too—and I hope you have a happy life."

"Come on," the man outside barks. "Stop wasting time!"

———✧———✧———

A few minutes previously, while Ernie and Gary were walking to the middle of the bridge for their discussion, James has walked toward the bank of the river.

It's summer. The river is drying up, and the water is not very deep, but he will still have to swim a bit from where he will land in the water before he gets back to shore. The bank on the other side of the river is covered with shrubs. This will be good for him.

The Palestinians will have to get through the shrubs before reaching the edge of the shore. That should give him a few more seconds to make his escape. He looks up and notices Ernie and Gary coming back.

Ernie lets out a deep breath. "OK, James, it's all set. Are you ready?"

"Yes. Let's go."

James, Ernie, and Gary are standing on the bridge as one of the Palestinians opens the back door of the sedan and helps Sam out of the vehicle. A smile broadens James's face as Sam comes into view. Another one of the men comes up alongside her and holds her arm. They begin walking toward James and his party. A huge smile forms on her face when she looks onto the bridge and sees James. They get within ten feet of him.

Sam breaks free and runs to James. She gets him in a bear hug and kisses him on the mouth. The Palestinians yank her off him.

"What's happening?" she asks James.

"Sam, you'll go back with Ernie and Gary," James tells her.

"What about you?"

"I'm going with them," he says, nodding toward the Palestinians. "That's the deal. We're exchanging me for you."

"No, James!" Tears start running down her face. "They'll hurt you!"

"Sam, we can't argue about this now—it's too dangerous. Please go with Ernie."

Ernie and Gary grab Sam and begin to pull her away. The two Palestinians grab James.

"No—I don't want to leave, James!" Sam yells and tries to break free.

Ernie and Gary forcibly pull her away, toward the car.

"Mrs. Coppi, please come with us!" Ernie shouts. "Don't make a scene. It's too dangerous—there are too many men here with nervous trigger fingers."

The Palestinians try to lead James away. James breaks free and tells them curtly, "I'm not leaving until I see my wife drive away safely. Then I'll come with you."

By now, Sam has reached the vans. Ernie opens the back door for her. Sam resists getting in.

"I don't want to leave without James!" she wails.

Anthony comes over and shoves Sam into the vehicle.

"Please get in, Sam. Don't argue," he leans down and whispers in her ear. "You'll spoil the plan." Anthony hops into the back seat with her.

"What plan?" she asks as the car drives off.

Ernie and Gary jump into their vehicles and the caravan follows the car with Sam. Ernie picks the radio up off the floor.

"Commence firing, over," he says.

"Roger, commence firing," the voice on the other end says back to him.

James watches as the cars drive off. The stopwatch in his head begins counting—*one Mississippi, two Mississippi*. There's a tug at his arm.

"Let's go," his captor says.

"Thank you for waiting," he says while continuing the count in his head. *Four Mississippi.*

On five Mississippi, James breaks free and shoves his captor aside. He bolts for the edge of the bridge and jumps off feet first, breaking the surface of the water and heading straight down to the bottom of the river. When his head rises above the water, he looks around to get his bearings, then begins swimming straight toward the underneath of the bridge and to the riverbank, where he's hoping to find shelter from the bombing that's about to rain down on their heads. He wants to get to the crevice where the bridge and the land meet—it's the best spot to protect himself from the falling debris.

The count continues in his head. *Eight Mississippi, nine Mississippi.* There are shots being fired from the bridge—wild shooting that's not getting anywhere close to hitting him. The plan is working, just as he had laid it out. *Twelve Mississippi, thirteen Mississippi.* He makes it to the shallow end of the river and stands up, wading through the shallow water. He can now see the spot where he will curl up under the bridge to shield himself from the bombs that are about to hit.

Eighteen Mississippi, he counts.

There's a man on the bank, pointing a rifle directly at James's head.

"*Waqfa!*" he shouts.

James stops, exhales, and raises his arms in the universal sign of surrender.

———✝————✝———

A few moments after giving the order to begin the artillery barrage, Ernie suddenly taps the driver of the vehicle on the shoulder.

"Turn around," Ernie says.

"Now?" The driver says. "The artillery hasn't begun."

"Yeah, now!" Ernie says and taps the driver again. "We can watch from a safe distance. I want to be there the minute the barrage is over."

The driver begins to make a U-turn. The car comes to a screeching halt when the first barrage is heard.

"Oh, James—I hope you made it," Ernie laments when he hears the bombs landing.

The van starts moving again and heads back toward the bridge, followed by the second vehicle.

"Stop here," Ernie tells the driver. "We don't want to get any closer."

The men watch as the second barrage hits the bridge. The ground under the car trembles. The smoke from the explosions completely obscures the bridge from view. When the structure comes back into sight, they can see the damage that has been done. The center has completely collapsed, and the bridge has been cut in half. Rubble from the bridge litters both shorelines.

"Damn," Gary utters. "The whole fucking thing has collapsed. That's not good!"

The third and final barrage hits the area. Once again, the ground quakes from the explosions. The smell of gun powder permeates the air.

"Move out!" Ernie yells at the driver. "That's it! It's done!"

Ernie leaps out of the car before it even comes to a stop at the foot of the bridge. Men from his other vehicle jump out and form a perimeter.

Ernie turns to Gary. "Secure the area just in case someone is still alive," he orders and hurries toward the riverbank. There's rubble littering the shoreline. He sees that a hand is sticking out from under the debris.

Cardiz comes up alongside Ernie.

"Who's that?" Cardiz asks, looking down at the hand.

Ernie doesn't respond. Instead, he slides down the shore on his backside and begins frantically removing the stones that cover the body.

Sam is kneeling on the back seat, looking out of the back window of the jeep in the direction of the bridge as it recedes from sight. Tears are still streaming down her face. She sees the flashes of light and hears the explosions.

"What's happening?" she hollers at Anthony.

"It's all part of the plan," Anthony tells her.

"What plan?" Sam yells. "Those explosions are part of the plan? Who's firing those cannons? James is there!"

"That's our side firing," Anthony tells her as another barrage goes off.

"Our side?" she yells. "They're firing on James. Do they know that?" Sam grabs hold of Anthony and shakes him. "Make them stop!"

"I can't, Sam," Anthony says as the final volley is fired. He turns to her. "There, that's it! It's over. That was the last."

Sam slumps in her seat and shakes her head. "He's dead! No one could have possibly survived that bombardment. My James is dead!" She closes her eyes. "My baby is dead!"

Ernie tosses aside the last stone and looks over at the body. It's a tall man with a moustache, wearing a Palestinian uniform—and he's dead.

"It's not Coppi," Ernie says to Cardiz.

"Well, where is he?" Cardiz asks, sliding down the bank to where Ernie is kneeling next to the body. Cardiz gets up, and he and Ernie wade into the river to get around the rubble and under the bridge.

"James, are you in there?" Ernie shouts.

There's no answer. Ernie wades around a large boulder. Once again, he hollers. "James, are you there?"

Still no answer.

"Coppi, quit fucking around and come out of there!" Cardiz yells. "I'm getting soaking wet! The water is fucking cold."

"It's about time you got here, Cardiz," James says as he comes crawling out from under the bridge, wiping the mud from his face.

Cardiz gives him a grin. "I was beginning to get worried. I'd started thinking I might have to look for a new job."

"Yeah, I know—and your new boss might not be a sap like me. You'd have to start working, for a change." James looks at Ernie. "Did Sam get out safely?"

"Yes," he replies. "Your wife should be arriving at the camp right about now." Then Ernie points to the Palestinian corpse. "Who was that, under the rocks?"

"That guy created my 'Oh shit! Didn't expect that to happen!' moment," James answers. "He was on this side of the bank with a rifle pointed at my head when I made it out of the water. The first volley hit and knocked him down, and I was able to overpower him and finish him off with his own gun.

"I jumped back under the bridge just before the second barrage. Come on, let's get out of here. I want to see Sam—she must be very frightened. Radio ahead and tell her that I'm OK!"

<hr />

The jeep carrying Sam has just arrived at the military compound. She is slumped in her seat with her head down. Sam still can't believe that James is gone. Just like that, he is no more—she'll never see him again.

Forgot to tell him that I love him on that bridge. How could I forget that?

Then a scary thought hits her. *How will I be able to tell our children? How will I ever have the strength to look into those little sad eyes and tell them that they'll never see their daddy again? I must be dreaming. This just can't be true. James is still alive—this is just a dream. I'll just close my eyes—and when I wake up, I'll be back in my bedroom with James lying alongside me.*

"Sam, we're here." Anthony is standing outside the vehicle with the door open.

She ignores him.

"Sam, we're here," he repeats.

"Please, Anthony—let me be," she answers. "Leave me alone."

After Anthony leaves, tears once again flow down her face. James's face appears in her mind's eye once more—and just as quickly, it fades away. *Am I dreaming? Is he really gone? This dream will end shortly. He'll walk up to the car soon.*

The back door opens again. "Mrs. Coppi," the voice says. "I'm Major Rubin. Welcome."

Sam raises her head. "Welcome to what? James is gone."

"Pardon me?"

"My James is gone," she repeats. "My darling is dead!"

"James isn't dead. They just radioed in. Your husband is on his way back here. Everything went just as he planned."

"What?" Sam sits up.

"Yes—James is on his way back. He should be here any minute." The major raises his head. "There! If I'm not mistaken, here they come right now. Get out and see for yourself."

Sam quickly jumps out of the vehicle. Men are piling out of the vehicles that have just arrived. That's when she sees James. He breaks into a smile when he sees her.

She runs to him and leaps into his arms. The force slams James back against the car. Both her legs and arms have wrapped themselves tightly around James's body. Sam pulls his face to hers and kisses him passionately. He breaks the embrace.

"Damn, Sam—I think you just broke my back."

Sam releases her hold on him and stands against his body, resting her head on his shoulder. Tears are flowing down her face.

"I thought you were dead!" she tells him, sobbing.

James lifts up her chin. "Well, I'm not," he says and gives her a kiss. "Are you OK?"

"I am now," she says, and kisses him again. Then she starts pounding on his chest. "Don't you ever, ever, ever, pull another stupid stunt like that again."

James laughs. "I wouldn't have had to pull this stunt if you had listened to me and not gone for a walk in Milan."

"I'm sorry to interrupt you folks," Major Rubin says. "We'd

like to speak to Mrs. Coppi about her captivity. It's important for intelligence purposes."

Sam looks at James. "Do I have to?"

"Yes, dear. I think you should. The Israelis have been very helpful in getting you freed. The information that you provide could be very useful to them. It shouldn't take long," James turns to the major. "Am I right?"

"No, not long at all," Rubin replies. But it's a couple of hours before Sam returns.

"What took you so long?" James asks when Sam gets back.

"The doctors wanted to check me over and they had showers, so I decided to wash up after the talk."

Major Rubin walks over to James and Sam. "A good day for our side—fourteen bodies were found. You should probably get going now—we're expecting a retaliatory rocket attack." Just before James gets in the jeep, the major pulls him over. "By the way—one of the dead was Aalam Savar."

James grins.

"I hope he burns in hell! Listen, major—I'm sorry about causing the rocket attack that's about to hit you guys."

Major Rubin laughs. "Don't give it another thought. We're overdue—we haven't been hit in over three days. This attack is inevitable. At least we know it's coming. Have a safe trip home, Mr. and Mrs. Coppi."

"Excuse me, major, was there a young woman among the bodies?" Sam asks.

"Yes, there was," he replies. "Why do you ask?"

Sam walks away without answering. James runs after her, gets hold of Sam's arm, and turns her to him. He sees that her eyes are full of tears.

"You know that she would've killed you if she had to," he says.

Sam smiles sadly. "No, I don't believe so."

16

Back Home

SAM IS RESTING HER HEAD on James's shoulder as they ride back to Tel Aviv in one of the jeeps. He's staring out the window at the Israeli countryside. Anthony is driving. Cardiz is in the front passenger seat, fast asleep.

"How are the children?" she asks.

"Everyone is fine. They miss you."

"What did you tell them about me?"

"The truth—that you were kidnapped by some really bad men."

Sam looks up at him, and James immediately recognizes the look.

"I had no choice!" he protests. "Your face was all over the television. Strangely, the children took the news pretty well. Molly was absolutely sure that I'd ride out and rescue you. Just like a prince rescued a princess in a story that I had just read to her."

Sam gives him a kiss. "Well, Molly was right—you did ride out to rescue me. You're my prince in shining armor." Sam sits up. "I can't wait to get home and get back to normal again," she says.

James looks over at her. "Sam, this isn't over. We still have a long way to go."

"What do you mean?"

"I mean, it isn't over. There are some pretty determined men behind what happened to you. They're not going to quit. This won't end until we destroy them."

"How do we do that? We don't even know who they are."

"No, Sam. I *do* know who they are—I just don't know *where* they are. Or, for that matter, how to get to them."

"James, you're scaring me. I'm starting to get very frightened."

"I'm sorry." He squeezes her hand. "Let's forget about those men for now. We'll figure something out when we get back home. Do you want to stay in Tel Aviv tonight? I can get us a room at one of the hotels."

"Why can't we leave? I'd like to get home to the children."

"No reason. I just thought you might be tired, that's all. We can leave any time. If you want to leave right away, we can do that—our plane is waiting for us at the airport."

"Yes, I want to leave," she says, and rests her head again on his shoulder.

An hour later, they have boarded the plane.

"I've never seen this plane so crowded," Sam remarks to James when they are in the air.

"It'll empty out once we get to London. Everyone is getting off except for you, me, Anthony, and Cardiz." He pauses. "I'm going to go and have a talk with Ian and Ernie. Would you like to join us?"

"Do you need me?"

"No, but you should know what's going on."

"James, I'm really tired," she says with a yawn. "I was hoping to take a nap. Do you mind?"

James gives her a kiss. "No, you're right—you should rest. You've been through a lot." He gets up and walks to the front.

"First of all, I want to thank all of you for your help," James says to start the meeting. "You guys really came through—I could never have done it without you. Now we need to discuss the next phase." James looks over at Ernie and Gary. "What plans do you guys have after we drop you off in London? Ernie, are you going back to South Africa?"

"Yes, James, I'm going to South Africa with Gary. There's that problem that needs cleaning up. Why do you ask? Do you need me for something?"

"Yes—I could use you when I get to this guy Faakhir. He is next on my list."

"This is the fellow in Afghanistan?" Ernie asks.

"Yeah, he lives in Mirabad," James replies. "I've got someone on the lookout for him. As soon as I get the word, I need to get back there before he disappears again."

"How are you going to do that, James?" Ernie asks. "This place, Mirabad, is pretty out of the way. There's only one road leading into town, and it's not even much of a road. By the time you respond to the notice that Faakhir is back, he could be gone again."

"Yeah, I know," James responds. Then he pulls out a map and spreads it on the table between them. "Here's my plan. Let me know what you guys think. When I get back, I'm going to call my man, Omprakash. He's going to get us a compound in Karachi. See? Right here. The compound will be fully stocked with weapons and provisions."

Gary looks at the map. "Where's Mirabad?"

"It's here." James points to a spot on the map. "Near the border with Iran."

"That's pretty far," Gary says. "A couple of hundred miles, at least. In fact, it looks like a lot more. How will we get from Karachi to Mirabad?"

"Believe me—I know it's far," James responds. "It'll take all day by truck just to get to the border of Afghanistan."

"Where are you going to get a truck?" Ernie asks him.

James let's out a sigh. "Can you guys have a little patience and wait for me to finish detailing the plan? Save your questions until after I'm done. OK—where was I? Oh yeah. Omprakash will get us the compound and the equipment that we'll need. He's also going to contract for two trucks to take us to the border of Afghanistan—see, right here." James points to another spot on the map. "It's only about thirty to forty miles from Mirabad. One truck will carry the men and the other will carry mostly extra petrol. The extra truck can also come in handy if the other truck breaks down."

"How many men are you going to need?" Ernie asks.

"Just you, Gary, me, and a squad of no more than ten. All light infantry." He pauses to let them take in the new plan. "What do you say? Can you guys join me? Will your affairs be over soon?"

"Yeah, we'll get there," Ernie says. "Whether or not the problem at home is settled. You can count on us."

"All right, good! Here's what I'm thinking. You guys get to Karachi in two weeks. That should give me enough time to get everything set. Can you guys be ready in two weeks?"

Ernie and Gary look at each other and nod. "Yeah, that sounds reasonable," Ernie says.

"Good. Give me a call at the ranch and I'll let you know where the compound is in Karachi."

"How long will we have to stay at that compound?" Gary asks. "Won't the Pakistani authorities begin wondering what's going on at this complex?"

"Yeah—I know, Gary. That's why it's important that no one leave the compound. The place will be fully stocked, so there'll be no reason to leave. But, really—I don't believe you will have to wait too long. I'm thinking this fellow Faakhir left Lebanon right after they brought Sam there. It'll take him two or three weeks to get home. That's my guess.

"As soon as I get word that Faakhir is back in Mirabad, we'll be moving from the compound. It'll take a day to get from Karachi to the Afghanistan border by truck. Three days to hike up to Mirabad and another three days to get back. The whole affair should be finished within three to four weeks after your arrival at Karachi. That's not enough time for anyone in Pakistan to get suspicious. Just in case, I'll have Omprakash spread some money around to the local police."

The group of men suddenly turns to the back of the plane as the sound of a piercing scream reaches them.

"James!" they hear Sam yell. "James, where are you?"

James leaps up and runs to the back. Sam is running toward the rear.

"James!" she screams again.

He grabs her and pulls her into his arms. "I'm right here, dear!"

Sam buries her head in his chest, crying. "Oh, James, I was so scared! I had the strangest dream that you were dead."

"It's all right, honey," he says, rubbing her back. "It was just a dream. I'm right here." James turns to the men standing behind him. "It's OK, guys. She'll be fine."

James escorts Sam to a seat. "Come on, sit down," he says, and she does.

Mary comes over. "Can I get you something?"

"Just get Sam a glass of water, please," James answers.

James sits next to Sam and pulls her to him. "Would you like to talk about it?"

Sam shakes her head no. After a moment, she adds, "I'm sorry."

"There's no need to say you're sorry. It's understandable. You went through a lot; I can only imagine the horror that you went through. Quite honestly, I was surprised at how easily you seemed to be taking it in your stride, earlier. This reaction is more reasonable."

She lifts her head and kisses him. "Thank you! Will you sit with me for a while longer? Do you need to get back to the meeting?"

"No, we're done. I'll stay right here with you."

Mary returns with the glass of water, but Sam shakes her head.

"Just put it down on the table, please, Mary," James tells her.

"What was your meeting all about?" Sam asks.

"We don't have to discuss it right now. I'll fill you in later."

"Let's talk about it now. Maybe it'll take my mind off how I'm feeling."

James smiles. "No, baby, I don't think what we discussed will ease your mind. We were discussing the next phase." He pauses and exhales. "You *know* this isn't over, right? We still have a lot more to do. The men who are targeting us aren't going to give up."

She frowns.

"So what's next? What did you guys decide?" she asks him.

"There's a name that's popped up—a man by the name of Faakhir," James says. "He's the next fellow that I need to get to, because my guess is that he was behind your abduction. This guy lives in Afghanistan—but he's not there right now.

"Omprakash has someone on the lookout for Faakhir. As soon

as he returns home, Omprakash is going to let me know. Then we'll pay Mr. Faakhir a visit and find out what he knows."

She looks at him suspiciously.

"You aren't planning to go to Afghanistan with the men, are you?"

"Yes, of course. I *have* to go."

"Are you fucking crazy?" she hollers, sitting up.

"Shush! Lower your voice."

"Do you have some sort of death wish?" Sam stands up and shouts. "You didn't get yourself killed this time around, so you're going to try again?"

"Come on, sit down—let's talk." James tugs at her and pulls her back into her seat. "Please lower your voice and let me explain."

Once she's seated again, James pauses for a moment. "Sam, I'm not doing things because I've gone crazy—I *have* to go. We need to get to these men. For some reason, they have targeted me, you, and our three children. The men we're facing are ruthless. You saw what they did to you. Ronan, our bodyguard, is dead. Regis is still in the hospital. These evil men won't rest, and we won't have any peace until the ringleaders are destroyed.

"Faakhir is next on the list. There are others after him. I don't know how many."

She wipes at her eyes.

"Why can't Ernie and Gary handle this without you?" she asks. "That's what you pay them for."

He takes a gulp from the glass of water she hasn't touched.

"What if they fail, Sam?" he asks. "What if they don't get the job done? It's you, me, and our family that'll be left with the problem." Gently, he turns Sam toward him. "Sam, you're losing track of how dangerous these men are that we're up against. How do you think they knew exactly where you would be? There is somebody in Colorado who told them exactly when your plane took off and where you were headed.

"Within a day of your leaving, these men were able to locate you in Milan, assemble a team, kidnap you, and have you on a ship to

Lebanon. They are extremely formidable enemies that we are facing. Governments can't control them.

"I know perfectly well how risky the mission in Afghanistan will be. I'm not delusional. But it's a lot more dangerous for me to sit at home in Colorado, doing nothing. Waiting for their next move. When will that next move come? Who will they hit? Will it be you again? Or maybe Molly, when she's in school? No, Sam—we can't live like this. We have to face our enemies and defeat them."

Sam pulls him to her and buries her head in his chest. "I'm just so frightened for you. I thought that you had been killed today, James. I don't think I can go on without you."

"I know it's a scary situation, dear—I know you're frightened," James says softly, rubbing her back. "Believe me—if there were any other way, I'd take it. But there isn't. People like Ernie and Gary are support players that we need in our fight. The ultimate responsibility for this war lies with us. We'll be the ones facing the consequences if we lose. Things are going to be bad for a while. We'll have to keep our guard up. But I'm confident that we'll win in the end. We have to!"

Sam leans her head on his shoulder and whispers. "James, will you make love to me?"

James lifts her face up and she mouths. "Please. I need to feel you."

James smiles. "Let me tell Mary that we'll be in the back of the plane and don't want to be disturbed."

———⫫————⫫———

After getting home, James and Sam are sitting on the patio at their ranch with the children. Baby Christopher is asleep in Sam's arms. Molly and Michael are sitting on the ground, playing with their toys.

"Do you want me to hold the baby for a while?" he asks. "You've been holding him since after dinner."

"No, it's all right. I'm fine." She tilts her head down and gives the baby a kiss.

Gilda comes out the back door. "Mrs. Coppi, would you like for me to get the children ready for bed? It's after ten."

Molly looks up. "Daddy, I don't want to go to bed yet."

"Molly, please, we're all very tired. We just flew in this morning from Washington."

"All right." Molly gets up. "Will you come and read the Bible to us?"

"Mommy will do the Bible reading tonight."

"Please, Daddy, *you* read it to us tonight. Read the story of the man and his daughters again."

"All right—I'll come read to you after you're ready for bed. But I'm not reading about the man and his daughters."

"Would you like for me to take Christopher?" Guadalupe asks Sam after the children run inside.

"No, Guadalupe—I'll bring him in. You start on Michael and Molly." After Guadalupe has left, Sam turns to James. "You've been reading the Bible to the children at night before bed?"

He pretends to be indignant.

"Somebody had to read to the children while you were sunning and funning in Lebanon."

Sam laughs, leans over, and gives him a kiss. "Thank you. That was really nice of you." They get up to go inside. "What's this story about a father and his daughters?"

"It's the story about Lot and his daughters."

"Lot and his daughters!' Sam stops and turns to him. "Did you really read that passage to her? It's indecent!"

"It was an accident," he says, trying to defend himself. "I didn't know what that chapter was about. I've never read the Bible before. Who expected a story like that in a religious book? It took me twenty minutes to put an end to all the questions Molly was asking."

"Well, I just hope she doesn't ask any more questions about it," Sam says. "Molly is a little too young for such a scandalous story. I can't believe you read that passage to her."

"You know, Sam—if I had known that the Good Book contained stories like that, maybe I would have read it myself a lot sooner."

17

The Letter

FAAKHIR SITS ON THE FLOOR with his back to the wall. Moshar is looking out the window. They have been back at the compound in Peshawar for six days. Moshar walks to the back of the room and sits next to Faakhir.

"I can't believe those stupid Palestinians screwed it up again!" Moshar tells him. "We handed them the prisoner on a platter. How could they have been so careless?"

"Maybe this American is a lot smarter than we realized," Faakhir says. "This is the second time we've dealt with him. And both times, he's come out on top."

Moshar puts his head in his hands and groans. "We're going to get the blame for this—you know that? We did everything they told us to do—but they're still going to blame us."

"I don't care who they blame," Faakhir says, raising his voice. "I just want to get back to my family."

"That's not going to happen" Moshar snaps. "Forget about seeing your family. They're going to send us right back out." Moshar stands up and returns to the window. "Where the heck are they?"

"What do you mean, they're going to send us right back out?" Faakhir asks. "What is there left to do?"

Moshar comes back and squats next to Faakhir. "Kill the American. The prince and Mafrouz won't rest until he's dead. Especially now that he's defeated us twice." Moshar stands back up. "No. Mark my words, Faakhir—they're going to send us right back out."

"Well, I'm not going! There's too much to do at home. I'm not going anywhere for a while—I'll tell that to the prince myself when he gets here."

"The prince isn't coming—it's just going to be Mafrouz. One of the men downstairs told me that the prince is on holiday. The royal likes to go to Monaco. The prince loves to gamble, and he especially has a fancy for those Western, busty, blonde women."

Moshar sits back down next to Faakhir. He nudges him and smiles. "Have you ever bedded a blonde, Faakhir?"

"No. I have not had any woman other than my wife."

Moshar leans closer to Faakhir. "They say those Western women are the best. I myself have never had one, but I've heard. How about that American we had as prisoner? Tell the truth—you desired her, Faakhir, didn't you?"

"No. I just did my job."

"I wanted her," Moshar tells him, gazing off into space. "I even thought about sneaking down to her room at night when we were on the sea, but I was too afraid to act. Someday, I will—someday, I will bed a blonde Western woman. That is a goal of mine."

"I only desire my wife," Faakhir says.

"But the American woman was beautiful, wasn't she?" Moshar asks. "What was her name—Samantha? I still dream of her. Don't you?"

"I told you, Moshar—I desire only my wife."

Moshar laughs. "I don't believe you. You must have wanted that woman at least some. She was beautiful," he repeats. Then he lifts his head and looks over to the window. "I hear something!" Moshar says, jumping up. "Sounds like a truck." He runs to the window and looks out. "He's here."

Faakhir gets up and joins him at the window. There are mujahedeen fighters jumping off the back of the truck, all armed with automatic rifles. Mafrouz steps out of the passenger side. He brushes himself off and heads for the building. Faakhir and Moshar head out of the room and down the stairs to greet Mafrouz.

Mafrouz gets a big smile on his face when he sees them. "Faakhir,

Moshar, welcome back! You are just in time. We're going to celebrate tonight. We just won a great victory. Killed many soldiers—and best of all, we didn't lose even one of our men."

"Glory be to God, it is wonderful news," Moshar hails.

"Yes, it is. It is wonderful news," Mafrouz agrees, but then the smile on his face fades. "I hear your news is not as good. The American defeated you once again."

"Not our fault," Moshar quickly defends himself. "It was the Palestinians. We did exactly as was planned. We got the woman and handed her over to the Palestinians. How could we foresee that they would mess it all up?"

"Well, no matter," Mafrouz says. "You'll just have to go back out and finish the job. The American must not be allowed to enjoy his victory."

"I'm sorry, sir, but I cannot go at this time," Faakhir tells him. "I have been away too long, and there is much to do at home. My family needs me."

Mafrouz waves his hand dismissively. "Your chores at home will have to wait. This is far more important."

"May I say something, sir?" Moshar asks. "It's my opinion that we should wait. The American had a lot of security in place before the kidnapping. After this affair, I'm sure he'll increase his security even more. Let's wait a few months. Let things calm down a bit. Who knows—maybe after a few months, the American might even start to believe that the danger no longer exists. At that time, he should make an easy target."

"Yes, I see your point," Mafrouz says. He turns to Faakhir. "How much time do you need to finish up your affairs at home?"

"I should be done by the beginning of October," he answers.

"All right," Mafrouz declares. "On October eight, you will meet Moshar at noon at the port in Karachi. From there, you two will make your way to America—and finish this man off once and for all!"

AA Freda

Sam walks into James's study with three of the household staff. "Gilda, you and Rosita dust the bookshelves. Guadalupe, you vacuum the rugs. I'll dust the desk."

Billingsley opens the door and hands her an envelope. "I forgot to tell you Mrs. Coppi that Kathy Percival was by yesterday and dropped off this envelop. Inside is the key to Mr. Coppi's desk."

Sam takes the envelop. "Thank you," she places the envelop on the desk.

Sam is dusting the desk after Billingsley leaves when she happens on a file. She tries to open the desk drawer to put the folder away but it is locked. She reaches over for the envelop and opens it to take out the key. Inside the drawer she notices another envelop, which is addressed to her. She opens the package and reads.

A tear makes its way down her face as she reads the letter. This was James's farewell to her if he had been killed during her rescue. So, touched by his words she has to sit to compose herself. After regaining her composure, she puts the letter back in the envelop and while putting it back in the drawer, she notices another envelop which has written on the outside. *For Kathy, Personal.*

Sam opens up that envelop and begins reading. A few minutes later.

"What do you think you're doing?" James shouts from the door of the study, looking around. The women stop what they are doing.

Sam looks up and freezes.

"Why are you going through my stuff?" James yells.

"I wasn't going through your stuff," she answers meekly and startled by his reaction. "I was moving it aside so I can dust the top of your desk."

James walks up and takes the letter from her. He looks at the letter. "Liar! You were reading it!" he barks at her.

"No, I wasn't!"

James tears the sheets up and throws them into the waste basket. "There! Now no one can read the letter!" With that, James storms out of the room and slams the door.

Sam looks at the closed door and turns to the women. "Go ahead, finish what you were doing."

She retrieves the torn papers from the wastebasket. She opens the desk drawer and pulls out a roll of Scotch tape. Carefully, she pieces the sheets together. When she is done, she takes the papers into the bedroom and opens up the chest that is against the wall. There is a metal box inside the trunk that contains James's Vietnam mementos. Sam opens the box and puts the papers inside.

When she comes out of the room, she runs into Billingsley in the hall. "Have you seen James?"

"I believe he's out back, on the patio."

Outside, James is sitting on the bench, looking out into the open space. Sam takes a seat alongside him.

"Do you want to talk about it?" she asks. "What was that all about?"

He turns to her. "You mean you didn't read the letter?"

Sam smiles. "No, I did read it. Why did you write it?"

"If you read it, you know why. It was written to Kathy in the event that neither of us made it back alive. I had appointed Kathy the person to look after our children and our estate. No one was supposed to read the letter's contents unless we didn't make it back."

There's a period of silence and finally James speaks up.

"Are you okay?" he asks.

"Yeah, I'm fine," she says without looking at him.

James smiles. "Liar." He gets up and squats down in front of her. Sam doesn't look at him. He turns her face to him. "Tell me what was in the letter that's upsetting you?"

"The way you signed it," she says.

He furrows his brow. "The way I signed it?"

Sam looks directly into his face. "Yes, the way you signed it! *Love, James.*" Sam fidgets with her hands. "James, do you remember when we first met? The night at the country honky tonk. The night that I walked up to you and introduced myself. Do you remember that night?"

"Yes, I do. What about that night?"

"You don't know this but Kathy also had her eye on you that night but I got to you first. I've often wondered what would have happened if she had gotten there before me?" Sam turns away from James.

James gently turns her face to him and smiles tenderly. "Sam that night was the luckiest day of my life. I met the most wonderful woman on the face of the earth. The woman who turned my entire life around. Without her, I wouldn't be the man that you see in front of you today. There's no one but you that could have done that." James takes a breath.

"Sam you're taking that letter all wrong. I was trying to express to Kathy why I had entrusted her with the task of taking on my family. Think about it Sam, I was asking Kathy, a young woman with a child of her own, to give up her life and take care of my family—our family. Kathy needed to know how special she was to me and why I selected her. When I signed the letter with love, it's not in the meaning that you're thinking of. Yes, Kathy is a special person to me and I do love her as a friend. Just the way I love my children as my children. But there is only one woman I love as my wife, my soulmate and that is you. No other woman. Why do you think I was prepared to die for you?"

Sam's eyes moisten. "I'm sorry."

"You don't have to apologize." James wraps his arm around her and gives her a passionate kiss. "I love you," he says after the kiss.

He gets up and sits back in his chair. "I'm still upset with you for going through my stuff without asking."

She leans over and her hand reaches down to his groin and begins stroking. "Is there anything that I can do to make it up to you?"

James looks down at her hand and back up at her smiling slyly. "Maybe. What are you offering?"

"Come on." She gets up and tugs at his shirt. "Let's go inside."

"Why?"

She gives him a knowing look. "Because I don't want someone coming out here and catching me with your cock down my throat!"

The next morning, Sam walks into the dining room where James is having breakfast.

"Why are you all dressed so early?" she asks him.

"I'm going into the office today," he answers.

"Weren't you the one who said that we should stay on the ranch?"

James picks up his coffee mug and takes a sip. "Yes, whenever possible. We shouldn't go out unless we absolutely have to. But I have to. There's a big meeting at the office, and we'll be discussing the purchase of the railroad. Greenwald has been very patient with us, but I think we need to start moving the transaction forward.

"Besides, I'll be well guarded," he continues. "There'll be Max and the new guy, Jerry, with me. Come on, darling, sit down."

Sam takes a seat. "I was hoping we'd go horseback riding."

"Weren't you just out yesterday?"

"Yes, but it was no fun—I had three men riding shotgun with me. I was afraid to make a move."

"We'll go out tomorrow. I can't do today."

Mr. Billingsley walks in. "Mr. Coppi, Mr. Vadivlastan is on the phone."

"Thank, you Billingsley. I'll take it in the study."

"Good evening, Omprakash," James says. "You're up late. Do you have some news for me?"

"Yes, James—good news. Your man Faakhir is back home. He arrived last week. I just got the news from my source."

"Does your source know how long Faakhir will be there?"

"No, he doesn't. All he knows is that the man is there now."

"Are Ernie, Gary, and the men at the house in Karachi that we set up for them?"

"Yes—they're all in place and have been for more than a week."

"OK, that's good. Do me a favor, Omprakash. Get word to Ernie. Tell him to be ready. I'm on my way. Make arrangements for the trucks that you hired to pick us up in three days in Karachi. Bright and early, five in the morning."

"OK, will do. Good luck."

"Thanks. And by the way, Omprakash—good job."

James walks back into the dining room.

"Who was that?" Sam asks.

"That was Omprakash. The man I was looking for just returned to his village in Afghanistan. I'm leaving right away."

"What about the office? The important meeting you just said you had?"

"I'm not going to the office. The meeting will have to go ahead without me. This is more important. I've got to pack," James says as he starts to leave the dining room. Then he stops and turns to her. "Do me a favor and call Kathy. Tell her to get my plane ready. I'm going to Karachi, Pakistan."

Sam gets up and runs after him. "Is this that mission you told me about?"

"Yes, it is."

Sam grabs him and pulls him into her arms. "Oh, James, I'm so frightened."

James gently pushes her off him. "Don't be. The operation is well planned. I've got a good team with me. I'll be just fine. You just be careful here at home. Be very vigilant. Don't take any chances. If anything looks suspicious or out of order, call our security man, Mark. I'll call him before I leave and tell him to keep an eye on this place.

"In fact, better yet, I'll have Mark stay at our guest house. It's empty now—Cardiz and his family moved out last week."

"How long will you be gone?"

"Three weeks—maybe four."

18
Faakhir

IT TOOK TWO DAYS AND three stops for James's plane to reach Karachi. He realizes now that he would have been better off taking commercial flights. The trip required an overnight layover in Cairo for the crew to get some rest. Both Ernie and Gary are waiting at the airport to greet him.

Ernie has a huge smile on his face. "I hear our man finally made it home to Afghanistan. Omprakash gave me all of the details."

"Yes, he's there right now," James says, hopping into the front seat. "We'll go over the plan as soon as we get back to the compound. The trucks will be here at five o'clock tomorrow morning to pick us up."

"Tomorrow?" Ernie asks, forcing out a laugh. "You sure as hell don't waste any time, do you?"

"No. We need to get to this guy—I don't know how long he'll stay put. Have you got all the maps that we need?"

"Yeah, I've got everything. We're all set."

When they're at the complex, Ernie opens the bag with the maps. "Which one do you want to see first?" he asks.

"The village," James replies.

Ernie unfurls the map onto a table.

"Which is Faakhir's house?" James asks.

"According to Omprakash, it's this one right here," Ernie says, pointing. "We can't miss it. It's one of the largest house in the town."

"Faakhir's house is in the middle of town." James leans over the map and looks at it closely. "We'll have to go through a lot of the city before getting to it."

"We should be all right," Ernie says. "Our plan is to get to Mirabad at around eleven or twelve at night. The good news is that his house is a little secluded, so no one should notice us—there are no other houses nearby. I think we'll be OK."

"How long will it take us to get to Mirabad?" James asks Ernie.

"I'm figuring it's a three day trek. We'll be walking mostly at night. This way, we won't be noticed, and we won't have to worry about the heat. The heat this time of the year is brutal—it tops a hundred every day."

"What about the Russians?" James asks. "Are they active in this area?"

"No, we're on the other side of Afghanistan. No Russian would dare show his face."

"All right—let me understand if I've got this right. This mission will last a total of six days. That's a lot of provisions."

"Yeah, but we don't have to carry much water. There are plenty of places to refill our canteens on the way. It's mostly food we need." Ernie looks at Gary. "Gary, you're responsible for the supplies. What do you say?"

"We've got enough for two weeks, James," Gary answers. "We'll be fine."

"What are we going to do with this guy Faakhir?" Ernie asks. "Do we just eliminate him?"

"No," James replies. "I need him to help me."

"There's no way we'll have enough time to work him over and get him to cooperate," Ernie says. "This guy is an ardent fighter, and he won't break easily. We'll need to bring him back with us."

"No—I'd rather not bring him back," James says. "That would lead to a whole lot more complications. Besides, I don't think torture is the answer for this guy. I've got something else in mind. Something that is quicker and much more effective."

"Like what?" Ernie asks.

James stands up. "I don't want to talk about that now. You guys will find out soon enough. You got any food? I'm hungry."

<hr />

Jeff and Billy are in the truck on the way back to the ranch from town, where they picked up supplies, when they notice a blue pickup parked on the dirt road about a quarter of a mile from the ranch. Jeff pulls alongside the truck and rolls down the window.

"Is there something wrong?" Jeff asks the driver. "Can we help you?"

"No, I'm fine," the man behind the wheel answers. "I just made a wrong turn."

Jeff looks back at the truck as it pulls away.

"Jeff, that's the same truck," Billy says and turns to look at the truck again.

"What same truck?" Jeff asks.

"The same truck that I chased off the ranch that day," Billy explains. "You know—the one with the two guys inside. The guys who cut a hole in the fence."

Jeff looks at Billy. "Are you sure?"

"Yes, I'm absolutely positive! That's the truck!"

Jeff makes a fast U-turn and tries to race after the truck. He stops when he realizes that it is gone.

"Damn!" he utters. "We'd better get back and tell Mr. Malone. I hope he's still at the ranch—I saw him there this morning."

Mark is talking with one of his security officers when Jeff drives up.

"Mr. Malone, may I have a word with you?" Jeff asks as he jumps out of the truck.

"Yes, Jeff. What is it?"

Jeff tells him about the truck. Mark turns to Billy. "Are you absolutely sure it's the same truck?"

"Yes—I'm positive," Billy replies.

Mark scratches his head. "You didn't happen to get his plate number, did you?"

"No, I'm sorry, sir," Jeff answers. "The guy left before we could get to him."

"What did he look like? The last time, you said the men looked foreign. Like Middle Eastern fellows."

"Yeah, I guess he looked sort of the same," Billy replies.

"The man spoke pretty good English," Jeff adds.

Sam comes walking toward them, wearing her riding breeches and boots.

"Are you going for a ride, Mrs. Coppi?" Mark asks. "You'll need an escort."

"No, I won't need the escort today, Mark. I'll just be riding in the training area nearby—I'm practicing my jumping. What are you guys up to?"

"We're just discussing some new security guidelines that I'm putting in place," Mark says.

"What new guidelines?"

"Oh, it's nothing important. You don't need to concern yourself. Have a nice ride."

Sam gives a suspicious look and raises her voice. "Yes, I do, Mark—I do need to concern myself. It's my family that's in danger. Now, what's up? Tell me the truth—not this baloney you're feeding me. What were you guys really talking about?"

Mark looks down and sighs.

"Jeff and Billy just noticed a blue pickup truck near the ranch," he responds, looking back up at her. "It's the same truck that Billy chased off the ranch."

Sam frowns. "So these people are still at it."

"I'm afraid so, Mrs. Coppi."

"And what are you going to do about it?"

"I'm going to beef up the patrols around the ranch. I'm also calling Charlie McGill. Have him run a check on all the blue pickup trucks in the area."

"That's a lot of trucks," she says.

"Yes, I know, ma'am. But you never know—we might get lucky. In the meantime, I'll increase the patrols."

"All right. And, Mark: in the future, don't hold anything back from me. You don't need to spare me—I need to know everything that's going on around here."

"Yes, Mrs. Coppi. It won't happen again."

After Sam walks off, Mark tells Jeff and Billy, "Thanks, guys. Let me know if you see anything else suspicious." Mark turns to the security officer. "I want someone patrolling up and down that road. Every hour, day and night. Also, twice a day, I want someone to ride in a jeep around the entire perimeter of this ranch. Once at night and once during the day. Alternate the times so that no one can get a fix on our watch schedule. Place all our men on high alert. I don't like the news I just heard. No, sir—I don't like this at all.

"I'm calling Charlie McGill," he adds. "I want his department to get involved. How many Middle Eastern guys can there be in the Colorado Springs area? With a blue pickup truck, no less? If he puts a couple of men on the case, they might find these guys."

The other men nod in agreement.

Mark looks at the security officer. "You got anything to add?"

"No. I'll get to working on the new schedule right away," the man says. "I'll tell the guys to be on the lookout."

James wakes up at four and turns on a lamp. He gets out of bed and stretches. He hears Ernie's voice barking orders in the courtyard. He looks out the window and gazes upon the silhouettes of Ernie and the men working. There's a knock on his door.

"Come in," he says.

Gary walks in and tosses a pile of clothes onto the bed. "Your dress code."

"What is that?" James asks.

"It's typical Afghan wear. Ernie and I think you should dress the part. When you're done, you'll look like a mujahedeen fighter."

Gary heads for the door but then stops and turns. "Also, you might want to wear a scarf to cover up that milky white face of yours—it's a dead giveaway."

James walks into the courtyard later, wearing his new outfit. The entire troop has a look and then bursts out laughing.

"OK," James says. "You've all had your laugh. Now get back to work."

"I love your *pakol*," Ernie yells out.

"My what?'

One of the soldiers takes the hat off James's head and points at it. "*Pakol!*" he says and hands it back.

The trucks honk their horns in front of the door to the compound. One of the men walks over and opens the wooden gates. The men pick up equipment and start loading it onto the trucks. James hops into the back of one of the trucks and takes a seat on the floor. He pulls the *pakol* over his face and goes to sleep sitting up.

19

Convincing a Killer

IT'S LATE AFTERNOON WHEN THE trucks reach the border of Afghanistan, northwest of Saindak, Pakistan. It was hot in the truck. It got so hot that James thought about taking off all the clothing he was wearing. *How do they wear all this garb in this heat?* He jumps off the truck and stretches his legs.

The trucks are quickly unloaded. Ernie tells the drivers to meet back at that spot in six days.

"If we're not here, keep coming back for us every day—you hear? We'll eventually get here." Ernie turns to James. "James, I know it's hot, but I'd like to get started, if it's all right with you. The men are well rested, so we can get going."

James looks up at the searing sun. "Are you sure? It's *really* hot."

"Yeah, I know—but it's just as hot sitting as it is walking."

"All right, Ernie—whatever you say. You're running this operation. Let's go."

An hour into the walk, James begins to appreciate the outfit that he's wearing. Although the sun is beating down on him, his body is not burning up, because the clothes provide protection from the sweltering rays. He's still sweating underneath all the clothes, but he's not being burned by the sun. The men are moving at a slow pace, and he's wondering if the slowness is because of him. Ernie may be worried that he can't keep up.

As the sun lowers in the horizon, Ernie yells out, "This is a good place to take a break. We'll continue after the sun sets."

Ernie walks over to James. "How are you holding up?"

James takes a seat and leans his back against a boulder. "I'm OK." He puts his hand up in front of his eyes to shade them from the sun and looks up at Ernie, squinting. "You're not deliberately going slowly because of me, are you?"

Ernie lets out a bellow of laughter and sits alongside him. "No, the thought never crossed my mind. We're moving at a good pace. There's no need to go any faster. The terrain is rocky. It'll become harder to see as it gets dark. I don't want anyone to trip and hurt himself. Someone getting hurt would throw a wrench into the operation."

"Yeah—especially if that someone is me," James observes.

Ernie lets out another laugh. "Yes, that's true. Don't worry about the speed. We're doing just fine. Three days from now, in the early morning hours, we'll be five miles from Mirabad. There's a river near the place. We'll make camp not too far from the river when we get there. Give us a chance to get washed up and replenish our water supply.

"We'll start out for Faakhir's place as soon as it gets dark. We should get there sometime before midnight, as planned. Everyone in the village should already be home for the night. The streets should be deserted. It should be easy to move in on Faakhir. Once we get this man immobilized, you can do your thing. We should be heading back that very next morning. We'll be back at the trucks by the sixth day, as scheduled."

"OK, good," James says. He unhitches his canteen from his belt and takes a drink. "How much time have we got before we need to get moving again?"

Ernie looks at the setting sun. "At least an hour."

"Good." James slides down and puts the scarf over his face. "I'm going to take a little nap."

From there, the walking at night gets rough. There are no real mountains to cross—just a lot of loose rocks. With no moon out, the path is difficult to see. The only light is from the thousands of stars in the sky. James trips twice. Fortunately, no serious damage is done—he just twists his ankle. It hurts, but he is able to keep up. The other men seem to do the trek relatively easily. The hardest part of the journey happens during the day, when they have to sit in a tent to temper the sun. But nothing can shield a person from the heat when the temperatures reach well over a hundred.

They get to the outskirts of Mirabad in the early morning hours of the third day, just as Ernie had predicted. Once they are near the river, Ernie looks for a good site.

"We're going to make camp in this little glen," Ernie declares. "It's covered on all sides and is away from the trail, so we won't get noticed. It'll be sunup in a few hours. I'll send the men to the river to replenish our water in a few minutes, while it's still dark. You might want to go with them if you want to clean yourself up.

"After that, we'll stay holed up until nightfall," Ernie continues. "We don't want to take a chance on anyone coming this way and noticing us. We don't want Faakhir to get tipped off about us and disappear, after we've come all this way."

"When are we leaving tonight?" James asks Ernie.

"Right after sunset. We're about five miles from the village. We should be at Faakhir's place around eleven, just as we planned. We'll take just our weapons and leave a few men here to guard our provisions."

"All right. I'm going to get a little shuteye. Wake me up when the men leave to get water—I'd like to get cleaned up. I hope the river isn't dry."

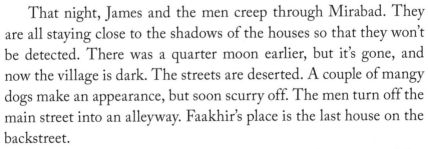

That night, James and the men creep through Mirabad. They are all staying close to the shadows of the houses so that they won't be detected. There was a quarter moon earlier, but it's gone, and now the village is dark. The streets are deserted. A couple of mangy dogs make an appearance, but soon scurry off. The men turn off the main street into an alleyway. Faakhir's place is the last house on the backstreet.

Ernie whispers to Gary, "Post two men at the beginning of this block." He signals to two of the other men. "You two, cover the rear of the house!" he says and then turns to James. "Wait here until I come out to get you."

Ernie turns to the other three men and whispers, "You guys ready?" They nod. Ernie points to two of his men. "You two take one of the bedrooms." He turns to the last. "You come with me."

When they have moved noiselessly to the front of the dark house, Ernie turns to the men,

"Are you ready?" he whispers. The men nod and he bursts through the door, charging into the house. James hears a brief scuffle—and a few moments later, Ernie comes back out. "All clear—you can come in."

Faakhir's wife and three children are huddled together in the corner. One of the men is pointing a rifle at them.

"He's in there," Ernie tells James, pointing to a room.

James goes into the room, where Faakhir is sitting on a bed. Another of his men is pointing his rifle at his head. Faakhir's right eye is beginning to swell from a sharp blow he took from Ernie. Ernie turns to the man. "Wait in the next room."

James pulls out a chair that was in the corner and sits across from Faakhir. "You know who I am?"

Faakhir nods as he rubs his face.

"And do you know why I'm here?"

Faakhir nods again.

"Why am I here?"

"You want to kill me," Faakhir says faintly.

"No. If I wanted to kill you, you'd already be dead. I wouldn't have needed to make the trip from America—I could have simply sent these men to do the job."

Faakhir's eyes widen. "You want me to talk?"

"No, not really. You don't have much to tell me that I don't already know."

Faakhir looks at James and shrugs. "I don't understand. What do you want? Why are you here?"

"I'll tell you why I'm here in due time. First, let me ask you—why do you want to kill me?"

"I don't want to kill you. Those were my orders—I have nothing against you. I'm just doing my job."

"Who gave you the orders?"

Faakhir looks down at the ground and doesn't answer.

James smiles. "Faakhir, I already told you that I don't need you to talk—I already know. The people who gave you the orders are Prince Aba al bin Faikil and Muhammad Mafrouz."

Faakhir looks up at James, startled.

"That's right, Faakhir—I know. I know the names of the men who are behind all this. What I don't know is: why my family? As well as me, why do you want to murder my family?"

Faakhir remains silent.

"Is that your family in the next room?" James points to the door.

Faakhir nods.

"Your wife and three children?"

Faakhir nods again.

"How old are your children?"

"My son is eleven, and my daughters are nine and thirteen."

"I also have three children," James tell him. "But you probably know that already. I love them very much. As much as I'm sure that you love your children. I'm very protective of my family; that's why I'm here. I want to make sure that nothing bad happens to them. Just as you would want nothing bad to happen to your family."

James pulls his chair closer to Faakhir. "You asked what I want from you? So here it is, Faakhir: I want you to switch sides. Work with me to get at the prince and Mafrouz."

"I will never do that!" Faakhir raises his voice. "I would rather die than betray."

"Really?" James asks, smiling. "You are more loyal to those two men than you are to your own family?"

A confused expression comes over Faakhir's face.

"That's right, Faakhir. If you don't agree to join me, I will take it out on your family. I will show them the same mercy you would have shown to my children. Infidels—that's what we are to you, isn't it? Worthless pieces of trash. Isn't that right? You would have slit my children's throats without blinking."

Faakhir doesn't answer.

"Well, I'm not as heartless as you, Faakhir—I'm not going to kill your family. Here's what I'm going to do. My men have not had a woman for a long time. Some have never had a woman at all. I'm going to let my men have their way with your daughters and your wife. The men will start with the youngest—the eleven-year-old. The oldest daughter will be next—and finally, after your wife has watched her daughters get ravaged, the men will get to her, too."

Faakhir doesn't respond. He continues glaring at James.

"After the men have finished with your women, they will release them naked into the streets so that the whole city will know what happened. Don't worry, Faakhir, you won't be around to share in their shame—because you'll be dead. Your women will have to face the humiliation all by themselves.

"Yes, and your son will face disgrace, too—for his whole life. After all, he did nothing to protect his mother and sisters."

Faakhir's eyes moisten, and James knows that his ploy is working.

"So do we have a deal? Will you work with me?"

Faakhir shakes his head no.

James turns to Ernie. "Tell the men to enjoy the youngest daughter."

Ernie takes a long look at James.

"You heard me!" James yells. "Get moving!" Ernie exits the room.

James and Faakhir can hear an argument in the next room There's a commotion. One of the girls screams, and someone is heard falling on the floor. The youngest daughter bursts into the room. Her thin blouse is torn. Tears are streaming down her face.

The young girl looks at her father and pleads, *"Baba, marasta!"*

Ernie walks in, grabs the child and drags her away.

"Darawem!" Faakhir yells out. Faakhir looks at James. "Please! Stop! No more!"

"You'll cooperate?" James asks. "You'll work for me?"

Faakhir's shoulders slump and he holds up his hands in defeat. "Yes—anything you say. Just leave my daughters alone."

James gets up and goes to the doorway and shouts, "Ernie, stop! Leave them alone."

James takes his seat again across from Faakhir. Ernie comes back in. The sound of a woman crying carries from the next room. James turns to Ernie. "Faakhir has agreed to cooperate and work with us. In return, we will not harm his family." James turns back to Faakhir. "Isn't that right, Faakhir? You will work with us?"

"Yes," Faakhir replies feebly, looking at the ground.

"What?" James says. "Speak up, Faakhir. I didn't hear you. What is your answer?"

Faakhir looks up. "I said that I will do anything you say" he says clearly.

"Good!" James says, settling back in his chair. "Let's talk for a while. How were you planning to kill me?"

"I was supposed to travel with Moshar to America. Meet up with two men who are already there."

"Who are the men that are already there?"

"I don't know who they are. Moshar knows the men."

"Who is Moshar?"

"Moshar is the man I've been working with. He helped in the kidnapping of your wife."

"Where is Moshar now?"

"He's back in Afghanistan, in Kabul."

"How do you reach him? If you need to talk to him, how do you contact this fellow Moshar?"

"I can't get in touch with Moshar. Everything goes through Mafrouz. I'm supposed to meet Moshar again in Karachi on October eighth and get onto a ship bound for America."

"And what about this fellow Mafrouz? Where is he?"

"Mafrouz spends most of his time in Afghanistan, fighting the Russians. He hides in caves in the mountains. When it gets too dangerous, he comes back to Pakistan. Mafrouz has a place in Peshawar."

"Do you know where the house is?"

Faakhir nods. "Yes. But if you're thinking of going to Peshawar, it won't do you any good. The place is heavily armed. Besides, Mafrouz is hardly ever there. He comes and goes. Even if you could get in, Mafrouz probably would not be there."

"What about the prince? Where is he?"

"Last time I heard, he was in Monaco, gambling and bedding blonde Western women."

James let's out a laugh. "I see. A real warrior and gentleman, that prince." James stands up and stretches. "All right, Faakhir—here's what's next for you. You'll meet this guy Moshar in Karachi, just as planned. When you get to the United States, you must find a way to get in touch with me. I'm guessing you should be there by the end of October. Other than that, there's nothing else for you to do."

James turns to Ernie. "We can head back now—we're done here." Before he leaves, James turns to Faakhir once more. "Faakhir, come find me when you get to the States. Don't try anything stupid. If you double-cross me, I will come back and find you. And then no amount of begging will stop me from destroying your family. You got that?"

"Yes," Faakhir looks up at James.

The men quickly get out of Mirabad. They make their way back to the camp, where the man guarding the provisions is waiting for them. It's three thirty and still dark when they start back out. Ernie comes alongside of James.

"What's the matter with your leg? You're limping."

"I twisted my ankle. I'll be all right—it only hurts a little."

"That was very cunning, how you got to Faakhir," he says. "I'm impressed. Very clever."

"Yeah, I impressed myself," he agrees. "I can't believe that Faakhir fell for it. It was the greatest bluff that I've ever pulled."

Ernie looks startled. Then he laughs and gives James a shove. "You were bluffing? I can't believe it. You had me completely fooled! Just how long were you planning on going along with what the men were doing to the little girl?"

"Not much longer. I almost gave up when she rushed into the

room with her torn blouse. It was very effective when she begged for her father's help. It even got to me. Good thing Faakhir yelled that he'd cooperate when he did."

"Do you really believe he'll keep his end of the deal?" Ernie asks.

"Yeah, he was pretty scared. I think he'll play ball. It doesn't really matter, anyway. I know his plans. Those two guys in Colorado Springs shouldn't be hard to find. It's the guys in Peshawar that I really need to worry about. They're the men calling all the shots. This thing they have against me won't end until I take care of both Mafrouz and the prince, and I've got to get to them."

"How are you going to do that? You heard Faakhir— Mafrouz's place is a well-guarded fortress."

"I'm not worried about the security of the place; there's always a way to get in. It's the schedule that I need to know about. When are the Prince and Mafrouz going to be there? And how can I get those two to be at that compound at the same time?

"Once we hit the compound, we won't get another chance," James continues. "We've got to get it right the first time. Anyway, I've got a lot to figure out when I get back. Thanks for all of your help; you really came through for me."

Ernie laughs. "I'm not done, am I? I could use more work."

"No, of course not. I'll need you again once I develop a plan for getting to Mafrouz and the prince."

"What if I go to Peshawar and have a look around for you?"

"No—it's too dangerous. The place is full of Afghan refugees. You won't be able to tell friend from foe. Besides, I have a better plan."

Ernie gives him a curious look. "Oh yeah? What's that?"

"I'm going to get an ally on our side."

"An ally? What Afghan do you know that is going to help you?"

James laughs. "No, not an Afghan. You're right; I don't know any Afghan that would help me, except maybe Faakhir. And, honestly, I don't believe he's capable of getting me the information—he lives too far from Peshawar. I'm going to rely on some old fashioned, surefire motivation—the best there is. Money!"

Ernie stops and looks at him. "Money! You're going to buy somebody off? Who?"

"Ernie, you know what's going on in this part of the world," James says, continuing to walk, and Ernie hurries to catch up again. "You've been here for a while. If you were going to bribe somebody, who would be the most likely to take a bribe? Who is the most corruptible in this area?"

Ernie thinks for a moment. "Either the Pakistani police or the Pakistani military."

"Exactly. The police or military. I'm going to buy off a Pakistani official. First chance I get, I'm going to call my man Omprakash and have him take a business trip to Peshawar. Have him talk to some businessmen there. Find out who the businessmen are paying off. You can't conduct business in Pakistan without paying someone off. I'll have Omprakash spread a little cash around and get someone on our side.

"That's the person that's going to get me inside the compound," James continues, shifting his heavy bag onto his other shoulder. "The man that's going to let me know everything about the place—and, most importantly, tell me when Mafrouz and the prince are inside the building at the same time." James looks at Ernie. "Ernie, you said you want another assignment, right? You got some time, don't you? Both you and Gary?"

"Yeah—sure, James. What do you need?"

"I want you to get two dozen Pakistani police uniforms and firearms. Official stuff, not junk. Also, recruit some more men. Make sure that they're Pakistanis. No Afghans. Afghans can't be trusted with this mission.

"Use the compound that you've got in Karachi for your base of operation. As soon as I have everything set to go in Peshawar, I'll give you a call."

"How long do I have to get this done?"

"I don't know. A couple of months, probably. I'll know better once Omprakash finishes his side of the business. I wouldn't waste too much time, though, just in case something breaks sooner."

20
Telephone Calls

JAMES IS BACK IN HIS study at the ranch. He's been home for a week. The operation in Pakistan has been set in motion. Omprakash is on his way to Peshawar. James has Charlie on the hunt for the two Afghans who are in Colorado—they shouldn't be hard to find. One of the men must have access to the airport. How else would they have known that Sam was on the plane heading for Milan?

James is feeling pretty good—he can see the light at the end of the tunnel, but there's still a lot of work to do. These are very dangerous enemies that he's made. But at least he's finally in control. His enemies aren't dictating what happens next.

Sam opens the door and looks in. "James, are you busy today? What's on tap?"

"No, not too busy—I have a meeting with Prince Firuz, but other than that, nothing much. The prince is on his way from California to visit his father. His father isn't feeling well. Why do you ask?"

"I thought we could take the horses out and go for a ride. It's a beautiful summer day. I'd like to get out before the afternoon thunder boomers. How long is the meeting?"

"Yeah, going for a ride is a good idea. I haven't been on a horse in months. The meeting shouldn't go on for too long."

"Can we go without taking all of the armed guards along? Just you and me?"

James laughs. "Yeah, we can do that this time. Nothing is supposed to happen until October."

"Good. I'll go pack us a lunch basket."

"How is your father?" James asks when Prince Firuz is sitting in front of his desk. "The shah must be very ill, for you to make the trip from California."

"You're right, James. He's not doing very well. It just doesn't look good."

James nods sympathetically.

"Where is your father staying right now? Is he still in Egypt?"

"No my father is at my home in Virginia."

"In that case Sam and I will arrange to pay him a visit."

"I suggest you get there right away if you want to see him—I'm told he could go into decline any day now," the prince says, sighing. "How is Samantha doing, by the way? Has she recovered from her ordeal?"

"Not yet. She still has trouble sleeping. Last night, she was tossing and turning."

"An ordeal like that can't be easy to get over."

"No, it can't. I'll keep that in mind when I finally meet up with this Prince Aba al bin Faikil."

Firuz sits up in his seat. "Who?"

"Aba al bin Faikil?"

The prince shakes his head. "That can't be right. Why would the prince have wanted to kidnap your wife?"

James's eyes widen. "Do you know him?"

"Not really. He's from a neighboring kingdom and our countries didn't get along too well. He's of a different sect, I'm Shia and he's Sunni. He's a lower level royal, not too high up in the chain. I met the prince a few times during Middle Eastern conferences. His family and mine get along a little better now that we have been ousted out of power. They no longer see us as a threat. But if you're so anxious to meet him, why don't you go meet him next week? The prince will be in DC."

"What?" James cries out, nearly jumping out of his seat.

"That's right. He'll be here as a guest of your government. They'll be discussing Afghanistan. I believe Prince Faikil will also meet with the president. If you like, I can arrange a meeting for you with the prince."

"Yes, of course—please arrange that meeting," James answers excitedly.

"James, I must caution you—you can't try anything. Prince Faikil is a guest of your country. There'll be massive ramifications if you try something."

"I'll behave," James says, smiling. "At least, I won't kill him. Set up the meeting. I'll tell you what—Sam and I will stop off to see your father first."

Prince Firuz stands up. "All right, James. I'll set up the meeting as long as I have your word that you won't try anything. Unfortunately, I won't be there, but my brother Farsad will make himself available."

"Where will you be?"

"I've got some affairs to take care of in the Middle East."

"This is that same matter that we spoke about in California? The counter-revolution?"

The prince smiles. "James, I'm not going to get into this with you again. You made your feelings perfectly clear when we last spoke. Farsad will get back to you on your meeting with Faikil."

After the prince leaves, James gets on the phone. "Rodney, you need to contact your CIA and State Department sources. Find out all you can about Prince Aba al bin Faikil—I need this report before next week."

After hanging up, James makes another call. "Frank, why hasn't the FBI followed up on the names Syed gave us? Prince Aba al bin Faikil and Muhammad Mafrouz."

"How do you know that the FBI hasn't followed up?"

"Well, if the FBI *has* followed up, why is the prince coming for meetings at the White House next week?"

"No shit. He's coming to the States?"

"Yeah. I'm trying to arrange to meet with him when he arrives. Call your sources at the FBI and see what you can find out. If this guy is a suspect, why would he be coming to the States as a guest of the president?"

James makes a third call. "Charlie, do me a favor. Call Syed's attorney. Find out if Syed is cooperating with the authorities as he promised he would. In particular, I want to know if he gave the FBI the names of Prince Aba al bin Faikil and Muhammad Mafrouz."

Sam comes walking in right after he's hung up. "Are we going? You said that you'd be done early."

James smiles. "Yes, I'm all done. Let me get changed into my riding gear." He gets up and walks over to her.

"I love your breeches," James says, kissing her. "You look very sexy. I hope those pants aren't too hard for me to pull off you when we get out there."

Sam slaps him playfully on the arm. "You better come back down to earth, mister. We're only going riding. Nothing else!"

They walk down to the stable, where two horses are saddled and waiting for them. Jeff walks over.

"You know, boss, we're breaking all the rules set up by Mr. Malone. We're not supposed to let you ride alone."

"I know, Jeff—but if Mark hollers about it, you can blame me."

"All right, sir. Your rifle is in the holster just in case there's any trouble."

"Where's *my* rifle?" Sam asks. "I'm a better shot than James."

"I'm sorry, ma am, I didn't know you wanted one—I'll go get a rifle for you," Jeff says and begins to walk away.

"Come back, Jeff," James says, laughing. "Sam is only kidding. Give her a boost up, will you? I wouldn't want her to tear those skintight breeches of hers."

"Very funny," she says, and hops onto the horse without help. "Let's see *you* make it!"

James turns to Jeff. "Give me a leg up." Jeff walks over and obliges.

"You better not fall off the horse," Sam tells him. "I'm not helping you back up. You'll end up walking back."

It's about an hour into the ride when Sam says, "Let's put down here and have lunch. There's nice shade under this tree."

"I'll eat in the saddle, since you're not helping me back up," he says.

"Stop being funny," Sam says. She hops off and ties her horse to a shrub.

James hops off and ties his horse to the same shrub. He takes a blanket off the horse and stretches it out on the grass.

Sam sets down the basket. "Do you want to eat?"

"Not right now. I'm not hungry."

"How about something to drink? I have some iced tea."

"No, I'm good." He lies down and pats the ground beside him. "Come and lie next to me. Let's talk."

She lies next to him. "Talk? Or have you got something else in mind?"

"No, only talk. There's no way I can get those breeches and those long riding boots off you."

Sam pulls him close and gives him a kiss. "I remember a time that you would have never given up."

"That's true, I'm getting old. But I really want to talk to you about something. I'll try to get into your pants after the talk. Can you tell me what's going on? You were tossing and turning again last night."

She sighs and furrows her brow.

"It's nothing, James. I'm just very anxious—that's all."

He smooths a stray tendril back from her face.

"Are you afraid that you might get kidnapped again?"

"No, not that! I'm just worried about you and the children. You know, with these men being so determined to harm us. It's very frightening. I just wish it would all come to an end. I know you're trying, James. But even your efforts scare me.

"Last week, you were in Afghanistan, of all places," she continues, propping herself up on one elbow. "I was so worried about you while you were gone that I sat up with the Bible and prayed my way to sleep every night." She lets out a long breath. "I'm trying, James. I'm trying to keep it together, I really am. But it's really hard."

James gives her a gentle kiss on the forehead. "I know you are, dear. And you're doing great. Staying positive in front of everyone, especially the children. It really helps."

"Will this ever end?" she asks with a sigh. "Will we win?"

"Yes—of course it will end, and we *will* win. There is no doubt in my mind. It's not going to be easy, but we'll win. We *have* to."

She smiles and pulls him close to her. "Come here. Let's figure out how to get these clothes off me."

Billingsley greets them when they get back to the house that afternoon. "Good afternoon, Mr. and Mrs. Coppi. I hope your riding was enjoyable?"

"Yes, it was very enjoyable, thank you," Sam replies.

"You had a call while you were away, sir," Billingsley informs James. "Mr. Vladivastan would like you to call him back."

"Isn't it awfully late in India for him to be calling?" Sam asks James, who looks at the clock.

"Yeah, it's after one in the morning."

"Mr. Vladivastan said that you should call no matter what the time," Billingsley tells him.

"Thank you, Billingsley," James says and heads for his study.

When James has Omprakash on the phone, he asks him what's going on. "Good news, I hope?"

"Yes, very good news," Omprakash says excitedly. "We now have an inspector general for the police department of Khyber Pakhtunkhwa working for us. That's the province the city of Peshawar is in. His name is Malik Toru."

"Can Toru be trusted?" James asks. "When the time comes, will he come through? Did you explain what we wanted—information on this compound?"

"Yes, I explained it all to him. Turns out that he's not too fond of those people coming into his city and basically taking over."

"All right—give him an assignment. Let's find out how helpful he will be. Tell him we need a complete layout of the place. Also, we need to know how many people live there. Let's see what he comes up with."

"OK, James. Will do."

As soon as James hangs up, the phone rings again.

"James, it's Charlie. I just heard back from Irving Finkelstein, Syed's public defender. James, there's something strange going on. When I called this guy Finkelstein, he said that he would call me back. When he did, he said he was calling me back from a public street phone. He said his office and house phones had been tapped. Someone broke into his office last week and rummaged through his files.

"Finkelstein suspects it's the FBI," Charlie continues. "The FBI is tailing him everywhere. Finkelstein spent half an hour ditching them before he called me. The lawyer assured me that Syed gave the FBI all the information that he gave to us. He doesn't know why the FBI is not doing anything with the material."

"OK, Charlie. Thanks." James walks out of the study and finds Billingsley. "Is Mark Malone at the ranch today?"

"I don't know, sir. Would you like me to call the station house for him?"

"Yes, please. Tell Mark I'd like to see him right away. I'll be in my study."

A few minutes later, there's a knock at his door, and Mark peeks in. "You wanted to see me, Boss?"

"Yes, Mark, please come in," James says. "Have a seat."

"What's up?" Mark asks after taking a chair. "I heard you went for a ride this morning without security."

"Yeah, I did. I'm pretty sure it's not needed right now. Nothing is going to happen until October."

Mark shifts uncomfortably in his chair.

"First of all, you don't know that for sure," Mark says, his voice starting to get louder. "The other side's plans could change at any time. Secondly, you're setting a bad example. Letting the staff know that the rules can be bent."

James bows his head and nods.

"I'm sorry, Mark! You're right—it won't happen again!"

Mark relaxes in his chair.

"Good! What did you want to see me about?"

James stands up. "Let's go for a walk."

When they are outside James looks up at the sun. "Man can you believe this heat. It's in the mid nineties. Let's go over there and stand in the shade of that oak tree. Listen Mark, I want you to check to see if we're being tapped. Both here at the ranch and at the office."

Mark's eyes widen. "You think we're being bugged? Who would do that?"

"Find out, first, if the places are wired. I'll tell you my suspicions once you get back to me. Check everything. You got that? A thorough exam."

"Yes, I've got it. I'll get on it right away." Mark walks back toward the station house.

After he leaves, James rubs his face. "What a mess," he mutters. He goes in his study and calls Charlie.

"Charlie, any news on those two Middle Eastern men I asked you to look into?"

"No, not yet. James, let me ask you—is one of these two Middle Eastern guys that you're looking for the same guy that Malone asked me to track down? A guy with a blue pickup truck?"

"What?" James almost yells. "What guy with a blue pickup truck?"

"Malone said that one of the ranch hands said he saw a guy snooping around the ranch. An Arab-looking guy. He was driving a blue pickup truck. Could he be one of your guys?"

"I don't know," James says, frustrated. He'd just spoken to Mark and wasn't told any of this. "The guy *could* be the same man. I don't know. Charlie, I believe that one of the men that I'm looking for works at the airport. Have someone snoop around at the airport and see what they can find out."

Once off the call, James runs out of the house and chases after Malone. "Mark!" he calls out when he sees the man a few hundred feet down the road. "Wait up."

"What's this about a man in a blue pickup truck?" James asks when he reaches him.

"Jeff and Billy saw this man parked a few hundred meters from the ranch. The man drove off before they could get to him. I'm having McGill search for him."

"A strange man is seen at the ranch—and you didn't think I should know?" James speaks in a terse, deliberate tone. "What the hell is wrong with you?"

"I'm s-s-sorry, sir," Mark stammers. "I was handling the matter—I just didn't think it was a big deal."

"Well, from now on, you tell me fucking everything!" James yells. "Let me decide what's important and what's not. It's *my* family that's on the line."

Mark looks down at the ground. "It won't happen again."

James realizes he has been yelling. "All right, I'm sorry. I came down a little too hard. It's just been a tense time for me." He puts his arm across Mark's shoulder. "Just keep me in the loop."

James goes back inside and gets on the phone again.

"Rodney, this fellow Bill Sester—he's an aide who is close to the president, isn't he?"

"Yeah, he is. Why do you ask?"

"I'm going to Washington, DC next week for some meetings. Can you set up an appointment for you and me to meet with him?"

"I'm coming with you?"

"Yeah, why not? Don't you have time? Are you busy with something else?"

"No, I can make time. What are we going to speak to Sester about? Is this about the people that I'm looking into with the CIA?"

"Yeah, probably—but don't tell Sester that. I don't want him to know in advance."

Rodney is quiet for a moment. "James, you know he's going to ask why we want to speak to him," he finally says. "Sester doesn't like surprises."

"Tell Sester that you don't know," James insists. "Tell him that I wouldn't reveal it to you. The meeting with us will take only half an hour of his time, at most."

"All right—I'll see what I can do."

As James comes out of the study, he bumps into Sam.

"You've been busy," she says. "What's going on?"

"Where are the children?" he asks.

"Outside. In the back yard."

"Outside? Isn't it too hot for them out there? I was just outside, it must be in the nineties," he says, walking toward the back.

"I've got a wading pool set up for them and plenty of sunscreen," Sam says, following behind him. "Are you going to tell me what's going on?"

"We're going to Washington next week. The shah is very ill. He's in Virginia, at Firuz's house. We'll be paying him a visit."

James opens the back door and walks out into the yard.

"Daddy, come into the pool," Molly calls to him.

James looks at his children in the wading pool and smiles. *This is what heaven must be like,* he thinks. *Seeing the smiling faces of my children, happy and playing.*

"I can't, dear," he tells her. "I'm not wearing my bathing suit." But he doesn't go back inside—he stays for a moment and watches them play.

21

Face to Face

THE NEXT DAY, JAMES IS inside the command center at the ranch with Mark, who is giving him a tour of the security setup. They are looking at more than a dozen television screens.

"How do you keep up with all the screens?" James asks the guard who is sitting behind the desk.

"It's not too difficult, Mr. Coppi," the guard answers. "All the monitors are right in front of me."

"What do you do when you see something suspicious?" James asks him.

"I get on the radio and dispatch someone to the site."

"What if you have to leave your post? You know—if you have to go to the bathroom? What happens then?"

"I radio someone to come and cover for me, sir."

"Good," James says. Then he looks up at the screens. "What's that?" He points to one of the monitors. "That's happening at the front gate, isn't it?"

Mark and the guard stare at the display. There are five cars stopped in front of the gate. Men have gotten out of the cars and are talking to one of the guards.

Mark goes over to the radio. "Martinez, what's going on?" he asks. "Who are these people?"

"These people say that they're here for some sort of social function, but they're not on my list," Martinez replies. "They say that Mrs. Coppi invited them, but I wasn't told anything about this. What should I do?"

Mark looks over at James. "Do you know anything about this?"

James is looking up at the screen. Two more cars have pulled up. "Give me the phone," James says to the man at the desk, and he quickly dials his house. "Billingsley, would you please get my wife on the phone?" he says when his butler answers.

"Hello?" Sam answers.

"What the hell do you think you're doing?" James shouts into the phone. "Who are all these damn people coming to the ranch?"

"They're coming for a charity luncheon! I'm having a fundraiser for the hospital. I'm expecting about a hundred people."

"Is there something wrong with you?" James yells again. "In the middle of this security crisis that we're having at the ranch, you go ahead and invite the whole of Colorado Springs?"

"Stop yelling at me!"

"Did you even bother to tell Malone? There's a line of cars outside the front gate, and the guards don't have a clue about who to let in," he continues to shout. The phone goes dead. James looks at the receiver and shakes his head. He hands the phone back to the guard.

"What should we do, Boss?" Mark asks.

"Let them in," James says, sighing. "These people are harmless."

"I hate leaving the children alone—what with all that's going on," Sam says to James as they sit on the plane, heading to Washington, DC.

"Yeah, I know. I don't like it either," he remarks. "But this couldn't be helped. It'll be brief—we're only staying over one night."

Mary walks over and puts mineral water onto the trays in front of them. "Will there be anything else?" she asks.

James looks over at Sam, who shakes her head.

"No, that'll be all, Mary," he says. "Thank you."

Sam turns to James. "I'm sorry about earlier today. I wasn't thinking of any security issues when I set up the party."

"Just be more careful, please," he says. "Mark has his hands full as it is, keeping up with everyone coming in and out of the ranch. How much did you raise?"

"Almost seventy-five thousand," she tells him.

He nods and takes a sip of his water.

"I can't believe you stuck me with visiting the shah all by myself," Sam complains. "You and I were supposed to visit him together."

"It couldn't be helped," he responds. "I've got meetings with Sester and this Prince Faikil character. I'm not going to have time to see the shah."

"What am I going to tell the shah about where you are? He's going to ask."

"Just make up any old excuse—it's no big deal. Tell him that I have to attend an important meeting. Which is the truth, by the way. This Faikil meeting is big. I've got to get a read on this guy." Then he squeezes her arm. "I've got to go now, dear—I've got to have a word with Rodney."

He gets up, walks down the aisle, and sits next to Rodney.

"What's the word at the CIA on this Faikil character?" James asks. "Were you able to find out anything?"

"Not much, James, and that's the strange part. Usually someone will leak something. But when it comes to this Faikil fella, everybody clams up. It's about the Russians and Afghanistan, that's for sure. That's become a big deal at the agency. They all feel this is an opportunity to give the Ruskies a black eye. A revenge thing for Vietnam."

"This Faikil guy must be very important in the CIA's plans," James says. "I mean, they've been willing to overlook Faikil's involvement in the church shooting."

"Yes, it's really odd," Rodney agrees. "By the way, what do you need from me at these meetings?"

"Just help me get a read on Faikil. I need another set of eyes to help me decide what's going on with him."

"James before we get started with what you came for, I need to speak to you about something else," Sester says when James and Rodney are sitting in his office.

"What's that?"

"I know that you're helping the shah and his family with the expatriation," Sester clears his throat. "My understanding is that the shah is in Virginia now. I've been told that the shah cannot stay in the country any longer. He must leave the US! It's not a request but an order. It's far better if the monarch leaves on his own free will—we don't want to resort to kicking him out of the country."

James can feel his blood boil. He takes a deep breath to calm down.

"Are you fucking serious? The shah is on his death bed. My wife is with him right now!"

Sester throws up his hands. "James don't take it out on me—I'm just the messenger. The order comes from on top." Sester looks at Rodney. "Give me a call tomorrow. We're working with the Mexican government—they've agreed to take him in, at least temporarily. We can find the shah a good place in Mexico—we'll even make arrangements for him to continue to get the medical treatments." Sester turns back to James. "Other than that, there's nothing much that I can do. The shah has to go! What did you want to speak to me about? What's the reason for this meeting?"

James sits there not saying a word. His face is tight, his lips are pursed.

"James," Sester calls out.

James shakes his head.

"I came here to get information on two individuals, Prince Aba al bin Faikil and Muhammad Mafrouz

"Why do you need information on these guys?"

"I'd rather not say."

Sester sits back in his chair and laces his fingers together.

"Well, James, if you won't tell me why, I can't help you."

James knows he's been backed into a corner. "I suspect these men were behind my wife's kidnapping."

"No, James—that can't be so," Sester says calmly. "Why would they want to kidnap your wife?"

"I don't know why, Bill. That's what I'm trying to find out," James says, raising his voice. "Are you going to help me or not?"

"Unfortunately, James, I'm not at liberty to share any information on Faikil. This is a top security matter."

"Why are you protecting these guys?" James asks, getting sterner. "They're fucking murderers. They were behind the church shooting that killed forty-three people."

"What?" Sester yells out, slamming his fists on his desk. "Why would you make such a baseless accusation?"

"It's not baseless. Two of the accomplices told me this. One of those accomplices is in jail in Texas. He told the FBI who was behind the attack."

Sester smiles at this. "James, when it comes to these matters, you're a neophyte. Many times, these men will drop names of important people just to throw you off the track. They know there'll be no way of proving that they're lying.

"Believe me, Prince Faikil had nothing to do with the church shooting," Sester continues. "As for your wife's kidnapping, it's my understanding that Palestinians were behind that. Prince Faikil hates the Palestinians just as much as we do. There's no way he'd get involved in one of their schemes."

"You seem to know a lot about this man," James observes. "Why don't you share something that I can really use?"

"I'm sorry, James. I'm not at liberty to disclose very much. Prince Faikil is working with us on some very delicate and important matters. As to his involvement with your wife's abduction, you're barking up the wrong tree. I'm absolutely certain that the prince had nothing to do with her kidnapping."

In the limo, on the way to the hotel to meet Prince Faikil, Rodney turns to James.

"As far as what you wanted, on these characters, I guess that was a complete waste of time," he says.

"Not really, Rodney. We got Sester to acknowledge that our

government is working with Faikil. And maybe even to admit that Prince Faikil was involved in Sam's kidnapping. I'll know for sure after I meet with the prince."

"Really? I didn't hear Sester say anything about that. When did he say it?"

"As I said, I'll know more after we meet the prince," James says and lays his head back in the seat.

Prince Faikil is occupying the whole top floor of the hotel. The prince's security guards frisk James and Rodney for weapons before they open the door for them. It is Prince Farsad who comes over to greet James.

Farsad has a broad smile on his face as he extends his hands. "James, it's nice to see you again. Did you pay a visit to my father?"

"No, Your Highness, I couldn't; I had to attend some urgent meetings earlier. My wife Samantha is there, paying our respects."

A tall man in a thobe comes out of the other room. Farsad turns to the man. "Prince Faikil, this is James Coppi. The fellow that I was telling you about."

"It is a pleasure to meet you, James," the prince says and gestures to the sofa. "Please, have a seat."

After they sit, Prince Faikil rubs his goatee, "I was sorry to hear about your wife's ordeal. I'm glad she got out safely. How is she doing?"

"My wife is doing fine. She is paying a visit to Farsad's father right now. Otherwise, I'm sure she would've liked to meet you."

"What these men did to your wife was most despicable!" Faikil says. "Totally uncalled for. Women and children should never be part of any disputes."

James tilts his head in acknowledgment.

"Thank you. I'm glad to hear you say that," he says.

"Both Firuz and Farsad speak very highly of you," Faikil says, looking over at Farsad. "They say that you've been a tremendous help to their family. Especially at these trying times. Farsad said that you'd like to have a word with me. What is it that you'd like to speak to me about?"

"It's very simple, really, Your Highness. All I want to know is why you want to kill me and my family."

Faikil lets out a laugh and looks over at Farsad.

Prince Farsad sits up on his seat. "James, why would you ask that?"

James doesn't look at Farsad. He's staring intently at Faikil.

"He hasn't denied it," James observes.

Prince Faikil smiles. "I categorically and unequivocally deny it. Please, answer Farsad's question. I'm curious, also! What makes you believe that I want to do you harm?"

"I've been told. Told by a man who has no reason to lie."

The prince is still smiling. "I believe that you may be referring to the man you have in jail. A fellow named Syed." The prince sits forward in his chair. "James, you are new to these types of affairs. When men try to save their own lives, they will very often drop names. Names of famous people that they know cannot ever show up to disprove their accusations. You can rest assured that I have no intentions of doing you or your family any harm." The prince then stands up. "Now, if that is all, there are a few other matters that I need to tend to."

James stands up and smiles back at the prince. "Thank you, Your Highness. It is a great relief to me to hear you say that you don't mean any harm to my family," James says. Then he looks straight into the prince's eyes. "Let me make it perfectly clear. I will find the men who are trying to destroy me and my family, and I will kill each and every one of them."

"James, are you threatening the prince?" Farsad calls out.

James smiles at Prince Farsad. "No, of course not. Prince Faikil means no harm to me and my family. Isn't that right, Prince? That is what you said, isn't it?"

Prince Faikil doesn't answer. He is staring at James.

James smiles. "We'll let ourselves out," he says. "I hope to see you again, Your Highness," he adds to Faikil.

In the limo, Rodney laugh and says. "Wow, that was intense. I thought you guys were going to come to blows."

"I wish we had," James responds. "I wish we had gotten it over with right then and there! It would've been nice to have ended it tonight. I'm worried that I may not get another chance."

"How did you know he was lying? What gave it away?"

James clears his throat. "Well, going in I was pretty much already convinced. The clincher was when he said that I was 'new to these types of affairs.' It was almost the same thing that Sester had said earlier. Faikil had been tipped off by Sester. I've got to assume, from now on, that the CIA is feeding Faikil information."

"Wow, it's a real mess."

"Yeah—a real mess," James says without looking at Rodney. "I wonder why Farsad and Faikil are so chummy?" He mutters to himself.

"What?" Rodney says.

James shakes his head and turns to Rodney. "Nothing, I was just talking to myself."

"What do you want me to do about the shah?"

"Call Sester tomorrow and find out how we can get the shah into Mexico. The US is abandoning this guy but we won't. We made a deal and we're going to stick to it! Contact the people in Egypt. At one time, they were willing to take the shah in, see if they're still willing."

Sam is being escorted down the hall to the king's room by Princess Yasmin. Outside his door, Yasmin whispers, "He may not be very alert—they are giving him morphine for the pain. I don't know how coherent he'll be. Call me if you need me."

The royal's eyes are closed when Sam walks in. There's a man sitting in an armchair on the opposite side of the room.

"I'm here to pay a visit to His Majesty," she says quietly to the man and points to the shah lying on the sofa.

The man gets up. "I'm Hassan Nassiri, his security chief. I'll leave you two alone."

"Is he asleep? Did I come at a bad time?" she whispers.

The shah begins to stir. "Are you the beautiful angel that's going to take me to the other side?"

She presses her hand to her heart and turns to the shah.

"No, Your Highness. It's just me—Samantha Coppi."

The monarch opens his eyes and smiles.

"Yes, I know, dear. Come closer. Let me get a good look at you." When she gets closer, the shah's smile widens. "More beautiful than any angel. Where is your husband?"

"He's sorry he couldn't be here. James had to attend some very important meetings in Washington, DC."

"So I have you all to myself," he says with a laugh, then starts coughing. After he recovers, he says, "Come, pull up a chair. Sit with me for a while."

"I'll be right outside if you need me, Your Highness," Nassiri says.

Sam takes a chair, pulls it alongside the shah's couch, and sits. He reaches out to her and takes her hand. His hand is ice cold.

"Thank you for coming," he says.

Yasmin walks in. "Father would you like me to adjust your pillow?"

"No, I'm fine," he responds.

"All right. Have Samantha come find me if you need anything," she says, and goes back out.

"She is such a beautiful daughter-in-law," the shah comments. "Attends to my every need. More attentive than any of my children." He coughs again.

"Speaking of your children," Sam asks, "where is Prince Firuz?"

The shah waves his hand dismissively and raises himself up from the couch, his face turning red with the effort. "He's back in our country, chasing a fool's paradise." Suddenly, the sovereign starts coughing violently. The shah turns to Sam as if to say something, but he can't speak.

"Can I do something for you, Your Highness?" Sam asks, slightly panicked.

The monarch clutches his throat and points at the door.

"Would you like me to get Yasmin?" Sam asks.

The shah nods up and down, his face is beet red. Sam rushes out of the room and runs into the nurse in the hall.

"Please, His Majesty needs help!" Sam says.

The nurse runs into the room, and Sam follows her. Immediately, the nurse sits him up and pats his back. The shah is still coughing, but he appears to be getting air again. Yasmin comes hurrying in.

"I'm sorry, Samantha, but you'll have to cut your visit short. We're going to give him morphine, and he won't be in any condition to speak to you."

"Oh, that's too bad. Is there anything that I can do?"

"No, we'll be fine," Yasmin says, smiling at her as she plumps the king's pillows. "Thank you for coming."

Sam reaches out and touches Yasmin's arm. "Are you sure? I don't mind. Really!"

"No, thank you. We'll be fine."

Sam looks at the shah. His eyes are closed, and he is pale, but the coughing has stopped. "I feel so badly—I was here only a short time. Please say goodbye to him for me."

"Yes, of course, my dear. Come, let me walk you to the door."

After Sam boards the plane, she walks down the aisle and sits next to James, who is already on board.

"How is the shah?" he asks.

"He's in pretty bad shape," she tells him. "He's heavily medicated on morphine. They don't believe he'll last much longer. We may have to come right back out for the funeral."

"No we won't?"

Sam looks over at him. "What do you mean?"

"I mean we won't. The shah is getting booted out of the US."

Sam sits up in her seat. "Who's booting him out? Do they know how sick he is?"

James shrugs. "They know but they don't give a shit!"

"How can they do this?" Sam's voice gets louder. "And why are you taking this so lightly? Don't you care?"

James sits up. "Of course, I care! I'm probably the only one that cares anything about that man! But there's really not much that I can do about it, can I? The politicians are in control. All I can do is find him a place that he can die in peace." James touches her arm gently. "Sam, believe me if there was anything that I could do for that man, I would. That family has been very good to us through the years. His son Prince Firuz is not only a client of ours, I consider him also a friend."

"What about the rest of your meetings? Did you get a reading on this character Faikil?"

"Yeah—he's definitely behind everything. There's no doubt. And we have another problem."

"Another problem? How many more can we handle? What is it?"

"Our government is supporting this guy. They need him in the fight against the Russians. He's basically untouchable, right now."

"Untouchable?" Sam asks in disbelief, getting louder. "What does that mean? Do we have to leave this guy alone?"

"No, he's untouchable by the US government because they need him in this Afghanistan fight, they'll overlook everything that he has done. The forty-three killings, your kidnapping—everything. But he's not untouchable by me. I'm going to kill that son of a bitch, first chance I get.

"What it *does* mean is that I won't get any help from the CIA in my fight against this man. I'm on my own. In fact, if they find out I'm out to get the prince, they'll probably try to stop me."

James turns to her and lowers his voice. "Sam, we have to play this very, very carefully. The CIA may already be watching me. I've got Mark Malone checking to see if any of our phones are bugged. From now on, no more talking about this on the phone. Be very, very careful not to mention any of our plans to anyone. We don't know who we can trust."

"OK, James. I understand."

James sees the worried look on her face. He pulls her close and gives her a hug. "It's you and me, dear," he smiles, "and that's more than enough to beat that one creep."

22

I'm Bugged!

"WHAT THE HELL DO YOU mean, all the phones are bugged?" James shouts when he's in his office the next day.

"I'm sorry to tell you, James, but they are," Mark answers.

James looks at the other men sitting in his office. "And none of you fucking guys knew anything about this? How the fuck did these men get into the office without anybody knowing? We're supposed to be the experts on security—and right under our noses, some people just walk in and tap our phones."

"James, telephone service people come in and out all the time," Charlie says. "No one suspects them."

"What about the ranch?" James asks Mark. "Is the ranch bugged, too?"

"Yeah, I'm afraid so," he answers.

James throws up his hands.

"Great—just fucking great!" James yells, standing up. "Get all our technical people working on this ASAP and get rid of all these bugs. While you're at it, take care of the ranch, too. And contact all of our other offices around the world—have them check for surveillance devices. I'm willing to bet their phones were also tapped."

"James, do you really want to remove the devices?" Rodney asks. "Now that we know that they're in, we can circumvent the system. If we take the taps out, they'll just come back and put in new ones."

"No, they won't, Rodney— because we're not going to let them," James says, looking at Mark. "Set up procedures that will allow no one to get to our phones. No more loosey-goosey bullshit. Every week, I want someone checking every inch of this place for wires. You got that? I'll see you guys in a little while." James heads for the door leading out of his office.

"Where are you going?" Charlie calls to him.

James turns around. "I need to make a call. Thanks to you guys, I've got to scour Colorado Springs to find a phone that isn't bugged." He shakes his head. "What a way to live."

James drives to a nearby motel and rents a room. He makes a credit card call to Ian Wadsworth in London.

"Listen carefully, Ian. Leave your office and get to a phone that is far from both your office and home. Don't ask any questions. Call me back when you get to a phone." He gives Ian the number of the motel.

"What's up, James?" Ian asks when he makes the call about thirty minutes later. "Why the cloak and dagger?"

"Where are you calling from?"

"I'm at my uncle's house."

"Good! The phones in my office are bugged. Your office may also be wired, and I couldn't take that chance. Ian, I need you to go to Monaco. Find a pimp who deals only with blondes. Very high-end."

"Why, James? Are you looking for some action?" Ian asks, laughing.

"Very funny, Ian. Go find this pimp. The pimp we're looking for deals mostly for Arab royalty. I'm especially interested in the man who provides women for a prince who goes back and forth to Afghanistan. He shouldn't be too hard to find."

"OK, James; will do. What do you want me to do when I find this chap?"

"Nothing. Just give me a call when you find him. I'll come and pay him a visit. Ian, it's the pimp that supplies blonde broads to this particular prince—you got that? That's the man I'm after."

"Yes, James, I got it. Do you have anything else?"

"Yeah, Ian, one last thing—don't use the phones at your office or at your house until they've been checked out."

When James goes back to his office, he finds his assistant at her desk.

"Kathy, where's Malone?" James asks her. "Is he still in the building? If he is, have him come see me right away."

"I'll find out," she replies and gets up from her desk.

A few minutes later, Kathy knocks and peeks into the room. "Malone is on his way, James. By the way, Vernon Dixon would also like a few minutes of your time."

"All right—as soon as I'm finished with Malone."

Mark knocks at his door. "You wanted to see me?"

"Yeah, I do. Come on in and close the door." When Mark is seated, James begins. "Can someone else take care of removing the wires? I need you for another assignment."

"Yeah, of course. Both Charlie McGill and Frank Gurney should be able to handle the problem. What about the security detail at your ranch? Don't you need me to stay on top of that?"

"No. We'll be all right for the time being. Nothing is going to happen until October at the earliest."

"What do you need from me?" Mark asks.

"Mark, I need you to get to Bombay right away. Leave tomorrow. Check the Bombay office for wires. It's very important. Don't call Omprakash and let him know that you're coming. Have Omprakash call me after you're absolutely certain the place is clean. After Bombay, you'll need to go to Karachi and do the same thing at our complex over there."

"I didn't know we had an office in Karachi!"

"No one else knows about that particular office, either—so keep it to yourself. Omprakash will give you all the details about Karachi when you get to Bombay. OK—you better get going. Tell Charlie that you're leaving for a few days on an assignment for me. Don't tell him where you're going." As Mark is about to leave, James yells to him, "No phone calls from you unless you're absolutely certain that it's secure!"

"Sure, James. I got it."

James buzzes Kathy after Mark leaves. "Kathy, I'm ready for Vernon."

After Vernon takes a seat across from James, he says, "I'm sorry to bother you, James. I just want to find out where we stand with the railroad. Are we still buying?"

"Yes, of course. Unfortunately, I've been sidetracked with some other problems. I'll tell you what—let's get started. How fast can we start on the financing?"

"I'll have to make a few calls, but we may be able to get going next week. Keep in mind, James, that finalizing the deal will take at least a month. Can you spare that much time?"

"Yeah—this is a good time. Let's get it resolved."

"How was your day, dear?" Sam asks when he gets home that night.

"You don't want to know," James replies, heading for the bedroom. "Where are the children?"

"They're out on the patio. We just finished dinner. You didn't call—otherwise, we would've waited for you. Are you hungry? We put your dinner aside."

"I'm not hungry yet. I want to spend some time with the kids. By the way—be careful what you say on the phone the next couple of days. They're bugged."

She walks over to him when they get to the bedroom. "What do you mean?"

"I mean that they're bugged. Your conversations are being listened to." He heads for the bathroom.

She calls out to him. "Who? Who's listening?"

"My guess? It's the CIA," James says.

She walks into the bathroom behind him. "Why would they want to listen to our telephone conversations?"

James smiles at her and points to his crotch. "Can I have a little privacy, please? I need to use the bathroom. I'll explain it all when I come out."

Sam is sitting on the bed when he comes out. Her arms are crossed over her chest. "Well?"

James sits on the bed next to her. "It's all concerning this Prince Faikil character that I went to see in Washington. The US needs him in the fight against the Russians in Afghanistan. We're in the middle. The government wants to know what we're up to. They're protecting this guy."

"What are we going to do?"

"Well, for starters, I'm having someone come over tomorrow to remove all the listening devices," James replies. Then he gives her a serious look. "Sam, I don't want to frighten you, but you need to know this: we've got to eliminate this guy Faikil. He means to do us real harm. We've got to get to him before he gets to us. If the CIA gets in the way, it's just too damn bad. They have their priorities, and we have ours. I've got plans in the works. If the CIA finds out about my plans to get rid of this guy, they'll try to screw them up."

"Why can't the CIA speak to this man?" she asks. "Have him back off. Leave us alone."

"Because this man is a manipulative liar. He's playing the CIA. Faikil is using our government in his fight against the Russians. As soon as he's finished with the Russians, he'll turn on the US, too. His goal is to have all governments that are not Muslim out of the Middle East. The CIA hasn't figured that out yet. Or maybe they have, and they believe that they have this guy under control—that they can handle him. In any event, regardless of what the CIA is thinking, we've got to look out for ourselves. Control our own situation."

"So what are you going to do?"

"The only thing that can be done. Kill Faikil—and also get rid of Mafrouz. I'm guessing the CIA hasn't figured out my plans yet. That's why they're keeping a close eye on me."

"This sounds very dangerous, James. Isn't there another way?"

James turns her to him. "Sam, we've already had this discussion. Yes, it is dangerous. But not as dangerous as doing nothing at all. This man Faikil wants to harm us. He'll keep sending men over here to do just that. The first wave will come in October—or maybe November.

"I've got that scheme under control," he continues. "I'm going to make sure that there's not going to be a second wave—I'm going to get to these guys before that can happen. I've already set the wheels in motion." James gives her a kiss and a hug, rubbing her back gently. "The family will be safe. I promise you. It'll all work out." He stands up. "Come on, I'd like to spend some time with the children."

Three days later, James gets a call at the ranch.

"Can we talk?" Ian asks. "Have the phones been fixed?"

"Yeah, we're good. What do you have?"

"Louis Finche," Ian says. "He's your man. He's the pimp that secures women for the prince."

"Are you sure? How do you know he's the one?"

"It's him, all right! I spoke to Finche myself. He told me that he set up a tryst a few weeks back for a prince who just came back from Afghanistan. Two blondes. Pays top dollar for the women. Who else could it be? It has to be the same prince. This fellow Finche says the prince comes to Monaco three or four times a year. Always demands blondes with blue or green eyes."

"All right, I'll fly over there tomorrow. Set up a meeting with this Finche character for tomorrow night."

"OK, will do. I'll see you tomorrow."

The next day, in Monaco, Ian meets James as he comes out of the airport with his bodyguard Max. They hop into a taxi.

"What, no suitcases?" Ian asks.

"It's in and out. I'm not staying overnight," James says and rolls down his window to let in the ocean breeze. On one side of the car there are Mediterranean style houses with their red tiled roofs. The yards of the homes are full of fan palms that proliferate the hills. On the other side, the waves from the clear blue waters of the Mediterranean are gently lapping onto the sandy beach. He's never been to Monaco. Hard to believe he's never been here.

James turns to Ian. "Where are we meeting this guy?"

"A bistro right outside of Monaco called Chez Joey," Ian answers.

"It's quiet; we won't be disturbed. We should be there in a few minutes. Can you bring me up to speed? What do we want with this bloke?"

"I need him to work with us on an assignment. You'll get the gist of it when I speak to Finche."

The taxi pulls up in front of the bistro. "Wait for us," he tells the cabbie. "The meeting shouldn't take long."

When they are inside the bistro, James asks Ian, "Where is he?"

Ian looks around and sees a man sitting alone at a table in the back. "There he is! That skinny fellow with the handlebar moustache." Ian says.

Finche stands up when he sees the three men coming over.

"Louis, this is my boss, James Coppi," Ian says in English "He's the one who called for this meeting."

"It is a pleasure to meet you, Monsieur Coppi," Finche says. "Please, join me." Finche makes a sweeping gesture toward the chairs. "May I offer you a drink?"

"No, we're fine," James replies.

"How may I be of help to you?" Finche asks James. "Your man, over here, says that you have a financial matter to discuss with me."

"Ian tells me that you set up liaisons between Arab royalty and some Western ladies?"

Finche smiles slyly and lights a cigarette with a slim, gold lighter. "Possibly! What is your interest in these affairs?"

"I know that you handle hundreds of Middle Eastern princes, but I'm only interested in one Arab royal in particular—a prince that spends time in Afghanistan. Are you the one who sets up his affairs?"

Finche exhales, sits back, and smiles. "Once again, I must ask you—what is your interest in such a matter?"

"The next time this particular prince is in town for such a liaison, I need to know. I'm willing to pay for that information. Say—ten times what the prince will be paying for the evening. You won't even have to share any of the proceeds with your ladies. I'll pay you half of it up front, right now!"

"I'm sorry, Monsieur Coppi, but I must respectfully turn you down. My reputation is of utmost importance in my type of business. My clients must trust me to be *très discret.*"

James leans forward and smiles. "Finche, perhaps you misunderstood me. I'm not asking you—I'm telling you. If you don't work with me, I will make sure that you never do business again. You are in no position to take me on. I can just as easily bribe the authorities to put you away. My company looked into your background Finche—you do more for these Afghans than supply them women. You seem to have a fancy for their poppy." James smiles shrewdly. "And I don't mean the flower." He sits back in his seat. "Or I could just as easily use my money to have something very bad happen to you. I don't believe that the police will spend too much time investigating the disappearance of a pimp and drug dealer. Now—do we have a deal?"

Finche stamps out his cigarette. "What do you need?"

"As I said, I need you to call me the next time this prince is in town. That's all—just a phone call." James smiles. "That shouldn't be too difficult."

Finche looks at the two men. "Just a phone call? Nothing else? My name won't be disclosed?"

"Just the call," James assures him. "Nothing else. No one will know of your involvement."

Finche pauses for a moment and finally lets out a deep breath. "All right—it's a deal."

"Good." James turns to Ian. "Go to the bank tomorrow and get Mr. Finche's retainer." James turns back to Finche. "How do you know that this prince has been in Afghanistan? I'm quite sure that he wouldn't have volunteered that information to you."

"To me, no! But, to my ladies, he's quite conversational. Loves to tell the women how he is taking on the Russians."

"OK, Finche," James says and stands up. "You contact Ian the moment you know that the prince will be in town." Then James glares hard at Finche. "You make that call, Finche. Don't even think of trying to double-cross me."

Outside of the bistro, James gets into the back seat of the cab with Ian.

"James, I don't get it," Ian says. "Why do you want to know when this prince is in town? What are you going to do with that information? Are you planning on getting to him here in Monaco? Because that probably won't work. I'm sure the Prince comes with a full security detail."

"Ian, I have to get to this guy. If I don't, he'll get to me. Originally, I was going to take him out in Pakistan. There's another character that I need to eliminate. I was hoping to get them both at the same time. But I'm worried that plan may take too long. I've decided not to wait—I will take out anybody that I can get my hands on as soon as possible."

"James, you're not thinking straight. Let's say you do manage to kill him, which is difficult enough. What about the police? How will you get away with the murder?"

"The plan is still taking shape in my mind. The first step is to get this guy to a neutral territory. I don't believe he'll have as big a security detail as you might expect. Maybe two men. Once I know where he'll be, I'll figure out the rest. Remember—his security guards will have guns. Who will know who shot first? Dead people can't talk.

"The living will be the ones to tell the story of what happened," James continues. "You know—some kind of a tale of chivalry, such as how an Arab prince insulted a beautiful blonde. How maybe a gentleman didn't take kindly to the insult and demanded an apology. The words between the men may have gotten a little heated, and suddenly gunshots rang out.

"Or maybe there was an argument over a gambling debt. Someone accused a person of cheating at the tables. Disputes of that nature have happened thousands of times in Monte Carlo. I'd be willing to bet that the Principality of Monaco would want to put a quick ending to the matter. Dismiss it as soon as possible. Are you understanding where I'm coming from?"

"Yeah, I'm beginning to get the picture," Ian replies.

The cab pulls up to the airport. As James is getting out, he turns back to Ian and smiles. "Take good care of Monsieur Finche; we'll need him. Get him his money first thing tomorrow morning."

23

October, the First Wave

SAM IS RIDING IN THE back of her limo on the way to the office. She is needed to sign the closing documents regarding the purchase of Greenwald's railroad, a transaction that James has been working on for the past month.

Sam has not seen James in over three weeks. He has been traveling around the country doing a dog and pony show, trying to line up institutions that will put up the money for them to do the deal. Aside from the kidnapping, this is the longest James has been away from her since he went to Vietnam. She really misses him.

Her dream after that first time that she met him was to marry that young man after he returned from the war. Live in a modest home on a quiet cul-de-sac here in Colorado Springs. Raise a family of four children and live happily ever after. A modest, quiet, and unassuming life.

That young man, however, had other plans. His dream was to build her a castle. And James not only constructed that castle, but also built her an entire kingdom. Thousands of acres of land in Colorado. A château in France. Accrued more wealth than she could have ever needed or even imagined. And, today, he is going to buy her a railroad. Not just any railroad, but the largest railroad in the entire Southwest.

"We're here, Mrs. Coppi!"

Sam notices that the limo has stopped, and Regis, her bodyguard, is holding the back door open.

"We're here," Regis says again. "Is everything all right?"

Sam gets out of the car and smiles at him. "Yes, Regis, everything is fine. I was just daydreaming. Thank you." She looks out at the office building, smooths her dress, and walks in.

Sam decides to go to James's office first. She knocks and lets herself in. The office is empty. She leaves the office and is walking down the hallway when she bumps into Vernon. A broad smile appears on Vernon's face when he sees her.

"Samantha, it is so nice to see you again!" he says.

"It's a pleasure to see you, too, Vernon. Do you know where I can find James?"

"James is in Jack's office, our head of finance. They're meeting with some investment bankers."

"Oh, I see. What is expected of me today? No one gave me the agenda and my secretary Helen isn't around."

"I'll have Jessica come to your office. She'll explain everything to you. I'll have her come by right away."

"By the way, Vernon, when is James's traveling going to come to an end?" Sam asks as they walk toward her office. "I haven't seen him in nearly a month. Isn't that the reason we hired you? To ease James's workload?"

"You know, Samantha, I haven't been home in nearly a month, either," Vernon tells her. "I was with James the entire time he was gone."

"I don't understand. Why were both of you needed? Couldn't you have handled the dog and pony show yourself?"

"It's not a matter of handling, Samantha. These institutions are investing a lot of money with your company. Hundreds of millions. Before they hand over that money, the parties want to meet and speak with the man who is ultimately in charge—and that is James."

Vernon holds the door to her office open for her and smiles. "It couldn't be avoided; there was no other way. It will soon come to an end, I promise you. You'll have James home again soon enough."

"I've heard that before," she says wryly, and walks into her office.

"I'll get Jessica for you," he says.

A few minutes later, Jessica knocks at Sam's door. "You wanted to see me?" she asks.

"Come in," Sam replies. She motions to a chair. "Fill me in. What's expected of me today? My secretary, Helen, is missing."

Jessica takes a seat. "Other than the press briefing scheduled for four this afternoon, I don't know much about your schedule," she says. "Helen is in the conference room helping Kathy get the documents ready for the closing later today. Kathy has been working every night past midnight, and also on weekends. Every staff assistant has been trying to help her. James won't deal with anyone except Kathy." Jessica stands up. "Come on, we'll go to the conference room and get your schedule."

When the women walk into the conference room, they see rows of files on the table. Kathy is sitting at one end of the table with two folders in front of her. Helen and another office assistant are at the other end.

"We thought you might need some help," Jessica tells Kathy.

Kathy moves a strand of her dirty blonde hair away from her face. "Thank you, but we've got everything under control."

"Would you mind giving Sam an update and her schedule for today? What time is the signing?"

Kathy looks at Sam once again. "Sure," Kathy says, standing and fixing her blouse. "The signing is scheduled for two this afternoon. That is, if we ever get the last changes from the law firm in Boston. That crappy fax machine we have is so slow. Every page takes forever to come in." Kathy looks at the women at the other end of the table. "Helen, what happened to the latest amendments? Where are the faxes?"

"Margaret went to get them," Helen answers.

"That was over half an hour ago. Go and look for Margaret. See if you can speed things up." Kathy turns back to Sam. "Where do you want to start?"

Sam points to the files on the table. "Why don't we start with the files? What are all these papers?"

"The small row of files on the left are the documents needed to set up the new holding and management company. That's the company that is going to acquire the railroad. You and James are the only stockholders of that company, and there's not much to those papers. Pretty simple." Kathy points to the next row. "These documents refer to a new union agreement with the railroad workers."

"A new agreement? What's that all about?" Sam asks.

"James negotiated additional concessions from the union. James asked for and got additional labor reductions. The manpower will be reduced by twenty percent over the next five years, primarily due to normal attrition and retirement of the union members. The new union agreement goes into effect as soon as the deal is signed this afternoon."

Kathy gestures to another row of documents. "These documents refer to the buyout of the railroad. When all this is done, the holding company, which is owned by you and James, will own eighty percent, and Henry Greenwald will own twenty percent."

"Henry is going to be an owner?" Sam asks. "Why is that? I thought Henry wanted to retire."

"I don't know the reason," Kathy replies. "You'll have to ask James. All I know are the terms of the buyout."

Sam points to the final set on the table. "What is this long row of documents?"

"Those are the subordinated debentures. The bonds that will be issued to raise the money to pay off the existing stockholders."

"All these documents are for the bonds?" Sam asks. "How complicated is this deal?'

Kathy lets out a laugh. "I don't know. I've been so busy making sure that all the documents are accounted for, I never analyzed what the contract actually said. These are the documents that had me working past midnight. The papers deal with transfer agents, fiduciaries, escrows, defaults, interest rates, and redemptions. I could go on and on. I hope someone knows what's in the agreement—because I sure don't."

At that moment, Helen walks back into the room. "I've got the faxes with the final changes," she says.

"Good," Kathy says. "I hope there are no more. That should do it." Kathy turns to Sam. "That's all I have; you're completely caught up now. If you have any more questions, you'll have to ask James."

"Thank you," Sam says and heads out of the room with Jessica. When she gets to the door, she turns around. "Thank you, Kathy," she adds. "You did a good job. I know you've been working really hard on this project. Thanks for all of your help."

Kathy smiles. "You're welcome."

Outside the room, Sam starts walking down the hallway. Jessica calls out to Sam. "Where are you going?"

"I'm going to James's office to see if he's in."

When Sam gets to his office, the door is open, so she walks in. James has his back to her. There are at least a dozen men standing up in the office. She hears laughter. Most of the men are smoking cigars. Sam looks around and recalls the day when James first opened the business. Only three people were there: James, herself, and Kathy. *Oh, how things have gotten so complicated!* she thinks.

"There's a rumor that my husband may be around," she calls out. "Or is that just office gossip."

James turns toward her. There is a broad smile on his face. "Sam!" he calls out and comes over to give her a hug. "You have no idea on how great it is to see you!" James whispers in her ear, "I've missed you so much."

"I've missed you, too," she whispers in return, then steps back to survey the room again.

"Henry!" Sam yells when she notices one of the men. She walks over and gives the old gentleman a hug and a kiss on the cheek. "I hear we're going to be partners."

"Yes. I hope you can tolerate me."

She laughs.

"Don't be silly; it will be wonderful."

"Let me introduce you to the rest of the people," James says to her.

James takes her around the room and introduces her to more than a dozen men—Wall Street brokers and investment bankers from New York, Boston, and other parts of the country. Lawyers from at least four law firms. Transfer agents and union representatives. When James has finished, he looks at the men.

"Gentlemen, would you mind continuing your discussions in one of the conference rooms." he asks. "I'd like to speak to my wife for a few minutes."

After the men leave, James gives Sam a hug and a kiss. "I'm sorry that I've been away for so long. I needed to get everything finished before October. How've you been? How are the children?"

"As I told you this morning, everyone is fine. How are you? You must be happy—you're finally getting a railroad. Isn't this what you always wanted? Ever since you were a little boy?"

James laughs. "Yes, I guess you're right. I'm getting a railroad." He goes behind his desk. "Come, have a seat." James gestures to a chair. "We have a few minutes; let's talk a bit."

When she sits, he asks her, "What do you think of the deal now? Last time we spoke, you seemed concerned."

"'Concerned' is putting it mildly," she replies. "I'm scared stiff. This is one monster of a deal. What about you? Any anxiety?"

"I'm a little frightened, too," he replies.

"You are? You know, James, it's still not too late to back out. If you believe that for any reason the venture might fail, we shouldn't do the deal. This is a lot of money."

James smiles at her. "Sam, I'm not worried about the money. The deal is a good one. I've done my homework. The railroad is going to make a whole lot of money."

"Well, what's worrying you?"

"The *size* of this deal, Sam. Can you believe I'm buying Greenwald's company? The man who gave me my first break?

"I'm still on a cloud," he continues. "I'm expecting that at any moment I'll wake up, and we'll be at our small house on a cul-de-sac.

You remember? The house that you showed me before we got married?"

She laughs, remembering.

"You didn't realize back then that you married a freaking lunatic. 'No modest little home for us,' I said. 'We're getting a ranch.'

"But it didn't stop there, did it, Sam? We got that ranch, but I wasn't satisfied. I just kept going and going. Now we're about to buy a railroad. And not just any railroad—one of the biggest rail systems in the world, stretching from Texas to California. Jessica tells me that after the purchase, we'll be considered one of the richest families in Colorado—if not the whole United States."

He pauses.

"That's what's scaring me, Sam. I don't know how I got here. Nor do I know what impact this wealth will have on you and me. What impact this new fortune will have on our children? Eleven years have passed, and I'm right back where I started—my life is spinning out of control."

"You don't have to do this, you know," she says. "We're doing fine without the railroad."

"Yeah, that's true, but you know me—I can't stop. We're going to do the deal. It's another mountain, and I can't resist a good climb." James stands up. "Come on, let's go sign the papers and buy us a railroad."

A week later, Sam knocks at James's study door and looks in. "James, your mother is here," she tells him.

James looks up. "Already? She got back from the airport quick." He stands up and walks through the open doorway and into the foyer.

"*Mamma, come sta?*" He gives his mother a hug and a kiss. "When did you get home? I didn't see the limo bring you to your house."

"About two hours ago," she answers.

"How do you feel?" James asks and gestures toward the sofa in the living room. "Come, sit down. Tell me all about Italy." After the three of them sit, he asks, "Where's Pop?"

"He's out in the back, yelling at the men," she says.

"Yelling at the men?" James laughs. "Why? Pop just got home—he's already fighting with my ranch hands?"

"Hanno lasciato caderi a pezzi il giardino."

"That's not true, Mom. The men didn't let the garden fall apart. I kept an eye on Pop's garden myself. It's being well maintained. We're getting nice produce."

Mamma waves her hand dismissively. "You know your papa—no one can do the job right but him."

"Forget about the garden," James says. "Tell me about Italy. How did you like being back in the old country? It's been years since you were back. How did Dad like working on his farm?"

"Your father was in heaven," she replies. "He loved being back in *Italia*. Worked on his land every day. I've never seen him work so hard."

"How about you, Mom? How did *you* like being back in Italy?"

Mamma shrugs. "Yeah, it was all right. I missed the grandchildren." She looks over at Sam accusingly. "You didn't bring the family to visit us in Italy, as you promised."

"How could we visit, Mom?" James asks, raising his voice. "You know what happened to Sam. She was *kidnapped*. It's been a very scary time for her—for us."

"Yes, I know. I'm sorry." Mamma looks over at Sam again. "How do you feel?"

"I'm fine now, Mamma," Sam answers.

Mamma stands up. "I've got to get back to your father." She looks at James. "You'll come for dinner on Sunday—I have gifts for the children."

"Yes, Mamma, we will come," he says, and they walk her to the door.

"Giacomo, who are all these men around here?" Mamma asks, stopping at the door. "They say I can't leave the ranch by myself. I need a guard to come with me if I want to leave. Why?"

"Because, Mamma, there are some really bad men who want to hurt me and my family. These men are here at the ranch to protect you. You listen to what they have to say, please."

His mother waves her hand up in the air. "Me? Who wants to bother with an old woman like me? You're making such a fuss for nothing."

James gives her another kiss. "Nevertheless, you listen to these men. Don't go off on your own. You hear?"

"Giacomo, I don't like having these people with me. Your sister Tina is coming tomorrow to take me shopping. They say we can't go by ourselves. Someone has to come with us."

James gives her a look. "Mom, don't you give me a tough time, too. You listen to what they tell you. I've got enough to worry about."

Mamma looks at Sam. "You agree with him?"

Sam gives her a hug and kiss. "Yes, Mamma, I do. Let's all be nice and play along with James. Your boy is worried about us. He wants to make sure no one gets hurt."

"OK, I'll be nice," she says as if talking to herself as she heads out. "But I no like."

Sam looks at him and smiles after his mother leaves. "It's getting to be quite a mess."

"Yes, it is. My parents couldn't have picked a worse time to come back," he says as he heads back to the study. "Listen, Sam—I need your help. You're going to have to coordinate everything around the ranch this month—I'm going to be very busy. This fellow Faakhir is due to come to the US at any time."

"James, you're asking for a lot," she argues as she walks alongside him. "I don't know if I can keep up with the comings and goings of everyone."

James pulls her to him. "I know, dear," he says, and rubs her back. "I know it's a lot to ask. Malone is at the guest house, have him help you.

"This situation can't be avoided," he continues. "These men who are coming to America are killers. Seasoned fighters. I've got to stay focused on them. Tomorrow, I'm going to the office to have a meeting with McGill. I've got to get moving. Time has run out."

"Sir, Mr. Vladivastan is on the phone," Billingsley says as he enters the living room.

"I'll take it in the study," James tells him.

"What's up, Omprakash?" James asks when he's on the phone. "Any news from Peshawar?"

"We're making progress," Omprakash responds. "The inspector general who's working with us was able to turn one of the Afghans working inside the compound. We now have someone on the inside working for us."

"How did he do that? Can the Afghan be trusted? You can't tell which side these Afghans are on, in that part of the world—they're always switching sides."

"Yes, absolutely, the Afghan will work with us. He was caught stealing—a very serious crime in this part of the world. Our inspector general has agreed to look the other way just so long as the thief provides information on what's going on in the compound. The source will work with us—I'm sure of it."

"Well, I hope this police chief gets this information soon. I'm paying a lot of money to have a team ready for action in Karachi. They need more to do than just pull on their peckers."

"I'm confident, James—now that we have someone on the inside, something should happen soon."

———————

Max opens the door of the limo for James when he arrives at the office later that morning. James steps out of the limo and they walk into the lobby. He looks over at two men sitting in the lounge.

"Good morning, Mr. Coppi." The receptionist stops typing and greets him from behind a massive counter.

"Good morning, Mattie," he responds and heads for the elevator. Max presses the button and the door slides open. James looks back at the two men in the lounge.

"Hold the doors," he says to Max and heads back to the desk.

James leans over the counter and whispers, "Mattie, who are those men waiting for?"

"Mr. Davis," she replies.

"How long have they been waiting?"

Mattie checks the sign-in log. "Eighteen minutes."

James looks at the papers on her desk. "What are you doing? What's with all the papers."

"I'm typing charts of the budget that Helen brought down."

"Since when have you been typing? You're the receptionist, not a secretary or a typist."

Mattie gives him a smile. "About two weeks, now. They give me some of their work when the other secretaries get too busy."

"Give me the papers," he says. "I'll give them to someone else—I don't want you typing. That's not your job."

"I don't mind, really," she says. "It's no bother at all."

"Give me the papers," he tells her, holding out his hand. "I don't want typing interfering with your job."

"It's not interfering," Mattie protests. "I can do both."

"Really!" James asks, getting sterner. "What about those men? They've been waiting for nearly twenty minutes. When were you going to call Davis to remind him that the men are still waiting? Give me the papers." James motions again.

Mattie gathers up the papers, puts them in a file, and hands it to him. "I really don't mind," she says abashedly.

James takes the file. "Forget the typing, call Davis and tell him to get his ass down here and greet the gentlemen who are waiting for him."

James walks to the elevator, where Max is still holding the doors.

"It's going to be one of those days, Boss?" Max asks as the doors close.

James smiles. "Oh yeah, Max. You better put in ear plugs."

James passes the cafeteria and looks inside. Three ladies are standing in the middle of the room, chatting and sipping cups of coffee.

James turns to Max. "Do me a favor. Go to my office and have Kathy come here." Then James walks to the open doorway of the cafeteria and calls out to one of the women.

"Helen, may I interrupt for a moment?" he asks.

"Of course, Mr. Coppi," Helen says and walks over to him. The other women move to leave the room, but he is blocking their path.

"Don't leave yet," James says to the women. "I'd like to speak to you, too." James turns back to Helen and shows her the file. "Why did you give Mattie this work?"

"We were busy, and Mattie was free," she replies nervously.

"Busy—really?" he looks pointedly at the coffee in her hands and then at the other women. "Not so busy that you can't stop to have a cup of coffee and a nice chat." James looks up at the clock on the wall. "At a quarter past nine," he adds.

Kathy comes to the doorway. "You wanted to see me, James?"

"Yeah, I did. Since when is the receptionist doing the typing?" he asks with a scowl. "Who came up with that bright idea?"

Kathy shrugs. "Well, it wasn't me! I didn't know that Mattie was doing the typing."

James turns back to Helen. "Whose big idea was it?"

"It was Gertrude's," she replies. "Gertrude felt that the receptionist had time and could fill in when we got busy."

James turns to Kathy. "Who is Gertrude?"

"Vernon Dixon's secretary," she replies.

Another lady comes to the doorway and tries to squeeze past him. "What do you want?" James barks at her.

"I need to get coffee for the men at the staff meeting in the conference room," the woman answers meekly.

"You're McGill's secretary, right?"

"Yes," she responds feebly.

"Tell McGill and those other fat asses that they can get their own coffee," he shouts. "Getting coffee is not in your job description."

The lady turns to walk away. "Wait!" he calls after her. James reaches into the file folder and pulls out a few papers. "Type these for Helen—since you've obviously got nothing better to do."

James looks at the other women and then hands them the remaining contents of the folder. "You ladies take the rest," James says. Then he turns back to Helen. "Go downstairs and take that typewriter away from the receptionist. Mattie won't be doing any more typing; that's not her job."

After Helen leaves, he looks at Kathy who is giving him a wry look. "What?" he snaps.

She shakes her head and laughs. "Nothing!"

"In that case, stop standing around doing nothing and get me a cup of coffee," he says and starts walking toward his office.

"I thought you said that wasn't in my job description," Kathy calls after him.

James turns around. "When did I say that?"

"Just now," Kathy says. "You said it to McGill's secretary."

James gives her a crafty look. "Well, that's right. It *isn't* in her job description. But it *is* in yours. Now get my coffee," he says.

After he has turned his back again, Kathy wrinkles up her nose and sticks out her tongue at him.

"I saw that," he says.

McGill's secretary returns to the conference room. "I'm sorry, Mr. McGill, but I couldn't get the coffee," she tells her boss. McGill looks perplexed.

"Why not?" he asks.

"Mr. Coppi said that you men should get off your fat asses and get your own coffee. Mr. Coppi also said that getting coffee is not in my job description. Then he gave me a bunch of charts to type, since, apparently, I wasn't busy."

"It's going to be one of those days," Charlie says to the others at the meeting after his secretary leaves. "James is on the warpath."

"I guess I better go and find out what's bothering James," Vernon says, standing up. He walks to James's office, knocks, and looks in. "James, may I have a word with you?"

"Sure, Vernon. Come in," James says and points to a chair. "Have a seat."

Kathy walks in with James's coffee and puts it on the desk in front of him. Kathy looks at Vernon. "Would you like a cup?"

"I don't know," Vernon says, laughing and looking at James. "Am I allowed?"

"Very funny, Vernon." James looks at Kathy. "Get him a cup, Kathy."

"What can I do for you, Vernon?" James asks after Kathy has left. "What did you want to speak to me about? Don't tell me it's about the coffee."

"Well, maybe," Vernon responds cautiously. "What happened this morning? What upset you?"

"The receptionist becoming a typist—that's what bothered me."

"Why would that make you so upset?" Vernon asks. "It seems like such a small matter."

James pauses and leans back in his chair.

"Vern, who made that decision? Whose idea was it?"

"Well, I believe it came from my secretary, Gertrude."

"Did you agree with the change?"

"Frankly, James, I wasn't even aware that a change had been made. It doesn't seem like such a big deal. What difference does it make if the receptionist is doing some typing?"

James sits back up in his chair. "Vernon, do you like the lobby of this building?"

"Yes, James—it's very impressive."

"Yes, I agree," James comments. "I spent a fortune on that lobby. And do you know why?"

Vernon shrugs. "Because you wanted to impress visitors?"

"That's right, Vernon. A visitor to our company gets a first impression of who we are by that lobby. It sends a clear message about our firm. The receptionist is part of that message. Her job is to convey to those visitors the manner in which they can expect to be treated by our company. The receptionist's role is to give our guests her undivided, professional attention. In that regard, I expect her to follow a clear code of conduct and behavior.

"Her attire is always very professional," he continues. "No gum chewing, no eating at her desk, no personal calls, and so on. The people visiting us are not to be kept waiting. Anyone kept waiting for more than five minutes, gets reported to Kathy. Making a good first impression is the start of winning people over."

"I see," Vernon says, and clears his throat. He stands up. "I'll have a talk with Gertrude."

"You do that, Vern," James says a satisfied smug is on his face.

A few minutes later, Kathy knocks at his door. "Are you in a better mood?"

"There's nothing wrong with my mood," he replies. "Come in and have a seat."

"How's everything going at home?" she asks, once seated.

"About the same. The hardest part is protecting Molly at school. I wanted to keep Molly at home and get her a tutor until this problem blows over, but Sam didn't like that plan. She doesn't want Molly to miss out on first grade. Feels it's important that Molly interact with the other kids.

"Sam and I let the school know of the danger that Molly is facing, so that they're on the alert. Every morning, I take her to school myself. I've got guards in the front and back of the building." James shakes his head. "What a way to live, right? I can only imagine what's going through little Molly's mind."

"Yes, I know," Kathy says. "What you guys are going through must be very frightening." She gives him a sympathetic smile and stands up. "Do you need anything else from me?"

"Not right now."

A few minutes later, Kathy buzzes him. "James, the receptionist just called. She says there is a strange man downstairs in the lobby asking for you. His name is—I hope I'm pronouncing it right—Faakhir. Should I call security and have them handle this?"

"No, Kathy. I was expecting him. Have him come straight up. In fact, go fetch Faakhir and personally escort him to my office."

"You were expecting him? He's not on your appointment schedule."

"I know. That's not important. What's important is that I see him. Please stop yapping and fetch Faakhir right away."

A few minutes later, Kathy is back at the door of James's office. "Mr. Faakhir," she announces and rolls her eyes. "Do you need me to take notes?" she adds.

James gives her a stern look. Kathy smiles. "I'll leave you two," she says and closes the door behind her.

Faakhir is dressed in western jeans and sneakers. James smiles as he recognizes that the man is trying unsuccessfully to pass himself off as an American.

James gestures to a chair. "Have a seat." Faakhir takes the chair in front of James's desk.

"It's nice to see you again, Faakhir. Well, I guess the time has come—are you here to kill me?"

"Not me, but the others are," Faakhir answers nervously. "I've come to warn you, as we agreed."

"All right—good. Where are the others?"

"Moshar and two other men are at a hotel in Denver."

"Which hotel? Where is it located?"

Faakhir takes out a card and hands it to James. "Here—the address is on this paper."

James looks down at the card. It's from a Holiday Inn on South Colorado Boulevard.

James looks up at Faakhir. "What is the room number?"

"322." James jots that onto the card.

"What is their plan?"

"They intend to wait outside of this office building. When you get out of work, they will attack your car. They have automatic weapons. The goal is to overpower your security detail."

"When are they going to do this? How do they know my schedule?"

"They don't know your schedule. Their plan is to stake out your office every day. Wait as long as it takes. When they see you leave the office, they'll come at you blasting. With automatic weapons, they should be able to outshoot your bodyguards."

James gets on the intercom. "Kathy, get McGill, Davis, and Gurney. Have them come to my office right away."

"Who are these men?" Faakhir asks James.

"These are men who work for me."

"What do these men have to do with me?" The timbre of Faakhir's voice rises and he stands up. "I'm done here. I've kept my end of the bargain. It's time for me to go."

James pulls out a pistol from his upper desk drawer and takes aim at Faakhir. "No, you're not leaving. Sit down!"

Faakhir looks at the gun. "You're going to shoot me?"

"Only if you force me to. You're going to be my guest for a while. At least, you'll be my guest until this confrontation with your friend Moshar and company is over."

Charlie knocks at his door and looks in and sees James holding a gun. "You wanted to see us, James? What's going on?"

"Yes, I did, guys. Come in."

The three men walk in.

"This is Faakhir. He and a few of his friends came over from Afghanistan for the sole purpose of murdering me."

"*I* did not come to kill you—Moshar came to kill you," Faakhir protests. "I told you the entire plan."

"Yes, I know, Faakhir," James says, smiling. "And I want to thank you." James turns to Charlie. "Here, take my pistol. Escort Faakhir to one of our empty rooms. Have security keep him in custody until after I've finished with his cohorts. After that, we'll turn him over to the FBI. Faakhir is one of the men who was involved in the church shooting in Texas. He was also behind Sam's kidnapping."

"This was not our agreement," Faakhir says to James.

James turns to Faakhir. "What agreement? I don't recall any agreement that said you would go free. Forty-three, Faakhir—that's how many people were killed inside that church. It's time for you to be held accountable. I hope you said your goodbyes to your family, because you'll never see them again."

Charlie grabs Faakhir and hauls him out of the room.

"Have a seat, guys," James says to the other two men after Charlie has gone. "We need to discuss what we're going to do with Faakhir's associates. They're at a motel in Denver, and they're armed with automatic weapons."

"James, you're not thinking about taking these guys on by yourself, are you?" Rodney asks.

"No, of course not," James says and looks over at Frank. "Frank, I want you to call the FBI. Give them the location of where these guys are holed up. Make sure you tell them that these men are armed and dangerous. They have automatic weapons—and maybe also explosive devices." James turns back to Rodney. "I want to be there when these men are taken down. I want to see the look on their faces when they see that I've defeated them once again. That is, if the men are still alive after this is all over."

James looks at Frank again. "Go make that call. The men are staying at the Holiday Inn on South Colorado, Room 322. Come back and get me after the call. You and I are going to take a ride up to Denver."

<hr />

"The FBI is over there in the RV," Frank says, pointing, when he and James reach the parking lot of the motel.

James and Frank knock at the door of the trailer. Someone peeks out. "Frank Gurney and James Coppi," Frank says to the man.

The man lets them in. There are five men huddled near a radio.

"Hey, Frank," one of the men says.

"How's it going, Pete?" Frank replies.

"We're finishing up evacuating the motel," Pete replies. "We've got a SWAT team ready to go. The bomb squad is also here, just in case. I've got guys in the front and back of the place so that nobody can escape. One of the accomplices came out earlier. We followed him to a fried-chicken joint. The man picked up some food and brought it back to the room. We're pretty sure they're all in there."

Pete looks at James. "We're waiting for the court order. How sure are you that these are the right guys? We're not breaking into a room for nothing, are we? We're gonna look pretty stupid if all we find inside the room is a bunch of regular Joes sitting around and eating fried chicken."

"Absolutely certain," James replies. "These are some pretty bad men. Take this seriously, and don't take any chances. I wouldn't want any of our guys hurt. How are you planning to pull this off?"

"We have a team ready to ram the door and burst right in," Pete tells him. "Catch them before they can make a move. Everyone is in place. As soon as we get the call that we've got the warrant, we're going in."

"I'd like to be there when you've got them apprehended," James says.

"Sure, why not?" Pete says. "If it weren't for you, we wouldn't have been able to nab these guys. Give us a little time to make sure the room is clean."

"Which room is 322?" James asks, looking out the window of the trailer. "Can I watch from here?"

"Yeah, you can watch. Third floor terrace. Right hand side, two doors from the end." The phone rings, and Pete picks it up.

"It's a go!" he yells. "We've got the warrant!" Pete immediately gets on the radio and gives the order.

James watches as six men in dark blue police uniforms jump out of another van that is also parked in the lot and make their way up the stairs. The men are helmeted and wearing bullet proof vests. One of the men is lugging a battering ram. They disappear from sight when they get to the stairway. A few moments later, they reappear on the terrace. They surround the door of the room with guns drawn. One of the men nods to the fellow carrying the ram. That man walks forward and heaves the ram against the door. The door bursts open, and the men rush inside.

James gets out of the RV and makes his way up toward the room. He listens for gunfire, but there isn't any. *A good thing*, he thinks, exhaling. *That means everyone is safe.* More uniformed men are now running up the steps in front of him. Frank has caught up to him.

"Maybe you should wait a bit, James?" Frank says. "Make sure it's completely under control."

James doesn't respond. He continues up the steps. On the landing of the third floor, there are what must be a dozen policemen standing around. James pushes his way through the men and enters the room. Two men are lying face down on the floor. Their hands are cuffed behind their backs. A third is sitting on a chair, also handcuffed.

"Which one of you is Moshar?" James asks.

"I'm Moshar," the sitting man replies.

James walks up to him. "Do you know who I am?"

Moshar nods.

"Faakhir sends you his regards," James says.

Moshar stares at him blankly. Then, after a moment, he smiles. "Very good. Very smart."

James turns to leave.

"You will lose," Moshar gives James a wry smile as he is stepping out of the room. James turns back to Moshar, who smiles again. "The fight isn't over. There will be others. You've won today. Eventually, you will lose. We only have to win once. You have to win all the time. And you won't."

James comes back into the room and walks back to Moshar. "No, Moshar, I *will* win. I know the men who were behind this attack, and I will get to those guys just as I got to you today. You're quite right. This fight isn't over—except it's over for you and your good buddy Faakhir."

James gives him a sly smile. "Maybe you and Faakhir will be cellmates. You guys can talk about how I defeated you both. You'll both have plenty of time in prison. Maybe not Faakhir; he's going to fry in the electric chair. You, on the other hand, will spend the rest of your days in an American prison. Which, by the way, is a lot better than what's waiting for the prince and Mafrouz. At least you'll still be alive. Those two won't be so lucky. Once I catch up with them, I'm going to put a bullet into each of their heads."

Frank does the driving all the way back to Colorado Springs. James is out of sorts and deep in thought. The last conversation with Moshar is weighing on him. *Why did I feel that I had to confront Moshar? What was the purpose? Show him that I had outsmarted him? Rub the man's nose in his defeat? Why was that important? It's not like me to act this way.* He thinks about it some more, and then he realizes why. *It's Sam. It's all about Sam. That's why I had to provoke Moshar.*

24

A Bloody Nose

WHEN THEY HAVE DRIVEN BACK to the office, James hops out of the car and turns to Frank. "There's my limo. I'm leaving—I need to pick up my daughter Molly at school. When you get upstairs, have Charlie turn Faakhir over to the authorities."

His limo stops at the school, and his bodyguard Max opens the door for him. Parents are standing by their cars, waiting for their children to come out of the building.

"Where's our security?" James asks Max.

Max moves his head to the right. "Here he comes now."

"Anything happen today, Steve?" James asks the security man when Steve gets to them.

"No, nothing, Mr. Coppi," he replies. "Will you be needing me any longer today?"

"No, you're done," James tells the man. "We'll take it from here."

The door of the school bursts open and the children come running out. James looks for Molly. Mrs. Constance, Molly's teacher, signals to James from the top of the steps.

"I'll be right back," he tells Max, and hurries off to see the teacher.

"Molly is inside," the teacher tells James when he reaches her.

James senses that something is wrong. "Is she all right?"

"Yes, she's fine," the teacher tells him. "Molly had a fight with one of her classmates. She's with the headmaster, Mr. Reister. He'd like a word with you."

Molly is sitting in front of the headmaster's office. She jumps up when she sees her father and runs right over.

"Hello, honey," he says, squatting down and giving her a hug. "How was your day?"

"Not good, Daddy," Molly responds, looking away from him. "I had a bad day."

James turns her face toward his. "What happened?"

"You promise not to get angry?"

James smiles. "I'm sorry, baby, I can't make that promise until I know what you did. I'll get angry for sure if you don't tell me."

"I punched Robbie in the nose and made him bleed," she reveals.

"Why did you do that?"

"Because Robbie said that I was a scaredy-cat," Molly yells out. "You too, Daddy! He said you were a scaredy-cat, too."

"We'd better go in and see Mr. Reister," the teacher says. "He's waiting for us."

James looks up. "Yes, of course."

Inside the office, the headmaster offers him a seat. "Has Mrs. Constance told you what happened?" the headmaster asks.

"No. Molly told me that she had a fight with a classmate."

"Gave him a bloody nose," Mrs. Constance adds.

"Is the boy all right?" James asks.

"Yes, he'll be fine," Mr. Reister says. "His mom was not too happy, I can assure you!"

"No, I'm sure she wasn't." James turns to the teacher. "What happened?"

"The young man was teasing your daughter," Constance replies. "It's about the security guards that you hired for her. The boy said that she needs the security guards because she's a scaredy-cat."

"I see!" James turns to the headmaster. "You'll be happy to know that you won't be seeing the security men again—I'm taking them off their duty. I don't believe Molly is in danger any longer."

"That's good to hear, Mr. Coppi," the headmaster says. "That's really very good news."

"What do you want me to do about that young man?" James asks.

"Well, you'll need to have a talk with Molly, of course," Mr. Reister replies. "Explain to her that hitting doesn't solve anything.

Molly will need to apologize to the young lad. You may want to call the boy's parents and apologize, also."

"Yes, of course. I'll do everything that you suggested."

On the way home, James sits in the back seat with Molly.

"Are you angry with me?" she asks.

"No. I'm not angry, but I am disappointed," James tells her. "You gave that boy a bloody nose."

"But he wouldn't stop teasing me, Daddy."

"You should've told the teacher." He leans toward her. "You hurt that boy, Molly. Made him bleed. Tomorrow, you'll have to say you're sorry."

"Daddy, please. I don't want to."

"I know you don't want to, but you need to." He turns Molly to face him and strokes her red hair. "Will you do that for me?"

"OK, I will."

Sam comes out onto the porch to greet James and Molly when they get home to the ranch. "Go inside and put your stuff away," he says to Molly.

"What happened?" Sam asks. "Why are you late?"

"There was a problem at the school," he says as they walk inside. James tells Sam the story of Molly's fight. "Do me a favor—call Robbie's mom and apologize to her," he says when he finishes the account. "I think it's better coming from another mother. You know, woman to woman. Maybe you can invite Robbie's family over for dinner? You know, smooth things over. Robbie and Molly can spend a little time together away from their classmates."

"That's a good idea," Sam says and turns to go inside. "I've got to speak to Molly first."

James grabs hold of her arm. "Go easy. She's very embarrassed."

When Sam is done talking to Molly, Sam knocks at the door of James's study and peeks in. "Can I come in?"

"Yes, of course. Come in and have a seat."

"You didn't tell me how everything else went today. I spoke to Kathy earlier. She said that you went to Denver. She didn't know why. You left in a hurry after a strange foreigner came into the office. What's going on?"

"That was the man I was expecting. That's why I went to Afghanistan a few months ago. That man was here to warn me about the men that were coming to the US to try and kill me."

"So what happened?"

"All the men have been arrested. I called the FBI, and they raided the motel where the men were staying. They're all in jail. One of the men was also involved in the church shooting."

"Well, is that it, then? Is it all over? Can we finally relax?"

"No, baby—it's not over. There's still the issue of the men who are giving the orders. They're still out there. This thing won't be over 'til I get those guys. Anyway, I'm pulling the security detail from Molly. She's no longer in any danger. After today, these men will be after me alone."

Sam shakes her head. "My God, this will never end. We'll have to live like this for the rest of our lives."

"No, dear. I've got a plan in the works. It won't take long. The next part of my plan is taking the fight to the men giving the orders. We'll win this fight, just as I promised we would."

The next day, James is in the conference room for a meeting with his senior management. He hasn't attended one of these meetings in months. Men are standing around, eating pastries and drinking coffee. James is staring at the four huge platters of breakfast food on the conference room table. One of the platters is stacked with assorted bagels. Others are piled high with donuts, pastries, and fruits. Three bowls contain different cream cheeses. There is another flat dish of Nova Scotian salmon.

"Is there something wrong, James?" Vernon asks him, seeing his annoyed expression.

"How many people will be attending this meeting?" James asks, looking around.

Vernon ponders for a moment. "Eight, I believe—not counting us," he replies.

Kathy walks in with her notepad and takes a chair next to James. She reaches over and puts a blueberry muffin onto a plate.

"Who ordered all this food?" James asks Kathy. "Was it you? There is enough here to feed the entire office."

"No, James, I didn't order the food. Vernon's secretary did."

"Don't you usually order the food?"

"I haven't been, lately. Vernon has told his secretary to do all the ordering."

James looks up at Vernon, who was listening to the conversation. "Shouldn't we get started?" James says.

When the meeting is over, James gets up and arches his back. He turns to Kathy and says, "Call Frank Gurney and have him come to my office, please."

After James leaves the room, Vernon pulls Kathy aside and whispers, "What's with James?"

Kathy furrows her brow. "I'm sorry, Vernon? I don't understand the question."

"At the beginning of the meeting, James asked about the food. Why was he preoccupied with the food?"

"Oh," she says and smiles. "You probably should explain to him why you ordered so much food for such a small gathering. If I know James, that's what was on his mind."

Frank Gurney knocks at James's door and looks into the office. "Kathy said you wanted to see me?"

"Yes, come in, Frank. Have a seat."

James tosses a newspaper in front of Frank. "Where's the news of yesterday's raid?"

Frank looks at the paper, looks up at him and raises his shoulders. "I don't know—where is it?"

"It's on page six."

Frank shrugs. "So it's on page six? So what?"

"There's an FBI raid where three armed men with automatic weapons are busted—and that news doesn't make the front page?

Don't you find that kind of peculiar? Such a major story doesn't make the headlines?

"And what about the story itself?" he points to the paper. "Do you know what the news article says?" James doesn't wait for an answer. "It says that three men were busted for having unregistered firearms. Unregistered firearms? Can you believe that? What about Faakhir? It doesn't even mention him. The mastermind of the church shooting that killed forty-three doesn't even get a mention?"

"What do you think is going on?" Frank asks.

"You were in the FBI. You tell me. What's going on?"

Frank is quiet. "Some sort of cover up?" he asks after a moment. "They're being told to keep this quiet."

"Exactly! Now how do we find out who is doing the covering up, and why?"

"James, it may be beyond my ability to find out. These orders are coming from much higher up. I'll ask around the Bureau, but I don't think I'll get anywhere. No one is going to risk his career. You're probably better off with Rodney. He might be able to help you."

James's intercom buzzes. "James, Bill Sester is on the line," Kathy tells him. "He says it's important."

James picks up the phone. "Hello, Bill. What's up?" he asks.

"First of all, I want to convey to you the personal thanks from the President of the United States for getting those men yesterday. We're all very appreciative. Once again, you've been able to ward off some sort of serious attack."

"OK, Bill—you're welcome. I'm glad that I could be of help. What else have you got? I'm sure this call is more than just to say thanks."

"I'd like to come out and pay you a visit. Have you got time for me tomorrow?"

"What's this all about?"

"I'll fill you in when I get there. Does tomorrow work for you?"

"Yes, of course—come out. When will you be here?"

"Is tomorrow afternoon good?"

"Tomorrow afternoon works for me, Bill. I'll see you tomorrow."

James hangs up and looks at Frank. "We won't have to dig around. We'll know everything tomorrow."

After Frank leaves, Kathy buzzes again. "James, Vernon wants to have a few minutes with you."

"OK, Kathy—tell Vernon I'll stop by his office on my way out. By the way—put Bill Sester on the calendar for tomorrow afternoon. Tell Rodney I'd like to have him at the meeting with Sester."

James drops by Vernon's office. "What's up, Vernon?" James asks. "You wanted to speak with me?"

"Yes, James, I did." Vernon clears his throat. "This may sound trivial, but I couldn't help but notice that you were somewhat chagrined at the amount of food in the conference room today. Which, by the way, was an error on my secretary's part. She misunderstood the number of people that would be attending the meeting."

"Vernon, please—don't take me for a dummy. That was the usual amount of food that you've been ordering. I asked Kathy after the meeting. Now, you want a second chance at an explanation? This time, no bullshit!"

"Maybe I'm just not getting it, James," Vernon gets defensive. "I really don't see the big deal. This is such a small matter. Why would you take such an interest? We're five percent ahead of our projections. That's the big picture."

"Because, Vernon, when I see waste like that, it gets me wondering. Are we five percent ahead because of our superior management style, or are we just damn lucky? And, if we are just lucky, what happens when our luck runs out?

"To my mind, Vernon, that food may be indicative of what's going on at the company. If we can overlook a small detail like that—aren't we also missing bigger issues?"

James gives Vernon a wry smile. "You know the old saying, 'Watch the pennies, and the pounds will take care of themselves.' Good night, Vernon." He turns around at the door. "And, Vernon—please don't ever lie to me again."

The next afternoon, Bill Sester and Rodney are sitting in James's office. After the usual small talk, James looks over at the guy with the blond crew cut. "OK, Bill, what did you want to speak to me about? I'm assuming it's something that comes from the very top. Am I correct?"

"Yes, you're right. It comes directly from the president."

"Well—what is it?"

"We need you to back off!"

"Back off! From what?" James says calmly.

Sester gives him a side glance. "Come on, James—don't get cute with me. Cut the dumb act. You know exactly what I'm talking about. We know the people that you're after. The president wants you to stop. We need those men as our allies in our fight against the Russians."

James scowls at him.

"So I'm just supposed to sit here and let those motherfuckers come and kill me?" James asks, his voice getting louder. "Terrorize my family and do nothing about it. Is that it?"

"No, James—it's all been taken care of. After this latest incident, we've spoken to the men. It's all been called off. There'll be no more attempts on you or your family."

"Really, Bill? It's all over? What about the men that we nabbed yesterday? What would've happened if I hadn't stayed alert?"

Bill leans forward. "James, I just told you. We spoke to these people after the incident. They assured me that there'll be no further attempts on you."

"Bill, the last time we talked, you told me that these guys were harmless, remember? The term you used was that I was a *neophyte*. You said that I didn't understand anything. Well, it's a good thing that I'm a little more clever than you realize—otherwise, right about now, you would be giving my wife your condolences.

"So stop the crap, Bill, and don't think for one second that I believe any of the shit you're trying to feed me," James says, banging his fist on the top of the desk. "And even if you don't give a fuck about me—what about the church shooting? What about some justice for the victims? These are the men responsible for their deaths. Don't you give a damn about the families of the dead at all?"

"No, James—they aren't responsible."

"If not them, who was it? Martians?" James shakes his head and looks over at Rodney. "Can you believe this guy? Listen to the truckload of crap he's trying to feed us. I'm supposed to believe all this bullshit."

"James, this is very complicated. You wouldn't understand," Sester says in defense.

"Well, Bill, if you want me to back off, you're going to have to *make* me understand," James tells him.

"Gaddafi was behind the church shooting. A revenge for something we did to him. He promised these guys a shitload of money for their cause if they carried it out. These men were desperate for money to help their cause, so they agreed. Believe me, they didn't want to do it. They hate Gaddafi as much as we do."

"So that's it." James throws up his hands. "Forty-three people are dead and it's all over, as far as you're concerned."

Sester leans forward. "No, it's not over. Believe me—we have big plans for Mr. Gaddafi. He's not getting away with this. Just let us handle the problem. We'll take care of the *real* problem—Gaddafi."

Sester waits for a moment as James sits in silence. "So is it a deal? Can I report back to the president that you'll back off?"

"What assurance do I have?" James asks. "How can I be absolutely certain that these men will leave me and my family alone and allow us to live in peace?"

"The president is giving you his assurance right now, through me. James, this is really a very big deal. The Russians, if successful in Afghanistan, can threaten the entire Middle East. They need to be stopped."

"OK," James gives him an assuring smile. "Tell the president I'll back off. As long as these men make no further attempts on me or my family, I'll cease and desist."

Sester smiles. "Great!" He stands up and shakes James's hand.

"That's really good news. Thank you, James. I'm sure the president will be very appreciative."

Rodney turns to James after Sester leaves. "You're backing off? That was quick."

James laughs. "Yeah, I couldn't see any point in arguing with him. Especially since I don't have any plans to back off. Might as well let Sester think that I won't do anything. Maybe they'll stop trying to figure out what I'm doing."

James looks over at the door and shakes his head. "They're all a bunch of bullshit artists. All of them. Gaddafi was responsible, not them? They must take me for some kind of fool. What about Sam's kidnapping? Did Gaddafi give that order? Fucking assholes—all of them."

"You know the president is not going to be happy when he finds out what you're up to," Rodney warns him.

"Yeah, well—tough shit," James says and smiles. "There's an election two weeks away. If the polls are right, I won't have to worry about the president for long. It doesn't look like he's going to be around much longer, anyway. Ever since that hostage crisis where the Iranians grabbed fifty-two Americans the president has been losing support. By the time the new guy takes office, I should have killed those rotten bastards."

James gets up from his chair and arches his back. "It still hurts when I sit for too long," he tells Rodney. "You know, this can work in my favor. Sester will report back to the guys in Afghanistan that I'm backing off. Maybe they'll relax when they hear the news. Come out in the open. Make it easier for me to find them. I've never wanted to kill a man in the past—but I do now."

25
Time for Action

JAMES IS OUTSIDE HIS HOUSE, putting training wheels onto Michael's bike. Molly and Michael are watching. Sam comes out.

"He's too young to be riding," she says. "He's only three."

James looks up. "He's nearly four. That's when Molly started riding."

"Molly is different; she's more coordinated than Michael."

"No, he'll be all right," James says and gets up. "There," he says to Michael. "It's finished. Come on, I'll help you up on the bike."

James lifts Michael onto the bike. At the sight, Sam starts laughing. "He can't even reach the pedals," she says.

"I'll lower the seat," James says. "Come on, Michael." He lifts his son off the bike and leans down to unscrew the bolt under the seat. "There," he says when he's finished. "That should do it. Come on, Michael—get back on." James lifts his son back up to the seat on the bike.

Michael just sits there, not moving. James leans over. "You need to peddle, son. The bike won't move unless you peddle. You know— just like you've seen Molly peddle her bike."

Michael looks at him. "Daddy, I don't know how."

"I told you he's too young," Sam says.

James turns to her and scowls. "Don't you have anything better to do?"

Sam smiles, turns and goes inside.

Half an hour later, Sam is back outside. James and the kids are about a quarter of a mile from the house. "James, you have a call," she shouts.

"I see you got him to start peddling," she says when James comes walking back with the children.

"Yeah, he's doing much better. Who's on the phone?"

"It's Omprakash. He says it's important. The call is in your office."

"Molly, I've got to go in and take a call," he tells his daughter. "You help Michael."

"I will, Daddy!" she says.

"What did Omprakash want?" Sam asks James when he comes out of the study.

"Let's go onto the patio," he tells her. "I need to speak to you."

"So what's up?" she asks when they are standing outside. "What did Omprakash have to say?"

"I'm leaving for Pakistan tonight," he tells her. "Mafrouz and the prince will be at their compound in four days."

"What do you mean?" Sam turns pale.

"I mean I'm leaving. This is it. This is the moment we've been waiting for. Both men are going to be at the compound at the same time. This is perfect. I can get them both at once—finish this once and for all. I've got to get going. I'll be meeting up with Ernie and Gary in Pakistan. This is our chance to finally get these guys."

"Oh my God, James, I think I'm going to faint," Sam says, sitting down on a wrought-iron chair. James squats in front of her.

"Are you all right?"

"No, I'm not all right." Sam starts fanning herself with one hand. Then she collects herself and looks into James's face. "Isn't there another way? Can't Ernie and Gary do this without you? They're professionals. This is their job. They're a lot better at this than you are."

"Sam, we already had this conversation," James says with a sigh. "You know I need to be there. Ernie and Gary will be with me—but I have to go, too. This is the final fight, and it's personal. When we win this, it will all be over."

Sam reaches over and pulls him to her. "Oh, James, I'm so frightened."

James rubs her back. "I know you are. But this can't be avoided. I have a good plan. If I didn't think this plan would work, I wouldn't be going." He stands up. "Come on—I need to pack and get my stuff together. I'm leaving in two hours."

Sam gets up. "Are you taking the company plane?"

"No. It's much quicker if I fly commercial. I called Kathy after I spoke to Omprakash. She has already booked the flights. The tickets are waiting for me at the airport."

"What about Max? Isn't he going with you?"

James walks toward the door. "No. I won't need Max this time."

Sam grabs James's arm and turns him to her. "You're going without a bodyguard?"

James smiles. "When I get to Karachi, in addition to Ernie and Gary, there'll be two dozen fighters waiting to assist me. That's more than enough to protect me. I won't need Max."

As the plane makes its approach to Jinnah International airport James is woken by an announcement to prepare for landing. He looks out his window, but all he can see is water. It's early morning, and the sun is just beginning to rise. Leaving the family behind had been stressful. Sam had insisted that she and the children come to the airport to see him off. Then she began crying inconsolably as he was about to board. The children noticed their mother's tears and immediately joined in. The whole scene was a mess. Exactly what he does not need imprinted in his memory at a time like this.

The operation itself will be simple. Disguised as Pakistani policemen, they will enter the compound where Mafrouz and the prince are holed up. They will round up everyone they find in the building and lock them away. Everyone except the two ringleaders. Mafrouz and the prince will be taken into another room where James will put a bullet in each of their heads. The whole operation shouldn't take more than an hour. After it's done, the entire raiding party will head to the Peshawar airport, where there will be a plane waiting to take them to New Delhi.

He and his men will be long gone before anyone in government has a chance to react. Tonight, Omprakash will fly down from Peshawar, bringing with him a map of the layout of the complex. The men will spend two days in Karachi, rehearsing the mission. Then it's on to Peshawar for a date with Mafrouz and Prince Faikil to settle the score—once and for all.

James disembarks the plane and a luggage porter immediately runs up to him to help him with his bag. He has only one carry-on bag—there is no need for more luggage. James would tell the porter that he does not need any help, but he knows from experience that in this part of the world, trying to decline the offer of help will be futile.

It is just not worth the effort of fighting the porter off. This man makes his living carrying luggage, and James—a clearly well-off Westerner—is the perfect customer. Without the energy to fight a losing battle, James offers the man his single carry-on. At that moment, two other men run up to grab his bag, too, and an argument starts between the three men. The first man shoves the other two away and smiles at James as he reaches for his bag. James laughs and starts walking toward the exit, the porter following him with his carry-on.

Outside, at the curb, he sees Ernie standing next to a black van. "Welcome to Karachi," Ernie tells James.

"Do me a favor, Ernie, and give the porter a tip. I don't have any local currency."

Ernie reaches into his pocket and pulls out a roll of rupees. He hands a bill to the porter, takes the bag, and tosses it into the trunk. Then he opens the car door for James.

"So I guess the mission is a go?" Ernie asks James as they drive off.

"Yeah, I got the word," James replies. "Faikil and Mafrouz will be at their headquarters later this week. This is our chance to get them both at the same time."

"Are you sure? How good is your source?"

"Absolutely certain," James replies. "My source is an inside operative. Omprakash will be joining us tonight to show us a layout of the place. He's in Peshawar right now, getting his hands on the blueprints."

Ernie smiles. "Well, all right, then. This will be over this week."

"Yeah—this is it."

"Good. I was getting fat and lazy just sitting all day. And I was beginning to feel a little bit guilty taking your money for doing nothing," Ernie says with a snicker.

James creases his brow and feigns concern. "Really, Ernie? You know, if you're feeling so guilty, you can give some of that money back. I wouldn't want you to lose any sleep over this."

Ernie laughs loudly. "I'm not feeling that guilty!" he says.

"Yeah, that's what I thought. You had me worried there for a while. For a second, I thought you were actually getting a conscience."

Late that evening, James hears a knock on the door of his room.

"James, are you still up?"

"Yes. Come in, Ernie."

Ernie opens the door and walks into the room. "Omprakash is here."

"Good."

"There's a guy with him," Ernie informs James. "A policeman. His name is Malik Toru. Do you know who he is?"

"Yeah, I do. He's the police chief who's been working with me up in Peshawar."

"Why is he here? Do you know what he wants?"

James smiles. "My guess is that this character is going to hit me up for more money. This mission is coming to an end, and this guy wants to ask for one final piece before it's over."

James heads for the door. "Come on," he says to Ernie, "Let's go downstairs and see how much this guy is asking for."

When they get downstairs, James smiles at his colleague. James genuinely and truly likes the fellow.

"Good evening, Omprakash," James says and walks over to shake his hand. "It's so nice to see you again. It's been a while. How have you been? How is your family?"

"I'm fine. My family is also well, Mr. Coppi," Omprakash replies. "It is nice to see you again, too."

James turns to the police chief standing alongside Gary and extends his hand. "And you must be Mr. Toru."

"Yes." They shake hands, and the man smiles. "It is a pleasure to finally meet you, Mr. Coppi."

"The pleasure is all mine," James replies, holding on to his hand for a moment and staring into his eyes, trying to get a read on the man. "Thank you for all of your help."

"It was my pleasure to lend some assistance to you," Toru says as he stares intently right back.

James releases his hold and gestures toward a table. "Why don't we sit and have a chat?"

After they have all taken their seats, Omprakash tells James, "Chief Toru accompanied me because he has some concerns."

"What are your concerns?" James asks the chief.

"I noticed a lot of men when I came here," Toru replies. "Men in Pakistani police uniforms. I'd like to know precisely what you will be doing in Peshawar."

"That's really none of your business," Gary answers curtly. "You've been paid for information."

"It is very much my business," Toru snaps back angrily. "This is happening in my city—I will be the one left behind to answer for what happened. It'll be me that will have to clean up the mess."

James looks over at Toru and studies him intently. Then he looks around the table. "Fellows, would you excuse us for a few minutes? I want to speak to Commissioner Toru in private."

When the others have left the room, James faces the chief. "All right, sir," he begins. "What do you want to know?"

"I would like to know exactly what you're up to," Toru responds.

"We are going to raid the compound and find the two men that you already know about."

"What will you do when you meet up with the men?"

"Kill them," James answers matter-of-factly.

The chief gets up and looks outside the window. "So the men I see out there are to help you get into the compound? Why the police uniforms? To disguise yourselves?"

"Yes, so the guards will let us into the facility without question. We are going to make believe that it's a police raid. Have the guards open the doors to us without a fight."

The chief lets out a sardonic laugh. "That won't work. Your men will immediately be recognized. The uniforms won't fool anyone. These Afghans have been in my city for years. They've had constant run-ins with my men. The Afghans can spot a real Pakistani policeman a mile away. They'll know immediately that your men are fakes."

"What are you suggesting that I do?" James answers. "Turn around and go home?"

"No, I've got a better plan," Toru offers.

James sits up. "What is that?"

The chief smiles. "Make it an official raid. Using real police authorities."

"An official raid?" James laughs in disbelief and sits back in his chair. "How the hell do I do that?"

"I'll set it up. I'll go back to Peshawar and order an official police raid of the compound. I'll lead it myself. You can send your men home—they won't be needed. You'll wait outside the building until I've rounded everyone up inside. Once the coast is clear, I'll give you a shout. You can do your thing and be out of there in minutes. That's all there's to it. You'll be out of the country before anyone has a chance to ask any questions."

James looks at the commissioner and smiles. "And how much will you charge me for your services?"

"One million dollars."

"I'll pass," James tells him without missing a beat.

"Why?" The chief hollers. "One million dollars is more than fair. Remember, in addition to setting this all up, I'll have to provide answers to the questions of how and why those men were killed. There will be a full inquiry into the matter. I'll have to expend a considerable amount of your money bribing officials to close the case."

"No, I'm sorry. One million is out of the question—I can do this operation a lot cheaper myself."

The commissioner leans forward. "Well . . . make me an offer."

"A hundred thousand," James says.

"A hundred thousand!" The chief throws up his hands. "That's ridiculous!"

"I've already paid you nearly fifty grand," James reminds him.

"Yes, but this will be much more difficult."

When James doesn't respond, Toru continues to argue his case. "Please, Mr. Coppi—you must understand that there are a lot of people that will need paying off—and not for small amounts."

James continues to remain silent and impassive, sitting back in his chair.

"I'll tell you what," the chief proposes. "I'll make it five hundred thousand. That's half of what I asked for—it's more than fair."

"Two hundred, and you've got a deal," James counters. "That's my final offer!"

Toru shakes his head. "I don't know why I'm agreeing to this." Toru looks at James with defeat. "All right—it's a deal."

James smiles. "Good! How much time will you need to set it up? The prince and Mafrouz are due at the compound the day after tomorrow. I don't want to wait too long and have one of them slip through my fingers."

Toru ponders this for a moment. "There's no reason that we can't be there the day they arrive. I'll fly up to Peshawar tonight and set up the operation tomorrow. We should be ready to go by the next day. How fast can you get me the money?"

"I'll take care of that right now," James says. He gets up, walks to the door, opens it, and calls out, "Omprakash, come in here, please."

"Have a seat," James says when Omprakash is in the room. "You'll leave today to go back to India. When you get back to the office, call Jack in finance. Have him wire two hundred thousand dollars to Mr. Toru's Swiss account right away. Tell Jack that you have my approval." James turns to Toru. "The money should be in your account in about three days. Is that satisfactory?"

"Yes, very satisfactory," Toru says and stands up. "Now, if you can arrange for a car to take me to the airport."

"Of course," James says, standing and shaking his hand. "You can share a taxi with Omprakash."

"When you get to Peshawar, give me a call," Toru tells James. "I'll give you all the details on the raid. You've got my number?"

"Yes, I do. I should be there by tomorrow night."

When Omprakash and Toru have left, Ernie and Gary come back into the room. "What's going on, James?" Ernie asks. "What did the cop want? Did he hit you up for more money, as you suspected?"

James laughs. "Yeah, of course he did. But it wasn't too bad. Have a seat, guys—I'll fill you in. There's been a new development.

"First of all, you can dismiss the men and send them home," James says when the guys are seated.

Gary and Ernie look at each other. Gary shakes his head and turns to James.

"What do you mean? Have you changed your mind about the mission? You no longer want to get these guys?"

"No, I'm still going to *kill* these bastards," James says calmly. "There's just been a change of plans as to how it will happen. Your men won't be needed in this new plot."

"What about us?" Ernie asks. "Are we being sent home, too?"

"No, I still need you guys. After I talked with the chief, I agreed to a new arrangement. Instead of using our men disguised as Pakistani policemen, we're going to use real cops. The chief is going to spearhead the raid. He's going to round everybody up in the compound."

James sits back and lets the men absorb this news. Then he continues.

"When the coast is clear, we're going in and doing our thing. It's a much better plan than the one we had before. Less chance us of being recognized as impersonators. And there's less for us to do. In and out and gone in no time."

"Do you trust the chief?" Ernie asks. "How do you know he won't double-cross us?"

"Because he's being paid good money to do the job."

"James, I've got to warn you," Ernie says. "This could blow up in your face. Guys in this part of the world are always switching sides. Your man Toru could already be talking to the other side. If they offer him more money, he'll sell you out. Toru is up for sale—he'll go to the highest bidder."

"Maybe," James answers. "I'm just going to have to take that chance." He stands up and stretches. "Anyway, let's get things wrapped up here. We won't need this place any longer. After this mission is over, we'll fly to New Delhi and then home. There'll be a plane waiting for us at Peshawar."

"How are we getting to Peshawar?" Gary asks James. "Are we still going up by truck?"

"No, no need. We'll rent a car. We'll leave here this afternoon. I'd like to be in Peshawar by tomorrow night."

James is in his hotel room in Peshawar, pacing. They have been there for a few hours, and now he's worried. He had immediately called Toru upon his arrival. Toru's office said he wasn't in and took a message. Ernie's warning about Toru switching sides is echoing through his thoughts.

Is this guy going to try to sell us out? Is he negotiating with the other side right now? James looks out his window at the busy street below. The phone rings, and James rushes to pick it up.

"Hello," he says.

"I see you made it all right," Toru says.

"Yeah, we're in Peshawar," James lets out a breath. "What's the word? Are we on for tomorrow?"

"Yes, we're on. Both the prince and Mafrouz have arrived and are now at the compound. My source on the inside confirmed their arrival. I'll meet you at five in the morning in front of the Fort Bala Hisar. Do you know where it is?"

"I'll find it."

"Good. Be there at five—don't be late. I'd like to hit this place nice and early—while they're still sleeping. Catch them completely by surprise."

"I'll be there at five. Do you want to meet first and go over the plan?"

"There's no need," Toru says. "We've hit that place before—we know what to do. Just make sure you're ready to carry out your part of the affair. You need to be in and out quickly. I'll have the prince and Mafrouz separated from the rest of the men. I'm assuming you'll do it silently? I don't want the rest of the men to hear what's going on."

"Yeah, I have a silencer."

"Good. Well, then, we're all set. I'll see you tomorrow."

26

The Three Blondes

THE LIMO ARRIVES AT THE Coppi office building, and Max opens the rear door. "Thank you, Max," Sam says as she gets out.

Max rushes ahead of her and opens the front door of the office building.

When she gets to her office, she greets Helen. "Good morning, Helen. Would you please get me a cup of coffee?"

"Yes, of course, Mrs. Coppi," Helen says, standing up.

"I'm expecting Penelope Campos," Sam tells her. "Please send her right in the moment she gets here."

"Miss Campos is already here, Mrs. Coppi. She's meeting with Kathy. They're in Mr. Coppi's office."

"Oh, can you get her before you get my coffee, please?"

"Yes—right away."

There's a knock at Sam's door and Kathy peeks in. "Are you free?"

"Yes, come in," Sam says.

Both Kathy and Penelope come into the office.

"I know you'll be busy with Penelope, but I need to ask you, before you get started, if you've heard from James," Kathy says to Sam. "Ian has called at least half a dozen times and says he needs to speak to him. He says it's urgent."

"No, I'm sorry, Kathy. I haven't spoken to James, and I have no way of getting in touch with him."

"Yeah, that's what I thought," Kathy says and turns to walk out.

"Kathy, wait!" Sam calls to her. "If you're not too busy this morning, why don't you stay in this meeting? We might need your help."

"All right—sure. My work can wait until later." Kathy takes a seat.

Helen comes in with Sam's coffee and places it on the desk in front of her. "Would anyone else like coffee?" she asks the other women.

The ladies shake their head no, and Helen turns to Sam. "Will there be anything else?"

"No, that's all for now, Helen. Please hold all my calls. I don't want to be disturbed."

"Yes, ma'am." Helen heads out and closes the door behind her.

Sam turns to Penelope and smiles warmly. "It's nice to see you again. Did you enjoy your time off? I see you got rid of the platinum and are back to your natural blond color. What've you been up to?"

"Quite honestly, Sam, I was beginning to worry. I thought you and James had forgotten about me—I thought maybe you had changed your mind on banking me on the new fashion line."

"No, Penny—we never forgot. We just had so many things come up. My kidnapping, among them."

"Yeah, that's what I figured. How do you feel?"

"Good, now. I was terrified when it happened." Sam pauses for a moment and collects herself. "Look who I'm complaining to about being kidnapped! You went through more horrors with your ordeal than I ever did with mine. I remember when James and I first rescued you, you were so skinny and frightened. You wouldn't even look at James."

Penelope gives her a smile. "Well, now we both have two things in common."

Sam looks quizzical. "What are the two things?" she asks.

"We both were kidnapped, and we both were rescued by James."

Sam laughs. "Yes, that's true," Sam says and clears her throat. "Are you ready to get started on your new business? It's the fall, and we need to get your designs ready for the spring fashion shows."

"I'm ready, Sam. I've already designed about a dozen ideas. I brought them in to show you. Do you have some time?"

"No. I'm sorry, darling, I can't go over your designs with you. James feels that he and I shouldn't get too involved in the everyday operations of your business. You know—because of the noncompete clause and all. We're just going to supply you the cash that you need. You'll have to do most of the rest by yourself. We can give you some direction and a little advice, but you'll have to do the majority of the work."

"Oh God, now I'm terrified," Penelope blurts out. "I don't know anything about setting up the business—I'll probably lose all your money."

"No, you won't, dear," Sam reassures her. "Both James and I have the utmost faith in you. We have an accountant ready to help you develop your business plans—also, Amelia, who used to work as a buyer for me but was laid off by the Cinellis after the sale, has agreed to come work for you. And so has Jonathan, who used to be the sales manager."

"Great! Those two will be a lot of help," Penelope says. "What about the clothes designs themselves? How do I know that they'll work? I've always had you and the Cinellis to look over what I've done."

Sam smiles at her. "Well, that's what we'll have to find out when you present your line at those upcoming fashion shows." Sam's smile widens. "But I wouldn't worry too much. I've seen your work. You'll do just fine." After a pause, Sam asks her, "Well? Are you ready to get started?"

Penelope sighs. "I guess so. I'm just really very nervous—I don't even know what the next step is. I've got these ideas—but now what?"

"Here's a suggestion," Sam volunteers. "Go to New York and find a good office to rent. Something in the fashion district. After that, arrange for a meeting with your new staff. Kick around a few ideas. I'm sure that after meeting, you'll know what that next step will be."

The intercom buzzer goes off. "Yes, Helen," Sam says.

"Mrs. Coppi, I know you said you didn't want to be disturbed, but Ian Wadsworth is on the line. Mr. Wadsworth says that it's extremely urgent. He needs to speak to either you or James."

"All right—put him through."

"Good morning, Ian," Sam says when he's on the speaker. "What's so urgent? You just interrupted a very important meeting."

"I'm truly sorry, Mrs. Coppi, but this is very important. It is imperative that I get in touch with James."

"I'm sorry, Ian, but there's no way to reach him. He's overseas, and I have no access to him."

"When will he be back? Sometime soon, I hope?"

"No—I don't expect him back for at least a week."

"Oh shit!" Ian falls silent.

"Is there anything that I can help you with?" Sam asks.

"No."

"Well, at least tell me what this is all about. Maybe I can be of some help."

"No, not really, Mrs. Coppi. The man will be long gone before James gets back."

"Who'll be long gone?" she asks.

"As, I said, Mrs. Coppi, it doesn't matter. Have James call me when he gets back."

"Ian, please tell me what this is all about!"

"James wanted to know when this prince would be in Monaco."

"What?" Sam asks, getting a sick feeling in her stomach. "What prince?"

"Some prince who has something to do with Afghanistan. I don't know much about who he is. James has been looking for him."

Sam's lips are quivering. "How do you know that the prince is going to be in Monaco?"

"James hired this guy to keep a lookout for him. Told this source to give me a call as soon as the prince showed his face in Monte Carlo. I got a call last night from our source that the royal is on his way there. That's why I've been trying to reach James."

Sam collects herself. "Ian, is your source reliable?"

"Absolutely."

"Who is your source? Why are you so sure you can rely on him?"

"His name is Louis Finche. James and I met with him a few months ago in Monaco. He's a pimp. The prince calls Finche when he goes to Monte Carlo. Has him provide call girls while he's here. The prince always wants blondes—he's got this thing for blondes. Finche says that the prince got in touch with him and told him that he's coming to Monte Carlo in a couple of days. The prince wants Finche to set him up with some girls. It's him all right, Sam. It's really too bad that James is going to miss him."

"Where's the prince staying?" Sam asks.

"The Hôtel de Paris in Monte Carlo."

"Ian, go to Monte Carlo. I'll meet you there. You can introduce me to this fellow Finche."

"I'm sorry, Mrs. Coppi—I don't understand. Why would you go to Monte Carlo?"

"I don't have time to explain now. I'll tell you all about my plans when I meet with you. Set up this meeting with Finche—I should be in Monte Carlo in the morning."

"Mrs. Coppi, I'm truly sorry, but I don't think this is a good idea. We shouldn't do anything without James."

"Thank you for your concern, Ian, but I must remind you—you work for both me and James. Please do as I am telling you and get to Monte Carlo. Set up this meeting with Finche."

"Yes, ma'am—right away."

"Good. Give my secretary a call and let her know where you'll be staying once you get there."

Sam buzzes Helen after she's finished the call with Ian. "Helen, is the company jet available?"

"Yes, Mrs. Coppi."

"Great! Call the pilot and have him get the flight crew ready—I leave for Monte Carlo this afternoon. Also, get me a hotel in Monte Carlo for a couple of nights. Any hotel except the Hôtel de Paris."

"Just what do you think you're doing?" Kathy asks after Sam hangs up.

"I'm going to Monte Carlo. This prince is in town. This is the man that's been after me, James and my family."

"And when you get there?" Kathy asks her, voice rising. "Just what do you think you're going to do? Confront this prince? Are you fucking crazy?"

"Kathy, I have to," Sam tells her. "This may be our only chance to get this guy."

Kathy takes a deep breath and exhales.

"Sam, sit back for a moment and think this through rationally," Kathy says in a calmer voice. "The prince will no doubt have bodyguards. If you try something, they'll blow your head off. Why not just wait until James gets back?"

"No, Kathy, I can't wait. Don't you see? James is in Pakistan. He thought the prince and this fellow Mafrouz were both going to be there. He went there for the specific purpose of getting to both men at the same time. James was afraid that if he only got to one and not the other, the other would go into hiding. It would make it that much more difficult to ever find him again. James will soon realize that he's wrong. There'll be only one man there: Mafrouz. The prince won't be there."

"Sam, you're missing the point," Kathy says. "You're not capable of confronting the prince by yourself. You'll be in a lot of danger."

"You know what, Kathy? That's a chance I'll just have to take. So far, I've let James do all of the fighting. He's been putting his life on the line constantly. It's time I stepped up to the plate." Sam stands up. "I can't talk anymore. I've got to get home and tell the children that I'll be gone for a few days."

Kathy stands up. "I'm coming to Monte Carlo, too."

"What?" Sam yells.

"You heard me—I'm coming with you! I'm going home to get my daughter Marlene and take her to your house. Your staff can watch her, too—along with your children."

"No, you're not coming!" Sam cries out. "There's no way you're getting involved."

"Oh yes she is!" Penelope pipes up, joining the quarrel. "And so am I! We're both coming with you. If you want to do this crazy thing, you'll have to do it with us coming along with you."

Sam and Kathy look at Penelope and ask in unison, "You?"

"Yes, me! You and James saved my life. Now it's my turn to return the favor."

"Neither of you is coming with me," Sam declares. "I'm going alone."

Sam begins walking toward the door, but Penelope jumps up and grabs her arm.

"Sam, get this through your thick head. You're not going alone. Now, we can all waste a lot of time arguing and fighting among ourselves, or we can get going."

Sam looks at the two women, then sighs. "All right—but what I say goes. Kathy, go home and get Marlene and bring her to the ranch." She turns to Penelope. "You might as well come with us to Monaco, too."

Penelope smiles. "That's much better. Let's get going."

As they pass by Helen's desk, Sam asks, "What hotel did you get me?"

"The Hôtel Hermitage Monte-Carlo," she replies.

"Call the Hermitage back. Tell them we'll need a suite large enough to sleep three. Kathy and Penelope are coming with me."

The jet has taken off after refueling in Newfoundland. The next stop is Monaco. Kathy and Penelope are in the back, sleeping. In her mind, Sam is going over the plan that has just occurred to her. She wonders what James would say if he found out what she was up to.

Sam stifles a laugh. She knows exactly what he would say. And, more importantly, she knows precisely what he would do. There is no way that James would allow her to try to carry out this scheme.

Kathy and Penelope insisting upon coming along has made her uneasy. Now she has to worry about *their* safety along with her own.

But she is happy that they're with her. She's not absolutely certain that she would be able to carry out the task without their support.

A calmness has come over her as she decides on her plan. She no longer feels the nervous tightness in her stomach that she had felt earlier. Now that she has developed a strategy on how to get to the prince, she's at peace with her decision. She becomes so relaxed that she actually manages to close her eyes and drift off to sleep.

Ian is standing by the car curbside when the women exit the airport terminal. He looks one by one at each of the blondes.

"Do you mind telling me what is going on?" Ian asks Sam. He gestures to the two other women. "What are they doing here?"

Sam smiles. "I will—in due time, Ian. Have a little patience. Come on—let's get going. We have a lot to do."

As they drive off, Ian turns to Sam, who is sitting in the front passenger seat. "You do know that James is going to fire me for this, don't you?"

Sam laughs. "Don't worry, Ian. I'll protect you."

Kathy leans forward from the back. "You've got nothing to worry about, Ian. James would never buck Sam."

"No way, ladies. I'm a dead man—I know it. No one can save me." Ian shakes his head and turns to Sam. "I don't know why I let you talk me into this."

"Forget about James," Sam says. "We'll worry about him later. What about this man, Finche? Were you able to reach him?"

"Yeah, we're meeting him at Chez Joey. The same place where James met with him. We'll head right out after you check into the hotel. Finche is expecting us."

"What about the prince?" Sam asks. "When does he arrive?"

"Tomorrow."

Sam sits back in her seat and closes her eyes. "Perfect. Everything is falling into place."

After dropping off Kathy and Penelope, Sam and Ian walk into the bistro. "There he is!" Ian points to a man sitting at a back table.

Sam looks around the place—it's almost empty. A bartender is talking with a lone customer at the bar, and a waiter is setting up the tables. Sam and Ian walk quickly to where Finche is sitting.

Finche jumps up when he sees Sam. "Who is this woman, Ian? What's going on—where is Monsieur Coppi?"

"Mr. Coppi can't be here," Ian replies, and gestures to Sam. "This is Mrs. Coppi. She's taking his place."

"I don't like this one bit! This was not the deal that was proposed to me." Finche waves his hand dismissively at her. "The deal is off!"

"Please, Louis, have a seat," Ian implores him. "Just hear us out."

"No! I've heard enough," Finche says and starts to walk off.

"Sit down, Mr. Finche!" Sam yells out. "You were paid well for your services. Unless you have the money in your pocket to pay me back, I suggest you sit and listen to what I have to say."

Finche looks at Sam and pauses. Then he sits down again. "Fine, I will hear what you have to say."

Ian and Sam also take seats at the small table.

"All we need from you, Mr. Finche, is *little* more of your cooperation—not much more," Sam tells him. "The deal is the same with me as it was with my husband. First, please tell me about what you have arranged for the prince."

The pimp looks from Sam to Ian and then back at Sam again.

"The prince has requested two women to come to his hotel for their services tomorrow night," he says at last. "Pretty blondes, as is his usual preference."

"What time tomorrow night?" Sam asks.

"Nine."

Sam smiles. "Good," she says. "Now we're getting somewhere." Then she leans forward in her seat. "Here is what I'd like you to do. Call the prince. Tell him that it's all set for tomorrow night. Say he's such a good client that you're throwing in an extra woman as a bonus. No extra charge. There'll be three blondes—it'll be a special night."

Sam smiles again. "That's all you have to do. We'll take it from there. Do you understand?"

"Yes, *madame*," Finche replies. "What about the women? Where will you find such professionals? I'm quite sure this is not your area of expertise."

"That's not your concern, Mr. Finche. We'll handle the rest. Just make the call as I have instructed."

Finche takes a long look at Sam.

"What's the matter?" she asks. "Is there something wrong?"

"This will not work," Finche voices. "The prince has armed security guards. You'll never get past the security. Those bodyguards can tell the difference between amateurs and professionals."

"Thank you for your concern, Mr. Finche, but that's not your problem. Just do what you're being paid to do. Do you understand?"

"Yes, of course," Finche says and turns to Ian. "Please get me the balance of the money you owe me by tomorrow. I'm going to get out of town—I don't want to be here when this affair blows up."

When they are back in the hotel lobby, Ian tells Sam, "You know, Mrs. Coppi, I didn't say anything in front of Finche, but he's absolutely correct. If it is your intention to confront the prince, you are in great danger. The prince has armed professionals."

"Once again, I thank you for your concern."

Ian sighs.

"Is there anything else you need?" Ian asks her.

"No. You're all done. You can go home—you're not needed anymore. Thank you for your help. Don't forget to get Finche the balance of the money we owe him before you leave."

"I'll pay him the balance, Mrs. Coppi—but I'm not leaving," Ian says. "If you don't mind, I'll stick around town until this is over. I'll be in Room 326 if you need me."

"I guess you're still going through with this?" Kathy asks when Sam gets in the room.

"Yes, I am." Sam tells her and looks at both women. "If either of you wants to go home, believe me—I'll understand. No hard feelings.

You guys must have figured out by now what I'm up to. I know it's a lot to ask of anyone. This is my problem, not yours."

Penelope looks at Kathy and then back to Sam. "No, we're going to see this through."

"All right, but you've got until tomorrow night to change your mind," Sam says, heading for the door.

"Where are you going?" Kathy asks.

"I need to go pick something up. Listen, girls, do me a favor. You guys go shopping. You'll need the proper attire for tomorrow night, if you know what I mean. Pick up a dress for me, too. Something chic, but slutty. Make sure it's low cut in the front. You guys know my size." Sam gives them a smile. "I should be back in a few hours. We'll have a nice dinner and go to the casino afterward. I'll spot you some money for gambling—that's the least I can do."

Sam goes downstairs to the concierge desk. "Where can I find a fine cutlery shop?" she asks the woman.

"There's a cutlery shop nearby," the concierge answers, reaching into a drawer and pulling out a map. "Here, let me show you where it is. Just take a right out of the hotel and walk four blocks." The concierge takes a pen and traces the route for Sam on the map. "Then take a left, and the store is halfway up that street. You can't miss it." She hands Sam the map.

"Thank you!" Sam takes the map and leaves the hotel.

Sam follows the concierge's directions and quickly arrives at the cutlery shop, Les Couteaux de Francois. The woman behind the counter is helping another customer. Sam walks around the store and looks over the silverware in one of the displays. A few minutes later, the customer leaves, and the saleswoman approaches Sam.

"*Puis-je vous aider?*" she asks.

"Do you speak English?" Sam asks.

"*Oui.*"

"Good! I'd like you to build me a pocketknife. Could you do that for me?"

"Of course," the salesperson replies. "What kind of knife are you requiring? Would you like me to show you some that we already have in stock?"

"No. There's one that I'd like for you to build custom for me. Let me show you." Sam opens her purse. She pulls out a nail file.

"I'd like it made out of silver, Sam says, showing the clerk the file. "Each side will have a file like this one. In between will be the blade. The knife should spring open by pressing on the sides. It must not look like a knife. The blade should be concealed."

"How big of a blade are you looking for?"

Sam lifts up the nail file. "At least as long as this file. It must be very sharp. Can you do that?"

"Yes, of course."

"Good! How much will it cost?"

"Two hundred francs," the saleswoman responds.

"I'm sorry but I have only dollars. How much is that in American money?"

"Fifty dollars. Is that acceptable?"

"Yes, that will be fine. Can I have it by tomorrow? I'm leaving to go back to America."

"No. I beg your pardon, *madame,* but that is not possible. Tomorrow is too soon."

"I'll tell you what," Sam says. "I'll pay you two hundred dollars if it's ready by tomorrow morning."

The woman stares at Sam. *"Excusez-moi. Un moment.* I will be right back. I will get my husband, Henri." The woman turns, walks to the back of the store, and disappears out of sight.

Sam hears two voices speaking in French. After a moment, the saleswoman comes back out with a man.

"Madame, what time tomorrow morning do you need this knife completed?" the man asks.

"By eleven," Sam replies. "Can you do it?"

"Yes, certainly—it will be ready."

"Thank you!"

Sam gets back to the hotel and walks up to the concierge. "Thank you, the directions were perfect."

The woman smiles "*Merci madame.* Did you find what you were looking for?"

Sam sighs. "No. I had a problem with the language." Sam opens her pocketbook and takes out the nail file. "I wanted the store to make me a silver file like this one. A souvenir for my trip here to Monte Carlo but the woman couldn't understand me."

The concierge reaches out. "May I see it?"

Sam hands her the file and the woman takes a look. She looks up at Sam. "I don't understand, this doesn't look too difficult to make. What was the problem?"

"I don't know, I couldn't understand her."

"Would you like me to send the piece over to the shop and have it made for you?"

"You would do that?"

The lady smiles. "Of course, that would be no problem. I'll put the charge on your hotel bill."

"I'm checking out of the hotel tomorrow so it has to be done before then."

"Yes, certainly madame."

Sam takes a step to walk away but turns and comes back. "Please don't tell the store owner that it's for me. I feel embarrassed that I couldn't understand the lady."

"Yes of course madame. They don't need to know."

Sam smiles. "Thank you."

27
Settling the Score

JAMES IS SITTING IN HIS hotel room in Peshawar in the dark, looking at the clock. It's twenty to four in the morning, and he hasn't slept at all. With his adrenaline rushing through his veins, he wouldn't be able to sleep even if he tried. *Plenty of time to sleep when this is over,* he assures himself. He's counting the minutes until four o'clock, when Ernie and Gary should come knocking at his door. The plan is to meet Chief Toru at five. But, before that hookup, James and the other two intend to ride by the compound to have a look around. Just take a final check to see if anything fishy is going on.

Neither Ernie nor Gary trust Toru—they suspect that Toru might sell them out, though they don't think that Toru has found a better deal than what James has offered yet.

Anyway, James has agreed to go have a look at the facility. A few minutes later, there's a knock at his door. James takes the revolver sitting on the counter and tucks it in the back of his belt, opens the drawer, takes out the silencer, and sticks it in his pocket. He grabs his bag and opens the door.

Ernie and Gary are standing outside. "Are you ready?"

"Yeah," he says.

Ernie drives the car and parks on the unlit street a block away from the compound. There are two men in front of the entrance to the compound. One is sitting on a chair, his rifle leaning against the wall. He is smoking a cigarette. The other guard is standing nearby and has a rifle strapped to his shoulder. The two men appear to be talking. The compound itself is completely dark.

"Well, if it's a trap, you wouldn't know it by those two men," Gary remarks from the back seat.

"Yeah—it looks pretty normal," Ernie says. "There's nothing unusual going on."

"Come on—there's nothing to see here," James says. "Let's go for our meetup with Toru at the fort. Time to get this show on the road."

There are a dozen police vehicles at the rendezvous site when James gets there. Dozens of policemen are milling about. James and Gary get out of the car. Toru comes walking over dressed in full police uniform.

"Good—you are here," he says to James. Toru turns to another man and has a brief conversation in Urdu. Then he turns back to James.

"The men are ready. Let's get started—we want to hit the compound early. You and your men will wait in the car when we raid the place. I'll signal to you when it's safe to enter."

Back behind the wheel, Ernie follows the police vehicles from a distance as they make their way to the compound. The police pull up to the front gate, and policemen come pouring out of the vehicles. They nab the two sentries that are in front of the place and stand them facing the wall. Then two of the policemen begin handcuffing the men. The remaining officers burst open the doors and go running in with their guns drawn. Toru, surrounded by three of his men, gets out of his vehicle and walks into the compound.

James gets out of the car and turns to Gary and Ernie. "Come on, let's go." He reaches behind him for the pistol at the back of his belt.

Gary and Ernie jump out. "Weren't we supposed to wait for Toru to give us the all clear?" Gary asks.

"If it's a trap, I don't want to give them time to set up," James says, walking quickly toward the entrance. Ernie and Gary draw their weapons and follow him.

The two Afghans who were guarding the compound are sitting on the ground at the entrance, their hands cuffed behind their backs. A policeman with rifle drawn is standing over the men. The Afghan men look up at James as he walks by.

Inside the courtyard of the facility, the scene is chaotic. There is a lot of shouting. Another dozen men are sitting on the ground with their hands cuffed behind their backs. Three cops are standing guard over the men, again with rifles drawn.

James looks around. There are two more policemen standing in front of the doorway to the building, across the courtyard from the front gate. James heads their way. Four men with their hands up in the air come walking out of the entrance as James tries to enter the building. Two cops follow behind with guns pointed at the men.

There is a stairway just beyond the entrance. Again, two more Afghans with their arms raised are coming down the steps. A Pakistani policeman follows behind the men. The men squeeze by James as they pass him.

James looks back at Ernie and Gary—they have their weapons drawn. James nods to them. They nod back. Nothing is said. Nothing needs to be spoken. Both Ernie and Gary know exactly what to do.

There is nobody that James trusts more on an assignment like this one than those two guys walking behind him. Those two are the ultimate professionals. True soldiers of fortune. They know precisely what needs to be done, without hesitation. Totally fearless.

On the landing of the second floor, three Afghans are squatting on the ground with their hands behind their heads. Half a dozen policemen are there. Toru comes out of one of the rooms.

"Good, you're here," he says to James. "I was just coming out to get you. The men you're looking for are in here."

James and his two escorts walk into the room. Two policemen are standing alongside Mafrouz and the prince, who are sitting in chairs with their hands cuffed behind their backs.

"I'll leave you alone," Toru says to him. Toru turns to his men and orders them out of the room. Ernie shuts the door.

James reaches into his pocket and takes out the silencer. As he's screwing the piece onto the barrel of his gun, he walks up to the men.

"Nice to see you, Your Highness," he says to the prince. "I bet you didn't expect to see me again so soon." James turns to the other man. "You must be Mafrouz—I don't believe we've been properly introduced. Although our knowing each other will be brief—I'm here to send you to hell!"

"This won't end here, you know," Mafrouz says. "We'll keep coming at you—and eventually, we'll get you."

James smiles. "No, I don't think so, Mafrouz. It all ends here." James puts the barrel of the gun to Mafrouz's forehead. "In any event—even if what you say is true, you won't be around to see it done. Say goodbye to this world, Mafrouz."

James pulls the trigger. The bullet goes right through Mafrouz's head with such force that his gray matter splatters against the far wall. Mafrouz slumps over and slowly drops to the floor. James steps over to Faikil and lifts the pistol.

"Wait! Wait! Please, wait! Just wait a moment!" Faikil yells out. "Hear me out! I have a proposal for you."

James puts the tip of the barrel to his forehead. "Speak fast, Faikil—death is calling for you."

"If you let me live, I will make you a rich man," the royal tells him.

"I'm already a rich man," James responds.

"Not this rich. You will have enough wealth to have your own kingdom."

James smiles. "No deal, Faikil. Say your goodbyes."

"Please, please, don't do this," Faikil pleads. "I don't want to die!"

"As much as I'm enjoying your sniveling and begging for your life, Faikil, it's time for you to leave this world."

James pulls the trigger. Faikil's brains also splatter against the far wall. His body falls to the floor

James exhales and turns to Ernie and Gary. "That's it—we're done! Let's get the hell out of here."

———— ⌇——— ⌇————

James is sitting in Pan Am's first class lounge at the Palam airport in New Delhi. He keeps looking at the clock. It's two thirty. His flight to Milan isn't due to leave for another hour. He's planning to spend the night in Milan. Good thing, too—he is exhausted. Has not had a good night's rest in a week.

Now that the danger to his family has finally been eliminated, he might be able to get a decent night's sleep. From Milan, he will board a flight to New York the following day and then switch to another flight that will head back to Denver.

"Don't you ever drink?" Ernie asks, sitting across a small table from him with a beer in hand.

"Sometimes," he replies.

Gary comes over and hands James one of the two beers he is carrying. "Well, you're having a beer now. When a job is well done, a man should be able to kick up his feet and have a nice, cold beer."

James smiles. "All right, I'll drink to that!" He lifts up his bottle and salutes the other two. "Here's to a job well done."

"Here, here!" Ernie bellows, and chugs half his beer.

James wipes the foam from his lips. "Thank you, guys, for all your help. It's been a long haul. I couldn't have done it without you—you guys really came through for me." James takes another swig of his beer. "So what now? Where are you guys headed?"

"We're heading back to South Africa," Gary says. "We're partners in a vineyard there, and it's time we paid a bit of attention to the farm."

"Vineyard?" James exclaims. "I didn't know you two were vintners. I'd never have guessed it in a thousand years. I've got to take a trip to South Africa and pay you guys a visit."

"Well, we're not quite vintners yet," Ernie says with a laugh. "We just started the farm two years ago. The vines are just beginning to develop." Ernie stops talking to listen to an announcement for boarding.

"Gary, that's us," he says, standing up. "They just announced our flight."

James stands up and extends his hand. "Once again, thanks for all your help, guys. Really—I couldn't have done it without you."

"No problem, James. Have a safe trip," Ernie says, and the two men walk off.

James watches as they walk away. He finishes his beer, puts down the bottle, picks up his bag, and heads for his own gate.

28

It's Sam's Turn

"DID YOU GIRLS GET OUR outfits this morning?" Sam asks Penelope and Kathy as they are having a late breakfast at the hotel restaurant.

"Yes, we did," Penelope replies. "They're altering the dresses as we speak. We'll pick them up this afternoon."

"Penelope tried on your dress," Kathy says. "She's only an inch taller than you."

"What kind of dress did you pick out for me? I hope it's something sexy—I want to make just the right impression."

Kathy laughs. "Let me put it this way. James would get very excited if he saw you in this outfit."

"Your dress is red," Penelope tells Sam. "The color fits in with the theme of the night, don't you think?"

"I guess we're still going through with this?" Kathy asks. "There's no way for us to talk you out of tonight?"

"Kathy, we already had this discussion. Please, no more. I'm scared enough as it is—I don't need more doubt feeding my fear. I know what I've got to do, and I know how to get it done. If you guys don't want to go along, I fully understand—you have until tonight to change your minds."

Sam looks at the watch on her wrist. "It's after eleven. I've got to get going; I've got an errand to run." Sam stands up. "Do me a favor—take care of the bill. I'll see you guys up in the suite in a bit. My errand shouldn't take long."

Sam leaves the hotel and heads for the cutlery shop. Inside the

293

store, Henri is taking care of another customer. He looks at Sam. "I'll be with you in a moment, *madame*."

When he is done with the client, Henri tells Sam, "I've got your merchandise in the back—I'll go get it for you."

Henri comes out a moment later with the saleswoman who helped Sam the day before. Henri places a rolled-up, gray cloth on the counter, unfurls the cloth, and holds out the knife.

"This is the knife." Henri hands her the knife.

Sam looks at the knife and then looks up at him. "Are you sure? It doesn't look like a knife. It's so thin!"

The man laughs. "Yes, I'm absolutely sure. Let me show you how it works." Henri reaches over and takes the knife from her. "You simply press on the two bottom sides of the piece." He shows her the spot and presses. "See?" A six-inch blade flips out.

Sam is startled and flinches.

"You try it." Henri closes the blade and hands her the knife.

Sam presses the sides as Henri had done, and the blade instantly springs out. "Is the knife functional? The blade doesn't look sturdy. Or sharp—it doesn't look like it could cut anything."

"Madame, the blade is very sturdy." Henri turns to his wife. *"Va me chercher la roue de fromage, s'il te plaît."*

The woman goes to the back of the store and comes out with a large wheel of cheese. Henri stands the cheese on its side and looks at Sam. "Go ahead, stick the knife through it!"

Sam stabs at the wheel with the knife. The razor-sharp blade easily slides through the thick rind and into the cheese.

"Are you satisfied?" Henri asks.

"Yes," Sam says, pulling out the knife.

Henri takes the knife from her and cleans off the blade with the cloth. "Should I wrap it for you?"

"No, I'll just put it in my purse. How much do I owe you?"

"Two hundred dollars as we agreed."

Sam opens her bag and pulls out her wallet. She counts two hundred dollars.

"Would you like a receipt?" he asks.

"No, thank you."

Henri hands her the knife and Sam places it in her bag. *"Merci beaucoup, madame.* Please come again."

When Sam gets back to the hotel she stops at the concierge desk. The woman looks up. "Oh, Madame I have the merchandise." The woman opens a drawer and takes out a box. "Is this to your satisfaction?" she asks opening the box.

"Yes that's perfect." Sam takes the box from the lady. "Thank you!"

"Merci, madame."

"It's seven o'clock," Penelope tells Sam and Kathy. "We'd better get dressed if we're going to make it to the Hôtel de Paris by nine."

"Sit down, guys. We need to talk," Sam says. "I've given this a lot of thought—I can't let you guys get involved after all. This is too much to ask of anyone. What I'm going to do tonight is more than a friend should ever be asked to do."

"Sam, Penelope and I know what we're getting into," Kathy says.

"Both of us talked it over," Penelope adds. "No more discussion. We're ready—we better get going."

"Stop it!" Sam shouts at them. "Please, just stop it!' she says in a calmer voice. "I'm already scared out of my wits—I don't need to be worried about you two as well. Just wish me luck—that's all I need.

"If something goes wrong, I would feel awful that I dragged you into this," Sam continues. "Even if something doesn't go wrong, think about what I dragged you into doing? No, you guys can't come. No way! Now, get out of my way and let me get dressed. I also need to do my makeup and my hair, so I need to get going." Sam heads for her bedroom.

An hour later, Sam emerges in the new dress. She is wearing frosted eyeshadow, and her blonde hair is up in a chignon.

"How do I look?" she asks.

"Wow!" Penelope exclaims.

"Look at that cleavage!" Kathy says and whistles.

"Yeah, I know," Sam says, smiling ruefully. "It's a little too revealing—I feel naked."

"You better wear a jacket," Kathy suggests. "You'll never make it through the lobby dressed like that."

"I have a shawl that I'll use to cover up."

"Well, I guess you'd better get started," Penelope tells her, looking at the clock. "It's twenty to nine. One last time, won't you reconsider?"

"No, I'm all set—my mind is made up. Let me get my shawl and purse. Do me a favor, girls. Call downstairs and make sure a cab is waiting for me outside the front door. I don't want to be hailing a cab on the street in this getup."

Sam heads into the bedroom and picks up the shawl that is lying on the bed. She adjusts her skimpy dress and makes sure everything is covered. One final look at the full-length mirror and she heaves a sigh, turns, and picks up her purse on the bureau.

She takes a final look in her purse to make sure the knife is still there. The plan that she has decided on is fully ingrained in her head—she's gone over it a hundred times. There will be no wasting time. As soon as she comes face to face with the prince, she will stick the knife into his gut. No small talk, no chitchat—she'll just get it over with quickly. No chance for anything to go wrong. And—most importantly—no chance for her to back down. She comes out of the bedroom.

"You guys are going straight to the airport after I leave," she reminds the ladies. "Captain Jeffrey has the company plane waiting for us."

"Yes," Kathy confirms. "What time will you get to the airport"

"Sometime between twelve and one."

"Well, if you're not there by one, we're calling the police," Penelope tells her.

"Wish me luck," Sam says and heads out the door.

Standing in front of the doors of the elevator inside the Hôtel de Paris before she pushes the call button, she thinks through one more time the plan she has settled on. The first thing she must do is to get into her head the fact that she is about to kill a man.

It's not as easy as it sounds, James had once told her. You must be fully convinced that the person needs to be killed. Any hesitation on your part, and your plan could fall apart. Sam closes her eyes and lets out a breath. *I'm ready.*

The next item is to rehearse in her mind, once again, exactly how she is going to do the deed. Her eyes close once more as she reflects on the plan. It is simple. The minute the prince comes up to her, she is going to stick the knife into his gut. *Remember, no talk—just do it and get it over with.* Sam lets out a breath again and presses the button to call the elevator.

The elevator doors open when she gets to the prince's floor. Sam arranges the shawl on her shoulders, exposing her bountiful breasts. She steps out of the elevator and smiles at the two men guarding the prince's door.

"I have an appointment with the prince," she tells them.

One of the men looks her up and down and then hesitates. "There were supposed to be three of you."

Sam smiles. "I don't know anything about that—I was just instructed to come here tonight." Her look becomes flirtatious. "Besides, when I get done with your man, he won't need anyone else."

The guard looks at her ample cleavage. "Yes, I'm sure you're right—but I've got to search you."

Sam makes a sweeping gesture toward her skimpy dress and smiles again. "Just where do you think I could hide a weapon"?

The sentry smiles back. "Your purse, please," he says and points to the purse in her hand.

Sam hands him the purse. The guard opens the small bag and rummages through it. Then he pulls out the nail file with the knife hidden inside and holds it up. "What's this?"

Sam gives him a small laugh and takes the item from his hand. "It's for filing my nails," she explains and demonstrates by filing one of her nails. Then she hands him back the file.

The guard puts the knife back in the purse, gives her the bag back, and opens the door to the suite. Inside, a man in a white jacket is arranging dishes on a dinner cart. The waiter stops to look at Sam when she comes in.

"The prince is on an important call in the next room," he says. "He asked me to tell you that he'll be out shortly. Help yourself to anything." The waiter gestures to the cart and lets himself out of the room.

Sam opens her purse and takes out the knife, palming it by her side and waiting for the door to open.

At the same time, James is in his hotel room in Milan, getting ready to hit the sack. It's just an overnight stay until the morning, when he will catch a flight back to the States. He takes a sip of his bottle of mineral water, kicks off his shoes, and lies down on the bed. The clock on the night table shows 9:05. *That means it's 1:05 in the afternoon in Colorado. Time to call Sam and give her the good news: the war is over—and we won.*

Billingsley answers the phone. "Good afternoon, Mr. Billingsley. May I speak to Samantha, please?"

"I'm very sorry, Mr. Coppi, but your wife isn't at home," he replies.

"Do you know what time she'll be back?"

"No, I don't, sir. She went on a trip overseas and won't be home for days. Her friend Katherine went with her. Katherine dropped off her daughter Marlene so that we can watch her."

What the fuck is going on? James wonders. *What are they up to?* "Do you know where they went?" James asks, trying very hard to remain in control.

"Monte Carlo. She is staying at the Hôtel Hermitage. I can get the number for you."

"Yes, please get me the number," he asks, trying to keep his voice calm.

James writes down the number after Billingsley gives it to him and, immediately after hanging up, calls the hotel.

"We're very sorry, sir—Madame Coppi and her party checked out a few minutes ago," the front desk tells him.

"Damn," James mutters after hearing the news. He calls his office and asks for Helen.

"Helen, do you know why Sam and Kathy went to Monte Carlo?"

"No, I don't, Mr. Coppi. Mrs. Coppi asked me to have the company plane made available and to book hotel reservations for the three of them."

"The three of them? Who's the third person at the hotel?"

"Penelope Campos," Helen tells him.

"Penelope Campos!" James cries out, his voice getting louder. "Helen, what's this all about? What's going on?"

"I really don't know, sir. It might have something to do with Mr. Wadsworth. They left suddenly right after he called."

"What did he say to Sam?"

"I don't know, Mr. Coppi."

"OK, thanks, Helen." He hangs up. Rubbing his forehead and then lifting up the receiver, he dials again.

James dials Ian's office in London but there's no answer. "Damn, it's too late," he mutters. An idea comes to him and he dials again.

"Hermitage," the woman answers.

"Is Ian Wadsworth staying there?"

"Yes, he is," says the operator. *Bingo!* James thinks. "I'll connect you to his room."

"Come on, Ian, please be in your room," he whispers to himself.

"Hello?" Ian answers.

"Ian, what the fuck is going on? Why the hell is Sam in Monte Carlo?"

"James!" Ian yells back. "Where the fuck are you? This thing is about to blow up!"

"What thing is about to blow up?"

"This thing with the prince!" Ian shouts. "Sam just went to meet with him."

"Ian, what the fuck are you talking about? Which prince?"

"The Prince that you planned to kill. Finche called me a few days ago and said that the prince would be in Monte Carlo today. James, I tried to reach you. I called you at least a dozen times. Finally, I got to Samantha. She said that she would take over for you—she's at the prince's hotel right now."

James shakes his head still confused. *What prince? Who the hell did Sam go see?* "For God's sake, Ian—why didn't you stop her?"

"James, I tried! Believe me, I tried. You know Samantha; no one can stop her when she's made up her mind. She threatened to fire me and do the job alone. I thought it best if I stayed in the picture. You know—just in case something goes wrong."

"Well, something's gone wrong!" James tells Ian. Then, suddenly, everything becomes crystal clear in his head, and he mutters to himself, "Firuz!"

"What?" Ian says.

"Nothing. Where is the meeting?"

"The Hôtel de Paris. Do you want me to burst in?"

"No—that may put Sam in even more danger." James pauses for a moment to think. The knot in his stomach is getting tighter. "Listen, Ian, I'm in Milan. I'm going to grab a car and get to this Hôtel de Paris. If I go fast, I can be there around midnight. You get to the lobby of the Hôtel de Paris and hang out there in case Sam needs you. Don't do anything else until I get there."

"OK, James. Hurry!"

James puts on his shoes, grabs his bag and bolts out of his room. Downstairs, he hails a cab.

"Hôtel de Paris in Monte Carlo!" he says to the cabbie. The driver turns his head and shouts back in Italian. "Monte Carlo? *Sono tre ore di distanza!* That's three hours away!"

James tells the driver. "*Sì, e se lo fai in due, ti darò duecentomila lire in più.* Yes, and if you do it in two, I'll give you two hundred thousand lire more."

The cabbie peels out.

Sam is sitting on the couch. She's been waiting for the prince for nearly twenty minutes. She's getting very nervous, and she is having second thoughts. The sound of the voice in the next room goes quiet and she hears the receiver of a phone being placed into the cradle. *It's time.* Sam stands up and presses the knife for the blade to come out. She takes a deep breath and stands by the doorway. The door opens and the man walks out wearing a white evening jacket.

"Firuz?" Sam blurts out in astonishment and freezes.

"Mrs. Coppi?" he says, looking equally surprised. "What are you doing here?"

"You're the one who's been trying to kill my family?" Sam is confused and paralyzed by fear. She can't move her limbs, but she also can't seem to stop talking.

"Samantha, you better leave," Firuz says, motioning to the door.

"How could you?" Still in a state of shock, Sam keeps trying to make sense of the scene in front of her. "What did we ever do to you? You were supposed to be our friend!"

"You wouldn't understand. There are moments in history bigger than a few people. I'm going to get the guards," Firuz says, walking toward the door.

As he passes by, Sam grabs hold of his arm and turns him around to her. She plunges the knife deep into his stomach. Firuz lets out a groan and grasps the hand that is holding the knife. A puzzled look comes over him as he stares into her face. He looks down at her hand, which is still pressing the knife into him. He looks back up at her.

His other hand reaches up and grasps her by the throat. Sam grabs his wrist and tries to pull the hand from her neck. With one hand on Sam's throat, Firuz uses the other hand to pry the blade out from within him, but Sam grits her teeth and pushes it deeper. She can feel the blade cutting through the flesh of his belly. Her hand is wet from the warm blood that is flowing out of his body. She is still trying to remove the hand that is clutching her throat.

Sam feels his grip around her throat weaken, and he suddenly collapses to the floor. She looks down at his lifeless body. A pool of blood is forming on the rug. Blood is still dripping from her hand.

She rubs her throat with the other hand and tries to get control of her breathing, which has become ragged. Staggering, she falls back onto the couch, continuing to gaze at the lifeless body.

Her mind has gone blank. Confusion sets in. She doesn't know what to do next. Suddenly, she feels freezing cold. She needs to move—needs to do something. But what, exactly? *Why am I here?* she wonders. She can't quite remember. It is nearly half an hour before Sam comes out of shock.

She heads for the bathroom. There is a full-length mirror that reflects a woman with red marks on her throat and a large blood stain on the front of her dress. She washes the blood from her hands, removes her dress, and lets it drop to the floor. Exhaling to relieve all of the tension that has built up inside of her, she picks up her dress and tries to wash the stain. She hangs the dress to dry and then takes a shower to clean the evidence of the crime off her body.

After the shower, she puts her bra and panties back on, goes back into the living room, and looks over at Firuz's lifeless corpse. The bleeding appears to have stopped. A chill goes through her body and she shudders. She sits on the sofa, on a side where she can't see the corpse and reaches for the magazine that was on the coffee table. It's only 9:56—too early for her to leave without arousing suspicion from the guards outside.

At midnight, Sam goes back into the bathroom. The dress is dry, the stain is barely detectable on her red dress.

I'll just have to take my chances, she thinks. Sam gets dressed, then goes back into the living room to get her shawl. Carefully, she drapes the shawl over her shoulders, making sure that her breasts are fully exposed, and holds her purse against her stomach, trying to cover the stain. Taking a look in the mirror a final time, she lets out her breath. The two bodyguards are sitting on a chair when she opens the door to leave.

Sam gives them a smile and says, "The Prince asked me to give you strict orders that he does not want to be disturbed. He's very tired."

Quickly, she walks to the elevator and presses the button, keeping her back to the men and saying a silent prayer. The elevator seems to take forever to arrive, but the elevator doors finally open, and she steps inside.

Sam exhales. *I did it. I can't believe I really did it!* she repeats all the way down to the ground floor.

The elevator to the lobby opens and Sam steps out—right into James's arms.

"Oh my God, you're here!" she cries out, and squeezes him tight. "I'm so glad you're here."

"Yeah—but unfortunately not in time, I see." He looks at the stain on the dress. "Are you OK? Never mind—no more talk. Let's get out of here. I told Ian to get us a taxi to take us to the airport and get on our plane that's waiting for us."

"Don't you want to know what happened?" Sam asks him in the cab.

"I do—but let's get out of this country first," he says. "You can tell me everything in the privacy of our plane." James leans over and kisses her. "I'm guessing by that stain on the front of your dress that's it's over, and our family is safe. We have nothing else to fear. We won!"

29

The Fallout

JAMES IS WOKEN FROM HIS sleep by Sam, who is tossing and turning and moaning something unintelligible. It has been five days since they returned home, and she hasn't had a full night's sleep since. James leans over and shakes her shoulder gently.

"Sam, wake up. You're having a bad dream."

Her eyes fly open. There is a blank expression on her face. She looks at James as if she doesn't know him.

"Are you all right?" he asks, and she seems to come back from whatever private hell she was in.

She sits up and holds his body to hers. He rubs her back.

"No, I'm not fine—I had another one of my awful dreams. His face keeps popping into my head." Sam breaks off the hug and searches his face. "How do you do it, James? How do you set aside the people you've killed . . . get them out of your thoughts?"

James pulls her to him again and caresses her back once more. "You never do, dear. Those faces will stay with you forever. You just need to learn to live with what you did. Come to terms with the fact that there was no other way." He breaks off the embrace. "Come on, get up. It's nearly six. Take those pajamas off—they're all soaked through. Go take a shower. I'll make us a pot of coffee."

James looks up from sipping on a cup of coffee when Sam comes into the kitchen after her shower. "There's a full pot on the stove," he says to her.

"Can we talk now?" Sam asks after she sits down at the kitchen table.

"OK."

"Why did Firuz want us dead? I thought he was our friend."

"He didn't want us dead. At least, not at first. After his father abdicated the throne, Firuz joined forces with these guys. It was his way of trying to get back into power."

"But how about Finche?" she asks. "He said that the prince from Afghanistan was coming in—I don't believe Finche even knew Firuz."

"I spoke to Ian about this—he believes that Faikil had a change of plans and Firuz must have taken his place. Faikil never told Finche about the switch."

"How did you realize it was Firuz?"

"I probably should've realized much earlier that Firuz may have been behind some of this. It was Firuz who set up for my meet with Prince Faikil in Washington. Why was Firuz friends with this guy all of a sudden, I'm now asking myself? The Shia and Sunni's hate each other. Even worse, the Arabs never trusted Firuz's country. They always felt it was a tool of the US government."

James shakes his head. "I let my friendship with Firuz cloud my judgement—I never thought that he would go that far to regain his power. Prince Faikil and Mafrouz were trying to build a theocratic society in the Middle East—I thought Firuz was against that idea. But Firuz got desperate, I guess? Maybe he thought that once he came into power he could outsmart Faikil and Mafrouz."

James lets out a breath. "In any event, at some point, Firuz joined their cause and I guess eliminating us became acceptable to him to reach his goal. It was Firuz that was in charge of the men in Colorado Springs. Those were the men that tipped off Faakhir and Moshar that you were headed for Milan. It hit me while I was talking to Ian on the phone in Milan—Firuz also loved blondes."

"What about the shah?" she asks. "What's going to happen to him?"

"We arranged to have the shah relocate to Mexico. I called Firuz's brother Farsad and told him that we wouldn't be representing his family any longer. The last I heard is that Egypt was considering taking in the shah."

Sam gets herself a cup of coffee. "What are you doing today?" she asks him.

"I'm going to the office."

She gives him a pleading look.

"Oh, do you have to? I was hoping that we could go for a ride. You know—have a nice day out on the ranch."

"It'll have to be tomorrow," he replies. "There're things that I have to do in the office. Kathy says that there are documents that they need me to sign."

"My goodness, you two are up early," Mrs. Billingsley says when she comes into the kitchen. "Would you like me to prepare some breakfast to go with your coffee?"

"Not for me." James stands up. "I'm going to take a shower." He walks up to Sam and gives her a kiss. "Do me a favor, take Molly to school for me today. I'd like to get into the office and get done early. Maybe I can be home for dinner."

James is at work reading documents when his speaker goes off.

"James, Bill Sester is on the line," Kathy says.

"Good, you're in today. I'm coming right over," Sester says when James is on the phone.

"Coming right over?" James looks at the clock. "It's a quarter to twelve. Where are you?"

"I'm at the Broadmoor Hotel—I got in last night. The president sent me. I've got to speak to you."

James knows what's coming. "You should have called first—I don't have the time."

"I really don't give a fuck if you have the time. I'm on my way." The phone clicks in James ear.

James buzzes Kathy. "Kathy, do me a favor. Have Rodney come to my office right away. When Bill Sester gets here, let him right in."

There's a knock at his door and Rodney looks in. "You wanted to see me?"

"Yeah, Rodney, come in." James waves to him. "Have a seat. Bill

Sester is in town, and he's on his way here. Should be here in ten or fifteen minutes."

"Sester is in town?" Rodney takes a seat. "Did he have an appointment with you?"

"No, this was unexpected. Sester called and said he was in Colorado Springs and wanted to meet with me right away."

"This can't be good! Do you know what this is about?"

James lets out a laugh. "Yeah, I've got a pretty good idea. I'd fill you in, but I don't want to spoil the surprise for you. Let me just say, things are going to get pretty exciting when he gets here."

A few minutes later, Kathy is on the horn. "Bill Sester is in the lobby."

"Go ahead and get Sester. Bring him to my office," James replies. "And, Kathy, you might want to put in earplugs."

"Mr. Sester," Kathy announces when she comes back up. She rolls her eyes and closes the door behind her.

"You really fucking did it this time, Coppi!" Sester yells at James. "You just couldn't let it go, could you? You had to do it your way!"

James stands up and motions to a chair. "Come on, Bill, sit down. Stop screaming! You'll have the whole office in here."

Sester sits down and looks at Rodney still shouting, "You were with the CIA! You, of all people, can appreciate what this clown just succeeded in doing. Do you know what this motherfucker did? He single-handedly gave the entire Middle East to the Russians."

"First of all, you can look directly at me when you speak." James's voice gets louder. "Secondly, you can lower your voice, or I'll kick you the fuck out of my office. And finally, stop being so fuckin' dramatic.

"Nothing has changed," James continues more quietly. "Those assholes were absolutely useless to you. They would have caused more trouble for America. They had a vision of setting the Muslim world back five centuries. There are others who are leading the fight against the Russians—people like Ahmad Shah Massoud. All he's looking for is a free Afghanistan—he has no designs on anything outside his country."

Sester looks over at Rodney. "Do you believe this guy? Now he thinks he knows foreign policy."

James stands up. "OK, Bill, I warned you—I told you to address only me. Now you need to get your sorry ass out of here."

Sester stands up and shouts, "Don't worry, Coppi—I'm leaving. I'm done, anyway. By the way, James, you know all of those government contracts your firm gets?" Sester asks with a sardonic smile. "Well, you can kiss them all goodbye. The president asked me to let you know that hell will freeze over before you ever get another government contract."

Sester heads out but, before he leaves, he turns and looks pointedly at James. "I hope you have better answers for the police of Monte Carlo when they come calling." His voice has taken on a menacing tone. "Goodbye, James."

At the mention of Monte Carlo, James falls silent.

When Sester is gone, Rodney turns to James. "What was that all about?" he asks.

"You really don't want to know," James says, distracted by what Sester said.

"What was that about the government contracts?" Rodney asks. "Are we in trouble or something?"

"What?"

"I asked you if we are in trouble on the government contracts. Do we need to take Sester's threat seriously? You know that the government side of the business represents a significant portion of our revenues."

James shakes his head as if trying to refocus on what Rodney is saying.

"No, we're good. There's an election coming up next week. If the polls are correct, the president is going to lose. The new administration is going to want to work with us. We have a lot of expertise around the world that they'll need. There's no chance of our company losing contracts. It wouldn't surprise me if Sester himself came back and asked us for a job after the election."

"Then what's worrying you, James?" Rodney asks. "Did Sester say something that's got you concerned? You look troubled."

"No, I'm fine," James says, smiling. "We're done here. You can go—I need to get back to work."

Two days later, James is in his study at his ranch when Billingsley walks in. "Mrs. Percival is on the phone for you, sir. She says it's urgent."

"What's up, Kathy?" James asks.

"Pete Simmons from the FBI called and wanted to speak to you."

"What's it's about?"

"He didn't say. He just left a number—he wants you to return his call."

"OK, thanks." James writes down the number and hangs up.

James pauses for a moment before calling Simmons back. It's about the remark Sester made—he's sure of it. But why is the FBI getting involved? They have no jurisdiction over something that happened in Monte Carlo. Or do they?

He's about to call his attorney, Michael Barret, but decides against it. He dials Simmons's number.

"Hello, Pete. It's James Coppi, returning your call."

"Hey, James! How's it going? Thanks for returning my call."

"No problem, Pete. What can I do for you?"

"James, I need for you and your wife to come to my office. It's about an investigation of a murder that happened in Monte Carlo. A Prince Firuz—I believe you know the man. The Monte Carlo police would like to speak to both you and your wife."

"A murder that happened overseas? Why is the FBI getting involved? And why us?"

"I don't know why the Monte Carlo police wants to speak to you two. The detectives I talked to wouldn't say. The agency is not really involved in this matter, James—we're doing it as a courtesy for the Monte Carlo police.

"The United Sates is a member of Interpol," the FBI agent continues, "and the member nations have agreed to work with each other when investigating crimes."

"When would they like to see us?"

"Next Tuesday. Say, around eleven. That's four days from now. Can you guys make it to my office?"

"Let me speak to Sam, and I'll call you back," James tells him. He hangs up the phone and immediately phones his lawyer Michael Barrett.

"Michael, do me a favor," James says when his lawyer is on the line. "Call Raymond Marr, the attorney who represented me last year. Tell him that I need him to come out to the ranch—I need to meet with him concerning an upcoming legal matter."

"What's up, James?" Michael asks. "Why do you need Marr?"

"Michael, I really don't want to talk about this over the phone. The FBI wants to interview Sam and me at their office on Tuesday."

"The FBI? Why does the FBI want to speak to you guys?"

"Just reach out to Raymond and have him call me. Better yet, don't have him call. Just ask him to come out to the ranch as soon as he can. It's really important—I'll fill him in when he gets here. Let me know if he's available."

James hangs up and comes out of his study, running into one of the maids in the hall. "Guadalupe, have you seen my wife? Do you know where she is?"

"I believe Mrs. Coppi is in Michael's room."

When James goes into the child's room, he finds Sam on the floor with Michael and his train set.

"Sam, can I see you for a minute in the bedroom?" he asks, beckoning to her.

"What's up?" she asks when they are seated on the bed with the door closed.

"We have a problem," he tells her "The FBI wants to speak to us about Monte Carlo."

Sam's face turns pale. "The FBI? Why are they involved? Don't they only handle things that happen in America?"

"There's some sort of agreement between the two countries. The police cooperate with each other. It's actually the Monte Carlo police that want to speak to us. The FBI is supposedly doing it as a courtesy to the Monte Carlo police."

"James, I'm frightened," she says, clutching his hand. "What do we do?"

"I've already called Michael and told him to get in touch with Raymond Marr. You remember Raymond? He's the attorney that represented you when you punched that senator."

"Yes, I remember Raymond. He's a good lawyer."

"Well, he'll be out here to go over our strategy." He gives her a quizzical look. "You must have known that this investigation was going to happen, didn't you? You didn't think that we would get off scot free?"

There's a knock at the door. "Mr. Coppi, I'm sorry to disturb you, but Mr. Michael Barrett is on the telephone. He said it's important."

James opens the door. "Thank you, Billingsley. I'll take it in the study."

"What's up, Michael?" James says when he takes the call. Sam comes walking in and sits on the opposite side of his desk.

"James, Raymond can't make it out to the ranch," Michael tells him. "He's in the middle of a trial and can't cut himself loose. He suggests that Vera Susskind take his place. You remember Vera, don't you?"

"Yes, I do. She was very good. I thought she left Marr's firm and went into her own practice?"

"Yes, she did. But Marr asked me to reach out to her. I've already spoken to Vera, and she's agreed to come out here—if you're comfortable using her."

"Yeah, that will be fine. I was impressed by Vera."

"Good. I'll give her a call and let her know. Expect a call from her."

James hangs up and looks over at Sam. "Did you hear?"

"Yes, Vera will be helping us." Sam takes a deep breath and sighs. "James, are we going to be all right?"

James gives her a smile and waves his hand dismissively. "Yeah, of course. After all we've been through, this is nothing."

The phone rings and James picks it up. "Hello?"

"Mr. Coppi, it's Vera Susskind," the caller says.

"Hello, Vera. How have you been?"

"I've been just fine, Mr. Coppi. And you? How is that lovely wife of yours?"

"Just fine, Vera. Sam is right here, across from my desk. I'll put you on the speaker so she can join the discussion."

"Hello, Vera," Sam says, speaking loudly toward the phone.

"Hello, Mrs. Coppi," Vera replies. "I guess I'll be seeing you again."

"Yes, Vera. I look forward to seeing you."

"James, Michael told me that the FBI will be conducting an interview with you. What's that about?"

"They want to speak to Sam and me about a problem that occurred in Monte Carlo," James says and then hesitates. "Vera, I really don't want to speak about this on the telephone. Can you get out here before Sam and I need to go their office? The interview is set for next Tuesday."

"Which office, and who is the contact?" Vera asks.

"Denver, and the agent is Pete. I forget his last name."

"All right, I'm going to call the FBI and rearrange the interview to be conducted at your ranch—if that's all right with you?"

"Why the ranch? Why not their office? What difference does it make?"

"Because at the ranch, it's a discussion. At their office, it's an interrogation. They may even have recording equipment set up.

"Besides, I want them all to experience that warm Coppi hospitality that you give all your guests. Let them know that this gracious, family-oriented couple would never commit a crime. Maybe Samantha can give the FBI agents one of her famous ranch tours."

James looks over at Sam.

"Yes, I can do that," Sam responds.

"Great. I'm going to grab the first flight out of DC tomorrow. I should be at your ranch by about one o'clock—we'll discuss everything at that time. Samantha, I hope you have some free time set aside after our meeting tomorrow—I'd love to go riding with you. I haven't been on a horse since I was out with you at your ranch."

"If you twist my arm, I might be persuaded." Sam says, laughing. "There's always time for riding."

"OK, Vera, have a safe trip." James hangs up. Then he looks at Sam.

"Riding?" he asks, incredulous. "You got over your fear of the police investigation that quickly, and now you're going horseback riding with Vera?" James shakes his head.

Sam stands up. "There's always time for a little riding. Besides, didn't you say that there's nothing to worry about?"

She walks out, leaving him to shake his head.

30
The Inquiry

SAM COMES WALKING INTO THE house the following Tuesday. She has just finished giving the Monte Carlo detectives, Henri Le Conte and Jacques Papadopoulos, a tour of the ranch. FBI agent Peter Simmons is also there, as are the attorneys Vera and Michael.

"Make yourself comfortable," Sam says when she, Le Conte and Papadopoulos get to the parlor. "Please help yourself to refreshments." She gestures to the table containing two trays of pastries, buns, rolls, and two urns of coffee. "If there is anything else that you want, please let Mr. Billingsley know. I'll go get James," she adds and walks out.

James has a broad smile on his face when he comes into the parlor. "I hope you enjoyed your tour."

Le Conte swallows and puts a half-eaten croissant down on his plate. "Yes, very much. Samantha was quite the tour guide. Your place is magnificent." Le Conte looks at Sam. "Where did you get these croissants?" he asks. "These are every bit as delicious as what we have in Monaco."

"There's a Polish bakery that opened up a few years ago in Colorado Springs—the baker who works there is quite a master. Although the word is getting out now, and he's becoming quite popular. There are long lines, and there's usually a wait on the weekends." Sam sits down on the sofa next to James.

"Well, Mr. Le Conte, you called for this meeting," Vera begins. "How can we be of help? As you can see, my clients are very cooperative and will assist you in any manner possible."

"Yes, I see that," Le Conte replies, and looks over at Sam and James. "Thank you for your hospitality and your cooperation. I'll get right to the point. We are investigating the murder of a Prince Firuz, who was killed while he was in Monte Carlo two weeks ago. Your names came up in our investigation."

"Mr. and Mrs. Coppi's names came up?" Vera asks. Before the meeting, Vera told James and Sam that she will be doing most of the talking and to not answer any questions unless she instructs them to do so. "In what manner did their names come up? Are they suspects?"

"No, Mr. and Mrs. Coppi are not suspects. Their names came up during the investigation, and we need to get their names cleared. It shouldn't be too difficult. Just routine." Le Conte looks back at Sam and James. "May I ask you what was your relationship with the prince?"

"Mr. Le Conte, let's immediately get some ground rules for this interview very clear." Vera says, her voice getting a little louder. "Mr. and Mrs. Coppi are compassionate folks who are quite eager to help you, but I'm not going to allow you to take advantage of their kindheartedness.

"If you want this interview to continue, you will have to be more forthcoming with us," she continues. "Don't try to give me this crap that they are not suspects and that you're just clearing up some minor matters. You wouldn't have travelled five thousand miles over something trivial.

"In other words, what I'm trying to say is this—don't get cagey with me, and don't play cops and robbers. These nice folks are not criminals. Now, in answer to your question, Prince Firuz and his family are business associates of Mr. Coppi's. But more than that, the prince was a dear friend of the Coppis. Indeed, the Coppis have a long and warm connection with the entire family, including Prince Firuz's father, the shah. The prince and his family have stayed over at the guest house here on the ranch."

Vera leans forward. "Now, shouldn't you be investigating the possible *real* culprits of this horrible crime? It's my understanding that the royal family has a lot of enemies. Powerful enemies that are much more likely to have committed this crime than my clients."

Le Conte looks at Vera. "Thank you for the advice. We will certainly take that into account." The detective turns back to Sam and James. "Do you know a Monsieur Louis Finche?"

"Louis Finche? Who is he?" Vera asks.

"It's a simple question," Le Conte replies. "Either Mr. and Mrs. Coppi know the man, or they don't."

"I guess you didn't understand my earlier instructions," Vera says. "You are continuing to be harassing I'm not going to allow the Coppis to continue this conversation." Vera stands up. "This interview is over!"

James smiles. "Vera, please, let's not be so hostile to these fine detectives," James says. "They're just doing their job. Please sit back down." James turns to Le Conte. "Yes, I do know Mr. Finche."

"In what capacity do you know Mr. Finche?" Papadopoulos asks, getting into the mix. "What is your relationship with him?"

"As you both know, Mr. Finche is a pimp," James replies and then turns to Sam, grinning. "I never used his services, I swear," James assures her and then turns back to the detectives. "Ian Wadsworth, the head of my European operations, felt that we could use a person like Finche.

"We have some very high-level clients in Europe, and these clients have certain wants and needs. I met with Mr. Finche once, a few months ago, to discuss his services. We haven't used him, as yet."

"What about you, Mrs. Coppi?" Papadopoulos asks. "What is your relationship with Finche?"

"What are you suggesting?" Vera yells out. "Why would Mrs. Coppi have anything to do with a pimp? She's a mother, and she has an impeccable reputation."

"We're not implying anything immoral," Le Conte cuts in. "We're just asking if she knows the man."

Vera looks over at Sam. "Don't answer his question." Turning to Le Conte, she says, "If you want her to answer, you need to be more forthcoming about exactly what you want. Stop being so evasive. What did Finche say about Mrs. Coppi?"

Le Conte looks over at Papadopoulos, who nods. "Finche contradicts Mr. Coppi's statement," Papadopoulos reveals. "Finche says that he was hired to notify Mr. Coppi the next time the prince was in Monte Carlo. Finche did notify Mr. Coppi's associate, Ian Wadsworth, a few days before Firuz came to town.

"Mr. Finche was approached by Mrs. Coppi the day before the prince was killed. Mrs. Coppi had Finche arrange for her to have a liaison with the prince at his hotel on the night he was murdered."

Vera is staring at the detectives in shocked silence. "Wow!" she finally lets out. "My clients are not only murderers, but Mrs. Coppi also prostitutes herself!" She shakes her head. "That is quite a story."

"Why would Finche lie?" Papadopoulos argues. "What does he have to gain by making this up?"

"What would he have to gain?" Vera fires back. "I don't know what this lowlife character would have to gain. Maybe he's involved in the murder somehow and is trying to pass this crime onto two unsuspecting, naïve people."

"How else would he know Mrs. Coppi?" Papadopoulos continues to press Vera. "Finche described her perfectly to us."

Vera frowns and lowers her voice. "You know, fellas, I'm becoming very disappointed in your police work. At first, you looked like gentlemen who know what you're doing, but now I'm having some serious doubts.

"Mr. and Mrs. Coppi are in the news all of the time," the lawyer continues. "You yourselves must have already read dozens of news articles about them before you came out here.

"Let's begin with Mrs. Coppi being in the news after she was kidnapped. And as if that weren't enough, Mrs. Coppi is well known through her fashion business. Samantha is in the major magazines all of the time. It would take Finche no effort at all to find a photograph of her." Vera pauses for a moment. "Now I ask you guys—what is more likely? That Finche—a known pimp and criminal—is lying, or that Samantha—a mother to three young children and a pillar of her community— is a prostitute and a murderer?"

"Let's put Finche aside for the time being," Le Conte says and turns Sam. "You were in Monte Carlo recently. What was the purpose of that visit?"

"Mrs. Coppi went there for pleasure with two of her friends," Vera answers, and reaches into her briefcase. "Here." She hands the detectives two sheets of paper.

"These are sworn affidavits from Kathy Percival and Penelope Campos, the two women who accompanied her on the trip. Both of the women swear that they never met with Prince Firuz on the trip, and they have itemized everything that they did while in Monte Carlo."

Le Conte puts the statements in his briefcase. "We will want to interview the ladies. You'll need to make them available to us."

"I can't help you with that," Vera says. "I'm not their attorney. If you need to speak to the women, you'll have to deal directly with them—although I don't see why that's necessary. They said they had no contact with the prince. The ladies have provided you with a sworn affidavit to that effect. An interview would be a complete waste of everyone's time."

Vera looks over at Sam and James who are sitting quietly with their best poker faces on.

Le Conte turns to Sam. "Mrs. Coppi, while you were in Monte Carlo, did you happen to visit Les Couteaux de Francois? It is a store that deals in cutlery."

"Why do you ask?" Vera interrupts. "Why is that important?"

"Miss Susskind, can you let your client answer for herself?" Le Conte replies.

"I will, as soon as you tell me why you asked that question," Vera says, giving him a tight smile.

"The store owner remembers Mrs. Coppi." Le Conte reaches into his briefcase and pulls out a photograph. "This knife," he says, handing a photograph to Vera, "was the knife found at the murder scene. The blade has the store's marking. When we interviewed the proprietor of this establishment, he stated that he had sold that exact knife to *Madame* Coppi."

Vera looks at the photo and hands it to Sam. Vera turns back to Le Conte. "This is obviously a mistake on the store owner's part."

"No, Mademoiselle—no mistake. Both he and the saleswoman remember Mrs. Coppi well. Both say that Mrs. Coppi specifically asked for this knife to be built. It was made just for her." Le Conte gives Vera a smile. "And they didn't recognize her from a magazine or television. The couple didn't even know who she was until we approached them." Le Conte looks at Sam. "Now, Madame Coppi, I ask again—did you shop at Les Couteaux de Francois?"

"Were Mrs. Coppi's fingerprints on the weapon?" Vera asks.

"No, the knife was too smudged," he answers.

"What about some paperwork?" Vera asks. "Something that shows that this knife was purchased by Samantha?"

"No, there were no sales invoices or receipts," Le Conte replies. "But, as I say, two people remembered selling this particular piece to your client."

"How do you know that it isn't a mistake?" Vera argues.

Sam stands up. "Excuse me for a moment. I'll be right back." Sam walks out and returns a few minutes later. She hands Le Conte a nail file. "I *was* at that store, Mr. Le Conte—I bought a souvenir of my trip to Monte Carlo. The store's markings are on the file." Sam sits down next to James and gives him a smile. James shakes his head and smiles wryly back at her.

Le Conte inspects the file and when he's done, he looks up at Sam. "No, I'm sorry, Madame, this is not right—you purchased a knife."

"Does the piece not contain the store's markings?" Vera asks.

"Yes, it does, but there's some sort of blunder. The proprietor was absolutely certain that Madame Coppi bought a knife."

"The slipup is on the store's part," Vera suggests. "They obviously have Mrs. Coppi confused with someone else." Vera waits for a moment. "Is there anything else?" When there is no response from Le Conte, she adds. "Well, I guess this interview is over."

After the group leaves, James turns to Vera. "What do you think? Is this matter finished?"

"I think so. I can't say for sure, but I think it's over. The Monte Carlo government wants this to end. This is bad publicity for their country. The police have to show that they did a serious investigation. Now they can go back and close the case."

After Vera leaves, Sam looks at James. "Well? Are we done? Can we put an end to this chapter of our lives?"

James pulls her into an embrace. "No, honey—I'm almost certain that we're not done. Who knows what the police will do? There was probably a lot of evidence left at the crime scene, so I don't believe this ordeal is completely behind us unless Vera is right, and the government wants to shut the investigation down.

"In any event, it doesn't matter what the Monte Carlo police do; something will always come up. You and I are destined to have a life that's unpredictable and challenging. One thing that I learned from this segment of our life together—no matter what springs up, we'll find a way to get through those challenges." James gives her a kiss and a broad smile. "Something tells me, honey, that the next episode is going to be just as thrilling—I can't wait."

"Me, neither." Sam gives James a kiss, breaks off the embrace, and walks away. Then she stops and glances over her shoulder. "By the way, speaking of a next episode—I just found out that I'm pregnant again!"

"What?" James stands with his mouth agape. "How did this happen? Aren't you on the pill?"

Sam smiles. "Well, I wasn't taking the pill while I was kidnapped and being held prisoner. And you and I forgot that—don't you remember our tryst on the plane?" She smiles at him, her eyes twinkling. "I guess we should've waited a few days after my coming home before celebrating my freedom!"